For my parents, Jim and Marie Halpenny, who sadly passed away while I was writing this book. Thank you for your unquestioning love and support always.

The Insider

The Insider

Ava McCarthy

W F HOWES LTD

This large print edition published in 2009 by
W F Howes Ltd
Unit 4, Rearsby Business Park, Gaddesby Lane,
Rearsby, Leicester LE7 4YH

1 3 5 7 9 10 8 6 4 2

First published in the United Kingdom in 2009
by Harper

A CIP catalogue record for this book is available
from the British Library

ISBN 978 1 40744 022 4

Typeset by Palimpsest Book Production Limited,
Grangemouth, Stirlingshire
Printed and bound in Great Britain
by MPG Books Ltd, Bodmin, Cornwall

ACKNOWLEDGEMENTS

My heartfelt thanks go to my agent, Laura Longrigg, for believing in this book, and to all the team at MBA Literary Agents Ltd. A huge thank you to Julia Wisdom and to my editor, Anne O'Brien, of HarperCollins, for their enthusiasm and sound advice, and to the rest of the HarperCollins team for all their hard work. And a grateful thank you also to Helen Corner at Cornerstones Literary Consultancy for her help in getting started on this path. Finally, love and special thanks to my husband, Tom, who always took my writing seriously, and to my children, Mark and Megan, for putting up with my occasional disappearances.

CHAPTER 1

Harry was about to do something that could put her in jail. This wasn't unusual in her line of business, but it still made her palms sweat.

She pushed her coffee away and stared at the glass doors of the building across the street. Her eyes watered in the April glare. The first time she'd tried anything like this had been sixteen years ago when she was just thirteen, and she'd almost been arrested. This was different. This time she was going to get away with it.

The doors across the street swung open and she jerked upright in her chair. It was just the motorbike courier coming back out. He'd been the only visitor in the last twenty minutes. Harry shifted on the hard aluminium seat, certain she'd be left with stripes like Venetian blinds chiselled across her backside.

'D'you want anything else?'

The café manager stood in front of her, squat like a bulldog, his arms folded across a stained apron. The message was clear. It was lunchtime,

1

and she had occupied the pavement table for almost an hour. Time to go.

'Yes I do.' She flashed him her best winsome smile. 'A sparkling water, please.'

He dumped her cup and saucer on a tray and slouched back inside. The doors across the street swung open again and five young women stepped out in a bunch, all wearing the same navy-and-green uniform. They strolled along the pavement, passing around a single cigarette, sucking on it like deep-sea divers sharing out their last canister of air. Harry squinted at their faces. They were all too young.

She sat back and uncrossed her legs. Her tights prickled under her navy suit and her feet had started to cramp. It had been a toss-up that morning between plain flat shoes and the kitten heels with gold buckles, but as always she'd been a sucker for anything shiny. She hoped she wouldn't have to make a run for it any time in the next forty-five minutes.

Harry flexed her feet and listened to the clang of beer barrels being unloaded down a nearby laneway. She could smell the stale lager from the open pub doors, musty like decaying fruit. A bus lurched to a halt right in front of her and blocked her view of the doors.

Shit, she should have noticed the bus stop before she sat down. The engine throbbed as one by one the passengers spilled out. The air quivered with hot diesel fumes, the bus and the building beyond it rippling like a mirage. She drummed her fingers on the table.

Jesus, was the whole of Dublin on this bus?

She tried to see past its dusty windows to the office building beyond, but could only make out the top of the doorframes. Sunlight flashed off metal as the doors opened again, but Harry couldn't see who had come out.

She scraped back her chair and sprinted a few yards up the street until she had a clear view of the entrance again. The pavement was deserted.

Harry checked her watch. It was getting late, but she couldn't risk making her next move. Not yet.

The bus revved up its engine and barged back into the traffic. Harry clenched her fists, waiting for it to move on. Then her view cleared, and she spotted a woman halfway down the street, marching in the opposite direction to the other girls. She was older than they were, in her late forties maybe, and she was alone. She stopped to cross at the kerb, and glanced back up the street.

Harry's fingers relaxed. The woman's blonde streaks were new, but otherwise she looked just like her photograph on the website.

She waited till the woman had disappeared. Then she flung some coins on the table and crossed the street.

It was cooler and quieter on this side of the glass doors. Harry strode up to the receptionist, checking out her surroundings as she went. A low table with business magazines stood against one

3

wall. To her left was a set of large double doors, and another to her right. Her only escape route, should she need one, was back out the way she'd come in.

Harry selected another smile from her repertoire, the grimace of an uptight businesswoman with no time for fooling around.

'Hi, I'm Catalina Diego,' she said to the girl behind the desk. 'I'm here to see Sandra Nagle.'

The girl kept her gaze fixed to the computer screen in front of her. 'She's just gone to lunch.'

'But I've an appointment with her for twelve thirty.'

The girl chewed on the end of a pencil and shrugged. Her lips were a sticky mess of pink lipgloss, and some of it had strayed on to the pencil.

Harry leaned in closer over the desk. 'I'm here to run the training course for the helpdesk. Just how long is she going to be?'

The girl shrugged again and clicked the mouse on her computer. Harry wanted to snatch it out of her hands and rap her on the knuckles with it.

'Well, I can't hang around,' Harry said. 'I'll have to start without her.'

She turned towards the doors on her left, as though she knew where she was going. The receptionist half stood from her chair, her pencil clattering to the desk.

'I'm afraid I can't let you in there without Mrs Nagle's permission.'

'Look –' Harry turned back and peered at the

4

girl's name badge '– Melanie, this course has taken a month to arrange. If I leave now, it'll be another month before I come back. Do you want me to explain to Sandra just why I couldn't get started?'

Harry held her breath and braced herself. If someone had tried to bully her like that there'd have been quite a backlash. But Melanie just blinked and sank back in her chair. Harry didn't blame her. She'd talked to Sandra Nagle for the first time that morning when she'd called the bank with a bogus customer complaint. She'd found her name and photograph on the bank's corporate website, in the section that boasted of its unrivalled customer service. After two minutes' conversation with her, Harry had the woman pegged as a complete bitch, and it looked as though Melanie agreed with her.

Melanie swallowed and shoved a visitor's book across the desk. 'Okay, but you'll have to fill this out first. Name and date here, sign there.'

Something flickered in the pit of Harry's stomach as she scribbled in the details. Melanie handed her an identity badge and pointed to the doors on Harry's left.

'Through there. I'll buzz you in.'

Harry thanked her and gave herself a mental high five. She remembered the high fives her father used to give her whenever her poker bluffs paid off. 'Nothing like the rush that comes from winning with an empty hand,' he'd say, winking at her.

Empty hand was right. She clipped the badge to her lapel and stepped over to the doors. The safety lock clicked and a green light blinked on the wall panel. She straightened her shoulders and pushed open the heavy doors. She was in.

CHAPTER 2

Leon Ritch hadn't heard from the Prophet in over eight years, and had hoped to Christ he'd never hear from him again. He scratched his two-day-old stubble and read the email again.

Maybe it was a hoax. After all, anyone could sign himself 'The Prophet'. He checked the sender's address. It was different from the last time, but just as obscure: an763398@anon.obfusc.com. He thought about trying to trace it but knew it wouldn't do any good. They'd tracked the Prophet's last address to some anonymous re-mailer system. A dead end. Whoever he was, he knew how to conceal his identity.

Apart from himself, only three other people knew about the Prophet. One of those was in prison and another was dead. That just left Ralph.

Leon dialled a number he hadn't used in a long time.

'It's me,' he said.

'Sorry, who's this?'

Leon could hear the rumble of men's voices in the background. Ralph was probably in a meeting

7

with the bank VIPs, fighting for elbowroom at the corporate party. It was a world he'd once thrived in himself.

'Don't be a prick, Ralphy.'

The men's laughter roared in his ear, and then grew gradually fainter until there was just an echoing hollowness. Sounded like Ralphy-Boy had moved into the gents.

'Comfy now?' Leon said.

'What the hell are you doing?'

'Just looking up old pals. Seems to be a day for calls from the past.'

'What are you talking about? I told you never to call me.'

'Yeah, yeah, I know. Listen Ralphy-Boy, are you near your office?'

'I'm in the middle of a board meeting and I don't –'

'Good. I'm sending an email to your private account. Go and read it.'

'What? Are you out of your mind?'

'Just do it. I'll call back in five minutes.'

Leon hung up and turned back to his PC. He brought up the email again and forwarded it to Ralph's alias address.

He swivelled his chair to stare out the window at the bottle banks and wheelie bins that lined the small car park behind his office. Directly opposite him was the grimy back wall of the local Chinese takeaway, the Golden Tigress. A classy name for a seedy health hazard.

A young Chinese man in white overalls trudged out of the back door and flung a bag of God knew what kind of crap into the wheelie bin beneath Leon's window. He wrinkled his nose at the stench of garlic and his gut clenched. Most of the shop-keepers around here gave off the same rank smell, filling Leon's tiny office with it when they came in with their accounts. His ulcer bit into him.

'Leon-the-Ritch', people used to call him. He'd worked sixteen-hour days and managed all the big deals. He'd been a real player then, with millions in the bank and a glitzy wife on his arm. Now his twenty-year-old marriage was down the toilet, right there alongside his reputation and his bank balance.

Leon squeezed his eyes shut. Thinking about his marriage made him think about his son, and that was worse than the ulcer. He focused on the searing pain in his belly, trying to obliterate the image of Richard at the train station that morning. It was the first time he'd seen his son in almost a year.

He'd been up all night at a poker game and had travelled to his office on the train, vacuum-packed with the city's commuters. Their looks of disgust had told him what he already knew: that his eyes were red-rimmed, his breath stank, and the bacteria in his armpits had metabolized up a storm.

His carriage had pulled up alongside a knot of schoolboys on the platform at Blackrock. He'd stared idly at them through the window. Then his breath had caught in his throat. Dark hair, round eyes, freckles like mud splats. Richard. Passengers pushed in front of Leon, but he elbowed them out of his way, straining for another glimpse of his son. A head taller than the other boys, Richard was easy to spot. He'd grown. Leon felt his chest swell. The boy would be tall like his mother, not squat like him.

Leon had pressed closer to the door. The first of Richard's friends pushed through into the carriage, and up close Leon recognized the crest of Blackrock College on his jumper. He frowned. Maura hadn't said anything about changing schools. But then they hadn't talked in a long time. He wondered who was paying the fees.

Richard was at the door. Leon half raised his arm, ready to catch his attention. He heard the well-bred accents of Richard's friends. At the same time, he became aware of the sourness of his own clothes, of his stained anorak and unshaven face. His hand faltered, suspended in mid air.

'Richard!'

The boy snapped his head around to look back at the station platform. Leon yanked his arm down and peered out the window. A blond man in his forties was jogging towards the train. He wore a dark wool overcoat and carried a red sports bag in one hand. He held the bag out to Richard, and ruffled the boy's hair. Leon saw the wide grin that spread across his son's face, and felt a jagged

10

twinge in his stomach, as though he'd swallowed broken glass. Slowly, Leon had turned and shuffled through the crowd until he'd reached the other end of the carriage. And there he'd stayed, hidden, until he was sure his son was gone.

The clink of bottles made Leon jump. Outside in the car park, the young Chinese man was back, this time firing glass jars into the bottle bank. Leon rubbed his face again and took a deep breath, trying to clear the curdling in his stomach. Maybe tomorrow he'd get cleaned up. Maybe he'd go and see Richard.

He checked his watch. Time to call Ralphy-Boy again. He cleared his throat and dialled.

'Did you read it?' he said, when Ralph picked up.

'Is this some kind of sick joke?'

'Took the words right out of my mouth.'

'You think I sent this? I don't want anything to do with it.' Ralph's mouth sounded dry.

'What's wrong, Ralphy? You scared?'

'Of course I'm bloody scared. I've a lot to lose, even if you haven't.'

Leon tightened his grip on the phone. 'It's down to me you didn't lose it all eight years ago, let's not forget that, okay?'

Ralph sighed. 'What exactly do you want, Leon? More money?'

Good question. At first he'd just wanted to make sure Ralph hadn't sent the email, but now another idea was uncurling itself.

'You read the email, didn't you?' Leon said.

'Yes, he says the girl has it. So what?'

'Well, maybe I want it back.'

'You think she's just going to hand it over? And what if he's wrong?'

'The Prophet's never been wrong about anything before,' Leon said. 'Says he has proof.'

'What's the matter with you? Do you want us both to go to jail?'

Leon gazed out the window again. Maybe hearing from the Prophet wasn't such a bad thing, after all. Maybe this was his way back.

'There's this fella I know,' Leon said. 'I've used him before. He'll take care of it.'

'I don't like this.'

'You don't have to, Ralphy.'

Leon slammed the phone down and looked out the window again. This time he didn't see the graffiti on the walls or the overflowing wheelie bins. He saw himself clean-shaven and twenty pounds lighter, wearing an Italian suit and seated at the head of a boardroom table. He saw himself dressed in a smart wool overcoat, cheering Richard on as he played rugby for his school. Leon ground his teeth and curled his fingers into fists.

This girl had something that belonged to him and he wanted it back.

CHAPTER 3

'Good afternoon, Sheridan Bank –'
'– it isn't showing up in your transactions, Mr Cooke. Would you like me to try another account for you?'

The drone of about thirty different conversations buzzed through the air. The voices were mostly female, filling the room like polite bumblebees. Harry moved between the desks, each one screened by blue padded partitions, and half-listened to the girls on the phones. She had an account with Sheridan herself. Maybe after this, she'd need to switch banks.

There were plenty of empty desks, but Harry wanted one at the back. She reached the end of the room and snagged an empty desk in the corner. She dumped her bag on the chair and waited for the round-faced girl at the next workstation to finish her call.

'Apologies again about that, Mrs Hayes. Bye now.' The girl typed something on her keyboard and winked at Harry. 'Another unsatisfied customer.'

Harry smiled. 'Is there any other kind?'

'Not around here.'

13

Harry stuck out a hand. 'I'm Catalina. I start work here this afternoon.'

'Oh, great. I'm Nadia.' She grasped Harry's hand. Her nails were long and crimson, and she wore a silver ring on every plump finger, including her thumb.

Harry gestured to the empty desk. 'Okay if I sit here?'

'Sure, no one's using it.'

Harry sat down and switched on the PC. 'I don't think I've been set up on the system yet. Any chance you could log me in?'

Nadia hesitated. 'I'm not really supposed to do that.'

Keep it casual. 'Oh, right. I just wanted another peek at the helpdesk system before Mrs Nagle gets back from lunch.'

Nadia chewed her bottom lip, and then smiled. 'Why not? Don't want her to catch you out on your first day, do we?'

She pulled off her headset and walked over, leaning across to type in her username and password. Harry could smell a mixture of Calvin Klein and peppermints.

'There you go,' Nadia said.

'Thanks, I owe you one.'

Harry waited until Nadia was back at her desk, busy with another call. She adjusted the angle of her screen so that no one could see what she was doing, and went to work.

With a few keystrokes, she broke out of the

helpdesk application into the computer's operating system. Harry shook her head and almost tutted. It should have been better protected.

She poked around inside the PC, dipping into its files and directories, but it was a standard desktop and had no secrets to tell. She clicked her mouse and soon had a view of all her network connections:

F: \\Jupiter\shared
G: \\Pluto\users
H: \\Mars\system
L: \\Mercury\backup
S: \\Saturn\admin

This was more like it. This was her way into the bank's central computers.

Harry stepped through the list of networked machines, trying to gain access. Some she could drop right into and view their files, but most of them blocked her at the first keystroke. She dug a little more, searching for something she could use. And then she found it: the system password file. Stored inside were the usernames and passwords of everyone on the network. It was her key into the system. She double-clicked with her mouse and tried to open the file. Locked.

Harry frowned and checked the time. Her heartbeat cranked up a notch. She'd been here twenty minutes already, and still had a lot of ground to cover. She discarded the password file and began ransacking the network, burrowing deep into its file system and sniffing every corner. She knew what she was looking for, and it had to be here somewhere. And sure enough, there it was, tucked away on a shared drive available for anyone to read: the unprotected backup copy of the password file.

The back of Harry's neck tingled. It was always the same whenever she hacked into a system that was supposed to be secure. She wanted to beat a drum roll on the desk, but there was a time and a place for everything.

She opened the backup file and scanned its contents. The usernames were in clear text, but the passwords were all encrypted. Harry glanced over her shoulder. Nadia was chatting with a customer on the phone, her nails clacking on the keyboard.

Harry slipped a hand into her jacket pocket and drew out a CD which she slotted into the computer. It contained a password-cracker program, and she fed the backup file into it. She hunched over a computer manual and pretended to leaf through it as she waited for the cracker to do its job.

It could take a while. Dictionary attacks often did. The program was stepping through the entire dictionary, encrypting each word and trying to match it against the encrypted passwords in the file. After that, it would try letter and number combinations. By the end of it, she'd have all the passwords she needed.

Harry peeked at her watch again. Gooseflesh broke out on the back of her neck and she massaged it with her fingers. She had maybe ten minutes before the supervisor got back, and the cracker could take fifteen. It was going to be tight. But then, breaking and entering always was. That was what made it so irresistible.

Her father had always said she'd end up a burglar, ever since the day she'd hurled a brick through the kitchen window and climbed inside. She'd got locked out after school, but all she could think about was the port scan she'd launched from her computer that morning and what it might have found. She tried to explain this to her father later, as he crunched about in the broken glass, his face incredulous. She was sure he'd confiscate her PC, but instead, he upgraded its processor and presented her with her own set of house keys. To eleven-year-old Harry, he'd acquired some serious kudos that day.

And she had acquired a new name, because that was when her father had first started calling her Harry. There were times when she longed for an exotic Spanish name, like the one her sister had been given. Amaranta was tall with ash-blonde hair. She'd been born while Harry's mother was still infatuated with her husband's half-Irish, half-Spanish charm. But by the time Harry was born, her father's financial disasters had forced them out of their mansion to a cramped terraced house, and her mother's taste in names had dulled. Harry was the one who inherited her father's sooty Spanish eyes and blue-black curls, but her mother had been unimpressed. Rejecting anything faintly

17

Spanish, she had christened her daughter Henrietta after her own mother, a prim woman from the north of England.

'But whoever heard of a burglar called Henrietta?' her father had declared after the incident with the window, and had insisted on calling her Harry ever since. Now she never answered to anything else.

Harry checked the cracker program. It was almost finished. She scanned the list of passwords broken into clear text so far. There was Nadia's. Username 'nadiamc', password 'diamonds'. And Sandra Nagle's: 'sandran', password 'fortitude'. She shook her head. No good. She needed a heavy-hitter account, one with privileged access.

And there it was, at the bottom of the list. The network administrator's password: asteroid27. Her toes wriggled inside her shoes. Now she was like a security guard with the master key to the building: she could go anywhere. She owned the network.

She logged in under her new privileged status, and immediately disabled the network's auditing program. Now her activities couldn't be recorded in the audit logs. She was invisible.

Harry prowled the servers and plunged into any file that looked interesting. Her eyes widened at some of the data she could access: customer credit ratings, bank revenues, employee salaries. She could view everyone's emails, including those belonging to the chairman of the bank.

She hopped into another database and tried to

make sense of the numbers in front of her. Her fingers froze on the mouse when she realized that she was looking at some of the bank's most confidential customer information: account numbers, PIN codes, credit-card details, usernames and passwords. The stuff of hackers' dreams, and most of it wasn't even encrypted.

Harry scrolled through the data. It would be so easy to lift money out of these accounts. No one would even know it had happened. She was a ghost on the system, and left no footprints.

'She's back early.'

Harry looked across at Nadia, who was nodding towards the other end of the room. Sandra Nagle was standing by the double doors, consulting a clipboard.

Shit. Time to move.

Harry's fingers jitterbugged over the keys. She copied the list of cracked passwords on to her CD, and dumped some customer account data and security PINs on to it for good measure.

The copy was slow to execute, and she looked up to check on Sandra Nagle. She was working her way down the room, stopping every few paces to check in with a helpdesk operator.

Harry knew she should wrap it up, knew she was taking a risk, but she still had one thing left to do. Manipulating the mouse, she disguised one of her own files and stashed it in a corner of the network. She always liked to leave a calling card.

The woman strolled in her direction, making

notes on her clipboard. She stopped to interrogate a girl sitting a few feet away from Harry.

Harry cleared the system event logs to obliterate any possibility that she could be traced. She re-enabled the auditing facility and then glanced up.

Sandra Nagle was looking right at her.

Moisture trickled from Harry's armpits. She heard the swish of nylon mashing against nylon as the woman marched towards her. She closed down her access to the network and flipped the helpdesk application back into view just as Sandra Nagle reached her desk.

The woman was breathing hard. She was so close that Harry could see the pale hairs on her upper lip.

'Just who are you, and what do you think you're doing?'

'Are you Sandra Nagle?' Harry stood up and flung her bag across her shoulder, snatching out the CD and slipping it back into her pocket. 'I've been waiting for you.'

'What –'

Harry brushed past her and marched towards the doors, trying to ignore the trembling in her knees.

'I've been sent in by IT to check the health of your systems,' she said. 'You've got serious virus problems here.'

Sandra Nagle was close behind her. 'How –'

'You don't need to cease operations right away, but I hope for your own sake you've been following the bank's anti-virus procedures.'

The woman's step faltered. Harry looked back over her shoulder.

'I see. No doubt you'll be hearing from IT in due course.'

She pushed against one of the double doors, but it wouldn't open. She tried the other one. Locked.

'Hang on, who did you say you were?' Sandra Nagle was stomping after her.

Fuck it.

Harry spotted the door-release button on the wall. She pressed it and heard a click. She shoved open the doors and raced across the reception area. Melanie stared at her, her mouth wide open.

Harry burst through the glass doors into the sunlight and raced down the street.

Electrified by adrenaline, Harry sprinted alongside the canal, her shoes smacking against the pavement and the blood drumming through her body. When she was sure no one was following her, she slowed to a walk and then perched on the canal wall to cool down.

Water hissed through the tall rushes by the banks and a light breeze buffeted her face. When the thumping in her chest had eased off, she fished her phone out of her bag and dialled.

'Hi, Ian? Harry Martinez here, from Lúbra Security. I've just finished the penetration test on your systems.'

'Already?'

'Yeah, I hacked in and got all I needed.'

21

'Jesus. Hey, lads, have we had any IDS alarms?'

Harry could hear some commotion in the background. 'Relax, Ian, your Intrusion Detection System is fine. I didn't come through from the outside.'

'You didn't? But we were expecting a perimeter attack.'

'Yeah, I know you were.' Harry winced. 'Sorry.'

'Ah Jesus, Harry.'

'Listen, a huge number of hacker exploits are inside jobs. You need to protect yourselves.'

'No kidding.'

'So I came in through the bank's own network, and got admin access –'

'You what?'

'– and found the customer bank accounts and PIN numbers.'

'Ah fuck it.'

'Let's just say your internal security doesn't look too good. But a few simple precautions should sort it out. I'll make some recommendations in the report.'

'But how the hell did you get in?'

'A bit of social engineering, and some hard neck. If it makes you feel any better, I nearly got caught.'

'It doesn't. What a mess.'

'Sorry, Ian. Just thought I'd give you some warning before your management gets wind of it.'

'Well, thanks, I appreciate that. But I'm still dog meat.'

'It's not as bad as it sounds.' Harry's phone

beeped. 'I left a stash of hacker tools behind, just to test your anti-virus software. But we can go through that later when we do a clean-up.' Her phone beeped again. 'Sorry, Ian, got to go. I'll talk to you tomorrow.'

She took the incoming call.

'Hey there, Harry, how's the break-in going?'

Harry smiled. It was Imogen Brady, a support engineer from the Lúbra Security office. She pictured her friend sitting at her desk, her feet not quite reaching the floor. Imogen looked like a Chihuahua, with huge eyes in a gamine face. She was one of the best hackers Harry had ever worked with.

'I'm just finished,' Harry said. 'What's going on back there?'

'Mister Loads-a-dosh is looking for you.'

She was referring to their boss, Dillon Fitzroy. Rumour had it that he'd become a multi-millionaire at the age of twenty-eight during the dot.com boom. That was nine years ago. He'd founded Lúbra Security shortly afterwards, expanding it by merging with other software companies until it was now one of the biggest in the business.

'What does he want?' Harry said.

'Who knows? Maybe a date?'

Harry rolled her eyes. Imogen may have looked as though a breeze could blow her away, but when it came to digging for gossip she was a terrier.

'Why don't you just put me through to him?' Harry said.

'Okey-dokey.'

A few seconds later, Dillon's voice came on the line.

'Harry? You finished over at Sheridan?'

Judging from the background acoustics, he was yelling into a conference phone from several feet away.

'I'm done,' Harry said. 'Except for the paperwork.'

'Ditch it. I've another job for you.'

'Right now?' She was starving and could smell the coffee and bacon rolls from the sandwich bars in Baggot Street. She stood up and strolled towards the canal bridge.

'Yeah, right now. Send me on the Sheridan details, I'll get Imogen to compile the report. I want you on another vulnerability assessment.'

Harry could hear the click of his keyboard in the background. Trust Dillon not to waste an opportunity to multi-task. His left hand was probably flexed across his laptop like a pianist's, while his right hand made notes on a pad.

'So where to this time?' Harry said.

'The IFSC, and the client has asked especially for you. I told them you're the best.'

'Thanks, Dillon, you're a gent.' Now she was glad of the kitten heels. The International Financial Services Centre was definitely upmarket.

'Call me when you've finished,' Dillon said. 'We'll grab some dinner and you can fill me in.'

She felt her eyes widen. Doubly glad of the kitten heels. 'Okay.' Before she could let herself wonder what dinner might mean, she said, 'So tell me more about the IFSC job. Do we know what kind of systems they have?'

'Nope, you'll find all that out when you meet them . . .' Dillon paused. 'If you ask me, I think they want to look you over first.'

Harry stopped in the middle of the pavement. 'Why would they want to do that?'

Dillon hesitated for just a second too long. 'Look, maybe this isn't such a good idea after all. Maybe I'll put Imogen on to it.'

Harry stuck a hand over her ear to block out the din of traffic. 'Okay, what's going on here? Who's the client?'

She heard him suck in air through his teeth as he thought about his answer.

'All right, it was a stupid idea,' he said. 'It's KWC.'

The adrenaline shot out of Harry's system like water from a burst main. She stumbled over to the canal wall and sank back on to the cold stone.

KWC. Klein, Webberly and Caulfield, one of the most prestigious investment banks in the city, servicing some of the wealthiest individuals and corporations in Europe. It was headquartered in New York, with offices in London, Frankfurt and Tokyo, as well as here in Dublin.

It was also the company her father had worked for before they sent him to prison.

CHAPTER 4

'Give me your worst-case scenario,' Harry said.

The man across the boardroom table looked at her through half-closed eyes. He was in his forties, with bristly grey hair cut like a US Marine's.

He shrugged. 'Someone getting access to our investment accounts.'

'Worse than that.'

He leaned back and folded his arms, flesh straining against his shirt. 'What could be worse than some hacker getting hold of our clients' money?'

'You tell me.' Harry sneaked a look at the business card he'd given her. Felix Roche, IT Procurement, KWC. She scribbled a note on the back: *hostile*.

Her gaze strayed to the window behind Felix. It wasn't just a window, it was an entire wall of glass that made the quays along the Liffey seem like part of the room. In the distance, she could see the peppermint green dome of the Custom House and the corrugated cap of Liberty Hall tower. Business must be good for KWC.

Felix leaned forward across the table. 'Okay, I'll give you a worst case,' he said. Harry could smell the onions he'd had for lunch. 'How about someone getting a look at our confidential M&A deals? That bad enough for you?'

M&A. Mergers and Acquisitions. The department her father had worked for before he was arrested. Harry swallowed and fiddled with her notepad. Then she flicked a glance at Felix. His pasty face looked unhealthy, like the underbelly of a dead fish. She was used to antagonism from the technical guys, but this was something different. She'd told Dillon she could handle this assignment, that KWC was just another client. Now she wasn't so sure.

The door swept open and a man in his thirties strode into the room. He was well-built, with light brown hair and shoulders that belonged on a rugby pitch.

Felix scowled at the interruption.

'Hi, Felix, I'm sitting in.' The man frowned at Harry as he pulled up a chair.

Her cheeks tingled under his gaze. What was up with these guys? She squared her shoulders and stood up.

'Harry Martinez.' She held out her hand.

His brow cleared and he grinned. 'Sorry, I was expecting a man. Probably happens all the time, right?' He returned her handshake. 'Jude Tiernan. I'm an investment banker here.'

His hand was warm and his citrus aftershave

27

perked up the room. What was an investment banker doing at an IT meeting? Then she remembered Felix's barbed comment about M&A deals.

'Let me guess,' she said. 'You work for M&A?'

'Let's say M&A work for me.'

Harry sank back down and worked it out. So he was Head of M&A, just like her father had been. One man's prison sentence was another man's career break. She felt their eyes on her, invading her. Her father was a legend in this bank. Had they made the connection and come to look her over? She chewed her lip, unable to meet their gaze.

Jude set his mobile phone on the desk and took a silver pen from his breast pocket. He twirled it between the fingers of one hand and gestured towards Harry with the other. 'Please continue.'

'I was really expecting someone from IT Security to be here,' said Harry. 'Someone who knows the systems.'

Felix snorted. 'IT Security. I know these systems better than anyone. I practically built the damn machines myself.'

'I see.' Harry checked the card again. 'And now you're in IT Procurement?'

He glared at her. 'The career move came up. Security were more than happy to let me handle this initial meeting, believe me. Saves them the trouble.'

Harry took a deep breath. She looked at her pad, although she'd written nothing down.

'Okay, well, I don't know how much Dillon covered with you on this,' she said. Not much, from the looks of things. 'We need to scope the penetration test, see which approach suits you best.'

Know the players at the table, her father had taught her. Adjust your style accordingly. Trouble was, she didn't know these guys at all, and they weren't giving her any clues.

'A pen test is a waste of time,' said Felix. 'Our systems are secure, I can personally guarantee it.' He glowered at Harry. 'Anyone who says otherwise is challenging my professional competence.'

Jude ignored him. 'What exactly happens in this pen test, Ms Martinez?'

Felix sighed. 'Ah, come on, Jude, I've been through this with her already. Besides, we both know she's only here because her boss is an old friend of yours and he wants the account.'

Harry looked back down at her pad. No wonder she was being fobbed off with someone from Procurement. They weren't even serious about the business.

Jude raised a hand to shut Felix up and smiled at Harry. 'Humour me. Tell me about this pen test.'

Harry suspected he was conducting some test of his own. She didn't smile back.

'A penetration test is when I use every dirty trick in the book to try and break into your computer systems,' she said. 'And once I'm in, I sniff around to see what kind of damage I can do.'

Jude stopped twirling his pen. 'In other words, you pretend to be a hacker.'

'Right.'

Felix leaned forward. 'And just what kind of hacker are you, Ms Martinez? A black hat or a white hat?'

Harry stiffened, and glared at him.

Jude looked from one to the other. 'Anyone care to fill me in?'

Harry cut in before Felix could take another swipe at her. 'Black hats are malicious hackers intent on causing damage. White hats aren't destructive. They're only interested in the technology and how far they can push it.'

She turned to Felix. 'To answer your question, Mr Roche, I'm a security professional, not a hacker.'

'Well, well, a hacker with ethics,' Felix said. 'Who'd have thought it?'

Jude scribbled something on his pad and shoved it across to Felix. Harry watched Felix's jaw tighten as he read the note, and she wondered if she'd passed the test.

'I'm intrigued,' Jude said. 'So how do we do this?'

'For a straight pen test, we can either do it as a black-box or a white-box scenario.'

'Everything's black and white with you, isn't it?'

Harry looked him in the eye. 'Pretty much.'

He raised his eyebrows. 'Okay, I'm listening.'

'Black-box testing is the closest thing to a real

hack from the outside. I start with nothing except your corporate name. I use outside sources of information to snoop around your network, and then I break in.'

She paused to make sure he was getting it. He nodded and smiled.

'For a white-box test, I know everything about your internal systems right from the start. Your firewalls, your network infrastructure, your data-bases, the works,' Harry said. 'In other words, I'm attacking from the inside.'

The door creaked opened and a man in his late fifties eased into the room. His grey hair fluffed out like a pair of wings on his balding head.

Coco the Clown, Harry thought.

'Please carry on,' the newcomer said and slid into a chair against the wall behind Harry.

God, how many more people were coming to gawp at her? She eyed up the conference table that could seat twenty people and feared the worst.

Jude watched the older man for a moment. Then he turned his attention back to Harry. 'So which approach would you recommend, Ms Martinez?'

Harry tried to concentrate. 'White box. In my experience, insiders are far more of a threat than external attackers.'

'And I guess you'd know all about insiders, wouldn't you?' Felix said.

Every muscle in her body went still. 'Just what are you getting at, Mr Roche?'

'Come on, let's put it on the table here. We're

all thinking it.' He spread his arms as though the whole room was full of people on his side. 'Your daddy was the master of all insiders, wasn't he?'

Harry blinked. Then she dropped her gaze and fiddled with her pad, willing her voice to be steady. 'What my father may have done is not part of this discussion.'

'*May* have done?' Felix said. 'He was found guilty of insider trading, wasn't he? Put away for eight years.'

Harry took in his clenched fists and the angry splotches on his cheeks. She stared at him. 'You're taking it all rather personally, aren't you?'

'Damn right, I am. Salvador Martinez nearly brought this company to its knees.'

'Felix, you're out of order.' Coco the Clown's voice behind her made her jump.

Jude shifted in his chair. Felix glared at Harry; it looked as if he had more to say.

Harry didn't bother turning to acknowledge the unexpected support. To hell with it. She'd had enough. She placed her palms on the lacquered boardroom table. It was smooth and cold, like a mirror. She pushed herself up and stood to face them.

'Mr Roche, I came here to talk about the security of your IT systems, and that's all I'm prepared to discuss with you.'

She grabbed her bag and turned for the door. Then a thought struck her. She knew she shouldn't say it out loud, but she was going to anyway. She swung round and faced them.

'Who knows, maybe my father wasn't the only insider trader around here. Maybe his arrest just spoiled the party.'

Felix's jaw fell slack. Jude drew himself up in his chair, his lips disappearing into a tight line.

Coco the Clown stood and held up his hand. 'Gentlemen, please –'

Jude cut in. 'Don't make accusations you can't back up, Ms Martinez.' He clenched the silver pen in his fist. 'Some of us still believe in the integrity of our profession, even if your father didn't.'

'Well, well, an investment banker with ethics,' Harry said. 'Who'd have thought it?'

She marched to the door as fast as she could without actually breaking into a run. The damn room was longer than a tennis court. She yanked open the door and slammed it behind her.

She was halfway down the corridor before she realized she was shaking. She blundered around a corner, searching for the way out. Dammit, the lifts must be back the other way. Her sense of direction was dyslexic at the best of times, but this was no time to get lost and call for help.

She doubled back, retracing her steps past the boardroom, and found the lifts. She punched the button, pacing up and down while she waited.

The boardroom door opened, and voices growled from inside the room. She checked the lift. Two floors to go. She scoured the corridor for somewhere to hide. No doors, no closets. Nothing but polished marble floors.

Someone came out. Coco the Clown. He saw her, and bowed his head.

'Ms Martinez, please accept my apologies.'

He walked towards her and held out his hand. His eyebrows were tilted upwards into his high domed forehead, his expression mournful.

'Ashford is the name,' he said. 'Chief Executive of KWC. You were treated very badly in there and I assure you the individuals in question will be reprimanded for their lack of professionalism.'

Harry ignored his outstretched hand. 'Since when does the Chief Executive sit in on routine IT meetings?'

Ashford dropped his hand. 'Good point. Very well, I admit it: I was curious. I wanted to meet you.'

The lift pinged and the doors opened. Harry stepped in and jabbed at the button for the ground floor.

'I've known your father for over thirty years,' Ashford said. 'Salvador's a great personal friend and a fine man.' He smiled. 'You're very like him.'

The lift doors started to close. Harry glared at him through the shrinking gap.

'I've known my father all my life,' she said. 'And I can assure you, I'm nothing like him at all.'

CHAPTER 5

Cameron knew he didn't blend in well with his surroundings. It was the colour of his hair that did it. Half a shade short of albino, a girl had once called it, as he'd rammed himself into her scrawny body. Afterwards he'd tightened his fingers round her throat and squeezed till she'd stopped moving.

He pulled the black woolly hat further down over his eyebrows and looked at his watch. He needed to get going before someone noticed him, but his instructions had been to wait for another hour.

He'd never been to the International Financial Services Centre before. As far as he was concerned, it was a place where rich people came to get richer. He could remember this part of the city before it had been redeveloped, when it was still the old Custom House docks. He'd preferred it then; vast faceless warehouses spread across bleak tracts of land. Now it was a landscaped city within a city, playing host to banks from all over the world.

Cameron stared up at the multi-storey office

buildings, all made from the same green glass blocks that sparkled in the sunlight. Like the fucking Emerald City of Oz.

He leaned against the steel barrier near the edge of George's Dock. It used to be a real dock that smelled of tar and dead fish. Now they'd transformed it into an ornamental lake. Jets of water crashed down on its surface from five spurting fountains. The noise was deafening, but it was the perfect position for observing the building opposite.

Cameron straightened up as a young woman stumbled through the revolving doors. He checked her out against the description of the Martinez girl. Five foot three, slim, with dark curly hair. Face kind of heart-shaped. She was clutching a black satchel with some kind of silver logo on it. It was her all right. She reminded him of the Spanish waitress he'd had in Madrid last year. He felt himself harden.

Cameron fell into step behind her. It was late on Friday afternoon and the city was clogged with people. He stared at her without blinking, fixing her in his sights.

He'd received his instructions by phone, his bowels clenching as he'd listened to the familiar voice. It was a voice he'd taken orders from many times before. He told himself he did it for the money, but he knew it was more than that. The blood had pounded through his body as he'd listened to the voice on the phone, anticipating the hunt.

The girl moved as if she was on the dodgems, slamming shoulders with other pedestrians, but she seemed not to notice. She walked out of the IFSC grounds and back on to the city streets. The crowd pressed in closer and he burrowed through, closing the gap between them.

'Will I do it like last time?' he'd asked on the phone. He'd savoured the memory of last time; the squeal of brakes, the smell of scorched rubber, the sickening crunch of metal and shattered bone. But the voice had cut into his thoughts.

'Not yet. I need her terrified, but I need her alive.' As if sensing Cameron's disappointment, he'd continued, 'But don't worry. Next time, you can kill her.'

Next time. Cameron swallowed hard as he gained on the dark-haired girl. Why did he always have to obey orders? He risked a lot to carry out his instructions. He needed gratification, and he needed it now.

The girl picked up the pace, and he lengthened his stride to keep up with her. His first chance would come at the busy intersection marked by the Eternal Flame sculpture, where the cars wheeled past the Custom House at top speed, heedless of pedestrians. It was less than twenty yards away, and she was headed straight for it.

Suddenly, she stopped and swung around. She stared straight at him, and then retraced her steps back towards him. What the fuck was she doing? She couldn't have seen him. He kept on walking.

She was face to face with him. Her breasts brushed against his arm, and he could feel her warmth.

'Sorry,' she said, without looking up, and swept on past.

He ran his tongue over his lips as he watched her walk away.

Cameron waited till she had put ten yards between them and then set off after her again. She headed back towards the river and crossed over the bridge. He followed her as she turned left along the cobbled quays. He could smell the rotting seaweed that hung like a fringe of oily hair along the river walls.

The girl turned down a narrow street lined with poky cottages and grimy blocks of flats. Cameron dropped back. There were fewer people here, less cover. He kept his distance until he heard the familiar whine of speeding traffic. They had reached the intersection with Pearse Street, where cars thundered in and out of the city centre.

The girl joined the knot of pedestrians by the kerb and he slipped in close behind her.

An old woman in a raincoat swayed in front of him. She was carrying a plastic bag full of old tennis shoes, and smelled like a urinal. He elbowed her out of his way and edged into position behind the girl. He could see the logo on her satchel more clearly now. The word *DefCon* was engraved in silver, the letter 'O' framing a black skull and crossbones.

It meant nothing to him, nor did he care.

He shot a glance at the lights and then back at the whirling traffic. Cars and motorbikes sped along Pearse Street. The lights changed from green to amber. A red truck barrelled on through. Behind it, a black BMW gunned its engine and prepared to make a run for it.

Cameron's scalp prickled. He raised his hand. Now.

An elbow jabbed at his arm and threw him off balance.

'Look at that speed. Should be locked up.' The old woman shoved her face into his. He could smell the stale wine on her breath.

The BMW roared past. The pedestrian lights bip-bip-bipped as the crowd spilled out on to the road.

Cameron glared at the stinking bag lady who had robbed him of his climax. The old woman widened her watery eyes and took a step back from him. He jerked away and strode across the street, squinting through the crowds.

There was no sign of the dark-haired girl anywhere.

He weaved his way through the bodies, straining for a glimpse of her. Then he stood still and dug his nails into his palms, ignoring the crush as he watched the flow of commuters, looking for patterns. They were scurrying past like rats, flooding from different directions. But they surged as one into the cavernous entrance on the left.

Cameron smiled and relaxed his fingers. Of course: Pearse Station.

What could be better?

He barged through the queue of people blocking the entrance and scoured the area. She had to be here. Trains rattled overhead and the air was a mixture of dust and sweat. Then he spotted her, on the other side of the ticket barriers. She was stepping on to the escalator for the southbound platform.

He checked the ticket queue. Ten bodies deep and it wasn't moving. He could vault over the ticket barrier, but that would get him noticed. He had to get to her before she boarded the next train.

Narrowing his eyes, he inspected the ticket barriers more closely. They were automatic turnstiles, all except for the one on the end. Passengers poured through it past a middle-aged man in a sloppy blue uniform, who flicked a glance at every second ticket.

It was Cameron's only chance.

He searched the crowd, looking for cover. Two Japanese students strolled past him, heading towards the barrier on the end. The taller boy held a large map of Dublin out at arm's length, as if he was reading a newspaper. Cameron ducked in behind them. They stopped in front of the ticket collector and wrestled with the folds of the map as they fumbled for their tickets. Cameron slipped unnoticed behind them through the open barrier.

He raced up to the southbound platform, taking

the escalator steps two at a time. He reached the top and held his breath.

The station was huge, like an aircraft hangar. People were lined up on both sides of the tracks, staring into the open mouths of daylight at either end.

The girl was near the edge of the platform, twenty yards to his left. He exhaled, and a familiar ripple of heat licked up his body. He basked in it.

He slunk over towards her, glancing up at the display that counted down the time until the next train.

Two minutes.

He sidled up behind her. Other commuters staked out their space on the platform beside him. He edged forward so that no one could get between them.

He was close now. Close enough to touch her. He could smell her flowery scent. He inhaled deeply, and was aware of his own musty sourness mixed in with her fragrance. He longed to press himself against her. He thought about what he'd whisper to her, just before she went over the edge.

The air moved. The rails clacked. Something small scuttled across them.

He looked up at the display. One minute. He raised his hand.

Any second now.

CHAPTER 6

Keep behind the line. Harry never bothered much with rules, but this was one she paid attention to. She stiffened against the bodies that packed in behind her, nudging her forward.

A pigeon curled its toes over the edge of the platform, dipping its head for a look at the three-foot drop to the tracks below. Her own toes curled just watching it. She checked the display: Dun Laoghaire, one minute.

She thought about the KWC meeting again and winced. Damn Dillon and his pop psychology.

'I thought it could help if you went down there,' he'd said to her over the phone, as she'd picked at the moss on the canal wall. 'You know, confront things.'

'If you use the word "cathartic", I'll scream,' she said.

'Come on, you never talk about your father. You haven't seen him since before he went to prison. What's that, five years?'

'Actually, it's six.'

'There you go, you see? You need catharsis.'

She laughed. 'Look, I appreciate the concern, but I'll sort it through in my own way.'

'You mean you'll put a lid on it and bury it alive.'

'Maybe.' She flicked a piece of velvety moss on to the canal bank. 'Look, my father comes and goes a lot in my life. Now he's just gone again. It's no big deal.'

'I'll put someone else on the pen test.'

'No, Dillon, I'll handle it. You just took me by surprise, that's all. Seriously, I'm fine.'

But she hadn't been fine. She'd been touchy and, worst of all, mouthy. Not an unusual combination for her, she'd be the first to admit, but she hated to let herself down like that. She'd tried to walk it off, turning away from the train station near the IFSC and choosing instead to march along the Liffey. She'd given up after ten minutes. Kitten heels just weren't built for cleansing power-walks.

Harry looked at the display again. The minute was up. A draught sliced at her cheek. The pigeon flapped into the air as though it had just seen a cat. People crushed in around her. Someone pressed against the length of her body and catapulted her six inches forward.

'Hey!' She made to turn her head, but felt herself rammed forward again, forced out on to the edge of the platform. She caught sight of the black tracks below and squeezed her eyes shut. Digging her heels in, she leaned backwards and drove her elbows into the crowd.

A shout came from behind her. 'Stop pushing!'

Hot breath whispered against her ear. A hard fist shoved her in the small of her back, and she pitched forward, weightless. Her eyes widened, transfixed. Steel rails accelerated towards her. She thrust out her hands and braced herself for the fall.

Her body slammed into the ground. Sharp stones pierced the palms of her hands, and her knee crunched against the concrete crossbar of the track. Somebody screamed.

Harry lifted her head and gaped at the winding tracks ahead. Her limbs were paralysed. The rails click-clacked.

Move!

She grasped the rails and tried to heave herself up. Hot pain shot through her knee as it gave way beneath her. She collapsed back on to the track, stretched across it.

The rails vibrated against her hands. A horn shrieked. She snapped her head up. A train roared round the bend into the station, blinding her with its headlights. Sweat flashed over her.

Harry dropped to the ground and rolled. Her shoulders hammered against iron and stone. Something yanked her back. She looked over her shoulder. Her bag had snagged on a bolt in the rail. The train thundered towards her. She whipped the strap off over her head and threw herself clear of the track.

She lay face down, breathing in the smell of dust

44

and metal and gripping on to the northbound track. Her whole body trembled. The first carriage crashed past. People screamed at her, but she couldn't move. Not yet.

Then there was another sound. Tick-tack, tick-tack. The rails buzzed beneath her fingers. She forced her eyes open, and her heart raced. Another train was screeching into the far end of the station and she was right in its path.

A yell froze in her throat. No time. She shot a glance at the northbound platform. She'd never make it. Behind her, the southbound train was still hurtling past.

There was nowhere to go.

She looked at the space between the two sets of tracks. It was only a few feet wide, but she had no choice. She flung herself down on to the stones separating the north and southbound rails. She knew she had to stay level with the ground. Any mistakes and the trains would slice her in two.

Harry turned her face to one side and stared at the black stones, waiting. Her breathing had almost stopped.

The two trains screamed past each other, catching her in their crossfire as together they blocked out the light. Gusts of air whipped her face. The huge roar of the engines filled her body and made her want to hunch her shoulders and cover her ears. But she had to stay still.

The joint in the rails beside her crick-cracked as each giant wheel pressed down on it. She focused on the undercarriage of the train, a mess of iron blocks and corrugated tubes charging by, inches from her face.

Brakes scraped against the tracks and the carriages hissed, until finally the trains squealed to a halt. Harry lay there trembling. The engines rumbled alongside her, like two old lorries. Her mouth was dry and tasted of iron and coal dust.

Doors slammed. People were screaming. Feet crunched over the stones towards her.

'Jesus! Miss? You all right?'

Harry closed her eyes. Bad idea. She snapped them open again. The back of her neck felt clammy and the world roared in her ears.

God, she couldn't faint now.

Strong arms lifted her to her feet, half-carried her across the tracks. More hands grabbed at her, heaving her on to the platform.

'Get back! Give her room!'

'Someone call an ambulance!'

Slowly, Harry eased herself up on to her hands and knees. She stayed there on all fours, swaying, as the blood drizzled back into her head. On the ground beside her was her battered satchel. Someone must have retrieved it from the track. She reached out for it, her fingers touching the silver DefCon logo.

Someone put a hand on her arm. 'Are you okay? Did you . . . was it an accident?'

Harry swallowed, and thought back to the fist in the small of her back, and the words someone had whispered in her ear before she fell.

The Sorohan money . . . The ring . . .

She shivered, looking up into the sea of strangers' faces. She couldn't deal with their questions. Not now.

'Yeah,' she said. 'It was just an accident.'

CHAPTER 7

'Are you sure that's what he said?'

Harry shivered and shook her head. 'I'm not sure of anything right now.'

She closed her eyes and sank lower into the seat of Dillon's car, trying not to mark the upholstery. Her suit was streaked with grime and black dust, like something that belonged in a skip, and she guessed her face must be the same. Her whole body ached, and her right knee had swollen to the size of a grapefruit.

She peeked at Dillon's profile. His nose always reminded her of Julius Caesar's, strong and straight with a high, aristocratic bridge. He was dark, almost as dark as she was, and his six-foot frame slotted easily into the driver's seat of his Lexus.

'So come on, tell me again,' he said. 'What exactly did this guy say?'

'It was more of a whisper, really. Sort of rough and sandpapery.'

Dillon turned to look at her. He had a habit of setting his mouth in a straight line, with an upward tuck in one corner as if he was holding back a smile. 'Okay then, what did he whisper?'

'I can't be sure, but it was something like: "The Sorohan money, give it back to the ring."'

'But what the hell does it mean?'

Harry shrugged, and examined the palms of her hands. They still stung where the gravel from the railway tracks had dug into her flesh.

'And he didn't say anything else?' Dillon said.

'There wasn't time to say anything else. I was falling, remember?'

'I can't believe someone tried to push you under a bloody train.'

'I'm finding it kind of hard to deal with myself. Not sure the police believed me, either.'

A tall young police officer with a bobbing Adam's apple had arrived at the train station to question her. Someone had wrapped her in a scratchy blanket, and she'd told her story between sips of hot sugary tea. All except for the words that she'd heard before she fell. That would have to keep for a while. When Dillon had phoned and insisted on coming to get her, she'd been glad for once to let someone else take charge.

Dillon swerved to avoid a cyclist and Harry's stomach flipped, taking a moment to catch up with the rest of her insides. So far, it had been a jerky ride. Dillon alternated between pumping the accelerator and slamming on the brakes, with no real let-up in between. At this rate, she'd be lucky not to get whiplash.

She'd worked for Dillon for less than a year. He'd head-hunted her the previous summer from

49

another software firm, hounding her with the same restless energy he seemed to apply to everything. It was the second time their paths had crossed in the last sixteen years. The first time, she'd only been thirteen.

That seemed so long ago. She leaned back against the headrest and closed her eyes, flashing on an image of herself at thirteen: fists clenched, wild hair, caught up in a kind of double life. Come to think of it, maybe she hadn't changed all that much.

She'd figured out early on in her childhood that she'd need a means of escape to survive her home life. Her solution had been to live two lives: one as the girl she called Harry the Drudge, whose mother opened her letters and read her diaries, and whose father wasn't around enough to be much of an ally; the other she lived as Pirata, an insomniac who sat in the dark and prowled the electronic underground where she was both powerful and respected.

That was in the late eighties, before the internet had taken off. Pirata spent her time dialling out over slow modem connections to bulletin-board systems, electronic message centres where people shared ideas and downloaded hacker tools. By the time she was eleven, she'd taught herself how to penetrate almost any kind of system. She trespassed lightly, never pilfering, never causing harm. But by the time she was thirteen, she was ready to take things to the next level.

Harry could still remember the night she did it. The room had been dark, the only light a greenish glow from her computer screen. It was two o'clock in the morning and she was war dialling, programming her computer to make continuous phone calls until it found a number that allowed it to connect. She sat curled up in her chair, hugging her knees for warmth, listening to the thin screech of the modem as it dialled and disconnected. She wasn't worried about her parents waking up to find her. They were too busy with their own problems to pay much attention to her.

Suddenly she'd had a hit. The caterwaul of chatty modems was unmistakable. Another computer out there had answered her. She straightened up, tapped out a command on the keyboard and hit Enter. Almost immediately the other computer spat back a message that made her clap a hand over her mouth.

> WARNING! You have accessed a Dublin Stock Exchange computer system. Unauthorized access is prohibited and can result in disciplinary proceedings.

Harry had curled her feet back up under her and chewed her fingernail. Up until now, the highest profile network she'd ever invaded belonged to the University College of Dublin. Security there was lax, mainly because there was no confidential data lying around. The Stock

Exchange, on the other hand, had to be crackling with sensitive information. She knew she should disconnect. Instead, she swung her feet to the ground and yanked her chair in closer to the keyboard.

She could tell by the characteristic 'Username:' prompt that the operating system was VMS. This was both good and bad. On the one hand, there were many ways to circumvent VMS security once she was logged in. On the other hand, logging in without a valid username and password wasn't going to be easy. And to make matters worse, she'd be disconnected after three bad attempts.

Her fingers hovered over the keys while she considered some likely account names and passwords. Best to stick to the obvious. She typed in 'system'. At the 'Password:' prompt, she typed 'manager', and hit Enter. Immediately the 'Username:' prompt re-appeared, challenging her to try again.

Strike one.

Next she tried 'system' and 'operator'.

Strike two.

She had one shot left. She flexed her fingers and in her mind ran through the passwords that had worked for her in the past: 'syslib', 'sysmaint', 'operator'. All were good bets, but there were no guarantees. Even the username 'system' might be wrong.

Then another possibility struck her; she shook her head – no chance. But it was so unlikely, she decided to give it a try. She typed in the username 'guest', left the password blank and hit Enter. A message unravelled on the screen:

Welcome to the Dublin Stock Exchange VAX server.

And there on the next line, waiting politely for her instructions, was the coveted VMS $ prompt. She was logged in.

She sat back and grinned. Administrators would sometimes create an unprotected 'Guest' account for new or infrequent users, but the practice was highly insecure. She was beginning to realize that the weakest point in any system was a lazy administrator.

She rolled up the sleeves of her pyjamas and started to type, sidestepping security blocks and dodging her way further into the system. Every time one of her commands outwitted the other computer, she bounced up and down in her chair.

When she figured out that she was inside a database server, she wiggled a thumbs-up sign at the screen. Goody. Databases were full of interesting information. She rummaged through the files. The records seemed to represent financial transactions of some kind, but the details made little sense to her. Then she found a list of vaguely familiar acronyms: NLD, CHF, DEM, HKD. It wasn't until she saw ESP in the list and recognized it as the symbol for the Spanish peseta that she understood what she was looking at. Foreign currency symbols. She must have stumbled on records of foreign exchange trades.

Harry scanned the data and blinked when she saw the sums of money involved. So many zeros. She itched to leave her mark, to let them know she'd been there. What harm could it do? With a flurry of fingers, she added a couple of zeros to some of the smaller trades.

Then she backtracked out of the system, shut down her modem connection and scampered into bed. But she couldn't sleep. She'd slipped a little further into the black-hat world, and now she wondered what she'd started.

She didn't have long to wait before she found out. The Stock Exchange discovered the security breach and recruited the services of an independent consultant to trace the source. The expert they hired was a twenty-one-year-old graduate who was a crackerjack in software security. It took him just a week to track her down.

His name was Dillon Fitzroy.

CHAPTER 8

'Tell me about KWC.'

Harry dragged her gaze away from the traffic and saw that Dillon was looking at her. KWC. Had that only been today?

She squirmed and made a face. 'I screwed up.'

Dillon frowned. 'What happened?'

'In my defence, they were a bunch of jerks.' Then she thought of Jude Tiernan, and something pecked at her conscience. Maybe she'd given him an unnecessarily hard time. 'One of them had a go at me about my father. I got a bit, well . . .'

'Don't tell me. Mouthy?'

'Sorry.'

'Shit, Harry, that could have been an important account. I had to pull favours to get that meeting.'

'Hey, you're the one who prescribed the cathartic therapy, remember?'

He sighed. 'Don't worry, I'll call them, see if I can patch things up.'

Harry didn't answer. She let her head sink back against the seat and closed her eyes again. Her neck had started to ache and she guessed her body

55

was covered in livid bruises that would hurt like hell in the morning.

'You shouldn't be alone tonight,' Dillon said. 'You're still in shock.'

She kept her eyes closed. 'I'm fine.'

'Come back to my house. I've got brandy, food and a change of clothes, strictly in that order.'

Harry shot him a quick look. She'd never been to his home, but, according to Imogen's sources, he lived in a gracious mansion in the Enniskerry countryside. Her sources also had him pegged as resolutely single, so Harry wondered where the change of women's clothes would come from.

Under other circumstances, she might have allowed her curiosity to get the better of her, but right now, all she wanted was to close her apartment door behind her and think.

'Thanks, but I'd be bad company,' she said. 'I just need to sleep.'

She felt his eyes scrutinize her face.

'You know what he meant, don't you?' he said.

'What?'

'The guy in the train station, the Sorohan money, all that stuff.' He flicked her a look in between watching the road. 'It means something to you, doesn't it?'

She shook her head and forced a shrug. 'It was just some nutter.'

He regarded her for a moment, and then snapped his attention back to the traffic. 'Suit yourself.'

His face had shut down on her. Hell. But she

couldn't do anything about it now. There were some aspects of her life she just wasn't ready to open up about yet. At least not until she understood them better herself.

Dillon swung right into Raglan Road. Harry's tension began to melt as they drove down the familiar tree-lined avenue. Victorian red-bricks stood guard on either side, some of them restored to elegant family homes but most converted into apartments. You could tell which ones were rented by the cracked paint on the sash windows.

Dillon peered out at them. 'Which one is yours?'

Harry pointed to a corner house with a canary-yellow door. She'd smartened it up herself with a fresh coat of paint the week before. One of these days she'd buy her landlord out. Her profession paid well, and she'd accumulated enough savings now to start thinking about a mortgage.

Dillon slammed to a dead stop, scuffing the kerb. Harry hauled herself up out of the car and led the way through the front door.

The building had a basement and three floors, and Harry lived in an apartment at ground level. It had once been an elegant drawing room where butlers served tea. Now it was a place where Harry ate breakfast in bed any time she felt like it.

She trudged down the hall, aware of Dillon's presence like a stalker behind her. They reached her apartment, and Harry froze. The door was open.

She edged up to the threshold, hesitating. Dillon stood behind her, looking in over her shoulder.

'Oh my God,' he said.

Her apartment looked as though a pack of wild dogs had been cooped up in it for ten days. Her sofa had been slashed, the black leather ripped apart to expose chunks of yellow sponge. All her paperbacks had been swept from the shelves and lay in slippery piles on the floor.

Harry took a deep breath. She stepped inside and picked her way through the carnage in the room. It was like wandering amongst the bodies of old friends. The mirror from over the fireplace had been hurled to the floor, the glass smashed. Her only picture, a playful print of dogs playing poker, had been wrenched away from the wall, splitting the plaster where the nail had been. The print lay propped up against the mutilated sofa, its brown-paper seal gouged out at the back. Harry stared at it, her arms hugging her chest.

Dillon's voice called out from the kitchen: 'Take a look at this.'

She dragged herself over to join him, her shoes making a crunching sound on the flagstones. It turned out to be sugar from a bag that had been dumped upside down on the floor, along with everything else from her kitchen cupboards.

Harry gaped. The entire contents of her kitchen – tins, saucepans, jars, food from the fridge – had been piled in the centre of the floor. The cutlery drawers had been upturned and chucked on to the heap. The cupboard doors stood wide open, empty shelves exposed. It was like a crazed attack of spring-cleaning.

Harry sank back against the doorframe. Jesus, who would do this? Dillon circled the mound of food, shaking his head. She sighed and trudged back along the corridor to check her bedroom. It was in the same disarray as the rest of the apartment; drawers ransacked, clothes strewn about. She'd never wear any of them again.

The red light blinked on her bedside phone, a mute demand for attention. She noticed a familiar, well-worn book that had landed face down on her bed. It was spread open so wide that its spine had cracked, and it lay there like a broken bird. She picked it up and some of the pages fluttered out. It was a book her father had given her when she was twelve: *How to Play Poker and Win*. On the inside covers, front and back, was a series of annotations written in blue marker. They recorded some of the poker games she'd played with her father. It was a habit she'd learned from him. After every hand, he'd make detailed notes, jotting down the cards that had been played. He never forgot a hand, and he never got beaten by the same bluff twice.

She'd been six or seven years old when her father first started taking her to his poker games, often staying out till three or four in the morning. She'd picked up some of her best swear words at those games. Usually she'd end up asleep on a sofa, her eyes smarting from cigarette smoke. Later, as a teenager, he'd brought her to London to visit the

59

casinos in Soho and Piccadilly. At the time it had all seemed grown-up and exciting, but in retrospect it was just bad parenting.

She turned over the flyleaf of the poker book in her hand. The inscription was still there, as she'd known it would be.

> *A mi queridísima Harry,*
> *Never be predictable. Play a random game and keep 'em guessing, but always fold on a 7-2 offsuit.*
> *Un abrazo muy fuerte,*
> *Papá*

She smoothed her thumb along the broad handwriting. Then she closed the covers and cradled the book with both hands so that the pages wouldn't split.

Dillon poked his head round the door. 'Your office and bathroom are both trashed.'

Harry swore. She'd seen enough. She slapped the book on her bedside locker and marched back out to the living room, ignoring her throbbing knee.

Dillon followed her. 'I'll call the police.'

'It's okay, I'll do it.'

Dillon paced up and down the room while she phoned her local police station. She reported the details to a sympathetic sergeant who said they'd send someone round. Then she snapped the phone shut and burrowed under the pile of books on the floor till she found the Golden Pages directory.

Dillon stopped his pacing to watch her. 'Now what?'

'Locksmith.' She flipped her phone open again and had a businesslike conversation with Express Locksmiths, who assured her that an engineer would be out in ten minutes. Harry could feel her energy levels pick up. Absurd how a burst of activity could fool you into thinking you were in control.

She perched against the sofa and massaged her neck and shoulders. They felt stiff and bruised, as though she was headed for a bout of flu. Then she remembered the blinking light in her bedroom, and went back to listen to her messages. There was only one. She recognized her mother's throaty voice, made low and fruity from years of heavy smoking.

'Harry, it's Miriam.'

There was a pause as she heard her mother pull on a cigarette. Harry had been addressing her mother by her Christian name since the day she'd left school. It was as though by unspoken mutual agreement the mother–daughter dynamic had dissolved once she'd turned eighteen.

'I've been trying to reach you all day, and all I get is this wretched machine,' Miriam continued. 'Could you please take a minute to pick up the phone and call me.'

Harry closed her eyes and fixed her lips in a tight line. Then she jabbed at the delete button and returned to the living room, where Dillon was still on patrol.

She looked at her watch. 'It's late. You head on home, there's no need to stay.'

Dillon waved a hand at her. 'I'm staying.'

She felt a tiny squeezing sensation in her chest and realized she was glad to have him there. Then she looked at the destruction all around her, and dared herself to cross a line.

'Is that offer of brandy still open?' Her voice had come out a little louder than she'd planned.

Dillon turned to look at her with his tucked-in smile. ''Course it is. Let's make it a double. You've had a rough day.'

He came to a sudden stop next to the damaged painting, and bent down to examine it. He poked his hand through the rent in the backing board. 'Why would anyone do this?'

Harry shrugged and shook her head.

Dillon scanned the room. 'This whole place – it's like they were looking for something.'

Harry threw him a sharp look. 'It strikes you that way, does it?'

'Doesn't it seem like that to you?'

She sighed and rubbed her eyes. They felt gritty. 'Yeah, but I was hoping I was wrong.'

She eased herself off the arm of the sofa and made her way over to the kitchen, keeping the weight off her bad knee. She leaned against the door jamb and stared at the incongruous heap on the floor.

What the hell were they after?

Then she thought of the man in the train station, of his hot breath against her ear, and shuddered.

CHAPTER 9

'So what did you find?' Leon said.

He swallowed and ran a finger along the inside of his collar. He was leaning against the back door of O'Dowd's pub, hunched over his phone as if he had cramps.

'Nothing,' came the reply. 'I told you it'd be a waste of fuckin' time.'

Voices roared from the bar at the other end of the passageway. In spite of the draught seeping in from the street outside, Leon was sweating.

'Are you sure?' Leon said.

'Course I'm fuckin' sure. I tore the whole place up, just for the crack, but there's nothing there.' There was a pause. 'So when do I get paid?'

'Stop worrying about your money, okay? You'll get paid.'

Someone opened the door of the nearby Gents' toilet, and Leon caught a whiff of disinfectant and stale urine. He turned his face to the wall and lowered his voice.

'Just stick with her. I want to know everything she does. But don't get too close. Blow your cover, and the deal's off.'

He disconnected the call and moved over to a door marked PRIVATE. He stood in front of it, rubbing his hands along his trouser legs. Then he eased open the door and stepped inside.

The room was the size of a prison cell and just about as well decorated. Light from a single overhead bulb bleached the walls and carpet of any colour. The door closed behind him with a thunk, blocking out all sound as though he'd been sucked into a vacuum. He stepped over to the green baize table where four other people were seated.

'Come on, Leon, are you in or what?' The dealer scowled at him, his sun-damaged skin corrugated with wrinkles. His name was Mattie, and Leon heard he spent most of his life crewing other people's yachts in the Mediterranean. The rest of the time he played poker.

Leon nodded and resumed his seat on Mattie's right. He slumped in the chair and closed his eyes, squeezing the bridge of his nose. The only sound was the slick-slick of the cards being dealt.

He hadn't expected the girl's apartment to be clean. There had to be a record of the money somewhere. Where the hell was she hiding it?

Mattie slapped the deck on the table beside him. Leon straightened up and tried to concentrate on the game. Being distracted was no way to play high-stakes poker.

They were playing no-limit Texas Hold 'Em. Each player was dealt two cards face down, which he had to combine with five communal cards to make a poker hand. Usually it was Leon's favourite game, every betting round another opportunity to coax money out of some loser's pocket. But tonight it felt as though he was the loser. And if he didn't win the next hand, he was fucked.

He slid his two cards towards him, lining up their edges, one on top of the other. He peeked at the bottom card. King of spades. He glanced around the table but no one was paying him any attention. He squeezed the top card out from behind the first, just enough to see one corner of it. Another king. His heartbeat broke into a little canter and he worked hard not to let it show.

The player on Leon's right tossed a handful of chips into the centre of the table. 'Raise a grand.'

Leon threw him a sharp look. The guy was built like a professional wrestler, with grey hair scraped back into a ponytail that reached halfway down his back. His face was unreadable.

Leon made a show of playing with his chips, but he didn't stall for long. With kings back to back in the hole, he intended to hit them hard. 'Yours plus another thousand.'

Mattie shook his head and flung his cards on the table. The old bald guy to his left consulted his hole cards and consigned them to the muck along with Mattie's.

Next up was Adele, the only woman at the table. Leon had played with her before. Blonde and in her forties, she always dressed in a smart business suit and played a tight game. She studied Leon's face for a moment and called his raise.

Leon waited for the Wrestler to decide if he was in or out. What the hell did he have? Leon was in no mood to work it out. Sal Martinez could have done the maths in an instant, but that kind of stuff made Leon's head hurt. All he knew was the pot was now over eight thousand euros, and he needed to win it badly.

It didn't help that he was playing almost entirely with his clients' money. A couple of businesses whose accounts he'd audited had sent him cheques for owed income tax, cheques that Leon was supposed to submit to the Revenue Commissioners. Somehow the money had made an unplanned pit-stop in his own pocket. Just for a few days.

The Wrestler's chips clattered into the centre of the table. 'Call.'

Leon took a deep breath and flexed his shoulders. He could hear the bones cracking at the base of his neck. Mattie flicked the three flop cards face up on the table, the first of the five communal cards. A king, a three and a five, all different suits. Electricity surged through Leon's veins. Now he had three kings.

Adele checked, and didn't look happy about it. The Wrestler was up next. With hands the size of baseball gloves, he grabbed a fistful of chips and raised by two thousand euros.

Leon examined the other man's face. The features were immobile, all apart from a tiny pulse in one eyelid that jumped like a sand flea. It was all Leon needed. He knew that at best the guy was holding a three and a five, giving him two pair. It didn't beat trip kings.

There were two more cards to come. Should he call or risk another raise? *Play the man, not the cards,* Martinez would've said. But then Martinez was a pretty loose player. Leon had seen him win half a million in a single pot, only to lose it minutes later on a bluff with a pair of threes.

Fuck it, self-confidence was half the game. Leon raised another three grand.

Adele chucked her cards on the table and settled in to watch the rest of the hand. The Wrestler took his time. He riffled his chips, separating them into tall stacks and then splicing them back together with a flick of his jumbo-sized fingers.

'Call,' he said finally, challenging Leon with a long stare. 'Just you and me now.'

Leon didn't like the smug look on his face. By now there was nearly twenty thousand euros in the pot, and eight thousand of it belonged to him. Or more precisely, to his clients.

Leon's stomach curdled. Christ. Reduced to pilfering funds from lousy shopkeepers. What the fuck happened? Nine years ago he was making millions, trading on nuggets of inside information. Between them, he and the rest of the trading ring had made over twenty-five million euros in a single year. Sweet deals, every one of them. Until the Sorohan deal, of course. That fucking Martinez.

He took a deep breath, trying to focus on the game. He still hadn't shaved and he could smell the sourness of his own body. Time for the turn, the fourth communal card. Mattie flipped it over on the table. Another five. Leon sat still. The table now showed a king, a three and two fives. It gave Leon a full house of kings and fives.

The Wrestler pushed a stack of chips into the pot. 'Five thousand.'

Leon saw the tightening around the other man's mouth and knew he was still ahead. The Wrestler could be making trip fives, maybe filling a house with threes, but not much else. He called.

Now for the river, the fifth and final card. Leon watched as Mattie rolled a five.

Shit. Now there were three fives on the table. He searched the Wrestler's face, looking for tells. Could he possibly be holding the last five?

The Wrestler's forehead glistened in the overhead light. He looked like a melting waxwork. He shoved out the biggest stack yet. Six thousand euros. The middle of the table was beginning to look like a model tower-block city.

Leon gazed at the pot. There was now over thirty-five thousand in there. He almost whimpered out loud. He knew that the thirteen thousand he had contributed was no longer his. It belonged to the pot, and to defend it with more of his own money would be downright stupid. The wise man would fold and walk away.

Leon scooped up his last remaining chips and piled them high in the pot. 'Call.'

He locked eyes with the Wrestler. Time to reveal their hole cards. The Wrestler went first. Almost in slow motion, he turned over his top card. The three of clubs. So far, that just gave him a house of fives and threes. Leon's back was drenched in sweat. He stared, transfixed by the second card. The Wrestler rolled it over. The five of diamonds. The only card in the deck that could beat him.

Leon sank back into his chair. Four unbeatable fucking fives. Nausea roiled like an eel in his stomach. His head started to pound, and his vision turned blurry at the edges. That fucking Martinez prick – he'd brought him to this. He'd ruined everything. Leon ground his teeth and choked back a howl of rage. That girl of his deserved everything that was coming to her.

CHAPTER 10

'ETA fifteen minutes,' Dillon said.

From the way he gunned the engine, Harry could well believe it. He swerved into the outside lane and she gripped the door handle with both hands. If he noticed she was bracing herself for impact, he didn't mention it.

The Lexus coasted along the open motorway and soon she felt her limbs relax. The car was warm, the murmur of the engine hypnotic. Harry closed her eyes and leaned back against the head-rest.

She'd spent over an hour with the police in her apartment. Two officers had arrived, one the same young Garda who'd spoken to her in Pearse Station, the other a plain-clothes detective who hadn't been introduced. The younger one did all the talking. The other had just watched her with quiet grey eyes as she answered questions about the break-in and explained again how she fell in front of a train.

Harry shifted in the passenger seat. Her legs grew heavy and she felt herself drifting. By the time she opened her eyes again it was pitch-dark, and the motorway had turned into a narrow country road lined with thick hedges.

Dillon slowed the car and rolled in through a pair of wrought-iron gates. 'We're here.'

Harry peered out the window. Electric lanterns lined the driveway up to the front door. Light splashed upwards along trees and bushes, illuminating everything from below like theatre footlights.

Dillon crunched to a halt and Harry hoisted herself out of the car, gazing at the house that took centre stage in front of them. It was shaped like a gigantic L, with a steeply pitched roof and dormer windows perched along the top like eyes. She could smell the fragrant cedar incense from the conifers that stood on sentry duty by the front door.

'Like it?' Dillon said.

Harry looked back at him. He was watching her with a self-satisfied smile, clearly enjoying her reaction to his magnificent home.

She raised her eyebrows. 'Are you showing off?'

He shrugged. 'Maybe. What can I say? No point in having money if you don't know how to spend it.' Then he guided her towards the door, his palm brushing against the small of her back. 'Come on, let's get you that brandy.'

The entrance hall was the size of her entire apartment. Dillon led the way to a room at the back of the house. Harry hesitated, suddenly aware of how she must look.

'Maybe I should take that bath first. I feel sort of grubby.'

Dillon's phone rang before he could reply. He checked the caller ID.

'It's Ashford, from KWC. You'd better hang on.' He took the call. 'Dillon Fitzroy.'

He stared at the floor, listening to the voice on the other end of the phone. Harry tried to read his face, and something squirmed inside her as she imagined what Ashford had to say. Then she remembered Felix's belligerence and stuck her chin in the air.

'Thanks, that's very understanding of you.' Dillon threw her a wry look. 'Unfortunately, Harry's been in a bit of an accident, but I'll put another engineer on to it first thing Monday morning.'

Dillon winced at the response on the other end of the phone. Harry flapped her hands to object. Dammit, she could finish the job. But Dillon ignored her.

'No, no, she's fine, nothing serious.' He shot a look in her direction, his expression puzzled. 'Yes, I'm sure. No, she's not in hospital. She'll be available to hand things over to Imogen Brady on Monday.'

Dillon began to wind up the call and finally disconnected. He stared at her.

Harry kept her chin in the air. 'I can do the pen test.'

'Let's not push it, okay?'

'What did he say?'

'He was full of apologies for today, said none of

72

it was your fault.' He folded his arms and considered her for a moment. 'He seemed very concerned for your welfare. Quite shocked to hear you were in an accident. Do you two know each other?'

Harry frowned and shook her head. Then her brow cleared. 'He knew my father. Old pals, apparently.'

'Ah.' Dillon checked his watch. 'I need to make some calls. You take that bath. Upstairs, second room on the left. The wardrobe has plenty of clothes.' He stepped into the room behind him and was gone.

Harry made her way up the stairs, checking out her appearance in the mirrors that lined the walls. Bed-hair, black streaks on her face and crumpled clothes. She looked like a teenage runaway up to no good.

Harry found the bedroom and closed the door behind her. Her eyes swept the room and she whistled. She'd stayed in five-star hotels that weren't as plush as this. She flung her satchel on the queen-sized bed, and was about to stretch out alongside it when her phone rang.

'Hello?'

'Hello, this is Sandra Nagle from Sheridan Bank Customer Services. Am I speaking with Ms Harry Martinez?'

Harry yanked the phone away from her ear as though she'd been scorched. Shit. The helpdesk supervisor she'd tangled with that afternoon.

Had she tracked her down and called her to bawl her out? Then she remembered the woman couldn't see her and put the phone back to her ear.

'Ms Martinez?'

'Sorry, yeah, that's me.' Harry perched on the edge of the bed.

'Our reports have shown up a slight anomaly on your current account. I need to check some of the details with you, if I may?'

Harry blinked. 'Anomaly?'

'I just need to confirm the size of the lodgement you made today.'

'What lodgement?'

There was a pause. 'Our records show that twelve million euros was lodged into your current account this afternoon.'

Harry's eyes widened. 'Are you serious?'

'Is the amount incorrect?'

Was she out of her mind? 'Of course it's incorrect. I didn't make any lodgements.'

'Perhaps it was lodged by a third party.'

A third party. Something cold dropped into Harry's stomach. 'I don't know anything about that money. Surely your records must show where it came from?'

Sandra cleared her throat. 'Well, that's the slight anomaly, I'm afraid.'

'What do you mean?'

'Our records seem to be incomplete. Your recent transactions are on the screen here in front of me, and the lodgement is there, but it's not coming up with any other information. Usually we can tell whether it's a cheque, an online transfer and so on, but that part is blank.'

'Doesn't it tell you anything? A branch number? A name?'

'No, just the amount. Twelve million.'

Harry flopped back down on to the bed. What the hell was going on?

'That twelve million euros doesn't belong to me,' she said. 'I don't want it in my bank account.'

She could almost hear the other woman draw herself up.

'I'm afraid I can't do anything about that,' Sandra said. 'The money has been credited to your account.'

'This is ridiculous.' Harry closed her eyes and massaged the bridge of her nose. 'People don't just lodge twelve million euros without leaving some kind of record. Don't you have any limit checks on what goes in and out of your bank? Wouldn't someone query an amount like this?'

'Normally, yes, which is why I'm on the phone to you now.' Sandra's teeth sounded clenched. 'There's obviously some problem with these trans-action details. I'll put the system-support team on it straight away. But in the meantime, the money stays in your account.'

'Can you send me out a bank statement? I'd like to see a record of this.'

'Of course.' The woman was all service.

Harry hung up. Then she grabbed her satchel

and whipped out her laptop, hooking it into a phone jack in the wall. Within minutes she was online, logged into her Sheridan bank account. She clicked the balance option and stared at the screen. Then she refreshed the web page, checking it again. Same answer.

12,000,120.42

Harry sank back on to the velvety bed. It had to be a mistake, a hitch in the bank's paperwork. These things happened, didn't they?

She examined the palms of her hands. The cuts from the gravel were like a row of teeth marks. She sighed and sat up. Who the hell was she fooling? She may not want to face it, but everything that had happened today just had to be connected. And her gut told her the connection was her father. If she was honest with herself, she'd known it from the minute the guy in the station had whispered in her ear. Sorohan was a name that had resonated with significance for her ever since her father's arrest.

She remembered the newspaper headlines: *Insider Trading Ring Exposed Over Sorohan Fraud; KWC Ring Leader Charged by Stock Exchange*. A hard knot burned inside her chest. That was almost eight years ago: 7th June 2001, to be precise. The day the shutters had slammed down for good between herself and her father.

But who the hell would lodge twelve million euros

into her account? Not her father, surely. He was locked up in Arbour Hill prison, and she doubted that online banking was a facility the inmates enjoyed. She slammed her laptop shut. Not only had someone stashed a chunk of money in her account, but somehow they'd done it without leaving any tracks. It didn't make sense.

She pushed herself up off the bed and trudged into the en-suite bathroom. Too tired to deal with a complicated-looking Jacuzzi shower, she made straight for the sunken bath in the corner and spun the taps on to full blast.

Harry stripped off her clothes and surveyed herself in the full-length mirror. Her legs were splotched with dark bruises, like blackening bananas. Her sooty face was hollow-eyed and anxious, with grazes along the cheeks. She looked like one of those waifs they used to send up chimneys.

She lowered herself into the steaming water an inch at a time. Then she closed her eyes and let her mind drift. She found herself thinking, not of her father nor of the twelve million euros, but of Dillon. And not the Dillon who was downstairs on the phone cutting a deal, but the boy of twenty-one who had once sat in her bedroom and held her by the hand.

CHAPTER 11

'Why do you want to hack?'

Thirteen-year-old Harry groped for an answer that would impress this dark, good-looking boy with the half-smile. She couldn't think of one, so she just told the truth.

'Because I can.'

She waited for his reaction, but there was none. Instead he seemed absorbed by the collection of soldering irons and screwdrivers that littered her bedroom shelves. He was dressed all in black, like a young priest, and his hair fell in a heavy fringe over thick brows. If only she wasn't wearing her brown school uniform and ugly lace-up shoes.

Her mother had shown him up to her room, acting as though the FBI had landed on their doorstep. When he'd introduced himself as Dillon Fitzroy, an investigator with the Dublin Stock Exchange, a whisper of fear had tickled Harry's spine.

She watched as he picked up one of the screwdrivers and tapped the business end against one hand.

'So tell me, why Pirata?' he said, referring to her hacker pseudonym.

'Pi-rrata,' corrected Harry, pronouncing the word with a rolling 'r' and rapid-fire delivery. 'It's Spanish for pirate.'

It suddenly sounded childish, but he nodded as though this were a sensible choice. He held her gaze, compressing his mouth into a neat smile. 'Is it okay if I ask you these questions?'

She nodded and felt the heat rise in her cheeks. She sat down on the bed and glared at her chunky shoes, willing her fiery colour to subside. She was acutely aware of her mother standing on the other side of the door, listening to every word.

Dillon's eyes swept the room, taking in the jumble of dismantled computer hardware and gutted radios. 'Are you building something?'

She attempted a casual shrug. 'Put me in a room with a box that has wires in it and I'll take it apart.' Then she bit her lip, regretting the flippant attitude. She was in trouble here, and she knew it.

Dillon wheeled out the chair from under her desk. There was a large red parcel on the seat. Harry snatched it out of his way and cradled it on her lap. He sat down facing her, arms folded.

'You understand why I'm here, don't you?' he said.

Now they were getting to it. She stared at the floor. 'Yeah.'

'Mind if I take a look?' He gestured towards her PC.

She shook her head, but he'd already turned

round to face the screen. His fingers sped across the keyboard. Harry edged further along the bed until she was close enough to see what he was doing. Text flew up the screen as he browsed through her files and checked out her hacking tools.

'Nice house you live in,' he said, without looking at her.

Harry raised her eyebrows. 'I suppose. We've only been here a year.' She looked at the frothy white curtains and the lacy bed linen. It was a princess's room. Absurd that she should still miss the poky converted attic she'd shared with Amaranta, with its narrow divans and the skipping rope her sister had stretched along the floor to demarcate her territory. But her dad had got this new job. Her mother harped on about how badly the Schrodinger job had ended, but her dad said this time everything would be different. He was right about that.

She turned back to Dillon to find him watching her. His gaze flicked over her school uniform and came to rest on the shoes that made her look like she had club feet. She closed her eyes in mortification.

'Did you move schools too?' he said, turning his attention back to her files.

Something gnawed at her insides the minute she thought about school. She shrugged, and made the kind of face that said it was no big deal.

'Yeah, but I can handle it. Except all they talk

about are skiing holidays and designer clothes.' She lowered her voice and nodded towards the door. 'Mum thinks I should be making more friends.'

'Mums are hard to please.'

She darted a quick look at him. There was no hint of mockery in his dark eyes.

He indicated the package on her lap. 'Christmas present?'

She shoved the parcel to one side. 'It's for my dad. Haven't given it to him yet.'

'He's away?'

'He played poker on Christmas Eve. He'll probably turn up in a day or two.'

Dillon stopped what he was doing. 'He missed Christmas?'

Harry shrugged. 'He misses most Christmases.'

Dillon was silent for a moment. She shoved the parcel on to the bed, the contents rattling. She'd bought her father a full poker set: six hundred plastic chips, two decks of cards and a thick rule book, all stored in their own shiny black case. She'd saved up for it for months.

Dillon turned his attention back to the screen. His eyes narrowed as he worked through one of her files, and Harry peered at the screen to see what had caught his interest. It was the code for one of the hacker tools she had designed herself.

With a staccato flick of the keys, Dillon snapped the file shut and opened up another one. He scrolled down through it, and then stopped to examine it line by line. He gave a low whistle, his eyes riveted to the screen.

He pointed to a line in the code. 'What's this bit doing?'

Harry read through it and then started to explain her design, the words tumbling over each other in her impatience to communicate her ideas. She had to lean across him to reach the keyboard, and she became aware of the warmth of his body and the light spicy soap that he used.

When she finished, he looked at her for a long moment, his eyes searching her face. 'Did you do all this yourself?'

'Yes.' Harry took a deep breath. 'Can I ask you a question now?'

'Sure.' His eyes never left hers.

'How did you find me?'

'That was easy. You posted too many details of your exploit on the bulletin boards. Security guys monitor those things all the time, you know. Stay online long enough and we can track you down, too.'

Harry felt like an idiot. So simple. She'd been careless. But then, she wasn't used to hiding.

Dillon tapped a few keys and closed down her files. Then he spun the chair so that he was facing her. He picked up the screwdriver again and began turning it end over end on the desk.

'You interfered with trading records belonging to the Dublin Stock Exchange,' he said. 'Do you know what happened when they found the error?'

'No.'

'The database administrator almost lost his job.' Dillon leaned forward, his face stern. 'He's only twenty-four and his wife is pregnant.'

Harry hung her head. Her skin crawled as though she had a nasty rash. 'I didn't think. It seemed such a small thing to do.'

Dillon shook his head. 'You're not just messing with computers here, you're screwing up people's lives.'

She couldn't look at him. 'I'm sorry.'

'So tell me about the other systems you've damaged.'

She jerked her head up. 'But I've never done anything like this before. I don't damage things, I just look around.'

He watched her for a moment. She couldn't tell if he believed her. Then he tossed the screwdriver on to the desk with a clatter and folded his arms, as though he'd made up his mind.

'Okay, I've seen how you hack,' he said. 'Now I want to know why.'

'But I've told you why.'

'No, you haven't. Your answer was a cop-out. Tell me again. Why do you want to hack?'

Harry's mind went blank. What kind of answer was he looking for? She felt as if she was back at school, with the teacher asking a series of questions designed to lead her to a single answer. But what was it?

She tried to analyse how she felt when she

started an exploit. 'Okay, well, maybe I love to break into things and be somewhere I shouldn't.'

'So you like taking risks. Why? Does it make you feel powerful?'

Harry thought of the way the hairs stood to attention on the back of her neck whenever she felt close to cracking a system. She thought of the exhilaration that pumped into her bloodstream like a drug as she unlocked the final door into someone's network. He was right. Hacking made her feel powerful in a way no other part of her life ever could. But there was something else.

She shook her head. 'That's part of it, I suppose. But mostly I just don't believe people when they tell me I can't break into a system. Just because it says it in the manual doesn't make it true.' She rubbed her nose, as if that would unscramble her thoughts. 'I know there's always a way in, if I stick at it long enough.'

'So it's about the technology? You want to find out what makes it tick?'

'Yeah, in a way. It's like . . . I dunno.' She looked into his face. 'It's like finding the truth.'

Dillon's eyes glowed and he sat very still. 'That's exactly what hacking is all about. The search for truth.'

Then he leaned forward with his elbows on his knees and clasped his hands in front of him. His face was inches from hers.

'People think hacking is all about destruction, but nothing could be wider of the mark. It's about exploring the technology, about pushing it to its limits and sharing the knowledge. A true hacker expands his mind beyond what's in the books or what he's been taught. He finds a way to do things when conventional thinking fails.' Dillon locked eyes with hers. 'Hacking is good. It's people that are bad.'

He grasped her hands in his. A flash of heat shot through her and something jolted inside her chest.

'Think of hacking as an attitude,' he said. 'We don't just hack computers, we hack our whole lives.' He squeezed her hands, pumping them for emphasis, and his eyes burned into hers. 'Never let yourself be limited by what other people tell you. Never accept their version of how things have to be.'

Harry listened, mesmerized. *Limited.* That described how she felt every minute of her day. Boxed in by her mother, who was always so disappointed in her; labelled at school where she failed to measure up. With a flash of insight, Harry realized he was telling her how to cope with her life.

Without warning, Dillon dropped her hands and sat back, as though suddenly embarrassed at his own intensity. 'End of lecture. Thanks for talking to me.' He jumped to his feet and headed for the door. 'I'll see myself out.'

Harry stood up, dizzy at the sudden change. 'But wait – what happens now?'

Dillon shrugged. 'Probably nothing. I'll need to inform your parents about everything you've been doing, but no one's going to prosecute a thirteen-year-old girl. Do it again though, and you'll be in trouble.'

He stood with his hand on the doorknob and looked over at her, his eyes still slightly feverish. 'Someday I'll have my own company, with the best engineers in the country.' His lips twitched, and he winked at her. 'Stay out of jail long enough and maybe I'll hire you.'

CHAPTER 12

Cameron stood outside the wrought-iron gates. The girl was inside the house, and had been there for almost an hour. He pressed himself up against the bars. He badly needed to finish what he'd started.

He dug his fingernails into his palms. The train station had been such a fuck-up. She'd been so light, like a child. But the instant he'd broken contact with her, the mob of commuters had barged in front of him, blocking his view. He'd heard the shrieking trains, seen them crashing by. But the crowd had robbed him of the sight of her fear.

Without that, it wasn't finished.

He peered through the gate. The driveway looked like a landing strip with all those fucking lights. He made out the shape of the house ahead, two lit windows glowing in the dark. He leaned his face against the cold metal and imagined the girl in one of those rooms. Heat filled his groin.

But he'd been told to back off.

He shook the railings, testing their strength. They stretched at least twelve feet into the air, welded on either side to a concrete wall that rolled away into the shadowy road. A pole-mounted surveillance camera rotated above him, panning its way down the driveway back towards the gate. Cameron ducked to one side, out of its line of sight. Houses like this were all the same. Prison walls, fence-mounted sensors, infrared cameras. Maximum perimeter protection. For all the good it did them. There was always a way inside.

He began to circle the property wall, trailing his hand against the ivy that had stitched itself into the brickwork. He could smell the damp woodiness of the forest around him. Something rustled in the undergrowth, a small mammal on the move. Cameron reached a side gate and gazed again at the long L-shaped house. How spectacular it would look swallowed up in flames.

But he'd been told no fire. Not yet.

Not many people understood fire the way Cameron did. Mostly they were afraid of it. But Cameron had spent time getting close to flames, so close that he could almost touch their trembling colours and slender tongues.

He moved further along the wall, caressing the ivy leaves. Trapping someone in fire was so much more satisfying than shoving them in front of a truck. You got to stay in the shadows and watch the effects of what you'd done. Not like a road accident, where everything was over in a single scream. With fires, the build-up of euphoria was gradual, ending in a trance-like state that sated his need to see things burn.

He'd heard that many serial killers were fire-setters in their adolescence. Son of Sam, for instance. He'd started thousands of fires. Cameron smiled. He wasn't in that league yet. One day, maybe.

He tried the latch on the side gate. It was locked, but the steel bars felt crumbly, the paint peeling away in his hands. He took a closer look. The gate was older and rustier than the other one, the welding not so secure. Cameron's breathing quickened.

He might have been told to back off for a while, but that didn't mean he couldn't get close to her.

CHAPTER 13

The wardrobe turned out to be a walk-in closet bigger than Harry's own bedroom.

She padded over to the rail that ran the length of one wall and browsed through the hangers. The clothes seemed to come in a variety of sizes, but all bore the same designer labels and glitzy evening style. Harry sighed. With her bruised face and battered shoes, it wouldn't be a good look.

She turned to rummage in the shelves behind her and found a pair of men's jeans, a wide belt and some crisp white shirts still in their cellophane wrapping. A few minutes later she was dressed, the shirt tucked in and the belt cinched tight over the loose-fitting jeans. She made her way downstairs, wondering about the women who'd left their clothes behind.

Harry found the room at the back of the house where she had left Dillon, and pushed open the door. There was no sign of him.

She peered around the room and guessed this was where he did most of his living. It was a combination of office and bachelor's den, and smelled of leather and grilled cheese. In front of the television was an oversized armchair complete with footrest and beer holder. Harry had a hard time picturing Dillon with his feet up watching TV.

Dominating one wall was a large black-and-white photograph, maybe five foot by four. It was a recent shot of Dillon, taken from an aerial viewpoint. He was sitting cross-legged on a deserted beach, and all around him were a series of lines and spirals traced in the sand. The pattern was Celtic in effect, and formed an ornate grid that took up half the beach.

'It's a simply connected maze.'

Harry spun round to find Dillon standing in the doorway watching her. He'd changed into smart chinos and a blue rugby shirt, and he carried a silver tray in his hands. He nodded towards the photograph as he moved into the room.

'I used to carve them out everywhere I went. In the grass, in the snow. Once I even built one with mirrors.'

Harry turned back to the photograph. The confusing swirls reassembled themselves into paths and dead-ends, and she recognized it as the sort of maze she used to do as a child.

'What does simply connected mean?' she said.

'Every path you choose leads either to another path or to a dead-end.' The tray rattled as he set it down on the coffee table. 'The paths never reconnect with one another, so it's the simplest kind of maze to solve.'

Harry squinted at the maze and tried to follow one of its paths, but her eyes started to cross and she gave it up.

'I never knew you were so hooked on mazes,' she said.

'Didn't you ever wonder how I named my company?'

She threw him a questioning look.

'Lúbra is the Irish for labyrinth,' he said.

Harry smiled. 'Nice.'

She eyed up the tray. He'd brought a bottle of brandy, two crystal balloon glasses and a plate piled high with sandwiches. Her stomach growled. She hadn't eaten all day.

Helping herself to a sandwich, she sank into one of the chairs. Dillon handed her a brandy. He raised his eyebrows at the men's shirt and jeans, but made no comment.

Harry slugged down a mouthful of brandy. 'Look, I'm sorry about all that stuff with Ashford.' She took a deep breath. 'And I'm sorry about earlier, too. When I clammed up on you. I do that sometimes.'

Dillon busied himself with a sandwich. 'That's okay, you don't have to tell me anything you don't want to.'

Harry sighed. She may as well come right out with it. 'It's because of my father. I think he's involved.'

Dillon frowned. 'In what? The break-in?'

'All of it.'

'The guy at the train station as well? But that's crazy. Why?'

'Because of what that guy said. The Sorohan deal, the ring – it all points to my father.'

'I don't get it.'

She held his gaze. 'The Sorohan deal was the one that blew up in my father's face and got him arrested.'

Dillon's expression cleared. 'Oh. I see. But what –'

She shook her head. 'Don't ask me any more, I haven't worked it all out yet. The point is, you know how I get about my father.'

Dillon rolled his eyes. 'Yeah. Prickly.'

She smiled and shrugged. 'Yeah, well.'

'Have you mentioned any of this to the police?'

Harry flashed on an image of the silent detective who'd come to her apartment that evening. She shook her head. 'I can't. They might start investigating him again.'

'Well, he's already in prison. What else can they do to him?'

Harry put her sandwich down. Suddenly she wasn't hungry any more. 'He's getting out.'

'I thought he got eight years.'

'Remission.' Harry's throat seemed to be closing up. 'He could be out any time.'

Dillon seemed to work it out. 'So if he gets investigated for any of this, his remission will be on hold?'

'Or thrown out altogether.'

93

There was a pause. She could feel Dillon's eyes on her.

'Look, you need to talk to your father,' he said. 'I've been telling you that for months.'

She shook her head and stared at her glass. She cupped it in one hand and swirled the golden liquid around in it. 'When I was a kid, I thought he was wonderful. He made all these marvellous promises, and the ones he kept were magical.' She traced a nail through the grooves in the diamond-cut crystal. 'Almost worth the disappointment of the ones that he forgot.'

'Sounds like you and he had quite a bond.'

She smiled. 'My sister Amaranta had a hand in that. When I was five, she told me our parents had found me on the street as a baby. She said they were going to keep me for a while, but that later, they planned to sell me on to the neighbours.'

Dillon laughed. 'Typical big sister stunt.'

'Trouble was, I believed her. For months I felt like an outsider in my own home. My mother was distant with me anyway, for reasons of her own, so that didn't help. I finally blurted it all out to my father, and he cleared things up for me. I suppose from then on, I saw him as some kind of ally.'

Dillon sipped his brandy. 'And that all changed when he was arrested?'

She shook her head. 'I'd already had enough long before that. Living with constant let-downs gets to you after a while. When he got sent to jail, that was kind of the end.' She shrugged and smiled. 'We don't get to choose our parents, do we?'

'I suppose not. Although you could say my parents chose me.'

Harry raised her eyebrows.

'I was adopted,' he explained. 'My adoptive parents couldn't have children so they took me in when I was a baby. But by the time I was two, my mother was miraculously pregnant.'

'Don't tell me, you got overlooked in favour of the natural child and it gave you a mass of complexes.'

Dillon paused. 'For a while, maybe. I certainly know what it's like to feel you're an outsider in your own home.' He shrugged. 'But then they tried to make amends and ended up over-compensating. I got all the attention, and it was my brother who got the complexes. He went right off the rails in the end. Drugs, prison – the works.'

She sucked down her brandy, not sure what to say. 'So we both have families with murky pasts?'

'Looks like it.'

Harry waved her arm around the room. 'Well, it hasn't done you any harm. Look at this house. It's amazing.' Her ears started to buzz and she wondered was she getting a bit drunk.

'It's not bad.' Dillon looked pleased with himself.

Harry scanned the room. 'Mind you, you seem to do most of your living in here.'

His smile slipped a little. 'Not when I have guests, which is most of the time. And when I don't, I can shut the world away. High walls, electronic gates – if there's one thing money can buy you, it's privacy.'

'Or isolation,' Harry said, and immediately wished she hadn't. Dillon frowned, and stood up.

'Come on, you look exhausted. You should get some rest.'

He grasped her hand and helped her to her feet. She stood facing him for a moment, only inches away from him, their body heat mingling. Then he turned away and strolled over to the French doors on the other side of the room, beckoning for her to follow. 'But first I want to show you something.'

CHAPTER 14

The first thing Harry noticed when she stepped outside the door was a pungent scent that reminded her of Christmas trees. It hung in the air like eucalyptus, and instantly cleared her head.

She peered into the darkness, waiting for her eyes to adjust to the gloom. Then she saw it. Inky black, looming up from the centre of the lawn, was a gigantic wall of hedge maybe twelve feet high and wider than a football pitch.

'My God,' Harry said. 'Is that a maze?'

As she spoke, the moon broke through the clouds and she could see that the dense evergreen had been planted in the shape of an enormous enclosed rectangle, extending as far back as it did across. There must have been over an acre of hedge out there.

'Awesome, isn't it?' Dillon said. 'The previous owners planted it about twenty years ago. I just had to have it. Come on, let me take you in.'

He strode across the lawn, his trainers making whispering noises against the dry grass. Harry followed, stopping in front of a red triangular flag that marked the entrance to the maze. She felt her brain dissolve into pulp, the way it always did when confronted with a navigational challenge.

'I feel like I need to throw a six to start,' she said.

Dillon laughed. 'Come on, before the moonlight goes. I want to show you what I built in the centre.'

She followed him in. The spicy pine fragrance was more intense inside the maze. All around her were curved, towering hedges. The rough clay path was only a few feet wide, so they were forced to walk in single file.

Dillon took a sharp left, and Harry trotted to keep up. The path followed a tight arc, and suddenly Dillon disappeared. The moonlight waned, and Harry's skin prickled. She quickened her pace.

'What do you do if someone gets lost in here?' she called out.

'We talk them in from the viewing deck.' He sounded close by, only a few feet ahead. 'It over-looks the whole thing. But if you do get lost, just follow the left-hand rule.'

'The what?' She clung to the main path, refusing to be tempted by left or right turns.

'Put your left hand on the hedge, follow the wall and keep walking. You'll get out eventually.'

By now, the moonlight had completely vanished, turning the hedges into black walls. Harry stretched her hands out in front of her, feeling her way around the blind bends.

'Don't worry, it looks worse than it is,' Dillon said. 'A lot of it's just an optical illusion.'

Harry's step faltered. Optical illusion. The phrase

triggered a snap of electricity in her brain, and an image of her bank account showing €12,000,000 flashed into her head.

'What do you mean?'

'The paths are designed to lead people down the wrong turns. Psychological trickery.' He sounded ten or fifteen feet away, but whether to her left or right, she couldn't tell. 'For instance, people tend to avoid paths that seem to go back the way they came. Stuff like that.'

Harry tried to see how this could have anything to do with her bank account. Could it have been some kind of trick? She shook her head. Some part of her brain had made a connecting leap, but she'd no idea why.

Feet scuffed against the clay behind her. She frowned. Had Dillon circled behind her? She checked over her shoulder, but all she could see was solid hedge. Her back tingled, and she geared up to a power-walk.

'Ever hear the story of King Minos and the Labyrinth?' Dillon's voice was growing fainter.

'King who?'

'Old Greek legend. King Minos of Crete built this huge mazelike building called the Labyrinth. He used it as a prison for the Minotaur.'

Harsh breaths cut through the darkness behind her. She whipped her gaze around, stumbling against the hedge. Where the hell was Dillon?

'What's a Minotaur?' she called out, not liking the note of panic in her voice.

'A man-eating monster, half man, half bull.'

She jogged along the narrow path. The scuffing sounds behind her grew louder, more urgent, the breathing laboured. Harry spun round again and stared at the dark empty path.

'Dillon? Is that you?'

Silence. A wood pigeon cooed overhead. The footsteps had stopped. Had she imagined them?

'Harry?'

She whirled round at the sound of Dillon's voice, straining to locate him. Somewhere far to her left.

'Wait there!' She lurched round a bend. 'And keep talking so I can find you.'

'Are you okay?'

'Just keep talking!' She broke into a run, her heart thudding. 'Go on about the Minotaur.'

'Right. Well, the king locked the Minotaur up in the middle of the labyrinth and every year he sacrificed seven youths and seven maidens into the maze.' His voice sounded stronger; she had to be nearly there. 'They'd get lost, and eventually the Minotaur would eat them.'

Feet pounded on the track behind her. Harry gasped. She wheeled around a corner, the disorientation making her head spin. The sound of ragged panting tore after her through the dark. The path began to spiral, the bends so severe she could only see one step ahead. Something warm and damp tagged her shoulder from behind. Harry screamed and shook it off, sprinting deeper into the maze.

'Harry! Are you okay?' Dillon sounded some-where up ahead. 'Stay where you are, I'll find you!'

Harry blundered out of her spiral and came up against a T-junction. Left or right? The scuffling behind her was like an animal sound. *Man-eating monster, half man, half bull.* She blanked the image out, and tore down the left-hand fork. The maze flung her into another twisting vortex.

She scrambled along the path, clutching on to the hedges. Rough branches cut into her palms. The firs snapped and she stumbled, her weak knee giving way. Someone thrashed through the hedges behind her, grunting. She clawed back to her feet, her head reeling.

Averting her eyes from the swirling path, she focused on the hedge. She grasped the woody stems, hauling herself round the tortuous bends. Suddenly, the twisting stopped, and she staggered into a wider stretch of path. She picked up speed, and crashed around the next corner. She slammed straight into someone's chest and screamed.

'Harry!' Dillon grabbed her by the shoulders.

Her heart banged against her chest. She clutched on to him. 'Someone's there, someone's running.'

He shot his gaze to the path behind her. The panting and crashing was closer than ever. Then suddenly the sounds died away.

'What the hell –' Dillon shoved her behind him and took a step towards the noise.

Harry yanked his arm. 'No!'

Who knew what lay behind those hedges?

He looked at her, then back at the maze, hesitating. Then he grabbed her by the hand. 'This way.'

He dragged her down a narrow path and plunged them both into a series of random turns, or that's how it seemed to Harry. She raced after him as he zigzagged through the maze, his navigation never faltering. Branches scraped her arms and face as she ricocheted against the hedges. Then the path straightened out and a gap opened up in front of them. Together they burst through it, emerging at the side of the maze.

Dillon hauled her across the lawn. She flashed a backward glance at the massive hedge. It loomed above her like a black fortress. Then she tore after Dillon around the side of the house, to where his Lexus was waiting.

CHAPTER 15

Leon turned the envelope over in his hands and studied it. It was slim and white, with the word PERSONAL printed above the cellophane window that framed his address. It was the type of envelope he'd normally toss into a corner with all his other unpaid bills, except for one important difference. This one was addressed to Harry Martinez.

He sank down on to the shabby sofa and tapped the envelope against one hand. The curtains of his bedsit were closed, even though it was almost noon, and the air smelled of stale sheets and chips from a brown paper bag.

How the hell had a letter meant for Harry Martinez ended up with his address on it?

Leon scratched his chest through his T-shirt. He needed to shower, but the thought of the vile bathroom across the hall made his bowels bunch up. He'd only got up so that he could call his wife, and after that he'd planned on crawling back to bed. But then the post had arrived.

Leon closed his eyes. Ever since he'd woken up, the enormity of last night's poker losses had been pressing down on him like a ton of wet sand. He'd left O'Dowd's pub with his wallet lighter by more than eighty thousand euros. Add that to the rest of his poker debts and his bill was now running close to a quarter of a million. Worst of all, he knew he'd be back in O'Dowd's again tonight.

He squinted at the envelope in his hand. He reached over to the faded drapes and dragged them back a few inches, the curtain rings rattling like chains. A wedge of sunlight pierced his eyes, and he held the envelope up towards it. All he could see were wavy blue-and-white lines, the contents of the letter totally obscured.

The Prophet was responsible, no doubt about that. This was how he operated. Inexplicable letters, anonymous emails. Leon turned the envelope over again. He should just go ahead and open it. Nothing left to lose.

He set the letter down on the coffee table and stared at it. He didn't like it that the Prophet knew where he lived.

The first contact Leon ever had from the Prophet had been through the post, ten years earlier in 1999. A thick brown envelope had arrived at his home in Killiney, and Maura had brought it up to him in his study, along with a glass of champagne.

'Time you changed into your tux,' she'd said, setting the glass by his elbow. They'd been invited to dinner by the chairman of Merrion & Bernstein, the firm of investment bankers where Leon worked.

'Yeah, in a minute.' He took the brown envelope from her and ripped it open. Inside was an official-looking document with a cover note attached.

'How do I look?' Maura's voice was as seductive as honey, as she swirled the layers of her silver dress around her tanned legs. Ignoring her, Leon read the note and frowned.

Maura fidgeted. 'Leon?'

'You go on downstairs,' he said, without looking up. 'I'll be there in a minute.'

She sighed. 'Richard wants you to say goodnight to him before you go.'

Leon shook his head. 'Tell him I won't have time.'

Maura stood still for a moment. Then she turned and marched out of the room. Leon read the note again. It was brief and to the point.

Buy Serbio stock. TelTech bid has been accepted and will be announced next week. It was signed *The Prophet.*

Leon flicked through the document, but had only to scan the first few paragraphs to know what he was looking at. It was a highly confidential proposal for a hostile takeover bid. A ripple of illicit fascination stirred in his groin, and he felt like a teenager with his first porn magazine.

He leafed through the pages, checking the details. The takeover was being launched by a company called TelTech Internet Solutions. Leon raised his eyebrows. He'd heard of them. Who hadn't? The Dublin-based software company had

105

floated on the NASDAQ a couple of months earlier, its founders making fortunes in a matter of hours.

The target for the takeover was an American company called Serbio Software, a well-established outfit with the misfortune to be operating in the same e-commerce space as TelTech. Leon sifted through the finances of the deal, and gave a low whistle. These TelTech guys had more money than God. Jesus, what was it about the word 'internet' that justified such crazy economics? He could remember when software start-ups meant a collection of techie nerds in need of a bath. Now they were breeding grounds for multi-millionaires. The fact that none of them had yet to rack up a profit just didn't seem to matter.

Leon set the document down on his desk as though it might explode in his face. Who the hell was this Prophet guy that he could access such a confidential document? And why had he sent it to him?

He checked to see which investment bank was managing the bid, hoping to Christ it wasn't his own. Being in possession of information leaked from Merrion & Bernstein would really drop him in the shit. But he needn't have worried. The document had been prepared by JX Warner. He'd worked for them a few years back, but they'd turned prissy about his ethics and fired him after three months.

Leon turned to his PC and checked the Serbio

stock price on the NASDAQ. Just under eight dollars a share, low enough to make them vulnerable to a takeover. He read the note again. Whoever this Prophet was, he was obviously expecting the price to go up when the announcement of the takeover deal came through. If the announcement came through.

He tapped his fingers on the desk. Anyone buying Serbio shares now, before the price soared, would make a killing later on. The notion teased him with its simplicity. He picked up the document and peeped at the numbers again. Then he flung it back on the desk. It was too big a risk. His personal trading activities were closely watched by Merrion & Bernstein's compliance department. Insider trading was a professional hazard that the investment banks worked hard to avoid.

He ground his teeth and locked the document away. He tried to forget about it, but every day for the next week he scoured the financial papers for any hint of the takeover. There was nothing. After two weeks he concluded that it had all been an elaborate hoax, and a curious mix of relief and disappointment washed through him.

And then, almost three weeks after the arrival of the brown envelope, Leon spotted a headline in the business press that made him clench his fists.

NASDAQ Darling TelTech in bid for Serbio.

He locked himself in his office and checked out

the Serbio share price from his PC. Ten dollars and rising. He poured himself a large whiskey, loosened his tie and settled in for a long wait. For the next few hours he sat transfixed by the NASDAQ ticker prices. By the end of the New York business day, at 9.30 p.m. Irish time, the Serbio share price had closed at nearly twenty-five dollars. Leon did the sums, and glowered at the numbers in front of him. On a 30,000-share trade, he would have netted over half a million dollars.

Two weeks later, Leon received a second brown envelope from the Prophet and this time he didn't hesitate. He set up a new trading account without disclosing it to Merrion & Bernstein, and made over $700,000. With the third envelope, the Prophet sent a demand for a cut of the takings and instructions on how the money was to be paid. That was how it had been ever since.

Someone retched in the communal bathroom across the hall and, not for the first time, Leon wanted to burn his bedsit to the ground. His hand shot out towards the white envelope on the table, but at the last second he snatched up the phone instead. Maybe things would be better this time when he talked to Maura. Maybe he could find a way back. Without the white envelope.

He wiped the palm of his hand on his T-shirt and dialled his old home number. He pictured Maura hurrying to answer the phone, her heels snapping against the black-and-white marble tiles that were laid out like a chessboard in the hall. Then he heard her voice.

'Hello?'

Leon straightened his shoulders and focused on the meagre fireplace across the room. 'It's me.'

There was a short silence. 'Leon. I'm on my way out.'

'Oh, sorry. I just wanted a quick word.'

'I really haven't much time.'

He heaved himself up and began pacing the few steps over and back between the fireplace and the sofa, like a demented bear in a zoo. 'Just thought I'd call round. You know, to see Richard.'

'What, now? I have a lunch appointment.'

'No, no of course not now, I know you're busy. Maybe later this afternoon?'

'Richard has rugby practice.'

'Well, how about this evening, then?' he said. 'I could come over for tea.'

She was silent for a moment. 'You want me to cook your tea?'

He stopped in front of the fireplace and squeezed his eyes shut, his fingers gripping the mantelpiece. 'No, no, I didn't mean that. After tea, then. I'll come after tea.'

'That's not going to work either, he's got studying to do. He's doing the Junior Cert this year, in case you'd forgotten.'

Leon opened his eyes and stared into the empty grate. It was cold and black. 'Of course I hadn't forgotten.' Shit, why hadn't he remembered that? 'I won't stay long. Just a quick chat.'

'Look, I really don't want him upset.'

Leon trudged over to his unmade bed and sank down on it. 'Come on, be fair, it's been months since I saw him.'

'It's been longer than that, Leon.'

He could see the kitchenette at the far end of the room, with its stacks of dirty dishes and take-away cartons. 'Yes, well, things have been hectic here.'

'I can imagine.' Her voice was flat, with no hint of sarcasm.

'Does he ask about me?' Leon gripped his knee with one hand.

'Not often.'

Something strangled his throat, and for a minute he couldn't speak.

'I don't encourage it, tell you the truth,' Maura said. 'What am I supposed to say? "Your father's doing great, apart from the white-collar crime and that little gambling problem he has?" You're not an easy topic of conversation.'

Shit. Things were slipping away from him, sliding out of control the way they always did. He dragged his fingers through his sparse hair. 'But that's all changing Maura, I swear.' He flicked a glance at the envelope on the table. 'I'm sorting it all out. Soon I'll be right back where I was. Leon-the-Ritch.'

'I really have to go.'

'But I mean it. Everything's going to be okay.'

'Can we do this another time?'

Leon took a couple of deep breaths. 'Of course. Sorry. Didn't mean to delay you. I'll call again later in the week.'

'Let's leave it till after the exams.'

'Oh.' Jesus, another two whole months. 'Right. Well, if you think that's best. Say hello to Richard for me.'

But she had already hung up.

Leon leaned his elbows on his knees and hung his head low between them. Hot tears stung his eyes, and he shook his head. Every time he talked to her it ended up the same way. No wonder he gambled, she drove him to it. Better to feel the gambler's rush than the pain of failure with his son. He lifted his head and took in the squalid bedsit, furnished from pieces of crap hauled out of a skip. He could never bring Richard here.

His gaze settled on the white envelope. He clenched his fists and moved back over to the sofa. He traced the finger and thumb of one hand around his mouth as though trying to make up his mind, but he knew the decision was already made. He picked up the envelope and opened it.

Inside were two sheets of pale blue paper. Leon stared at them for a moment, and then he understood. This was the Prophet's proof. Adrenaline sparked through him like a lit fuse. So the girl really did have the money. Well, not for long. Wait till he told Ralphy-Boy about this.

But first, he had another call to make. He

grabbed the phone again and punched in a by now familiar number.

The call was picked up after two rings. 'Mr Ritch. I was about to phone you.'

'What's happening? Where's the girl now?' Something about this fucker made Leon's skin crawl, but right now he was the only option he had.

'Back at her apartment.'

'Look, we need to make a move. There's been a development at this end.'

'Yeah, well, there's something funny going on here too.'

'What do you mean?'

'I mean whatever your next move is, you'd better make it fast.' There was a pause. 'We're not the only ones following her.'

CHAPTER 16

Harry huddled over a mug of tea and thought about optical illusions. Now you see me, now you don't.

An image of the maze reared up inside her head, and her chest tightened. She shoved her tea away and scurried down the hall to check her apartment door. It was still locked. Then she prowled through the rest of the rooms, testing the windows, listening for unfamiliar sounds. It was the fourth patrol she'd made that morning.

Dillon had driven her back to the apartment the night before and stayed with her till she fell asleep on the couch. When she woke, she found a quilt pulled up to her shoulders and signs that he'd slept on the floor. He was already up, on his way to the office. He'd knelt beside her and stroked her hair, ordering her to take some time off.

She cast an eye over the empty apartment and shuddered. She'd spent the last few hours cleaning the place up, but it still didn't feel like home.

Dillon had called the police from his car soon after they'd fled the maze, but by the time they got there, the intruder was long gone. The only trace the police had found was a rusty gate buckled at the hinges.

Harry reached out to check the window lock on the living-room sash, but at the last minute she clenched her fist. Goddammit, enough of the neurotic rituals. She marched back to the kitchen and brewed some coffee strong enough to juice up her brain. She paced the kitchen floor, gulping the coffee down. Her swollen knee felt stronger, her body less tender. The need for action jerked through her limbs like an electric current.

What she needed was hard information. What had happened with the Sorohan deal? Who were the other members of the ring? How had her father operated? If she understood the mechanics of her father's insider trades, maybe she could work out where the twelve million euros had come from. And who the hell was after it.

As for optical illusions, she dealt in science and technology, not smoke and mirrors. The twelve million was no illusion. She'd seen it on the screen with her own eyes, and the bank had confirmed it. No Houdini tricks there.

Unless someone had tampered with her account records.

Harry's pace slowed. But how would anyone do that? And why? Rigging the bank's database to show a false lodgement wouldn't make the money real. Sure, it would show up temporarily on a snapshot of her transactions, but the bank's reconciliation procedures would soon catch the error.

No one could ever access the money, not a sum of that size. Harry shook her head. It made no sense. The money had to be real. The question was, who put it there?

She hauled her satchel up on to the kitchen table and rummaged through it. Dillon had told her to talk to her father. He was right. She needed explanations, and what better place to start? But she couldn't face it, not yet. There had to be another way.

She pulled a fistful of business cards out of the satchel and thumbed through them till she found the one she was looking for. She scrutinized it, chewing at her bottom lip. She'd already had a run-in with this guy and didn't feel like asking him for any favours. But she had no choice. Apart from her father, he was the only investment banker she knew.

She dialled the number on the card and waited. He was bound to be there, even on a Saturday. Weekends didn't mean much to investment bankers.

'Hello, Jude Tiernan speaking.' His voice was deep, like a woodwind instrument.

Too late Harry realized she hadn't prepared her story. She'd have to play this out cold. 'Oh, hi, this is Harry Martinez.'

The silence at the other end went on a shade too long. She prompted him. 'I met you yesterday?'

'Oh, don't worry, I remember you all right,' he said. 'I just can't believe I've got to have another conversation with you.'

Harry shut her eyes. Maybe she deserved that one. She decided to stick with the truth. 'Look, I owe you an apology. I was probably out of line yesterday.'

'You were more than out of line, you were downright slanderous.'

Harry's eyes flared open. 'Hey, I was seriously provoked, remember? Your colleague wasn't exactly mincing his words.'

'Felix Roche is a dickhead, I'll give you that much. But, as I recall, your accusations seemed to include the entire room.'

Harry flopped down on a chair and sighed. 'Look, can we start again? I'd really like to talk to you about something else.' She picked at the corner of his business card. 'It's about my father.'

There was a pause. 'Go on.'

'I'd like to ask you some questions about what he did.'

'Why can't you ask him?'

Harry winced. 'That's a bit tricky. If I could meet with you this afternoon, I could explain.'

'That's not going to happen. I'm tied up all day and then I leave for the airport. So if that's all –'

'Yesterday someone tried to push me under a train.' Damn, she hadn't meant to blurt it out like that. She aimed for a more businesslike tone. 'The guy who pushed me said something about the Sorohan money.'

Another pause. 'The takeover deal that got your father arrested?'

116

'Yes.'

'I don't understand. And I certainly don't see what you want from me. Have you told the police?'

'Of course I have.' She crossed her fingers at the lie. 'But if I could just ask you a few questions, it would really help. I promise I won't take up much of your time.'

He hesitated, and she knew she had only one last chance to hook him. He was an investment banker. He may not care about her, but he had to be interested in the money. She took a deep breath.

'My guess is the Sorohan money amounted to about twelve million euros, and I know exactly where it is.'

There was silence at the other end. Then he said, 'You can come along for the ride to the airport with me. I'll pick you up outside the IFSC car park at six o'clock. That's the best I can do.'

She leaned back in the chair. 'Thanks, I really appreciate your doing this.'

'Oh, I'm not doing this for you – make no mistake about that. I'm doing it for your father.' His tone was challenging. 'I liked him.'

CHAPTER 17

The Irish Times archive. Please enter your search query.

H arry peered around the box room she used as an office, her fingers suspended over the keyboard. Then she gritted her teeth and stabbed at the keys. *Salvador Martinez, Sorohan, insider trading.* She gripped the mouse and clicked 'Search' before she could change her mind.

A list of articles published about her father rolled up the screen. The first was dated 7th June 2001. *Senior KWC Investment Banker Arrested for Insider Trading.* A familiar ache constricted her throat as she scanned the next few headlines in the list: *Banker Martinez Denies Accusations*; *Insider Trading Ring Exposed, Major Investment Banks Implicated*; *Martinez Made Millions from Insider Deals.* Harry paged down through the list, tracking her father's descent to disaster, until she reached the last entry. It was dated 14th April 2003. The headline was stark, with none of the sensationalism of earlier articles.

Salvador Martinez Jailed.

She'd been in her mother's kitchen the day she found out her father had been sent to prison. Miriam and Amaranta had returned from court where they'd been present at the sentencing. Harry hadn't gone with them. In the last few months, she'd given up attending the court sessions or even reading the newspaper accounts of the trial. No longer able to believe in her father's innocence, she'd felt equally unable to face the extent of his guilt.

Harry had stood on the threshold, her arms strapped across her chest as if she was wearing a strait-jacket. Miriam was sitting upright at the kitchen table, fiddling with a tea-towel. Her pale hair was gripped into a tight knot that stretched her skin taut, revealing the almost Slavic planes of her face. Unable to look her mother in the eye, Harry focused on the tea-towel. It had red and white stripes, and reminded her of the shepherd's costume in her first school play. She'd wanted to be one of the angels with wings and a halo, but her mother had told her you had to be blonde to be an angel.

'Your father's been sent to Arbour Hill prison for eight years,' Miriam said. She'd looked around at her own sparkling kitchen. 'I hear it's mostly full of murderers and rapists.'

Harry shivered at the memory, and tried to focus on the screen in front of her. She scrolled back to the top of the list and stepped through the headlines again, this time studying the full text of each article. Bit by bit, she pieced together the details of the story, most of which she already knew, but some parts she hadn't heard before.

It had all been triggered by the Sorohan deal. In 1998, Sorohan Software had been just another start-up company, with colossal investor backing and no trading record whatsoever. What it lacked in hard revenue, however, it made up for in clever marketing, and by 1999 the company had floated on the stock market with record gains its first day out of the stalls. For almost a year, the Sorohan share price defied gravity.

Then, in April 2000, the company was side-swiped by the dot.com pileup. Worldwide sell-off of technology stocks left the Sorohan share price languishing, and it was no longer of any interest to investors.

Until six months later, that is, when the stock suddenly began changing hands in a flurry of trading so unusual that the Dublin Stock Exchange picked up on it. At first, it just triggered a routine inquiry. Two weeks later, however, the press announced that Sorohan was to be taken over by the software giant Aventus, and the Sorohan share price took off like a torpedo. The Exchange geared its inquiry up a notch, mobilizing its legal team. They sniffed out the scent of leaked information and began to track down the fraudulent trades. They quizzed the banks managing the suspicious trading accounts. They interviewed the key players in the Aventus–Sorohan acquisition. Eventually, their investigations led them to a man called Leon Ritch.

There was a photograph of Ritch in one of the newspaper articles, and Harry studied it with interest. His gaze was averted from the camera, his mouth pulled down like a growling bulldog as he tried to escape the press. He was in his late forties, short and stocky, maybe twenty pounds overweight.

Leon was an investment banker with Merrion & Bernstein, the firm hired by Aventus to manage the Sorohan takeover. When the Exchange examined his trading history they discovered that not only had he purchased high volumes of the Sorohan stock prior to the takeover announcement, but all of his previous trades displayed the same suspicious pattern. The case was referred to the Director of Public Prosecutions, and Leon was arrested soon afterwards.

But Leon had no intention of going down alone. He claimed to be operating as part of an insider-trading ring, and he was prepared to expose his colleagues in exchange for considerations in court. He claimed that the ring extended across three leading investment banks: KWC, Merrion & Bernstein and JX Warner. This network of investment bankers exchanged confidential information and used it to make vast trading profits. They specialized in technology sector mergers and acquisitions, taking advantage of the easily inflated prices of tech stocks, and the cash-rich internet companies who seemed determined to acquire other businesses no matter what the cost. According to

Leon, the ring had been operating undetected for almost two years and had made trading profits of more than eighty million dollars.

Leon had protected himself well. He'd compiled a list of names, along with incriminating documents, emails and taped conversations, which he handed over to the authorities. The list of names was never published, but was rumoured to include some of the most senior banking figures in the country. And one of those figures was Salvador Martinez.

Harry blinked. Without warning, her father's face had rolled up on the screen in front of her. He was standing with his back to the courthouse, smiling into the camera like a celebrity. His greying hair and beard were neatly trimmed. His eyebrows made a startling contrast, so dark they looked as if they'd been inked in with black marker. His smile was relaxed, its warmth picked up in the brown eyes that always looked so trustworthy.

Harry put a hand to her lips and stared at the screen. It was the first time in over six years that she'd seen her father's face. She hugged her waist and took a moment to steady herself. Then she scrolled down the page until the photograph slipped out of view.

She scanned through the text of the article. The journalist described her father as 'affable and courteous, but with the air of someone who believes he is above the law'. Harry raised her eyebrows and checked the reporter's by-line. Ruth Woods. She'd noticed the same name on many of the articles. Harry wondered if Ms Woods had ever met her father. She'd certainly got his attitude nailed.

She took a deep breath and clicked on the final article. It was terse and to the point, and summarized the bald facts that tidied away the end of the story, at least as far as the press were concerned. After a lengthy trial that lasted almost two years, Harry's father and Leon Ritch had each been found guilty on twelve counts of insider dealing. Both had been instructed to pay forty million euros in forfeitures and penalties, and sentenced to eight years in prison. In recognition for his co-operation with the authorities, Leon's sentence had been commuted to one year. No one else had ever been arrested.

Harry studied the photograph attached to the article. It showed a man about her own age, staring into the camera, on his way out of the courthouse. She frowned, and took in the dark hair, the fine-boned features and the watchful grey eyes.

She stiffened. He looked younger, but it was the same man. The detective who'd come to her apartment the previous day. Her eyes flew to the caption: *Detective Lynne, Garda Bureau of Fraud Investigation.*

Fraud. So he'd worked on her father's case nine years ago. But what was a detective from the fraud squad doing on a routine burglary inquiry in her apartment? She thought of the money lying in her bank account, the money that might be linked to the Sorohan deal. Was Lynne still working on her father's case?

She sighed, and massaged the corners of her eyes. Then she leaned back and propped her feet up on the desk, listening to the whirr of her laptop as she let all the information sink in. Although her newspaper search had filled in some of the gaps, it had raised more questions than it had answered. Who were the other names on Leon's list? What had happened to the Sorohan money? More to the point, with all those forfeitures and penalties, how could there possibly have been any money left?

She thought about Leon's list. Then she thought about reporters, and how close they must get to police investigations when they follow a story. She swung her feet down off the desk and looked up the phone number of the *Irish Times*. Then she called the newspaper office and asked for Ruth Woods.

While she was put on hold, Harry wondered what tack she should take with the reporter. She didn't particularly want to reveal who she was and risk stirring up something with the national press. Time to trot out Catalina again.

Catalina Diego had started out as an imaginary friend when Harry was five years old. She took most of the blame for Harry's misdeeds, and had all the things Harry never had: she was blonde and beautiful, she was popular at school and her parents loved her. And she had a great name. As Harry got older she abandoned Catalina in favour of Pirata, but later reinvented her when she began her hacking scams. By the time Harry was fourteen, Catalina had her own email account, a driving licence and even a credit card.

'Woods.' The word shot like a bullet from the other end of the phone.

Harry scuttled in closer to the desk and picked up a pen. She always lied better with a pen and doodle-pad in front of her.

'Hi, Ruth, this is Catalina Diego, I'm a reporter from the *Daily Express*, and I wonder if you can help me out. I'm doing a follow-up piece on Sal Martinez. Remember him, the guy who –'

'Yeah, yeah, I remember. Jailed for insider trading. So?'

Harry pictured the woman making get-on-with-it signals at the other end of the phone, and decided to cut out the chat. 'Right. That's him. Well, I need to confirm a few facts and I know you were close to the investigation at the time. I thought maybe we could do a trade.'

There was a pause. Harry had hoped to bull-doze her pitch through before Ruth had time to pick up on the bullshit, but the woman clearly wasn't going to be pushed. Harry drew a three-dimensional dollar sign on the pad in front of her while she waited for the reporter to respond.

'The *Daily Express*,' Ruth said finally. 'Thought I knew everyone over there.'

Damn, snagged at the starting post. 'Well, I'm

new on the job, but I intend to make a splash with this one. So what do you say to a trade?'

'What kind of trade?'

'I've a new angle on the story. Fresh evidence.'

'And you'd pass that on to me?'

Harry laughed. 'I may be new, but I'm not stupid. I could let you in on some of it, though, in exchange for information.'

Ruth seemed to consider the proposition. Then she said, 'What kind of information?'

Harry gripped the pen in her hand and thickened the outlines on the dollar sign. 'Did you ever see the list of names handed over by Leon Ritch?'

There was a long pause. 'No, I didn't.'

'But you must have heard rumours.'

'What if I did? There was a lot of stuff going round about that case, but we couldn't print half of it.'

Harry frowned. 'Why not?'

'Gag orders from the authorities, in case we jeopardized investigations.' Ruth's tone turned dry. 'Likewise from my editor, in case we were sued for libel.'

'What kind of stuff are we talking about?'

Ruth didn't miss a beat. 'First tell me more about this fresh evidence of yours.'

Harry could hear the snap of pages being turned and guessed the reporter was getting ready to take notes. She raked through the data she had collected so far, in search of something that would draw out the journalist's hand without revealing too much of her own. She began to shade in the

S-shape of the dollar sign. 'What if I told you that someone close to Martinez was almost killed yesterday?'

'So? People die all the time. What's your point?'

'My point is, it looks like the trading ring was responsible.'

There was silence on the other end of the phone and for a moment Harry thought she'd been cut off. Then Ruth cleared her throat and said without conviction, 'That's impossible.'

Harry sat up straight. If she'd had antennae, they would have been trembling with incoming signals. 'Come on, you know something. Just give me one name.'

'Forget about the stupid list. You can't print anything without evidence.'

'Look, supposing I give you a name and you just say yes or no?'

'That's crazy. You've nothing to trade.'

'Just try this one on for size . . .' Harry thought back to her meeting at KWC, and drew a big 'F' with a circle around it. 'Felix Roche.'

There was another long pause. There was information in that silence, Harry was sure of it.

Then Ruth said, 'Okay, this is a waste of time. But you know what? I've nothing better to do this afternoon, so I'll play along. You know the Palace Bar in Fleet Street?'

Harry stopped doodling. 'Yes.'

'Meet me there in twenty minutes.'

CHAPTER 18

Harry paid off the taxi driver and looked across at the entrance to the Palace Bar, wondering how she was going to recognize the reporter.

She shifted the weight of her satchel into her left hand and set off across the cobbles. She'd packed her laptop, not wanting to leave anything of value behind in her apartment. She whipped a glance over her shoulder, checking out the crowds, and a crop of goose bumps crawled along her arms. It was the first time she'd been out alone since the incident at the train station.

She pushed open the door, stepping out of the sunlight and into the Palace Bar. Inside it was dark and oddly hushed, and it took her a second or two to figure out what sounds were missing. No loud music, no braying crowds. Just the slap of the cash register and the occasional murmur among the handful of patrons at the bar. Harry scanned their faces and realized she was the only woman on the premises. She checked her watch. She was only a few minutes late. Surely Ruth Woods hadn't left already?

'I checked with the *Daily Express*,' a voice said behind her. 'They never heard of any Catalina Diego.'

Harry spun round. A thin, dark woman in her early forties was peering down at her, her head jutting forward like a bird inspecting a worm.

'You're Ruth Woods?'

'Yes.' The woman narrowed her eyes. She wore round black-rimmed glasses, and her hair was chopped in a chin-length bob with a blunt fringe at eyebrow level. The overall effect was of someone wearing a neat black crash helmet with matching goggles.

She pointed a finger at Harry, the bracelets on her wrists jangling. 'You're his daughter, aren't you?'

Shit. Harry should've expected this. She'd been told all her life how much she looked like her father. She could even see it herself. The same dark eyes and brows, the same straight nose. And, according to her mother, the same disregard for rules and regulations.

She shrugged and nodded. 'Okay, I'm Harry Martinez. Does it make a difference?'

'It certainly makes it more interesting. Go and grab a table.' Without waiting for a reply, Ruth turned and stalked up to the bar.

Harry looked around. There was hardly going to be a stampede for seats. She made her way to her favourite part of the pub, the small square room at the back with its scarred wooden floor and arched roof. A stained-glass skylight crowned the dome, and a pyramid of sunlight beamed

129

through it, projecting into the room like a lantern. The place was empty.

Harry sat down at a corner table. A portrait of Brendan Behan looked down on her from the back wall, his Roman nose and dark looks reminding her irrelevantly of Dillon. She felt a sudden dull ache and found herself wishing he was there. Then she shook herself. Neediness wasn't her usual style.

Ruth returned and plonked two coffees on the table. She sat down and stared at her. Harry made herself stare back.

Eventually, Ruth said, 'Now why would the daughter of Sal Martinez come to me for information?'

Place your bet with confidence, Harry's father always told her. Especially when you're bluffing. She picked up a sachet of sugar and gave it a smart flick before ripping it open. 'Because I want to know the real story, the stuff that was never made public. You were close to the investigation, you would've heard things.'

'Of course I heard things, but what does it matter? Your father was convicted and now he's in prison where he belongs.'

'But the rest of the ring is still out there.'

'So? You think justice rounds up all the guilty parties until the streets are clean?' Ruth shook her head. 'They collar a couple of major players and then they're done with it. Game over.'

'It's hardly a game if the ring is trying to kill people.'

Ruth's eyes scanned Harry's face, taking in the grazes on her cheeks. 'So now we're getting to it. Who did they go after? You?'

Harry bit her lip. The last thing she needed now was to end up at the centre of a front-page news story. 'Maybe.'

Ruth waved her evasion away. 'Why don't you go to the police?'

'Maybe I will. But first I want to know about Felix Roche.'

Ruth sipped her coffee, taking her time about answering. 'If I tell you what I know, I want an exclusive shot at the whole story.'

'When I have a story, it's all yours, I guarantee it. So tell me about Felix Roche. Was he on the list of names Leon Ritch gave to the police?'

'No, the police dug Felix up all by themselves. But they couldn't make anything stick.'

'But where does he fit in?'

'He was just a lowly system administrator in KWC back then, but he had access to everything. Emails, documents, the lot. Thought he was God. Seems he intercepted a few emails and stumbled on to the ring by accident.'

'So he joined up with them?'

'No, the ring never even knew he existed. He just kept quiet and piggy-backed on their trades. Anytime he caught information coming through, he traded on it. Made quite a bundle for himself – or so I heard.'

So the collapse of the ring had put an end to

some lucrative freeloading for Felix. No wonder he'd been surly when Harry met him. She'd been closer to the truth than she'd known.

'How come KWC kept him on?'

Ruth shrugged. 'They couldn't sack him; nothing was ever proven against him. Besides, they didn't want the publicity. One crooked employee was bad enough, but two and the corruption would've looked out of control. I heard they side-lined him instead, put him someplace where he couldn't access any sensitive information.'

'Actually, he's in IT Procurement.'

Ruth smirked. 'That must've killed him.'

'So if he wasn't on Leon's list, then who was?'

'I never actually saw it, but from what I heard there were only three names. Your father was one. The second was an anonymous source they called the Prophet. He came up with the information for some of the biggest deals they pulled.'

'First I've heard of him. How come he wasn't mentioned in any of the papers?'

'The police put a lid on it. They wanted to track him down without tipping their hand. They tried tracing him through his emails and letters, but it never led anywhere.'

'They've no idea who he is?'

'His insider information was always connected to JX Warner deals, so their best guess is he was an investment banker there.'

Harry remembered the newspapers reporting that three investment banks were involved. She counted them off on her fingers. 'So Leon operated out of Merrion & Bernstein, my father was the contact point in KWC, and the Prophet worked inside JX Warner?'

'That's right. There were rumours that some other investment banker was involved, someone high up that only Leon knew about, but I didn't hear any names. Whoever it was didn't feature on Leon's list and he denied they ever existed.'

'Why would he hold back on anyone when he was already spilling his guts?'

'Could be he kept someone in reserve, in case he needed favours later when things got rough. From what I saw of Leon, his survival instincts were pretty highly developed. He covered his tracks better than your father ever did, that's for sure.'

Harry broke off eye contact and fiddled with another sachet of sugar.

'Did you ever meet my father?' she said, still not looking up.

'I tried to. Called him a few times. He was polite, but he wouldn't meet me. Spoke to me in Spanish half the time, which I thought was a bit pretentious.'

Harry could well believe it. Her father had always made much of his Spanish ancestry, aware that it gave him an exotic appeal, especially to women.

'Then I finally collared him coming out of the courthouse,' Ruth went on. 'He was jaunty and elegant, very gracious.' The corner of her mouth twitched. 'Told me I looked like Cleopatra.'

'You sound like you admire him.'

'I despise him and everything he did. But I could still recognize his charm.'

Harry tossed the sugar sachet on the table. 'Okay, so my father was charming. Let's get back to Leon's list. You said there were three names on it. My father, the Prophet and who else?'

'A guy named Jonathan Spencer. He worked in KWC with your father. The police investigated him, but they couldn't prosecute.'

'Why not?'

'Because he was dead.'

Harry blinked. 'What happened to him?'

Ruth took another sip of coffee, her eyes never leaving Harry's face. 'Tell me, when you say the ring tried to kill you, how did they do it?'

Harry didn't see any harm in telling her the truth at this point. 'Someone pushed me in front of a train.'

Ruth was still for a moment, and then nodded. 'This guy Spencer, he was pushed in front of a truck a few months before your father was arrested. Shot out right in front of the rush-hour traffic. Splat. Never had a chance.'

For a split second, Harry was back on the railway tracks, face-down on the cold steel, her whole body clenched against the scream of an oncoming train. She suppressed a shudder. 'Where did this happen?'

'Just outside the IFSC, by the Eternal Flame memorial. He was on his way home, heading towards Connolly Station. The police wrote it off as an accident at the time. Then his name turned up on Leon's list.'

Harry's heart seemed to trip over itself for a couple of beats. She thought back to her own route home after she'd left KWC. She too had been heading for the frantic traffic next to the Eternal Flame, until the need for a walk to clear her head had taken her back towards Pearse Station.

Ruth was still talking. 'I ran some checks on the guy. He was in his twenties, married with a young family, clean record. This was probably the first time he'd ever broken the law. God knows why he did it. Debt, maybe. Anyway, he got sucked into the ring, but after a few months it seems he got cold feet. He wanted out, and he went to your father for help.'

'When was all this?'

'October 2000. About the same time the Prophet leaked the information on the Sorohan takeover. That deal was set to be the ring's biggest coup yet, but now Spencer was suddenly a loose cannon. He could've ruined everything for them.'

Something cold prodded at the base of Harry's spine. 'So they killed him?'

'The police never proved anything.' Ruth fixed her with a stare. 'All I know is, the day after he talked to your father, he ended up dead.'

CHAPTER 19

Harry stood beside the Eternal Flame and steeled herself to cross the street to the IFSC. Cars screamed past in a semicircle around the Custom House, their drivers intent on nothing except getting in lane. Harry flinched, and thought about the guy who'd pushed her in front of the train. Had his first choice been to catapult her on to this racetrack?

She shivered and hung back behind the other pedestrians, pretending to examine the memorial while she got herself under control. She could feel the warmth of the flame flickering inside the gigantic wrought-iron sphere. She checked out the people beside her. A couple of middle-aged men in suits, a younger man in a woolly hat, women with buggies. None of them looked as though they were out to kill her.

The traffic growled to a halt and suddenly everyone was on the move. Harry followed at a distance, her heart pounding. By the time she hit the kerb on the other side, her whole body was trembling. She backed away from the edge of the pavement, her mouth parched. God Almighty, was it going to be like this every time she tried to cross a street?

She checked her watch. She was early. Balancing her satchel on the ground between her feet, she settled in to wait for Jude Tiernan.

Before she'd left the Palace Bar, she'd quizzed Ruth about the money trail surrounding her father's trades, but the reporter had only shrugged. According to her sources, the money trail was a dead-end. Harry's father and Leon Ritch went bankrupt paying the penalties imposed by the courts, and any profits made by the rest of the ring were now untraceable.

Harry thought about the twelve million euros lodged anonymously in her bank account. Maybe Jude would have a better insight into the ring's financial operations. The money had to lead somewhere.

A silver Jag purred to a halt in front of her, the passenger window rolling down. She went towards it, stooping to peer in at the driver. Peaks of grey hair stood out around his domed head. It was Ashford, Chief Executive of KWC.

'Could I have a word?' he said.

Harry hesitated, the tips of her ears burning as she remembered their last meeting. Then she shook her head, making one of those I'd-love-to-but-I-can't faces.

'Sorry, but I've an appointment with someone,' she said.

'It'll only take a moment.'

Harry flashed a glance at the traffic but found nothing to help, so she lowered herself into the car. She left the door open and kept one foot on the kerb, just to show she wasn't staying.

She felt Ashford's eyes on her face, studying her bruises.

'I believe you were in an accident,' he said. 'What kind of accident?'

'It's nothing, I'm fine.'

'But what happened? Did someone –'

'No one did anything.' She took a deep breath. 'Look, I think I owe you an apology.'

He shook his head. 'I spoke to your CEO. I told him that KWC accepts full responsibility for what happened.'

'Yes, I know.' She remembered her churlishness with Ashford outside the KWC boardroom, and couldn't meet his eyes. 'I appreciate that.'

He waved her gratitude away. 'I've known your father a long time. It's the least I could do.'

She shifted in her seat at the mention of her father. Her left thigh ached, and she began to regret her foot-on-the-kerb gesture. She felt his eyes on her.

'I'd like to tell you something about your father, if I may,' he said, after a moment.

Harry looked down at her hands and felt the urge to block her ears.

'He was always a maverick, you know,' Ashford said. 'Courageous or reckless, depending on your point of view. But a genius, nonetheless. He was working for Schrodinger when I first knew him. Before you were born.'

Harry frowned. Schrodinger. The name seemed familiar, but the context shadowy.

Ashford gazed out at the swirl of traffic. 'He saved my career once, you know.'

Harry's grip tightened on her satchel. 'Look, I should go –'

'I was in over my head,' Ashford went on. 'Went long on a stock I thought was ripe for acquisition, only to find no one wanted it. Chevron, it was called.' He shook his head. 'I'd never risked so much on one stock. When the price started to drop, my entire career was on the line. But then your father came along.'

Harry felt her jaw tighten. 'Let me guess. He offered to buy you out and then sold it all later at a huge profit?'

'Actually, he just told me to sit tight and keep an eye on the papers.'

Harry shot him a surprised look. Ashford continued.

'Two days later there was a small article citing rumours that KSA was acquiring Chevron. It wasn't true, but it set off a flurry of buying on the markets, enough to make the price climb for a few days. I managed to offload the stock before it dropped back down.'

She worked it out. 'So my father leaked false information to the press?'

He nodded. 'He knew any speculative trading in

Chevron would help me out. It wasn't ethical, but it saved my career. And it could have cost him his.'

'Well, it's a nice story.' Harry snatched up her bag and began to climb out of the car. 'But breaching ethics has never been much of a sacrifice for my father, believe me.'

Ashford put a hand on her arm, and she turned to look at him. His large, doleful eyes met hers.

'He may not have been the best father in the world. And God knows, Miriam deserves a better husband.'

Harry frowned. 'You know my mother?'

He paused, and seemed to look past her for a moment. 'I know her very well. And I know what she's been through all these years.' He re-focused on her face. 'But you see, to me, Sal was still a good friend. And whatever you say, you are very like him indeed.'

Harry shook her head. 'That's what my mother thinks. It's why she doesn't like me very much.'

She ignored his look of surprise and turned to go. Then she stopped. She'd remembered about Schrodinger.

'Schrodinger fired him in the end, though, didn't they?' she said, looking back at him.

Ashford sighed, dipping his large head in acknowledgment. 'About six months later. For an unrelated episode.'

An unrelated episode. Her mother had spoken in bitter tones about that unrelated episode, and Harry could understand why. Her father had been

140

caught embezzling money from clients, and the bank had fired him into oblivion. He was left with no income, no home and crushing debts from his high-roller lifestyle. With a baby daughter and a pregnant wife, his solution to the problem had been to absent himself for a couple of years and tour the gambling circuit. He'd missed Harry's entry into the world, and left his wife to cope alone. No wonder her mother had run out of romantic Spanish names.

Harry frowned. 'Was it you who helped him get back into banking after all that?'

He nodded. 'That was many years later. Our paths crossed and by then I was in a position to help him. I owed him a debt, so I gave him a chance.'

She sighed. That was the problem. There was always someone willing to give her father another chance.

Including herself.

CHAPTER 20

Cameron opened a packet of Marlboros and pulled out two cigarettes. One was for him, to smoke when he was ready. The other was going to help him kill somebody.

He tossed the pack on to the kitchen table in front of him and rested both cigarettes in the ashtray. In the middle of the table was a glass fruit bowl. He pulled it towards him. Inside was his collection of souvenir matchbooks. He stirred through the pile of cardboard folders with his finger, listening to them scratch around in the bowl. He had almost two dozen of them by now, each one a memento.

He picked a matchbook out at random and studied its cover: a pious-looking white bird on a green background. He turned it over in his fingers and nodded, remembering. The Dove Bar and Grill, Galway. Four years ago. A young bar girl with spiky blonde hair and a smart mouth. Cameron's right leg began to jiggle up and down, bouncing on the ball of his foot. That girl had been difficult. Too much blood.

He fished in the bowl and plucked out another

matchbook. This one showed a smirking matador dressed in blue, with a dumb-looking bull wrong-footed behind him. Cameron smiled. El Torero. He stroked the matchbook cover with his thumb, remembering the dark-haired waitress in Madrid. This was the second time in two days he'd thought of her. An involuntary shiver rippled down his frame. With her, he'd used his hands around her neck. He squeezed his right knee, clenching it until the jiggling stopped. Then he dropped the Spanish matchbook back in the bowl. Pity to waste that one. The Dove would do for now.

Cameron pulled over an empty metal wastepaper bin and set it between his feet. He leaned over it, elbows on his knees, and opened up the green matchbook, bending the cover backwards so that it was fully straightened out. Inside were two layers of matches, one closely packed on top of the other. One by one, he prised up the topmost matches, easing the layers apart. Then he tore out a single match and lit first one cigarette and then the other, pulling deeply on them both. He closed his eyes for a moment and savoured the dizzying nicotine hit.

The first cigarette he set back in the ashtray; the second he slotted lengthways into the matchbook between the two layers of matches. He adjusted it so that the rows of pink match-heads clasped the cigarette along its length, leaving its burning end poking out a couple of inches to one side. Then he placed the matchbook flat on the bottom of the bin and checked his watch: 18.35.

Cameron leaned back in his chair and sucked on the other cigarette, watching the ringlet of smoke that curled upwards from the bin.

The phone call had come earlier that afternoon. He'd been tempted to just hang up and curl foetal-like into a chair. But he'd been taking orders for too long to say no to anything now. Then he'd heard what he was being asked to do and hadn't wanted to say no.

Cameron tapped his cigarette ash on to the floor, his eyes skimming the cramped kitchen. The entire cottage was built on a pygmy scale. Great if you were an undernourished dwarf, but for his rangy frame it was just a fucking nuisance. Through the midget-sized window he had a view of Deansgrange Cemetery, with its doleful archangels and faceless tombstones. He didn't pay the rent on this doll's house; that was done for him. Even so, it was time he moved on. Maybe he'd mention it on the next phone call. He crushed his cigarette into the ashtray, screwing it into a tight zigzag. His leg started to jiggle again. No getting away from it. There would always be another phone call.

Cameron bent over to inspect the cigarette in the bin. The grey and white ash was almost an inch long. He watched as the glowing ember devoured the cigarette paper, advancing closer and closer to the plump match-heads.

As a time-delay device, it was pretty basic, but that was its appeal. Make a thing too complicated and chances were that something would go wrong.

He'd known a guy once who'd tried to torch his warehouse by filling up a balloon with paraffin, suspending it from the ceiling and then setting it swinging over a lit candle. His theory was that, once the oscillations died out, the balloon would stop over the candle, the flame would melt a hole in it and the paraffin would seep out and ignite. By this time, of course, the guy would be miles away, setting up his alibi.

Naturally, it had all gone arseways. Fucking idiot had used so much paraffin that it had cascaded down like Niagara Falls and snuffed the candle out.

Far better to keep things simple. Cameron had used the matchbook device once before, but had miscalculated the length of time he'd have to get to safety. He'd taken too long and the flames had slid past him, blocking his exit. The flickering tongues had shadowboxed with him as he'd tried to get through, jabbing at him whenever he got too close. He could still remember the smell of his own scorched flesh. He looked down and massaged the puckered skin on his right arm where the flames had branded him. He'd been lucky to get out alive. This time he wasn't taking any chances.

Cameron checked the cigarette again. The ash was over two inches long. It reminded him of the way old people smoked, gluing the cigarette to their lips and leaving it there till the ash was nearly as long as their own fingers. His mother used to do that. She'd shuffle along behind her walking frame, squinting in disapproval at him through the smoke that trickled from the cigarette clinging to her lips, the ash precarious but never dropping to the floor. She'd always seemed old. So old in the end that it took her nineteen minutes to hoist herself up out of a chair. He knew because he'd stood over her once and timed her.

He bent over the bin again. The burning tip was nearly there. The pink match-heads waited like ripe berries ready to burst. He edged away, just in case. The hot orange ember touched the first pink head. The match hissed and flared alight. The second match blazed, then the third and the fourth, until every match was burning. A ribbon of flame an inch high danced across the matchbook, and the smell of sulphur scented the air.

Cameron checked his watch: 18.44. Nine minutes. He nodded. Nine minutes to set up the rest of the fuel and get out of the apartment before it burned to the ground. He closed his eyes and smiled. He'd been told to make it look like an accident. A wave of pleasure rolled over him. No problem.

After all, accidents were his speciality.

CHAPTER 21

Harry stood on the kerb and watched Ashford's Jag sweep away. Not for the first time, she wondered how people could have such contrasting views of her father. Staunch friend versus absconding father; financial genius versus bankrupt fraudster. But then, she had trouble telling the difference herself sometimes.

'Quick, hop in.'

A sleek red Saab had purred to a halt in front of her, and Harry recognized Jude's boxy shoulders behind the wheel. She climbed into the passenger seat, settling her satchel on her lap. She glanced over at Jude, but he had turned away to check the traffic behind. His linebacker physique seemed too big for the car. His left hand gripped the gear stick, his shirt sleeve rolled up to reveal a chunky wristwatch and sturdy forearm. No wedding ring.

Harry listened to the ticking of the indicator and wondered how long he was planning to ignore her. Finally, Jude eased the car into the outside lane, saluting the driver behind. They drove in silence for a while.

How the hell was she going to get any information out of this stiff-necked guy?

Then Jude nodded at the satchel on her lap and said, 'What's that?'

'My laptop.'

'No, I meant the logo.'

'Oh.' Harry brushed her fingers across the silver *DefCon* emblem on her bag. The skull and crossbones etched inside the letter 'O' had once been inky black, but were now worn away to a mottled grey.

'DefCon,' she said. 'It's a hackers' convention held every year in Las Vegas. I won the satchel in a contest over there when I was thirteen. My father took me.'

Jude threw her an incredulous look. 'Your father took you to a hackers' convention?'

She nodded. 'Yeah, well, he knew I was determined to go. I'd made all kinds of elaborate plans to skip the country in the middle of the night. Got laryngitis the day before, but even that didn't hold me back. In the end, my sister ratted me out, but instead of forbidding me to go, he just came along.'

She smiled to herself at the memory. DefCon was one of the world's most notorious annual hacker conventions, and she'd been mortified at the prospect of turning up with a parent in tow. But by the time they'd arrived at the Alexis Hotel to register for the convention, all her truculence had melted away. There she was, thirteen years old, in the heart of the Vegas strip, where neon lights flickered twenty-four hours a day and the heat made it hard to breathe. The hotel foyer was buzzing with teenage hackers, and exhilaration had flared through her at the notion that she was a part of it all.

She'd gazed around her, drinking in every detail. At that time, the hacker underworld was male dominated. Dudes with tattoos and leather jackets mixed with kids who looked like they'd been dressed by their mothers. Some sat in corners discussing the latest hacker tools, while others were already drunk at two in the afternoon.

There had been two registration queues; one for white hats and one for black hats. Harry and her father joined the respectable white-hat queue, but she couldn't help sneaking fascinated looks at the bad asses in the other line. She eavesdropped on their swagger and recognized some of the most infamous hackers of her time.

'See that guy over there?' she'd said to her father, nudging him. 'The one in black? He's called Tomahawk. He broke into the AT&T telephone network. Caused havoc.' She tugged at his sleeve again. 'And the geeky-looking one beside him? That's Apollo. They say he infiltrated the FBI.' She had a hard time keeping the reverent awe out of her voice, and hoped the laryngitis would disguise it.

Her father had studied her for a moment. Then he'd grabbed her by the elbow and marched her over to join the black-hat queue. 'Let's live on the edge, shall we?' he'd said.

A horn blared somewhere in front of them and Harry re-focused on where she was. With Jude's steady driving style, they'd covered good ground and the airport wasn't far away.

A gap opened up ahead of them, and Jude slowed down to let a minivan slip into the stream of traffic. Harry glanced at his profile and noticed the blond flecks in his brown hair. She bet he always drove the same way: courteously and with no showing off, but with all the pizzazz of a tortoise.

'Do you never accelerate?' she said.

'Not in this kind of traffic. No point. Anyway, speed is dangerous.'

Harry rolled her eyes.

'So what kind of contest was it?' Jude said.

'What?'

'The bag. How did you win it?'

'Oh. A social-engineering contest.' She saw his blank look and explained. 'Social engineering is when hackers trick people into giving them confidential information. Sort of like hacking human beings instead of hacking computers.'

Jude raised an eyebrow. 'Seems unethical to me.'

'Oh, it is. That's half the fun.' She was needling him and she knew it.

He kept his gaze fixed on the road ahead. 'So what did you have to do?'

'We were each given a name and phone number,

and the first one to find out the person's bank account details and ATM PIN number was the winner.'

'Sounds like a training ground for scam artists.'

'I suppose it was, in a way.' Harry watched a low-flying plane as it tilted in to land. The airport was just ahead.

'Well?' Jude said. 'Aren't you going to tell me how you did it?'

'It wasn't difficult. I called the guy up and said I was from his bank's Fraud Prevention Department. The laryngitis added a few years to my voice, so I had no trouble convincing him. I told him his ATM card had been used to make withdrawals in the middle of the night for the past week totalling over $3,000, and I wanted to check that it was legit. Poor guy nearly fainted.'

'I don't blame him.'

'Oh, I was very sympathetic, but I pointed out he was still liable for the debits to his account. Then I said maybe just this once I could break the rules and get rid of the charges for him. Made it sound like I was doing him a big favour. All he had to do was give me his bank account details and his ATM PIN number and I'd clear the charges there and then. He couldn't read the numbers out quick enough.'

Jude shook his head, and Harry could have sworn she heard him tutting.

'So you won?' he said.

'Actually, I came second. I spent too much time

at the end reassuring the guy that it wasn't for real, that I was just conducting some kind of fraud prevention exercise. I got pretty cross with him. He really should've been more careful.' Harry shook her head and did some tutting of her own. 'People should never give bank details out over the phone like that. He won't do it again, that's for sure.'

She felt his eyes on her and returned his look. 'You know, none of this is what I came here to talk to you about and we're almost at the airport.'

He held her gaze for a moment, as though reassessing her. Then he said, 'Don't worry, there's plenty of time.'

'I thought you had a plane to catch.'

'Who said anything about catching a plane?'

CHAPTER 22

They were in a part of the airport Harry had never seen before, and from the neglected look of the place she guessed few people ever had.

They had followed the main route to the Departures block along with all the other traffic, but at the last second Jude had swung left on to a narrow side road that led away from the airport's main concourse. He'd driven without explanation for two or three miles and they were now bumping along a rough track with no other vehicles in sight.

Harry looked around. 'Where exactly are we going?'

The airport buildings were far behind, and in front of them stretched a wilderness of unkempt grass, criss-crossed by ribbons of grey runway that looked seldom used. No holidaymakers with matching luggage sets out here.

'You'll see,' Jude said.

He veered off the dirt track and headed across the lumpy terrain. Ahead of them was a corrugated metal structure that resembled a disused aircraft hangar. Jude rounded the side of it and slowed to a halt, killing the engine.

Squatting in front of them on an apron of tarmac was a sky-blue helicopter, its engine silent and its rotor blades drooping low over the cockpit.

'Come on,' Jude said, and jumped out of the car.

Harry followed at a slower pace, watching as a man in green overalls rolled out from underneath the helicopter. He caught sight of them and waved, giving Jude a thumbs-up sign before making his way back into the hangar. Jude saluted him and strode over to the aircraft. Without a backward glance at Harry, he heaved open the door and climbed aboard.

Harry hesitated. Then she marched across the tarmac and hauled herself up into the cockpit after him. He was leaning forward in the pilot's seat, inspecting the instrument panel as though he knew what he was doing. Harry made a move towards the row of seats behind him, but Jude beckoned her over.

'Sit up in front,' he said. 'You'll get a better view.'

Harry winced. Her head for heights was about as good as her head for navigation, and already she found herself taking a few deep breaths. She edged around Jude and sat next to him. She took in the 180-degree view of coarse flatlands and deserted runways. She felt like she was at the edge of the world.

'So, someone pushed you under a train,' Jude said, still studying the bank of screens and dials in front of him. 'What was that all about?'

154

'They were trying to frighten me,' she said as she checked out the cockpit. It looked like the bridge of an inter-galactic starship, and certainly not something that should be in the hands of a stuffy banker who didn't like accelerating.

She leaned towards him, her hands clasped in her lap. 'Are you really going to try and fly this thing?'

'Well, one of us has to.' Jude grinned at her. 'Don't worry, we're not going far. I just need to put her through her paces.'

He handed her a set of oversized earphones with a microphone attached, and she was reminded absurdly of the call-centre girls on the Sheridan Bank helpdesk. She adjusted the headset into place over her ears, her gaze fastened on Jude as he flicked switches and punched buttons. He had loosened his collar and tie, and rolled his sleeves further up his arms. A hint of well-developed bicep formed a curve beneath the white cotton of his shirt. The engine started to throb, and the vibrations drummed through Harry's frame.

'Why would anyone want to frighten you?' Jude's radio-transmitted voice sounded tinny and far away.

'They think I have money that belongs to them. Twelve million euros, to be precise.'

'And do you have it?'

'Maybe.'

The rotor blades began to spin, lifting and straightening, slicing shadows through the sunlight.

'And how do I fit into all this?' Jude said.

The blades whirled faster and faster, thudding across the roar of the engine. Harry resisted the urge to hunch her shoulders. Even with earphones, the noise was almost unbearable.

'You fit into it because you're an investment banker,' she said, trying not to shout. 'You understand market trading, how money gets moved around.' Her whole body buzzed from the vibrating aircraft, and she gripped the armrests to keep her hands still. 'According to the guy who pushed me on to the train tracks, the money belongs to my father's insider trading ring.'

The helicopter pulled straight up into the air and Harry's stomach slammed down into her groin. Jude glanced over at her.

'Ever been in one of these before?' he said.

Harry shook her head, not trusting herself to speak. They hovered for a moment in mid-air, and then banked steeply to the left. Harry swallowed hard. The ground veered up towards her and for a moment she viewed the world on its side.

When the helicopter levelled out, she looked across at Jude. He was guiding the chopper along a steady path, using fingertip sensitivity on the controls. His eyes scanned the horizon as he leaned forward, in tune with his aircraft's vital signs, his expression alert and full of intelligence.

What had happened to the stuffy tortoise who'd driven her to the airport?

'Where did the trading ring get twelve million euros?' he said.

156

'Okay, here's what I think,' she said. 'The trading ring received insider information that Sorohan was about to be taken over by Aventus. They bought Sorohan shares when the price was low, knowing it would shoot through the roof when news of the takeover leaked out. Then, when the takeover was announced, they sold high and made a fortune . . .' She frowned. This next bit was where the guessing started, but she felt sure she was right. 'Somehow my father managed to hide some or all of the profits from that deal. And now the other ring members want it back.'

'You're saying your father cheated them?'

'Wouldn't surprise me. My father cheated everybody.'

Jude regarded her for a long moment. 'Well, he never cheated me. He was one of the most talented investment bankers I've ever known, and too smart for any of this shit.'

She glared back at him. 'Not smart enough, obviously. He got caught, don't forget.' She dropped her gaze. 'Anyway, his guilt isn't up for debate here.'

The helicopter pitched suddenly to the right. The ground hurtled towards Harry, and she froze. At the last second, they pulled up into a dizzying vertical lift, and the horizon plummeted out of sight.

Harry's limbs were rigid. 'Would you give up all the macho manoeuvres and just fly in a straight line?'

Jude threw her a startled look. He levelled the aircraft out, righting the world back on its axis. 'This any better?'

157

'Yes. Thanks.' She relaxed her grip on the seat and took a few deep breaths. Silence fell between them and Harry began to think it wasn't possible to talk to this guy without turning surly.

Jude cleared his throat. 'So, if your father had the money, maybe he was the one who put it into your account.'

Harry shifted in her seat. She'd considered this already. Perhaps her father did have a way to access his funds from prison. After all, if there was one thing he knew about, it was money. Maybe he needed to move it, hide it from detection. It was possible. It made some kind of sense. It also meant her father was prepared to put her life in danger.

'Maybe,' she said.

'It may sound obvious, but why don't you just ask him?'

Just ask him. How simple. How tempting to just go and see him, to blurt out everything that had happened and then bury herself in his warm bear hug, the way she used to when she was five.

Harry crossed and uncrossed her legs. Who was she kidding? She'd be on one side of a table, her father on the other. 'But I don't know anything about it, Harry, I promise,' he'd say. Then he'd give that little shrug with his palms turned upwards, as if that could prove how little he had to hide.

Harry turned to Jude and gave him a wry smile. 'Trust me, asking him is not an option.'

Jude sighed. 'So what do you want from me?'

'I need to understand how my father and the

rest of the ring members conducted their insider trades. How did the money come and go?'

'You talk like I'm supposed to know.'

'Look, all I'm asking is that you use your imagination. Pretend you're not this upstanding investment banker who never breaks the rules. Imagine you're a conman, a crook.' Harry fixed her gaze straight ahead. 'Imagine you're my father.'

He was silent for a moment. Then he said, 'Okay. Let's suppose I'm an investment banker and I have some price-sensitive information I want to take advantage of. Problem is, I can't use any of my normal trading accounts.'

'Why not?'

'Because they're being watched. Investment banks keep an eye on their employees' trading accounts. One shady deal and the alarm bells would ring.'

'So what would you do instead?'

Jude shrugged. 'If it was me, I'd open a secret account, most likely a Swiss bank account, and trade out of there.'

'A Swiss bank account?' Harry raised an eyebrow. 'Isn't that the stuff of espionage and money laundering?'

'Not necessarily. You don't have to be a criminal to open a Swiss bank account. Anyone who wants to keep their finances private can do it.'

'So it's completely anonymous?'

Jude shook his head. 'No, that's just a myth. There's no such thing as a truly anonymous account. All Swiss banks know the identity of their customers.'

'But what about numbered accounts? I thought the whole point of them was that your name doesn't appear anywhere?'

'It doesn't. But the bank still holds a file somewhere in the archives with your name and address on it. Only a few senior managers have access to it, but it exists all the same.'

'It's confidential, though?'

'Oh, absolutely.' Now that he'd got started, Jude seemed almost chatty on the subject. 'The Swiss have made it a criminal offence for a bank to disclose client information to anyone. Bank employees sign a secrecy clause as part of their contract. If they so much as acknowledge the existence of an account, they risk going to jail.'

As an incentive to keep your mouth shut, Harry reckoned that would just about do it. 'So, if a foreign government approaches a Swiss bank with proof of criminal activity on one of their accounts, what happens?'

'Well, the Swiss have their own ideas about what constitutes criminal activity. Tax evasion and divorce disputes don't cut much ice with them, but they'd probably co-operate for crimes like drug trafficking and insider trading.'

'So, how do you go about opening one of these accounts?' She peered out the window. Below them, the terrain was changing. The sparse scrubland had given way to soft hills, and straight ahead were the gentle slopes of the Sugarloaf. They were heading south towards the Dublin Mountains.

Jude shrugged. 'Much the same as opening up any other bank account. You fill in some forms, provide proof of identity – usually your passport. A lot of Swiss banks insist on a personal interview. But apart from the secrecy stuff, it's much the same as any other bank account. You can get VISA cards, ATM cards, internet access.'

'So if my father had one of these accounts, he'd have gone to Switzerland to open it?'

'Or to the Caribbean. The Bahamas, Bermuda, the Cayman Islands. The Swiss banks have branches there that operate under the same secrecy laws.'

Harry thought of all the transatlantic business trips her father had made over the years and figured the Caribbean was more likely than Europe. 'So how did he manage the account from here? How did he trade out of it?'

If Jude noticed the switch from hypothetical what-ifs to direct questioning about her father's operations, he gave no sign of it.

'Assuming he had a numbered account, then it was probably assigned to a personal account manager,' he said. 'Relationship Managers, they call them. Your father most likely would've given this account manager his trading instructions by phone.'

'That doesn't sound too secure. Anyone could have phoned up pretending to be my father.'

'Not really. He'd have to quote not only the account number, but also a secret code to verify his identity.'

'A secret code?' Now they were back to espionage and double agents. 'Like what?'

'Like anything. He might have arranged that all instructions must incorporate a particular phrase, like, I dunno . . .' Jude shrugged. 'Mickey Mouse, or Abracadabra. Anything, so long as just he and the Relationship Manager knew what it was.'

Harry squinted at him. 'A bit James Bond, isn't it?'

'But confidential.'

What would her father have used as a secret code? Something slick, easily remembered. Something related to a significant part of his life. But then, his life had so many aspects: investment banker, criminal, poker player, father. Not necessarily in that order of priority, of course. To be fair, he was probably a better poker player than he was a criminal.

She gazed down at the fields far below. A large L-shaped residence swung into view, and it wasn't until she saw the Celtic swirls of hedges that she realized it was Dillon's house.

The maze seemed to lunge up towards her. Her breath died in her throat, and her pulse went into overdrive, hammering through her.

'You okay?' Jude was staring at her.

She nodded, and tried to tear her eyes away from the maze, but it was as though her head was clamped in a neck brace. The chopper lurched closer to the giant hedges, and she found herself trying to catch a glimpse of what lay in the centre.

All she could make out was something large and dark that glinted now and then in the sun.

Jude followed her gaze. 'That's Dillon Fitzroy's house, isn't it?'

'Yes.' She remembered Felix had said Jude and Dillon were old friends. 'How do you two know each other?'

'We were in college together.' His eyes were still on the house below. 'He always said he'd end up with a mansion in the countryside. Called it his "Fuck You" house.'

Harry's eyebrows shot up at the profanity. It seemed so out of place, coming from Jude.

'Where did that come from?' she said.

Jude shrugged. 'He was adopted, did he ever tell you that?'

'So?'

'If you ask me, it left him feeling he had something to prove. Don't ask me what.'

'You don't like him much, do you?'

He glanced over at her, and then swooped the chopper into a sharp turn. 'Time we headed back.'

Dillon's house disappeared from view. Harry leaned back in her seat and breathed deeply, waiting for her pulse to slow down.

'You know, you haven't asked me who any of the ring members are,' she said eventually. 'Don't you want to know?'

Jude shrugged. 'If you plan on telling me, I assume you'll get around to it. If not, then there's no point in asking.'

163

Harry regarded him for a moment, unsure how much to confide in him. After all, ultimately he was an investment banker, just like the rest of them. But there was still something she needed from him.

'You know some of them,' she said finally.

'I do?'

'Felix Roche, for one. Your man in Procurement.'

The helicopter lurched to the left. 'What? Roche was a member of the trading ring?'

'Well, not exactly,' said Harry, watching him closely. 'The ring never knew about him. He spied on their emails and piggy-backed on some of their insider information.'

Jude frowned, and squeezed the control levers as he tried to recover the chopper's equilibrium. 'Where did you hear that? And if it's true, how come he was never arrested?'

'Not enough proof. The police probably didn't think he was that important. But I do.' She leaned forward. 'I want to see his files. His emails, his archives.'

'Why?'

'Because he may have been just a freeloader, but he still had access to the ring members' emails. He knew who they were. Or, if he didn't, then he had information that could help me track them down.'

'But you can't see his emails. That's confidential information.'

She sighed. The tortoise was back. 'I know it is. That's why I need your help.'

'Are you kidding? What makes you think I'm going to help you with a stunt like that?'

Harry turned to watch the helicopter's shadow tracking them against the sunlit hills. 'Ever hear of a KWC investment banker by the name of Spencer?'

'Jonathan Spencer? What's he got to do with it?'

'You knew him?'

'Sure, I knew him. We used to beat each other at squash a couple of times a month. He was a good guy. He was killed years ago in a car accident.'

'No, he wasn't.'

Jude looked at her as though she'd lost her mind, but she held his gaze and continued.

'He was shoved in front of a speeding truck before he could sabotage the Sorohan deal.'

Jude yanked the headset away from his ears and dropped it on to his neck. He glared at her for a moment, then shoved the headset back in place.

'That's just crazy,' he said. 'Who's your source of information on all this? I don't believe a word of it.'

'If I end up dead under a speeding train, will you believe it then?'

Jude stared straight ahead, his mouth set in a grim line.

'I need to see those files,' Harry said softly. 'I need you to help me hack into KWC.'

CHAPTER 23

The odds favoured the hacker.

After all, time was on the hacker's side. Harry often spent days and weeks executing a game plan. She'd trawl the internet on lengthy reconnaissance, gathering information about her target. She'd scan the system perimeters, knocking on its walls, looking for holes. Then she'd get in close and jiggle the door knobs, rattle the locks. Inevitably something would give, and she'd slip inside.

A good hacker could break into just about anything, given enough time. But time was the one thing Harry figured she didn't have.

She glanced over at Jude, whose grip on the Saab's steering wheel seemed unnecessarily tight. His mouth was clamped shut, as though his lips had been tacked together with a staple gun. He'd hardly said a word since they'd left the airport.

'Look, it's not like I'm asking you to rob a bank,' she said. 'All you have to do is sign me in past security and I'll do the rest.'

'There is no way,' said Jude, emphasizing the last two words with karate chops on the wheel, 'that I am smuggling you into the KWC building. God knows what kind of damage you'd do.'

'Damage? God, all I want is to take a look at Felix's old emails. They're probably archived off somewhere. It'll take five minutes.'

'I'm sorry, but it's too risky.'

Harry slumped back in her seat and folded her arms, her gaze drifting over the streets outside. At nine in the evening the darkness was thickening, and soft lights glowed from the bars along Townsend Street. She was going to do this, with or without him. It just made no sense to go about it the hard way.

They drove past the Long Stone pub, with its warm red frontage and Celtic lettering, and past White's Bar, with its signs boasting cocktails and Wi-Fi access.

Harry gripped Jude's arm. 'Stop the car.'

'What? It's double yellows.'

'Just pull over.'

He eased the car down a side street and slotted it into a vacant spot. Harry yanked open the door before he'd even had time to kill the engine.

'Come on,' she said. 'I need a drink.'

She led the way back to White's Bar. She'd only been there once before but could still remember the low, dark ceilings and the smell of wet duffel coats that had saturated everything. It had been like drinking in a bear's cave.

She took a look over her shoulder and quickened her pace. For the first time in several hours, she was out in the open, completely exposed, and the notion almost made her whimper. She scanned the dark streets, but saw nothing out of the ordinary. Behind her she could hear Jude, taking a call on his mobile phone. The sound was oddly reassuring.

She pushed open the door of White's, and the first thing that hit her was the smell of fresh paint. She stood in the doorway and took in the bar. The low wooden beams were gone, and the ceiling was now alabaster white. Spotlights blazed down on to cream leather chairs, and the tables were dotted with flickering candles, as if someone was getting ready to say Mass. Harry stepped into the room. Where did all the bears go to drink these days?

Business looked slow for a Saturday night. She made her way over to a table in the corner, with Jude close behind her, still talking into his phone. Harry scooted in along the leather sofa and sat with her back to the wall. Shoving the candle out of her way, she hauled her satchel up on to the table.

'We need to wrap this up before tomorrow,' Jude was saying. He stood to one side, half-turned away from her. She noticed the way his hair was clipped in a precise track around the back of his ears.

She took out her laptop and, while she waited for it to power up, she considered her options. There were a hundred different ways she could do this; but most of them would take time. She wanted access to the KWC network now. The ring members' emails were an important link to their

168

identity. She already knew about Leon Ritch and Jonathan Spencer. The character that interested her most was the shadowy figure of the Prophet.

'Check your email, Frank,' Jude said into the phone. 'StarCom mailed us the meeting minutes this afternoon. Give me a call before you head home.'

Harry shot him a look and something inside her brain clicked into gear. Her eyes followed his mobile phone as he set it down on the table.

'I'll get the drinks,' he said. 'What'll you have?'

She blinked and dragged her gaze up to his face. 'Oh, a white wine. Thanks.'

She watched him as he headed off to the bar. He looked more like a nightclub bouncer than an investment banker. When she was sure he wouldn't turn around, she snatched up his mobile phone. She held it under the table and used her thumb-nails on the keys, looking for the name of the last caller. She flicked a glance up at the bar. Jude was handing cash over to the barman. She peered down at the phone again. There it was. Frank Buckley. She slid the phone back along the table just as Jude returned with their drinks.

Harry held out her hand to him. 'Lend me another one of your business cards.'

He frowned. 'What for?'

'Come on, just humour me.'

He extracted a card from his wallet and held it out to her. 'I don't suppose there's anything confidential on it.'

'You'd be surprised.' She scrutinized the details

on the card and then handed it back to him. She started tapping on her keyboard. 'Take a look at it and tell me what you see.'

He cast his eyes over it and shrugged, lowering himself into a chair opposite her. 'My name and phone number, my email address. KWC contact details.'

'Right. Now let me tell you what a hacker sees.' Harry reached over for the card and pointed at the phone numbers. 'See that? The main switchboard number is 2411200. And here's your direct line: 2411802. That gives the hacker an idea of the range of numbers your switchboard supports. Hundreds, in KWC's case.'

'So?'

'So, with that many employees, there's a pretty good chance that one of them has connected a computer directly into the phone network through a modem. It's probably unauthorized and most likely insecure.'

'Why would anyone do that?'

'Usually it's so they can access the internet without the company monitoring what they're up to. Maybe they're downloading pornography, that kind of thing. All the hacker has to do is keep dialling the switchboard numbers till he hits a modem. Then, bingo, he's hooked into that PC and your network is his.'

'Jesus. Is that what you're going to do?'

Harry shook her head. 'Not this time.'

She pecked at her keyboard and began drafting

an email with the subject heading 'Urgent: Revised Minutes from StarCom meeting'. She attached a bogus Word document to the body of the message.

Jude shifted in his seat. 'What exactly are you up to?'

'Just sending an email.' That was the other handy thing about business cards. They told you how the company constructed its email addresses. If Jude's address was jude.tiernan@kwc.com, then the chances were Frank Buckley's followed the same rules. She addressed the memo to frank.buckley@kwc.com and hit the Send button.

'Don't you need any cables?' Jude said, peering under the table.

Harry pointed up at the wi-fi signs on the walls. 'Wireless.' Then she cocked her head to one side, and regarded him for a moment. 'You don't know much about computers, do you?'

'About as much as you know of corporate finance.'

She dipped her head in acknowledgement. 'Fair point.'

'Are you going to tell me what you're doing?'

Harry scanned his face and decided she might as well explain. After all, he couldn't stop her now. 'I'm infecting someone's PC with a RAT.'

Jude froze, his pint halfway to his lips. 'A rat?'

'R-A-T – Remote Access Trojan.' She smiled at his bewilderment. 'It's named after the wooden horse of Troy. It's a malicious program that gets past a system's defences by disguising itself as

171

something innocent. Basically, it brings the enemy inside the camp.'

He blinked, and then took a long draught of Guinness. He wiped his mouth with the back of his hand and seemed to be puzzling it out. 'So yours is disguised in an email?'

She nodded. 'To anyone else, it looks like a harmless Word document. But the minute the guy launches it, he'll kick-start the RAT.'

Jude's brow cleared, then furrowed again. 'But what's this RAT of yours going to do?'

'First, it's going to scurry off into a dark corner and hide. Then it's going to open a back door in the guy's computer and let me in.' She leaned forward and smiled at him. 'And once I'm in, I own that computer. It's as if I've broken into the KWC office and I'm sitting down at that keyboard.'

Jude dragged a hand backwards and forwards through his hair until it stood up in short tufts. 'I'm not sure I should be sitting here listening to this.' He took another swig of his pint. 'Aren't there virus scanners or something that'll stop this stuff getting through?'

'Oh sure. They'll recognize any known Trojans and send them packing straight away.' She smiled. 'But they can't recognize one they haven't seen before. This little RAT is a zero-day exploit, fresh out of the hacker underworld. Very few people know about it yet. I usually leave something like it as a calling card whenever I penetrate a system. You never know when you might need to sneak back in again.'

She took a peek at her laptop, but there was no signal from the RAT. Come on, Frank Buckley, read your mail.

Jude fiddled with a beer mat, bending it over on itself until it was the size of a postage stamp. 'Do you really think Felix is stupid enough to get involved in insider trading? I mean, what if your information is wrong?'

'Haven't you ever wondered why Felix got side-lined into Procurement?' Harry watched him as she sipped her wine. 'When we were in that meeting in KWC and he was being obnoxious, you scribbled him a note. What did it say?'

He blinked, and then gave a rueful smile. 'I told him to stop being such a prick. You're right: he's stupid enough.'

She smiled back at him, and then checked her screen. Still nothing.

'So tell me about this helicopter of yours,' she said. 'Is that the latest investment banker's toy?'

He shook his head. 'I never wanted to be an investment banker. Ever since I was a kid, all I wanted was to be a chopper pilot.'

'What changed your mind?'

He shrugged. 'Investment banking was a family tradition, so there was a lot of pressure.'

'And you just caved in?'

'No.' He glared at her. 'I made a deal with my father. Told him I'd do it for a year and then I'd quit. After that, I'd get my pilot's licence.'

'So what happened?'

'Turned out I didn't want to quit. Seemed I was good at investment banking, and secretly I quite enjoyed it. So I stayed on.'

'But you still got your pilot's licence?'

He nodded. 'I used to fly all the time.'

'Used to?'

He paused. 'I had a bad accident in fog a couple of years back.' He stared down at his pint for a moment and his thoughts seemed to turn inwards. Then he looked up. 'You want to know the truth? That chopper scares me shitless.'

'What?' Harry thought of his expert handling of the aircraft. 'Didn't look that way to me. Why do it then?'

He shrugged. 'Investment banking is too safe. Sometimes you need to do things that scare you.'

The hairs rippled on the back of her neck. She thought about her hacking exploits, about the exhilaration of taking risks. Her eyes flicked over Jude's solid build. She thought of his cautious driving style, and of the acrobatics he'd put her through in the air. Tortoise or stuntman? She studied his face. Which one was he?

Suddenly, her laptop pinged and her gaze flew back to the screen. Her RAT had sent her an email. She read it and let out a long breath. The message contained detailed instructions for locating Frank Buckley's computer over the internet.

The backdoor was open and her RAT was standing by, ready to let her in.

CHAPTER 24

Fuel, oxygen, heat; the triangle of fire. Remove any one of the ingredients, and the fire would die.

Cameron licked his lips and groped for the rucksack on the passenger seat beside him. He squeezed the rough canvas between his fingers as if to reassure himself that it was still there. It contained all the ingredients he was going to need.

He slunk down lower in his seat and stared at the ground-floor apartment across the road. The windows were dark, the curtains open. No one was home. He checked his watch. Almost ten o'clock. His right knee began to twitch and he jammed it in against the steering wheel to keep it still.

He'd parked under a tree to shield himself from the street lights. The road was quiet, but he still wore his woolly hat pulled down low over his eyebrows. Without it, his hair would glow like a pale moon.

He tugged the rucksack towards him and checked through its contents one more time. A putty knife, two matchbooks, a copy of yesterday's

Irish Times, a pair of surgical gloves, two rubber suction cups and a small plastic container of paraffin. They all nestled together inside the largest item, a wicker wastepaper basket, the kind that would ignite in an instant, crackling like a bunch of dry twigs.

Cameron lifted out the container of paraffin and unscrewed the lid. He closed his eyes and inhaled deeply on the heady fumes, letting them flood his brain. Then he replaced the lid and tightened it. The container was less than half full. The amateur arsonist nearly always used too much accelerant, but Cameron knew that a small amount was enough. Use too much and some of it would soak into floorboards and carpets, escaping combustion from the rising flames and leaving clues for the arson investigators. Cameron lodged the container back inside the rucksack and took out the surgical gloves. There'd be no forensic evidence from this accident.

Rain spattered against the windscreen, and Cameron rolled down his window to get a better view of the apartment. Cool air trickled in and sweetened the staleness inside the car. He could hear the slap of wet tyres from distant traffic, but no one had passed him on this road since he'd arrived. He peered at the building across the street. The sash windows looked old, the putty cracked. Getting in was going to be easy.

Heels clacked on the pavement behind him, and he shot a look into his rear-view mirror. A young, dark-haired woman wearing jeans and a blue jacket was crossing the road, heading towards the apartment building. Cameron slid further down in his seat, shielding his face with his hand. He peered at her between his fingers, watching her as she climbed the steps to the front door. His gaze lingered on her petite frame, and caressed the neat waist and trim thighs. He swallowed, and his breathing quickened. The girl unlocked the front door and went inside.

Cameron watched the ground-floor windows, waiting. His right knee trembled against the steering wheel and he gripped it with his hand. His breathing grew so shallow that it almost stopped. Suddenly, lights blazed on in the top-floor apartment and he could see the girl stretching across the front window to close the curtains. He pushed himself up in his seat and punched his knee with his fist. The ground floor was still empty.

Cameron took a deep breath and rubbed the palm of his hands along his jeans. Then he began to pull on the rubber gloves. He flexed his fingers and stretched the thin, tight latex over his knuckles, snapping it up to his wrists. The pale fabric made his hands seem inhuman somehow. They looked bloodless and waxy, the way his mother's hands had looked after she'd been dead for a few hours.

She had been his first accident. He could still see her broken body sprawled at the bottom of the stairs, her legs bent at unnatural angles and the walking aid perched on top of her like a cage. He could remember the eerie mixture of fascination and fear that had crawled all over him. It was the first time he had ever killed anyone.

The twitch in his knee was uncontrollable now and Cameron jiggled his leg up and down like a kid who needed to go to the toilet. He peered over at the apartment again, and tried to imagine how it would look when the fire had taken hold: orange and saffron flames leaping forty feet into the air, black smoke belching out through the windows, the smell of scorched wood, the thunderous roar of devastation.

He exhaled a long breath and leaned back in his seat, stretching his legs out straight. His knee was finally quiet. The ground-floor apartment was still in darkness, but he knew he could wait. He felt sure someone would be home soon.

CHAPTER 25

The RAT had done its job well. Harry typed in the connection details, and the back door to Frank Buckley's computer swung wide open. She slipped inside and, with a few keystrokes, locked the door behind her. If she'd been a burglar committing B&E with a house key, it couldn't have been any easier.

She glanced up at Jude. He was swirling the dregs of his pint in his glass, studying them as if he were reading tea-leaves. The pub was almost empty, and she could hear the squeak and clink of glasses being polished and put away behind the bar.

She turned back to the keyboard and tiptoed her way around Frank Buckley's files, sidestepping the personal stuff and heading straight for his network connections. From there, she plunged into KWC's central computers and launched a search for the company's email archives. Just for good measure, she launched a parallel search for the system password files. She didn't think she'd need administrative access, but it wouldn't hurt to have it.

'What exactly are you looking for?' Jude said, his gaze still fixed on the bottom of his glass.

'The name of the guy who wants me dead.'

He stopped sloshing his beer in the glass and stared at her. Then he jerked to his feet and swung round to her side of the table, peering over her shoulder at the screen. There was something very male about his blend of tangy aftershave and warm beer.

Her archive search had netted her hundreds of filenames, listed in alphabetical order. Each one was named after an individual person, with dates going back as far as 1999.

'Hey, that's a list of KWC employees,' Jude said, leaning in closer.

'Actually, it's their email archives.' She beamed at him. 'Even yours is there.'

Jude planted himself beside her on the sofa and scowled at the screen. She sneaked a glance at him. From a certain angle, his upper-body bulk reminded her of a cartoon super-hero.

'Surely you need a password to open these?' Jude's voice seemed to echo in the empty bar, like someone speaking too loudly in church.

'You'd think so, wouldn't you?' Harry scrolled through the list and found a bunch of files belonging to Felix Roche. There were eight of them, one for each year from 1999 to 2007. 'People are so paranoid about their email, tying it up with usernames and passwords. But when it's backed up, it often just gets dumped in a file that anyone can read.'

180

She nudged her mouse so that it hovered over the archive from the year 2000. The year of the Sorohan deal. Her hand froze over the mouse. Her whole body seemed to clench, and she fought an overwhelming urge to bolt home and hide. Then she thought of the dark streets and shadowy laneways that stood between her and her apartment. She jerked the mouse back to life and opened the file.

According to Ruth Woods, Felix had eavesdropped on the ring's activities by intercepting their email. Harry was betting that he'd copied those emails straight into his own mailbox. She searched the archive for mails originating from Leon Ritch. There were dozens of them, and none of them with Felix as the intended recipient. She was right.

Harry opened the first email. It was dated 17th January 2000, and was addressed to her father, salvador.martinez@kwc.com. Something shrivelled inside her when she saw her father's name.

Sal,
   Mercury Corp gave the nod on KeyWare deal today. No public announcement yet! Snap up KeyWare and let's make another killing.
   Leon

Jude shifted in the seat beside her. 'I can't believe Felix would hold on to something as incriminating as this.'

181

Harry shrugged. 'Maybe he thought he needed a little insurance policy.'

She opened another email, this one dated 28th April.

> Sal,
> My source tells me that Dynamix Software have retained JX Warner to manage their acquisitions. First target is either Zephyr or Sage Solutions. Watch this space!
> Leon

Jude sat bolt upright.

Harry shot him a look and then snapped her gaze back to the screen. 'What?'

'Dynamix. I worked on all their deals. Nothing went public on that one till at least July or August. How come this little shit knew about it back in April?'

Something sparked in Harry's brain and she studied him for a moment. 'You worked for JX Warner?'

He nodded, still staring at the screen. 'For a few years. I left after the Dynamix deal to join KWC.'

Her stomach jolted the way it did when she missed her footing on the stairs. She tried to keep her expression neutral as she thought about what Ruth Woods had said. According to the reporter, the Prophet's insider information had always been connected to JX Warner deals, and the police had him pegged as an investment banker there. Now it turned out that the man she'd gone to for help matched that description exactly.

But so what? There must have been dozens of investment bankers in JX Warner at that time. Still, Harry didn't like the coincidence. She scrutinized Jude as he glowered at the email.

'Notice anything else about this one?' she said.

'Like what?'

She tapped the screen with her fingernail, pointing at the list of mail recipients. The email had been addressed to her father, but a copy had also been sent to Jonathan Spencer. There could be no doubt about his involvement.

Jude's face took on a crumpled look, as though she'd told him his dog had died. 'Ah shit.'

She scoured his body language for signs of pretence. Her father had taught her to read poker bluffs like an expert, and she could usually spot when someone was lying. But there were no false notes, and his regret seemed sincere. Still, the JX Warner coincidence jarred with her, and she stored it away to be re-examined later.

They spent the next forty minutes trawling through the rest of Leon's emails. The extent of the ring's activities was overwhelming. Deal after deal, trade after trade, Leon, Jonathan and her father had leaked and exploited privileged information, and racked up millions in the process. By the time Harry hovered her mouse over the last email, she felt squeezed dry. And so far, she'd learned nothing about the Prophet's identity.

'It's unbelievable.' Jude rubbed his hands over his face. He looked as if he'd been stunned with a baseball bat. 'The breach of ethics, it's just so blatant.'

Harry slumped back against the seat. 'Ethics were never a priority for my father, believe me.'

'People think insider trading is a victimless crime, but it's not.' He gestured at the screen. 'Manipulating prices like that, it just destroys all faith in the markets. All the fairness is gone.' He blinked and gave her a dazed look. 'These were three senior investment bankers, highly respected. What the hell were they thinking?'

Three senior investment bankers. Plus the Prophet makes four. Harry's gaze whipped back to the screen. She'd been so intent on tracking down the Prophet that she'd forgotten about the rumoured fifth ring member; the one whose identity Leon had protected in case he needed favours later on. Not that it mattered. Leon's mails hadn't mentioned him either.

'Go on,' Jude said. 'We may as well read the last one.'

Harry clicked her mouse and opened Leon's last email. It was dated 8th August 2000, and, like most of the others, was addressed to both her father and Jonathan Spencer.

184

Why don't you guys ever answer your
phones?? Dynamix–Zephyr deal is OFF!
Dump Zephyr ASAP or we're all in the shit!
Leon

Appended to the memo was another email, this
one addressed only to Leon:

Leon,
Dynamix having difficulty raising funds for
Zephyr acquisition. Negotiations on hold.
Press release being prepared. Suggest you
reverse your Zephyr position immediately.
The Prophet

Harry's gaze flew to the sender's address:
2877bp9@alias.cyber.net.

'The Prophet?' Jude said. 'Who the hell is he?'

Harry hesitated, and then told him what she
knew, including the rumours of the fifth uniden-
tified banker. Naturally, it occurred to her that
none of this was news to him, but she shoved the
thought aside for now.

'Is this Prophet character the one who's after
you?' he said.

She shrugged. 'Maybe. It could be any or all of
them.'

Jude nodded towards the screen. 'That's a pretty
weird-looking email address.'

'He sent it through a re-mailer.' Before he
could give her one of his blank looks, she went on:

'A re-mailer strips your name and address from your email before sending it on, so there's no evidence of where it came from.'

'Surely you can trace it somehow?'

Harry shook her head. 'It's tricky. Re-mailers are usually chained together, so your mail hops from one re-mailer to another before reaching its final destination. Each hop could be to a different country with its own legal jurisdiction and privacy laws. Try tracking your way through that litigation nightmare.'

'So it's anonymous?'

She threw him a wry look. 'About as anonymous as your Swiss bank accounts. In the less secure re-mailers, there's always a database somewhere with your real name on it. They can be hacked into, or an employee could be bribed to leak the information.' She pointed at the screen. 'But I know this one. It's been shut down now, but it was a hard one to crack. It hopped into about twelve different countries, and used advanced cryptographic designs. I'm not surprised the authorities had trouble tracking the Prophet down.'

'So now what?'

Harry sighed and checked the clock at the bottom of her screen. It was almost eleven. She massaged the corners of her eyes. They felt dry and gritty, and her whole body ached. She longed for the oblivion of sleep, and the chance to let her subconscious deal with things for a while. But she wasn't finished yet.

She tapped the keyboard and searched Felix's archive again, this time looking for emails from Jonathan Spencer. There were none. The man had clearly been cagey about his involvement. Then she remembered her search for the system password files. She checked the results. Nothing.

There was still one more thing she had to do. Knowing she couldn't put it off any longer, Harry flexed her fingers and jabbed at the keys, launching a search for emails from her father.

There was only one, dated 5th October 2000.

Leon,

Sorohan stock has bottomed out. Now's the time to buy, before Aventus leaks to the press. This is the hand we've been waiting for. Let's raise the stakes this time.

Sal

Harry felt a dull ache in her chest, as though she'd prodded an old bruise. Good old Dad. She could picture him now: the relaxed smile and the tanned face; the jaunty left eyebrow always slightly uplifted as if to say, *Who, me?*

She looked at Jude. He was squinting at the screen, re-reading the mail as if he had misunderstood it the first time. She knew the feeling.

'I don't get it,' he said. 'I thought I knew him. He was my mentor in KWC. I admired him, for God's sake.' He dragged his gaze away from the

187

screen and turned to face her. 'Why the hell did he do it?'

Harry's thoughts turned inwards. How could you explain someone like her father? Dealmaker; hustler; a man addicted to gambling and taking risks; a man utterly careless of the consequences to other people.

She shrugged. 'Because he could.'

Jude frowned and shook his head. 'But he had so much to lose.'

'That was part of the attraction. The bigger the gamble, the better.' She fiddled with the stem of her wine glass. 'He bet our house in a poker game once and lost. It wasn't much of a house – the area was pretty rough – but it was still our home.'

Jude shot her a startled look. 'What did you do?'

'We had to move out. My mother took myself and my sister to stay in a B&B for three months.'

Harry had been nine years old at the time. She could still remember the broken-down house in Gardiner Street, and the smell of stale cabbage and onions on every landing. She could picture the rickety bed she'd shared with Amaranta, and the fat, wheezing man who'd come every Friday to collect money from her mother.

'Where was your father?' Jude said.

'Staying in a suite in Jury's Hotel. Playing poker.'

Jude stared at her for a long moment, and then gestured towards the screen. 'I haven't been much help to you with any of this, have I?'

Harry smiled. 'Not really.' Then she thought about

188

the hidden system password file and chewed her bottom lip. 'There's still something you could do.'

'Oh?'

She nodded at the screen. 'I know what happened nine years ago. But what's happening now? What's happened in the last few days to stir things up again?'

She leaned forward and scanned Jude's face. 'I need to see Felix's current emails. I need to see if he's intercepted anything more recent from the ring.'

'But he's not in IT Security any more. How could he intercept anything now?'

'Do you really believe he'd just walk away from all that knowledge and power and not leave himself a way back inside? I'm betting that, before he left Security, he cranked open a few backdoors of his own.'

'But the new Security guys would spot anything like that, surely?'

She shook her head. 'Not necessarily. Don't forget, he built the systems. No, take it from me, he still has access. That's probably why he was dead-set against me sniffing around.' She contemplated Jude for a moment. 'This is where you come in: I need to see Felix's current emails. And for that I need his password.'

He looked blank. 'But I don't have his password.'

'No, but you can get it.' She leaned back and folded her arms, throwing him a challenging look. 'I think you're ready to try a little social engineering.'

189

CHAPTER 26

'Well, well. So my old buddy Jude needs a favour.'

Felix's voice sounded thick and sibilant over the loudspeaker on Jude's phone. Harry leaned in closer. She was sitting at the desk in her own study. Beside her, Jude's bodyguard physique made the room look small. It had been her suggestion to move things back to her apartment. This stage of the scam needed privacy.

'It's not often we do each other favours, is it?' Felix continued.

Harry could make out a low thrumming noise in the background, as if Felix was taking the call inside a giant beehive. Her eyes flicked sideways at Jude. He was glaring at the phone on the desk between them, a tight muscle bulging in his lower jawline.

She snatched up her pen and pad, and scribbled him a note. *Be nice.* After all, ingratiating yourself with the mark was part of the social-engineering game.

Jude met her gaze and nodded.

'I just need five minutes of your time, Felix,' he said. 'Minor problem that you can help me with.'

'At this hour? And since when do I work week-ends for KWC?'

'I appreciate it's late –'

'Late? It's practically tomorrow.' Felix laughed. It started as a prolonged bronchial wheeze, and ended in a rattling cough that made Harry wonder if he had tuberculosis. Instinctively, she leaned away from the phone.

Still coughing, Felix said, 'Hey, Judy, d'I tell you it's my birthday today?'

Jude raised his eyebrows at Harry. 'No, I don't think you did.'

'Those fuggers back in the office. Told 'em it was my birthday, but none of 'em turned up.'

Harry picked up on his slippery consonants and the gathering hum of voices in the background. Whatever pub Felix was in, it was doing a good trade.

'So what's the favour?' Felix's tone told Harry he was going to enjoy saying no, whatever the favour was.

'It's something really stupid,' Jude said. 'I'm in the office and I've forgotten my network pass-word. My mind's just gone blank.'

'What're you bothering me for? Call one of those Security jerks, the ones that are just out of short trousers.'

'Believe me, I've tried. All I get is voicemail.'

'Well, I'd love to help, really I would, but I'm just a lowly Procurement guy now.'

'Don't give me that, Felix. You know more about

191

the KWC network than all of IT Security put together.'

Felix paused. 'You're flattering me, Judy. You must be desperate.'

'Come on, help me out here, I can't do anything without a password.'

'So go home. It'll come back to you in the morning.'

'The morning's not an option. I've a deadline to meet tonight, and I need to get hold of a document on the network now. Can't you reset my password or something?'

'Not without a laptop, I can't. And believe me, I'm not leaving this old bar any time soon.'

Jude threw Harry a questioning look, and she nodded. He leaned in closer to the phone. 'Well, how about giving me another login ID? Something that has access to private files on the network.'

A raucous holler blasted out through the loudspeaker, followed by the clamour of jeering male voices. Harry winced, straining to hear Felix through the din.

Jude lowered his face closer to the phone. 'Felix? You still there?'

''Course I am, Judy. Wouldn't leave you hanging. Hey, guess what age I am today. Go on, take a guess.'

Jude sighed and cast his gaze heavenward. Harry rolled her hands in frantic play-along-with-him signals. They couldn't let him slip away.

'Okay,' Jude said. 'You're forty.'

'I'm forty-five. Forty-five years old today. Know how long I've been with KWC?'

Jude shrugged. 'Ten, eleven years?'

'Too fucking long, that's how long. But guess what? Not any more.'

'You're leaving?'

'In style. I've got plans.'

Jude took a deep breath. 'Look, Felix, how about you just give me the Administrator password? That would do it, wouldn't it?'

'Are you out of your mind? And let you loose on the whole network? You stick to your mergers and acquisitions, let me handle the technology.'

'Come on, Felix, I'll be in and out in five minutes.'

Felix belched into the phone, long and loud like a barking sea lion. 'Judy, I'm getting tired of this conversation. You're invading my drinking space.'

Jude threw Harry a desperate look. She closed her eyes for a moment, and then scribbled a single word on the pad, underlining it twice: *CEO.*

They'd gone over this. If Felix didn't respond to normal persuasion tactics, then they'd have to play their final card: the figure of authority.

Jude yanked at his tie, dragging it loose. 'Look, if I don't get this business wrapped up tonight I'll need to explain why to the CEO. Believe me, you don't want Ashford breathing down your neck.'

'Ashford? You think I'm scared of him? It's not even my job to help you with this. Besides, there's nothing he can do to me. Not any more.'

193

Jude cocked his head to one side and squinted at the phone. Then he turned to Harry and shook his head, his face creased in puzzlement.

Harry tossed the pen on the desk and slumped back against her chair. So that was that. They'd played their last card. She closed her eyes and massaged the back of her neck, aware of a dull throb spreading along her spine and pounding into her skull. She opened her eyes to find Jude watching her. She shook her head and tried to smile, then sliced her hand in a cutting motion across her throat, telling him to give it up. If Felix had information that could help her, she'd just have to get to it some other way.

She started to shut down her laptop while Jude turned back to the phone.

'I can make it worth your while,' he said.

Harry froze, and then whipped her gaze back to his face. His mouth was rigid, and the bulging muscle in his jaw was back. What the hell was he doing? They hadn't discussed this.

'Oh?' Felix said. 'How?'

'I'll do a trade. You give me a log-on ID and I'll give you information.'

'What kind of information?'

'Privileged information. Information nobody else has.'

There was a pause. 'Go on.'

Harry held her breath, her gaze fixed on Jude.

'This deal I'm working on,' he said. 'It's with Nectel. They're acquiring another company.'

'Everyone knows that. They're taking over BridgeCom. It's been in all the papers.'

'Not any more. They're switching targets. I just confirmed it with Nectel's CEO. They're dropping BridgeCom and gunning for someone else.'

Harry could hear the ragged sound of Felix's breathing over the phone. What was Jude thinking? Was he actually going to give Felix insider information? Her palms felt slippery. She knew she should stop him, but she couldn't move. It also crossed her mind that maybe he had done this kind of thing before.

Jude leaned into the phone, his mouth almost touching it. 'This won't be on record anywhere for another month. That's a whole month for someone to make a killing, and nothing to link them to the information.' He met Harry's gaze. 'Give me a log-on I can use, Felix.'

The phone crackled with background voices.

'You must need this pretty badly,' Felix said, after a moment.

Jude didn't answer. His face was stony. Harry watched him, transfixed.

Then Felix laughed. 'Okay, I'll trade. This is fun. You tell me the name of the target and I'll give you a log-on ID. And, Judy . . .?'

'Yes?'

'Don't fuck with me, okay?'

'Banker's honour.'

Felix snorted into the phone. 'Yeah, right. So what've you got?'

'The target is Aslan Technology.'

'Aslan. Well, well. Okay, I reckon that's worth a username and password. But not the admin account.'

Shit. Harry squeezed her eyes shut. She needed Administrator access. Other than using Felix's own password, it was the only sure way to get into his current email.

'I don't trust you,' Felix continued. 'You'll bring the whole fucking place to its knees.' He cleared his throat with a thick, guttural cough. 'You can use my account. It doesn't have as much clout as admin, but it'll read your files.'

Harry's eyes snapped open, and she could feel the blood surging back into her face. She wiggled a double thumbs-up sign at Jude and he smiled back at her.

'That's great, Felix,' he said, holding her gaze. 'Thanks.'

'Username is froche.' Felix spelled it out for him. 'And the password is rasputin45. Now fuck off and don't call me again. I'm going to switch off my phone. I'm about to get lucky.'

The line went dead. Harry finished scribbling down the account details and then grinned at Jude. His face was flushed and he looked pleased with himself.

'I'm impressed,' she said. 'You'd make a good hacker.' Then a small knot pinched at her insides. 'But what about those ethics you talked about? Or maybe that stuff about Aslan isn't true?'

'Oh, it's true all right.' He leaned back and laced

his hands behind his head. 'Nectel really have dumped BridgeCom and they really are going after Aslan. But they'll never make it. The fact is, Nectel are in the shit financially and haven't a hope of raising funds for any acquisition.'

'So Felix won't profit from the information?'

'Nope. But by the time he finds that out, it'll be too late.'

Harry stared at Jude for a moment. If he was comfy with the ethics of the situation, then so was she. But she knew the exchange had cost him.

'Thanks,' she said, turning back to her laptop before he could reply.

She reactivated her RAT connection into Frank Buckley's computer. Her fingers flitted over the keys, and soon she had logged out of Frank's network account and signed back in as Felix Roche. Within seconds, she had pulled up Felix's current emails on the screen.

She stepped through his messages, scanning the addresses for anything that looked relevant. If Felix was still intercepting emails, there was a chance he'd caught something that could help her.

She found it almost straight away. It was a mail from Leon, dated the previous day.

Ralphy-Boy,
  Know anything about this??
Leon

197

Appended to that was a second memo:

Leon,
The Sorohan money is on the move. The daughter Harry has it. I'll send you proof. I think that money belongs to us, don't you?
The Prophet

Harry shuddered, staring at her own name on the screen. She wanted to wrap her arms around herself to ward off the sense of violation.

'The Prophet's address is different,' Jude said.

Harry squinted at the screen. He was right. The Prophet's mail to Leon had been sent from an7623398@anon.obfusc.com, and not the alias.cyber.net address he'd used before.

She began to massage her forehead. 'He's changed re-mailers. He had to. The other one was shut down two years ago after some big legal wrangle with a couple of governments.'

She read Leon's email again. Who the hell was Ralphy-Boy? She checked the recipient. ww483554@realXremail.com. Another impenetrable alias. Was Ralphy-Boy the final trading-ring member?

A sharp pain pulsed through her head. She urgently needed to curl up in her bed and let oblivion take the wheel.

Jude touched her on the shoulder, and when

he spoke his voice was gentle. 'You look like you're about to collapse. You should get some rest.'

Harry didn't feel like objecting, and reached out to shut her laptop down. Then her hands went still. For the first time, she noticed the system information message displayed at the top of the memo.

> You sent a reply to this message on 10/04/2009. Click here for all related messages.

Felix had replied to the email? What the hell was he doing, emailing the ring?

Harry clicked on the yellow information bar, and found herself staring at an email sent by Felix Roche the previous afternoon. It was addressed to the Prophet's anonymous address, an7623398@anon.obfusc.com.

> Well well, Mr Prophet, so we finally communicate. Let me start by saying I know who you really are. I've got friends in anon.obfusc. They're not as tight on security as they should be. Unlucky, Mr Prophet.
>
> I miss the old days. Buy low, sell high. You guys were good. You should do it again. Before someone finds out who you are.
>
> I'll be in touch.
>
> Felix

A flash of heat swept over her. She grabbed the pen and scribbled down the re-mailer address. Then she snatched up Jude's phone and hit the redial button. Nothing. Shit. Felix had switched off his phone.

Adrenaline pumped through her, blasting away the aches and pains, at least for the time being. So Felix knew who the Prophet was.

Tomorrow he was going to give her a name.

CHAPTER 27

C ameron crept closer to the bedroom door. It stood partly open, and he leaned into the crack and listened. The breathing was heavy and regular, with the drugged, slow-motion rhythm of someone who'd been asleep for a while.

He'd waited until after midnight for the lights to go on in the ground-floor apartment. Then he'd waited another hour for the windows to flip back into darkness and for all signs of movement to die away. After that, he'd made his move.

Cameron eased away from the bedroom door and hitched the rucksack a little higher on his shoulder. He crept along the short hall, feeling his way through the dark, passing the doors to the kitchen and the bathroom, and moving on into the living room.

The darkness there was dense and suffocating. By his reckoning, the window was dead ahead, but there were no chinks of streetlight to give him any clues. Cameron closed his eyes and let the rest of his senses take over. He inched forward, hands outstretched. His fingers brushed against something smooth and cold: leather upholstery. He kept moving.

His hands struck against a tall, light-framed structure that wobbled and almost fell. He took a step to the right and edged forward again. A car swished past outside, the tyres slick on the wet road. Cameron's hands pushed into pleats of thick fabric, and he opened his eyes. He'd reached the window. He tugged at the curtain until a shard of light sliced through the darkness, stabbing his eyeballs. Then he turned to survey the room.

Fuel, oxygen, heat; the triangle of fire. The words hummed through his head like a mantra, hypnotic and seductive. He squinted into the gloom, searching for potential ignition sites. Selecting the correct starting point for the fire was crucial. Cameron knew that, just as heat travelled upwards, so did fire. But the flames had to be fed. They had to rise continuously into fresh fuel in order to survive.

He looked up at the high Victorian ceiling. The fire would spread across its underside faster than anywhere else in the room, but it had to get up there first. He fingered the curtains, checking their length. They ran floor-to-ceiling. Cameron smiled. They were the perfect conduit.

He reached over and touched the cold surface of the wall, and frowned. Hard exterior walls never offered much in the way of fuel. Once the paint and paper burned off, the fire tended to die away, unless it had something else to latch on to. He scanned the adjacent wall, and nodded slowly. It was panelled in wide wooden planks, and formed a path of perfect kindling that led straight to the apartment's front door. That was the escape route taken care of.

By now, the dark shadows inside the room had resolved themselves into recognizable shapes, and Cameron saw that the tall frame he'd bumped into was a collapsible clothes-horse draped with a couple of towels. The leather upholstery turned out to be a sofa and two chairs with sleek, modern lines. This was good news. The horsehair stuffed inside older furniture was difficult to ignite, but the foam padding inside these would burn better than brushwood.

Cameron ran his tongue over his lips.

Fuel, oxygen, heat.

He stepped over to the clothes-horse and lifted it back towards the window. Then he grasped the nearest armchair and yanked at it. Its castors shrieked against the carpet, and Cameron froze. He held his breath, listening for sounds from the bedroom. Down the hall the fridge hummed, and a radiator ticked from somewhere behind him. He counted to thirty. Nothing. He exhaled slowly and wiped his hands on the seat of his jeans. Then he tugged and nudged at the chair until it touched the clotheshorse.

Cameron swung the rucksack off his shoulder and knelt on the floor. He extracted the wicker wastepaper basket, yesterday's newspaper, cigarettes, matchbook and paraffin. He lodged the empty wastepaper basket in between the curtain and the clotheshorse. Then he tore up strips of newspaper and scrunched them into the basket. He adjusted one of the towels so that it dangled inches above the paper, and trailed a second towel across the armchair, tucking it loosely under the cushion. Then he lifted the end of the curtain and draped it over the clotheshorse, weaving it through the rods.

Cameron knelt back on his haunches to admire his handiwork. The curtain, clotheshorse and armchair were dovetailed together in a deadly flammable chain, with the basket at its core, waiting to be ignited. A blaze of excitement seared through him.

He unscrewed the top of the paraffin container and poured a small amount of liquid into the cap. The pungent metallic scent filled his nostrils as he sprinkled a few drops over the paper and the trailing curtain and towels. Turning away from the basket, he lit a cigarette and wedged it inside the matchbook. Then he set the device on the bottom of the wastepaper basket, coaxing aside the balled-up paper so that none of it touched the burning tobacco.

He stood up and checked his watch: 1.41 a.m. He had nine minutes to get out of here.

He slipped a hand into his pocket to retrieve the batteries he'd removed from the apartment smoke alarms, and dropped them into the rucksack. Then he packed up the rest of his things, and slung the rucksack over his shoulder. He crossed to the window and heaved the sash up about six inches, just enough to let in some air.

Fuel, oxygen, heat.

He stole across the living room and back out to the hall. Through the shadows, he could make out the door to the small study where he'd forced his entry into the apartment. He'd have to pass by the bedroom to get back to it. Slowly he edged along the wall, planting his feet flat on the ground to keep his weight evenly distributed.

A phone shrilled into the darkness, and he jumped. The ringing jangled on and on, loud enough to wake the entire building. The phone must have been nearby, probably on the hall table. Forcing his limbs to move, he shrank back against the wall. Who the fuck made calls at this hour?

His heart slammed into his chest. He waited for the inevitable sounds from the bedroom, for a blaze of light to illuminate the hall. He counted eight rings. Nine, ten. His body heat seeped upwards from inside his jacket, pungent and sour like the stench of boiled onions. On the twelfth ring, the phone stopped.

Cameron was paralysed. He counted to sixty and then squinted at his watch. Three minutes left. He inched his way down the hall, limbs stiff, knowing he had to get out of there. On reaching the bedroom door, he hesitated, straining to hear the breathing. The pattern was undisturbed. In, out, drag, blow, like someone working a small pair of bellows.

Cameron slipped into the study. He climbed through the empty window frame and landed with a crunch on the gravel below. The pane of glass was lying against the wall where he'd left it, along with the suction cups and putty knife. He lodged the glass back into the frame, and stowed the suction cups and the knife into his rucksack. The window wasn't secure, but that didn't matter. Any evidence of forced entry would soon be burned to the ground.

He jogged back across the street and ducked into his car, tossing the rucksack on to the passenger seat beside him. He crouched down low behind the steering wheel, and closed his eyes. Adrenaline pulsed through him and his breathing came in hard, burning rasps. He pictured the scene he had left behind. By now, the match heads would have sputtered into flame, igniting the paper. The wastepaper basket would have dissolved like candyfloss in the rain. He imagined the angry flames stretching tall, licking at the end of the curtain, tasting it, then spurting along its length to devour the rest of the room.

Cameron opened his eyes and stared at the apartment. An orange glow flickered through the gap in the curtains. He rolled down his window. The rain had stopped, and the tangerine gleam of the fire was already reflected across the wet pavement. He watched the flames as they intensified into a quivering frenzy, gyrating against the glass and lapping at the curtains. Cameron's breath became shallow and rapid, and an odious exhilaration rippled through him. For now, he would savour it. The self-loathing would come later.

He gazed at the fire for as long as he dared. The windows shattered, belching black smoke into the night sky. The blaze hissed and crackled and spat fountains of sparks. He could feel the heat on his face, and smell the sweet smoky scent of charred timber. Then he heard a gathering roar, like a fleet of overhead jets, as part of the ceiling collapsed. Flames burst through the windows, leaping thirty or forty feet into the air, their tapered heads looming high above him.

He tried to imagine the searing heat inside the apartment; the choking, the suffocation, the noxious fumes. And the paralysing fear of being burnt alive. Cameron closed his eyes and smiled.

Nobody was going to survive that inferno.

CHAPTER 28

'Felix Roche is dead.'

Harry shot upright on the bed and swung her bare legs on to the floor. 'What?'

'His apartment was burned to the ground last night, with him in it.' Jude's voice was low on the other end of the phone, as if he didn't want to be overheard. 'The police have been round. I've kept your name out of it so far, but it's not easy. Damn detective is like a cat, just watches and waits for you to talk.'

Lynne. Nausea stirred in the pit of her stomach and she swallowed hard. 'Was it an accident?'

'So far, no one's calling it anything else. But they asked a lot of questions.'

Shit, shit, shit. Harry squeezed her eyes shut and wrapped her arm around her waist. How could Roche be dead? They'd only talked to him a few hours ago.

'Harry? You still there?'

'Mm-hmm.'

She hunched her shoulders and began rocking back and forth as if she had cramps. Yesterday

Felix Roche had told the Prophet that he knew who he was. Today he was dead.

She tried to picture Roche: overweight, wheezing, obnoxious. She hadn't liked him much, but she didn't want him dead. And she'd desperately needed to talk to him.

Then she remembered something, and stopped rocking. 'I called him last night.'

There was a pause on the other end of the phone. 'You what?'

'It was late, nearly two in the morning. I couldn't sleep.' She remembered sitting on the edge of the bed in the dark, letting the phone ring out, willing Felix to pick up.

'What happened?' Jude said.

'Nothing. He didn't answer.' Her legs trembled and her T-shirt felt cold and damp. The slithering sickness in her stomach was gathering momentum. 'Do you think he was already dead?'

'God knows. At least you didn't talk to him.'

'I wish I had. He knew who the Prophet was.'

'Seems to me, the more you know about this Prophet character, the more danger you're in.' Jude's voice was harsh. 'If I were you, I'd just stay away from him.'

Harry frowned at his tone. Was he concerned for her safety, or was that a threat? She shook her head and breathed deeply through her nose. Jude had helped her last night, for God's sake. He'd taken a big risk, giving Felix insider information like that. It had put him in the other man's power. She stared at her toes.

Unless, of course, he'd known that in a few hours Felix would be dead.

'Are you going to talk to the police?' Jude asked. His voice was wooden, unreadable.

'Not about my father. I can't.' Speaking was suddenly difficult. Her mouth was so dry her words seemed to come out in a series of clicks.

'Isn't it too late to worry about him? Anyway, what do you care? I thought you hated him.'

'I don't hate him.' Was that really true? 'He's still my father.'

'Even if he's involved in murder?'

Harry swayed, and for a moment she thought she might faint. She dropped the phone and made it to the bathroom just in time. She retched into the sink until her throat was raw. Her whole body shivered as she braced herself against the cold enamel sink. She splashed water on her face and then staggered back to her bed, pulling the duvet over her. Belatedly, she checked her phone, but Jude had already disconnected.

Now what? She had no more leads to investigate. The only person who knew the identity of the Prophet was dead. And she had the distinct feeling that she was next.

She curled herself into a foetal ball, and puffed on her hands to get warm. Her limbs were heavy from lack of sleep. After her phone call to Felix the night before, she'd sat down at her laptop and probed the defences of anon.obfusc, the anonymous re-mailer used by the Prophet. Hour after hour, she'd prodded and poked, scanned and experimented, but its perimeter security was airtight. Social-engineering exploits were out of the question. The re-mailer crowd were seasoned experts on software security, and would be wise to any bogus approaches. By six thirty in the morning, she'd come to the conclusion that Felix must have had a personal contact in the company, someone who'd leaked the information to him. The notion depressed her. The re-mailer operated out of several different countries; identifying and cracking Felix's mole would be next to impossible.

Harry huddled further under the duvet. Daylight glinted through the curtains. She closed her eyes against it. Why couldn't the trading ring just take their damn money and leave her alone? She'd hand it over in a heartbeat if she could only get her life back.

Her eyes flared open and an idea took shape. Give the money back. Why not? Once the Prophet had his money, he'd leave her alone, wouldn't he? After all, she didn't know who he was, she was no threat to him.

She jerked upright in the bed. Her stomach felt lighter, and the clamminess had evaporated. She swept the duvet on to the floor and flew down the short hall into her office. Her laptop was still set up from the night before, and she sat down in front of it, flexing her fingers.

The tone of the email was crucial. It had to sound as if she was in control, as if she knew what she was doing. Her chest pumped as she drafted the email. It took several attempts, and in the end she wasn't wholly satisfied with it, but it would have to do. She read it through one last time.

> I have your 12 million. Tell me where to send it and you can have it back. One condition: call off your thugs and stay out of my way. I'm no threat to you – going to the police is hardly in my father's best interests. And handing them my dead body is hardly in yours.
> Harry Martinez

She would have liked it to sound punchier, but in truth, her position wasn't that strong. Once she handed over the money, all her leverage would disappear.

She typed in the Prophet's re-mailer address, and hesitated, just for an instant. Then she hit the Send button.

She leaned back in her chair and exhaled a long breath. For the first time in days, she felt as though she was in control.

Her phone rang, and she snatched it up. 'Hello?'

'Hey.' It was Dillon. She hugged her arm around her waist.

'Hey, yourself.'

'Are you okay?'

'Yeah, I'm fine.' Even to her own ears, the words lacked conviction. Hell. Where were her scamming skills when she needed them?

'You don't sound fine.'

'Stop worrying.' She scanned her email. 'But maybe I should take a day or two out of the office, if that's okay.'

'No need to ask, Harry, you know that.' His voice was gentle. 'Forget about the office. Imogen sent off the Sheridan report. They're happy, no follow-up, so take all the time you need.'

Harry frowned. No follow-up. Something sluggish stirred in her brain but wouldn't surface. Something left undone. The thought got bogged down like a fly in treacle. She shook her head and let it pass.

'Thanks,' she said.

Dillon paused. 'Could you face coming back out to my place for dinner tonight? I'll cook.'

Harry hesitated, and closed her eyes. Suddenly she was back in the darkness, whirling inside the maze. Her mouth went dry.

'Sorry, that was stupid,' Dillon said into the silence. 'That's the last place you want to be. It's just . . . I don't want you to be scared of my house forever, you know? In case you'd like to come back sometime.'

Harry's heartbeat did a bunny-hop routine which she tried to ignore. 'I'm not scared, I'd like to come back. Anyway, I didn't know you could cook.'

'I can heat things up. My housekeeper can cook.' There was a slow smile in his voice, and she pictured it flitting around his lips. 'I'll pick you up at seven, then?'

Harry remembered the rally drive she'd taken in his car two days earlier and winced. 'It's probably better if I drive myself. I've some stuff to do first. I could be there for half eight?'

'Half eight's fine. I'd better give you directions. You fell asleep on me last time, remember?'

Harry listened to his brief instructions, sketching out a rough map on the back of an envelope. When she'd hung up, she sat on the edge of the bed and found herself wondering what to wear. It took effort not to fast-forward through the evening ahead and anticipate where dinner might lead. Right now, she could probably do without the complications of an affair with her boss.

The last time she'd worried what to wear for Dillon had been the previous summer. He'd called her up out of nowhere to offer her a job, fifteen years after he'd sat in her bedroom and taught her the ethics of hacking. They'd met in the foyer of the Shelbourne Hotel, where they'd had coffee and sandwiches and sized each other up.

Harry could still remember the fizzing sensation she'd felt in her chest, as though someone was pouring champagne over her insides. The passionate, good-looking boy had grown into an attractive, self-assured man, who looked more than a little pleased with himself. The intensity was kept under wraps, but it still glinted occasionally in his eyes. In the face of his poise, Harry had been reduced to a thirteen-year-old once more, afraid to eat the sandwiches in case something green stuck to her teeth.

Her laptop beeped, and she checked her email again. Her spine hummed. One new message.

> You're a sensible girl, Harry. Your daddy wouldn't thank you for bringing the police in. There are a whole lot of questions about the Sorohan deal he doesn't want answered.
>
> We'll do it your way. I get my money back, you get your life back.
>
> But don't let me down, Harry. Your father double-crossed me. I'd hate to think you might do the same. Be smart. Otherwise you and everyone you care about will be in danger.
>
> I'll send you instructions about the money.
>
> The Prophet

Harry's palms were damp and her breathing had grown shallow. Had her plan really worked? With slow, heavy movements, she logged into her online bank account and checked her balance.

She studied the numbers and blinked. Then she refreshed the web page and studied them again. No change. Her insides went into freefall, and she almost stopped breathing.

Now you see me, now you don't.

The money was gone.

CHAPTER 29

'What do you mean, the money doesn't exist?' Harry said.

She paced up and down her living room, the phone jammed against her ear.

'It has to exist,' she went on. 'I saw it with my own eyes.'

'I'm afraid what you saw was an error in our banking software.' Sandra Nagle's tone was excessively polite. 'I just confirmed it with Technical Support. It seems that, for a couple of days, all our online systems showed an incorrect balance on your account.'

'An incorrect balance?' Harry's insides started to sink. 'But someone lodged twelve million euros into my account on Friday. You saw the transaction record yourself.'

'Yes, but I'm afraid it was invalid.'

'What does that mean?' But Harry already knew the answer.

'It means the transaction never happened.' Sandra's words were becoming thin and clipped, as though she was holding on to a mouthful of pins. 'Our records confirm it without doubt. No actual funds transfer for that amount was ever made to your account.'

Harry stopped pacing. Her muscles felt rigid. 'So you're telling me the twelve million was just a software glitch? It wasn't real money?'

'Exactly.' Sandra seemed pleased that Harry was getting it so quickly. 'And on behalf of Sheridan Bank, please let me apologize for the error. Your account has been adjusted, and I can assure you this won't happen again.'

Harry sank down on to the arm of the sofa. The money didn't exist. She felt as though a spider was crawling up her spine. She'd just made a deal to hand over twelve million euros to the Prophet. What was he going to do when she couldn't deliver?

Her heart pounded. This was crazy. Someone looking for the Sorohan money had pushed her under a train, and the same day her bank account happened to show a glitch of twelve million euros? Bullshit. That money did exist. But where the hell was it?

Harry thrust her chin into the air. 'Sorry, but that explanation's just not good enough. Can I talk with someone in Technical Support?'

There was a pause at the other end of the phone. 'I'm afraid our support engineers are not permitted to discuss the details of our banking systems with external parties. For security reasons. I'm sure you understand.'

Harry closed her eyes and scrambled around in her head for a way past this constipated woman.

Then she decided to let it go. She was tired of talking to her. And besides, she'd just thought of a better way to find out what had happened to her account.

She was about to disconnect when she remembered something else. Harry knew it was petty, but she hated to leave the conversation with Sandra Nagle scoring points.

'One last thing,' she said. 'I asked for a bank statement to be sent out to me a couple of days ago. I never got it.'

The other woman sniffed, and Harry could hear her working the keyboard at the other end.

'Yes, I processed your request myself,' Sandra said. 'In fact, according to our system, you'd already requested a statement earlier that day and it went out in the afternoon. You should have got it yesterday.'

'Well, I didn't. And I certainly didn't request it twice, either.'

'Let me check the address we have for you.'

Harry heaved herself up on to her feet and plodded over to the window, the phone still pressed to her ear. The sky had darkened, and fat drops of rain plopped against the glass. She rested her forehead against the cold window pane. Why the hell had she ever contacted the Prophet?

'Flat 4, 13 St Mary's Road, South Circular Road, Dublin 8.'

Harry jerked her head up and frowned. 'What? That's not my address.'

'Well, that's what we have on our system for you. It's where your statement went on Friday.'

Harry grabbed a pen and notepad from the bookshelf beside her and scribbled down the address. 'Can you check if someone changed that address recently?'

Another pause. 'No, there's no record of anyone updating your personal details, not since you were first registered on the system five years ago.'

Harry ripped the page out of the notepad. 'That doesn't make any sense. I live in Ballsbridge. My statements have been coming here for the last five years. It must have been changed.'

The other woman offered to check it out, but by now Harry had little faith in her. She thanked her and disconnected, then stared at the address in her hand: 13 St Mary's Road. It could be just a software error, but at this stage she was inclined to believe it meant something.

She strode into the kitchen and rummaged through the cutlery drawers, tossing out matches, candles and a box of old Christmas cards. Finally she found a street map of Dublin. She skimmed through the index. St Joseph's, St Lawrence's, St Martin's. There it was – St Mary's. She studied the map until she got a fix on the area. Then she grabbed her black leather jacket and headed out the front door.

The sharp afternoon air sliced through her, and the rain made polka dots on her yellow T-shirt. She shrugged into her jacket and trotted out the gate, speed-dialling the number for Ian Doyle, the System Administrator from Sheridan Bank she'd spoken to after completing the pen test on Friday.

'Hi, Ian? It's Harry Martinez again, from Lúbra Security.'

'Hey, Harry, I was just thinking about you.'

'You were?' Her car was parked by the kerb, a jaunty blue Mini Cooper with a white roof and trim. She tossed her bag on to the passenger seat and slid in behind the wheel.

'Yeah, I read your report yesterday,' Ian was saying. 'I hate to say it, but it's a nice piece of work.'

'Thanks. Hope it didn't ruin your day.'

'Well, they didn't exactly give me any medals.'

'I did try to warn you.'

'Yeah, cheers, I appreciate that,' Ian said. 'Gave me time to cover my tracks a bit. Hey, let me buy you a drink to say thanks. How about tonight?'

'Sorry, Ian, I'm up to my eyes. But I could do with your help on something else.'

'Fire away. I'm on weekend support here with feck all else to do. You'll brighten up my Sunday.'

She filled him in on the disappearing money from her bank account and the mysterious change of address.

'I'm getting nowhere with the dragon lady on the helpdesk,' she said finally. 'Any chance you could nose around and find out exactly what happened?'

'Yeah, 'course I can. Give me an hour or so. I'll call you back.'

Harry dropped the phone on to the seat beside her, and almost immediately it rang. She checked the caller ID: Jude Tiernan. She stared at his name, her heart thudding. Maybe he was just calling to check she was okay. Or maybe just to check how much she knew. The phone buzzed against her fingers. She took a deep breath and stuffed it back inside her bag.

She pored over the map one more time. Then she switched on the ignition, leaving the map spread open on the passenger seat for reference. The route was almost a straight line, but when it came to following directions, she needed all the props she could get. In her experience, navigational decisions were a bit like long division: impossible to do in your head without wanting to black out.

She checked her rear-view mirror. She was boxed in between two Volvo saloons. Any other car would have been in trouble, but the Mini could turn on a thumbtack. She yanked the steering wheel hard to the left and scooted out into the traffic.

Dillon often asked her why she didn't buy herself a real car, but she was never tempted. To him, owning a luxury car was a way of keeping score, but for Harry, other people's perceptions didn't come into it. The Mini was perfect for zipping about the city, as long as you didn't need to carry passengers or move any furniture. And besides, it made her smile just to look at it. She surveyed the round, old-fashioned gauges and aircraft-style toggle switches, and for a moment was reminded of her recent helicopter ride. She patted the dashboard. Real cars were for grown-ups. This baby would do her just fine.

She shoehorned the Mini on to Leeson Street, concentrating on her route. Twenty minutes later, she'd made it to the South Circular Road without mishap. She slowed down, peering at the street signs until she found St Mary's Road. It was a narrow residential cul-de-sac with a sagging, run-down air. Many of the houses were boarded up, and the local graffiti artists had daubed their bubble-writing across the plywood.

Number 13 was part of a two-storey red-brick terrace, with a basement visible through the flaky railings that fronted on to the pavement. The blue door could have done with a lick of paint, and the array of bells beside it indicated the house had been converted into flats.

Harry scanned the area for a parking space with a good view of the house. Parking was at a premium this close to the city, and all the spots were occupied. One, however, was only partially filled. A black motorbike was propped up near the kerb, its rider busy stowing his helmet in the back carrier box. Harry waited for him to finish and move off down the street. Then with a tidy reverse manoeuvre, she tucked the car in next to the motorbike. Another virtue of the cute car. She could park it in a broom cupboard if she had to.

Her phone chirped at her from the bottom of her bag, and she scooped it out. It was Ian.

'I've done some digging, Harry, and I hate to tell you this, but it looks like the dragon lady was right.'

'What?'

'There never was any twelve million euros.'

'You're kidding.'

''Fraid not. I spoke to the guys in tech support, even checked the audit trails myself. Seems our central database got screwed up on Friday, and your account was corrupted.'

'Corrupted? How did that happen?'

'Well, they won't commit themselves on that one. But they know for a fact there was never any money. See, they launch this reconciliation job every night that runs checks and balances on all the day's money movements, and on Friday night it triggered alarm bells all over your account. Seems there were no corresponding funds to match the numbers the database had for you.'

'Was it just my account, or were others screwed up as well?'

Ian paused. 'Actually, yours was the only one.'

'Hardly a random corruption then, is it?' Harry chewed the inside of her right cheek. 'Come on, Ian, you're a smart guy. You saw the audit trails. What do you think happened?'

There was another pause. 'If you ask me, a new record was illegally inserted into your account.'

'Illegally inserted? In other words, someone tampered with the database?'

'Looks that way. Hard to see how it could have happened by accident.'

'Can you tell when it happened?'

'From the files I saw, I'd say it was about 1.30 p.m. on Friday,' Ian said. 'What's more, the record was illegally deleted from the system today.'

'What? I assumed you guys got rid of it when you cleaned up my account.'

'Nope, someone got to it before us. They inserted it Friday, deleted it today. Flagged your account for a statement request, too.'

Harry stared at the blue door across the street. 'What about the address? How was that changed?'

'Same way, same time.' Then Ian laughed. 'Hey Harry, you sure you didn't mess with things yourself? After all, you were roaming pretty freely round our systems on Friday. I'd add a few zeros to my own bank balance if I thought I could get away with it.'

'Nice idea, but I'm afraid it wasn't me.'

Ian sighed. 'Well, if it wasn't an accident and it wasn't you, then you know what we've got here, don't you?'

Harry fixed her gaze on Number 13 and nodded slowly, letting Ian continue.

'We've got ourselves a hacker.'

CHAPTER 30

Harry punched the steering wheel with her fist. *Now you see me now you don't.* Her subconscious had figured it out long before she had.

The first time she'd called the helpdesk, they'd told her the lodgement record was incomplete; no date or time against it, nothing to say where the money had come from. Manipulating databases was nothing new to Harry. Some part of her brain had recognized the symptoms and known it wasn't real.

Had Felix been the hacker? Or Jude? He claimed to be computer-illiterate, but he could easily be lying. Ian had promised to dig through the files for clues to the hacker's identity, but Harry had the feeling there wouldn't be any trail.

She fixed her gaze on the blue door across the street. Who the hell lived there? She drummed her fingers against the wheel and reviewed her options. She could skulk around the rear of the terrace, looking for a way inside. She chewed her lip, not liking the idea much. Or she could wait until someone else let themselves into the house, and coast in behind them. She checked up and down the street, but it was deserted. Her gaze slid up to the rear-view mirror and she stared at the motorbike behind her.

Supposing she just walked up to the front door and rang the bell?

Before she could change her mind, she whipped round in her seat and stretched into the back of her car. She burrowed under a sliding pile of technical magazines until she found a gold A4-sized envelope, padded on the inside with bubble wrap. It had once contained software CDs she'd ordered from Amazon, but now she stuffed it with four back-issues of *Security Technology & Design* and tucked in the flap. She examined the result: the package looked bulky enough to be important. Satisfied, she rummaged in the glove compartment for her screwdriver, then grabbed her bag, switched her phone to silent mode, just in case, and climbed out of the car.

The clouds were lead grey and swollen with rain, and made the evening darker than usual. She could hear the grumble of buses hauling themselves along the South Circular Road as they got a run at the traffic, but St Mary's Road was desolate by comparison. All it needed was tumbleweed.

Harry buttoned up her leather jacket and sidled over to the motorbike, her gaze darting in all directions. She wedged the screwdriver under the lid of the carrier box, prising it upwards. The plastic was light, and a few sharp twists were all it took to wrench the box open. With a silent apology to the biker, she lifted out the helmet. Underneath was a pair of stiff biker gauntlets that smelled of oil and leather, and when she pulled them on they reached almost to her elbows. She tucked the helmet under her arm, then strolled across the road and climbed the steps to Number 13.

The bells were numbered one to four, with no name tags. She inspected the front of the house. City grime and age had muddied the red Victorian bricks to a rinsed-out shade of pink, and the gutters were beginning to crumble. She took a deep breath, and wedged the helmet on her head. It smelled stale and musty, like an old dishcloth, and she could feel her scalp creep. She pushed the bell for Flat 1, which she guessed was probably in the basement. Someone was going to be pissed off with her for dragging them all the way upstairs.

For a moment she stood there, listening to the sound of her own breathing amplified inside the helmet. Then the door opened, and an elderly man peered out at her. He had a short-sighted look about the eyes, like Mr Magoo without the glasses.

'Yes?' he said.

Harry caught a waft of concentrated beer fumes, and was tempted to flip down her visor. Instead, she held up the envelope.

'Courier delivery for Flat 4.' Her voice sounded loud in her own ears.

The old man squinted at her, his nose whistling as he breathed through it. Harry was about to repeat herself when suddenly he turned and ambled away from the door. She hesitated, and then followed him inside.

The hall was narrow and poorly lit, the weak lamplight staining everything a dirty, nicotine yellow. She shut the door behind her, and became aware of a muffled, ticking sound that seemed familiar but which she couldn't identify right away.

The old man was shuffling away down the hall. She stepped towards him, but he flapped a dismissive hand at her.

'Upstairs,' he said, without looking back. He disappeared through a door at the far end of the hall.

Harry shrugged, and stood at the bottom of the staircase, craning her neck to peer upwards into the dark. She could make out two flights of stairs leading up to the first floor. She had her foot on the first step when the lights went out.

She froze. The darkness was thick and absolute, and so was the silence. Even the ticking had stopped. She pressed her back into the wall. Her rapid breathing was making her face sweat under the helmet, and she dragged it off. Then she listened. Nothing.

She groped along the wall behind her and felt a round plastic fixture, like an old bell push. She pressed it hard, and the weak yellow light came back on. The steady ticking resumed behind her, and she looked at the light switch. It was the size of a tin of shoe polish, and its centrepiece was slowly pumping outwards, making soft clicking sounds as it moved. Harry leaned her head back against the wall and let out a long breath. The lights were on a timer.

She made a face at herself for being so jumpy, then started up the stairs, punching the light switch again to buy herself more time. She found herself counting as she climbed, wondering how long she had before the next blackout. What a cheap landlord.

She reached the return landing and passed an open doorway on her left. From the musty smell of urine, she assumed it had to be a toilet. Still counting, she crept up the next flight of stairs, and found herself standing in front of the door to Flat 4.

Now what? She'd conned her way into the house, but this was where her improvisations ran out. She pulled off the biker gloves and stuffed them inside the helmet. She tiptoed closer to the door and pressed her ear against it. The sound of muffled voices reached her. Men's voices. How many, she couldn't be sure. She checked left and right. There were no other doors on this landing, nowhere else to go except down.

Suddenly she was pitched into blackness again. Jesus. Thirty seconds of light was all you got around here. No wonder the old guy downstairs had abandoned her in such a hurry. He hadn't wanted to get stranded in the dark.

The voices behind the door were growing louder. Harry took a step backwards. The doorknob rattled, and she jumped. She scrambled down the stairs and darted into the foul-smelling toilet, flattening herself against the wall just as the door to Flat 4 opened.

'I'm paying you for results, and so far you haven't delivered.'

'Hire someone else, if you think it'll make a difference. I'm telling you, there's nothing to fuckin' find.'

Harry clapped a hand over her mouth. She inched closer to the door and peeped through the crack. The landing was illuminated by an oblong of light spilling out from the flat. A man in a dark jacket stood at the top of the stairs, his back half-turned to her, his head glistening in the light. It was as smooth and hairless as an egg.

'Get me something on her, Quinney, I need leverage,' the other man said. Harry tried to make him out, but the bald man was blocking her view.

'It'll take time.'

'Everything takes time with you.'

'You want it done right, don't you?'

'I want it done quick.'

The man called Quinney shrugged, and then headed down the stairs in Harry's direction. She snapped her head back and pressed herself further in against the wall. Her throat constricted as she tried not to inhale the stench of the toilet.

'Bring me some dirt on her, and I'll make it worth your while.'

Quinney's footsteps halted right outside the toilet door. Harry could hear him breathe. She still had her fingers pressed to her mouth to stop herself from humming with fear. She had no doubt they were talking about her.

She risked another peep, but all she could see was the back of Quinney's head. The flesh between his collar and the base of his skull was packed into thick pink rolls, like a row of uncooked sausages.

'There's a boyfriend,' he said, eventually. Harry raised her eyebrows. This was news to her.

'Can we use him?'

Quinney shrugged. 'Maybe.'

As Harry eased her head back into the shadows, she spotted a rectangular shape on the carpet, next to Quinney's feet. She stared at it, her mouth open. It was a padded envelope. She did a quick inventory of the items she had on her: shoulder bag, helmet, gloves. No envelope. Shit!

She sank down on her hunkers and patted the cold tiles around her, recoiling as her fingers touched soggy clumps of hair and tissue. She should have kept the gloves on. She closed her eyes and felt her head spin a little. She must have dropped the envelope when she ran down the stairs.

'Who is this boyfriend?'

'Some fuckin' bigshot. I can run a check on him.'

Harry's gaze travelled across to the package on the floor. It was only a few feet away from her, but impossible to reach without getting caught. Maybe it didn't matter. After all, it was only an envelope.

Then her eyes widened, and for an instant, her

heart stopped beating. In plain view on the front of the package was a label with her name and address on it.

'Okay, do it,' Quinney's companion said. 'Dig up everything you can. Look at her boyfriend, her family, her friends – anyone you saw her with. Get me something I can use.'

'First, I need to be paid. No money, no digging.'

'I'll pay you when you finish the job, and not before.'

There was a pause. 'Maybe my fees just went up.'

She heard the other man tramping down the stairs towards Quinney. The oblong of light began to shrink as the door to the flat drifted to a close behind him. Harry leaned forward. In another second, it would be dark enough to make a lunge for the envelope. But the man was too quick for her. He must have punched the switch on the wall because the landing was suddenly flooded with light.

She held her breath and instinctively began to count, listening to the two men argue. She felt oddly detached from the situation. How absurd to be crouched in a rancid toilet, eavesdropping on two strangers as they bickered over how much it was worth to mess with her life.

Nine, ten, eleven. She shot a glance through the door again. Quinney was looking down at the man standing in front of him, but his advantage in height didn't seem to be winning him any arguments. She still couldn't get a clear view of the other guy.

Sixteen, seventeen, eighteen. She flexed her

fingers and kept on counting. The men seemed to be reaching some kind of agreement and had started to wrap things up.

Twenty-one, twenty-two, twenty-three. Harry swallowed, then with one hand splayed on the wet tiles to support herself, she inched the other hand forward through the crack in the door, keeping it low to the ground.

Twenty-eight, twenty-nine, thirty.

The landing blacked out and both men cursed. In the same instant, Harry shot out her arm and grabbed the envelope. She clutched it to her chest and huddled back in against the wall. The men were momentarily immobilized by the darkness, but two seconds later they'd found the light switch. Harry's heart hammered in her ears, and it took effort not to pant out loud.

The men moved past her towards the next flight of stairs, where they took their leave of each other. Quinney carried on down to the front door, while the other man turned and trudged back up to the flat. As he passed the toilet door, Harry caught a glimpse of his face.

She knew him, of course. She'd seen his photograph in the newspaper archives. He'd gained a couple of stone and had swapped the suit for a grubby T-shirt, but it was him all right.

It was Leon Ritch.

CHAPTER 31

Harry drove along the South Circular Road, questions buzzing around in her head.

What the hell was Leon Ritch doing with a copy of her bank statement? Was Quinney the guy who'd trashed her apartment? Maybe he was the one who'd pushed her under the train. She hadn't recognized his voice, but it was hard to tell.

One thing was clear: Leon had seen her rigged bank balance, and was convinced she had the money. Now he was looking for a way to get to it.

Harry shuddered. The earlier tension was seeping away, leaving her cold and shivery. She thought about Quinney's plan to dig up dirt on her boyfriend, and wondered whom he'd fingered for the role. She'd spent time with both Jude and Dillon over the past few days, so to an outsider, it could look as though she was involved with either one of them. Then she rolled her eyes at herself. Except, of course, that Dillon had stayed the night. That probably made him favourite.

As she dodged through the traffic, it occurred

to her that she should have followed Quinney, but in truth, she'd been too terrified to move. In any case, he was more expert at surveillance than she was. He'd clearly been following her for days.

Maybe he still was.

Her eyes darted to her rear-view mirror. A black Fiesta was close on her tail, and behind that, a silver Jag. Harry frowned. Didn't Ashford drive a Jag? Her fingers tensed on the steering wheel. The city was full of prestige cars, it didn't necessarily mean anything. She experimented with changing lanes, but neither car followed suit. As she swung right on to Harcourt Street, the Fiesta peeled away and the Jag disappeared behind a van.

Harry tried to concentrate on the road ahead, but the questions and what-ifs zigzagged through her until her eyes began to cross. What she needed was someone to talk to, someone to confide in. Someone who wouldn't just tell her to go and visit her father.

She thought about Amaranta, but knew all she'd get was a list of bossy instructions. Her mother was out of the question. Miriam didn't invite confidences. Not from her, anyway.

Harry tapped her fingers against the wheel, cruising into the stream of traffic that would take her south, back to her apartment. Then she made up her mind. She barged her way across two lanes of traffic and headed north back into town. It was Sunday and she made good ground. In less than ten minutes, she'd pulled up across from the red

Georgian door that fronted Lúbra Security's office.

She crossed the street, remembering to switch her mobile phone back on. It beeped, announcing she'd missed three more calls from Jude. What the hell did he want? She shoved the phone back in her bag. The last thing she needed was a chat with a banker whose profile fit the Prophet.

She fished out her office keys and unlocked the door, making her way past the empty reception and on through the glass doors that led to the main office. Her glance travelled the length of the room.

Dillon's company occupied the entire ground floor of the restored Georgian house. The hum of computers filled the air, even though the desks were empty. The padded partitions surrounding each workstation suddenly reminded Harry of the Sheridan Bank call centre.

She frowned. There it was again, that formless nag at the base of her skull that said something had been left undone. She made a mental note to check out the Sheridan report for herself.

Harry headed towards Dillon's office, a glass enclosure in the far corner of the room. It was empty. Beside it was a large desk, the only one in the room that was occupied.

'I thought I'd find you here,' Harry said.

Imogen looked up, eyes growing round in her dainty face. Two pigtails flared out like butterfly wings from the side of her head, reinforcing the Chihuahua image.

'Harry! I didn't hear you come in.' She started to smile, but then peered at Harry's face. 'What happened to you?'

She hopped off her chair and bustled over, pushing Harry firmly into the nearest seat. Then she stood in front of her, hands on hips, inspecting the grazes on her face. Harry always felt like a lumberjack beside Imogen's petite frame, even when she was sitting down.

'Look at you, you're a mess,' Imogen said.

Harry smiled at the mother-hen tone. 'It's not as bad as it looks.'

'Don't give me that. Did you have an accident?'

'Sort of.'

Harry felt tears stinging her eyes, and immediately blinked them away. She wasn't used to being mothered.

'Come on, Harry, out with it.'

The promise of a listening ear was hard to resist. So, in a tumble of words, Harry told her everything that had happened, from the disastrous meeting in KWC, to Felix's death and the deal she'd made with the Prophet. Imogen listened without interruption; no questions, no melodramatics.

When Harry had finished, they sat in silence for a while.

'Someone actually pushed you in front of a train?' Imogen said eventually.

'It was a slow train. Just bruises.'

'God, Harry, I don't know what to say, but I'm

glad you came to find me.' She paused. 'How did you know I'd be here?'

Harry managed a weak smile. 'You're in between boyfriends. You always work Sundays when you're single.'

Imogen made a rueful face, then looked solemn again. 'You should've come to me sooner, I could've helped. I could've cracked KWC for you in minutes.'

Harry smiled again. Mother hen was losing out to baser hacker instincts. She tucked her feet beneath her in the chair and hugged her chest. She felt warm and sleepy, like a child with a hot drink before bedtime. Imogen's advice wasn't always sound, but it was comforting just to be on the receiving end of it.

Then she remembered the vague stirring at the base of her skull.

'Actually, there is something you can do to help,' she said. 'Could you mail me that report you did for Sheridan?'

'Is there a problem with it? Dillon sent me your pen-test details; it seemed pretty straightforward.'

'It was. I'm sure it's fine, there's just something I need to check.'

'Okay.' Imogen folded her arms and began tapping her foot. 'In the meantime, what are you going to do next?'

'I'm open to suggestions.'

'Rubbish. You know perfectly well what you need to do.'

Harry swung her feet to the floor. 'I'm not going to the police, and you can't either. I told you –'

'I know, I know. But if you ask me, your father's remission isn't worth the risks you're taking here.'

'Now look –'

Imogen flapped at her to be quiet. 'I wasn't talking about going to the police.'

'Oh?'

'Isn't it obvious? You need to go and see your father.'

Harry sank back against the chair and closed her eyes. She felt a childish urge to stick her fingers in her ears and start humming.

'I know your relationship with your father is complicated,' Imogen went on.

Complicated didn't cover it. Harry waited for Imogen to continue, and when she didn't, she opened her eyes.

Imogen was staring past her to the other end of the room. 'Did you leave the door on the latch?'

Harry whipped round.

Ashford was walking through the office towards them.

'One of my employees died in a fire last night.'

Ashford closed the door to Dillon's office behind him and continued, 'You met him: Felix Roche.'

'I'm sorry to hear that.'

Harry played for time, settling herself in the chair behind Dillon's desk and gesturing for

Ashford to sit opposite. The psychology might have been a little obvious, but so what? She had a feeling she might need to look as though she was in charge.

Ashford sat down, his Coco the Clown hairdo at odds with his business suit. 'And I understand your accident was far more serious than you led me to believe.'

Harry frowned. 'How –'

'Jude Tiernan mentioned it. He phoned me about Felix, naturally. Then we had a little chat about you.'

He leaned back in his chair, keeping his eyes on her.

Damn Jude. How much had he told him? And why had Ashford come looking for her? She remembered the silver Jag she'd spotted behind her.

'How did you know I'd be here?' she said.

He paused. 'Your mother often complains that you work too hard, that you're never around at weekends. I took a chance.'

'You've been talking to my mother about this?'

'Good lord, no. I wouldn't dream of worrying her.' He fixed his solemn eyes on hers. 'So instead, I shall worry about you on her behalf.'

Harry pushed herself away from the desk and folded her arms. 'There's really no need.'

'I think there is. You may be getting involved in things that don't concern you.'

She raised her eyebrows. 'I could say the same about you.'

'Point taken. However, the consequences for you could be far more serious.'

'What exactly did Jude tell you?'

'I pressed him for details about your so-called accident. I was concerned.'

Harry took in his benign expression and the kind, basset-hound eyes. With the tufts of hair around his head, he could have been somebody's grandfather.

'He'd no business telling you anything,' she said.

Ashford looked thoughtful for a moment. Then he said, 'Several years ago, another employee of mine was tragically killed. A traffic accident near the IFSC.'

Harry's jaw tightened, but she said nothing.

'First young Jonathan, now Felix,' Ashford went on. 'And, according to Jude, someone tried to push you under a train.'

'That's quite a leap, isn't it?' She tried to keep her tone light. 'From my accident in Pearse Station to whatever happened your employees?'

'Did I say they were connected?' He leaned forward, his hands together as if in prayer. 'I'm simply urging you to be careful, that's all. For your mother's sake, if not your own.'

Harry frowned. 'You seem to know my mother very well.'

'I've known Miriam longer than I've known Sal.' His gaze shifted past her. 'I introduced them, as a matter of fact.'

Harry examined her nails. 'Were you and she . . . I mean, are you . . .?'

He shook his head. 'Not now. Now, we're just two old friends who look out for one another.'

'But before?'

He hesitated. 'Once, I admit, long ago, we were close.'

'What happened?'

'It's almost thirty years ago, it's not important.'

'Please – I'd like to know.' Harry picked at a ragged nail on her thumb. 'My mother mentioned something about it once, now I'd like to hear it from you.'

She shot him a look. How to get somebody to tell you a secret: fool them into thinking someone else already told.

Ashford looked doubtful, and shifted in his chair. 'But it was so long ago. Amaranta was only a baby.' He brushed a speck of invisible dust off his coat. 'It's not something I'm proud of, I can assure you.'

Harry kept her eyes on her nails. It shouldn't have surprised her that Miriam had had an affair. God knows, being married to her father can't have been easy.

'So what happened?' she said.

Ashford cleared his throat. 'Nothing. It only lasted a few months. Then we put an end to it.'

'Why? Because of my father?'

'I wish I could say that was the case.' He paused. 'No, it was because of you, Harry.'

242

She snapped her eyes to his face. His expression was more doleful than ever.

'Miriam became pregnant with you,' he said.

Harry stared at him for a moment, her head reeling. Ashford must have picked up on her look of panic for he immediately shook his head.

'No, no, Harry, you needn't worry,' he said. 'You're Sal's daughter, there's absolutely no question about that. Look in the mirror, for heaven's sake. You're a Martinez through and through, you couldn't possibly be anything else.'

Harry blinked at him. Speech was beyond her, just for a moment. Then she nodded and said, 'So Miriam put an end to it because I was on the way?'

'I'm sure she would have, eventually.' Ashford dropped his gaze. 'The truth is, I got cold feet.'

'You mean, it was you who finished it?'

'I wasn't ready to take on another man's family. Especially Sal's. Her pregnancy made me realize it. So yes, I left.' It was his turn to examine his nails.

She felt dazed. She thought of how remote her mother had always been, of how nothing Harry did was ever good enough. She'd always assumed it was because she was too much like her father. But now she saw that wasn't the only reason.

'You mustn't blame your mother,' Ashford said. 'Your father's financial scrapes were difficult to live with, especially when she had Amaranta to consider.'

243

'But if it hadn't been for me, Miriam's life could have been very different. You could have given her the security she needed.'

He shook his head. 'She would always have gone back to your father in the end, I'm convinced of that.'

'But she never got to make that choice, did she?' Harry bit her lip. 'Because of me.'

Ashford didn't answer. He didn't need to. She knew she was right. Not only did Harry remind her mother of the husband she resented, but she'd also destroyed her only chance to leave him.

As mother and daughter, they'd never stood a chance.

CHAPTER 32

It was almost six o'clock when Harry got back to her apartment, but closer to eight by the time she remembered her dinner date with Dillon.

She smacked her hand against her forehead, then stripped and jumped into the shower, adjusting the water until it was as hot as she could bear. She shampooed her hair twice to get rid of the helmet smell, and tried not to brood about her mother.

Ashford had left the Lúbra office with a final appeal to her for caution, and a look that told her he was sorry he'd ever come. She'd sat in Dillon's chair, unable to move, until Imogen had come and ordered her home.

Harry hopped out of the shower, pulled on jeans and a white cotton jumper and headed for the door. Brisk activity usually straightened out her moods, but she had a feeling it wouldn't work so well this time.

She passed by her office, and hesitated. Then she stepped into the room and checked her email. Nothing.

She slumped down into her office chair and kneaded her forehead with her fingers. It was only a matter of time before the Prophet contacted her again with instructions about the money. What in God's name was she going to do then?

Harry slammed the desk with her fist. Damn her father and his dirty deals. What the hell had any of it got to do with her? For years now she'd managed to block him out, disconnect all her emotions. But it seemed that even from prison he could still fuck up her life.

She slapped down the lid of her laptop and marched out of the apartment, banging the front door behind her. Climbing into her car, she gunned the engine, flipped on her headlights and swung south in the direction of Enniskerry.

Usually she wasn't given to introspection about her father. She'd done enough of that over the years, and it never did any good. But now she was aware of a tumble of emotions churning up inside her, like milk coming to the boil. She took a shuddery breath and tried to focus on the road.

The traffic was light and she hit the dual carriageway in less than ten minutes. As she cruised along the open road, she felt her hands loosen their grip on the wheel and her brow began to clear. Maybe dinner and a glass of wine were just what she needed.

She exited the main road and made her way towards Stepaside Village. The floodlit motorways and petrol stations had given way to winding roads and grassy front lawns, and she reduced her speed.

She cut through the village and found herself climbing a narrow hill that was barely the width of a single car. There were no more streetlights, and the sky was blocked out by a ceiling of knitted trees. Harry shifted down a gear and switched her headlights to full beam. Ditches and dense hedges lined the road on both sides, and the blind corners slowed her to a crawl.

Suddenly, a blaze of lights dazzled her from behind, and she squinted into her rear-view mirror. Some maniac was driving close on her tail and, judging from the height of his headlights, he must be in a Jeep. Harry tapped the brake pedal with her foot, hoping the flash of red lights would warn him off. She rounded the next bend and checked her mirror again. The Jeep had fallen back out of sight.

The Mini's engine was labouring, and she cranked it down to second gear. Up ahead, the lights of Johnnie Fox's pub burned in isolation through the darkness. Harry frowned. Dillon hadn't mentioned it as a landmark. She chugged on past it with a twinge of misgiving, as though she was leaving the last of her guardian angels behind. She shivered at the notion.

For fifteen minutes the car dipped and climbed. She kept her speed at thirty kilometres an hour, her eyes widening at the landscape that her headlights picked out around her. To her left, the road was bound by low stone walls that separated her from the vertical plunge into the valley below. To her right was a rising hill of dense fir trees. And dead ahead was nothing but black bends.

As she rattled down into first gear, Harry had to face the fact that somewhere along the way she'd taken a wrong turn. Dillon hadn't said anything about steep climbs and it was clear to her that she was headed up the Dublin Mountains. She cursed her internal compass and began looking for a lay-by where she could do a U-turn.

When the thud came, Harry's first thought was that a falling boulder had crashed against the car. The force of it slammed the Mini forward, catapulting Harry out of her seat. Her safety belt jammed and snapped her backwards. For an instant she was paralysed, and then she hit the brakes. Immediately the car slewed sideways towards the stone wall. She swivelled the steering wheel, trying to correct her course before the next bend. Then she shot a look in the rear-view mirror, and let out an involuntary moan.

The Jeep was back, and was bearing down on her hard. Harry stared in disbelief as its headlights closed in on her. The Jeep bulldozed straight into her and Harry screamed. The Mini fishtailed wildly, smashing off the stone wall. The passenger window shattered. Harry rammed her foot on the brake, almost levitating out of her seat to get her full weight behind it. The car swerved across the road and juddered along the edge of a ditch.

Branches scrabbled against the windows. Her arms vibrated against the wheel, aching as she strained to steady the car.

The Mini responded, and blundered back out on to the road. Harry snapped her eyes back up to the mirror. The Jeep was only a few yards behind her. She switched her foot from the brake to the accelerator, and the Mini took off. She felt herself being sucked backwards against the seat as the car pulled up the hill. Please God there'd be no oncoming trucks.

The Mini dug into the hairpin bends, tyres squealing. Harry pitched from side to side, her hands clamped on the wheel, all her muscles clenched. Every particle of her body was on high alert, dedicated to the task of keeping her car on the road. She pushed her speed into triple digits, ignoring the screaming engine. Her headlights flashed on the words DEAD SLOW painted in huge luminous letters on the road. Harry swallowed and tightened her grip on the wheel.

She checked on the Jeep. It was struggling with the tight bends, and she'd gained some ground. Who the hell was this guy? Was it Quinney? Maybe he'd spotted her car outside Leon's flat and had been on her tail ever since. But why would he be playing bumper tag with her on the side of a mountain?

Harry screeched into a straight section of road and the Jeep roared up behind her. The stone walls on her left had disappeared, and all that separated her from the plunging gulley was a knee-high grass bank. A low hum started up in her throat. In brute-force terms, her Mini was no match for the Jeep. It was like pitting a go-kart against a juggernaut, and Harry didn't much like her chances.

The Jeep stampeded towards her, so close now that she could see the glint of its bull-bars in her mirror. A violent thwack propelled her forward. Her neck whip-lashed once, and then suddenly she was airborne.

Harry screamed and braced herself against the steering wheel. The car sailed upwards over the bank and, for a moment, everything flipped into slow-motion. The engine cut out, and there was an eerie silence, broken only by the sound of spinning wheels. Harry's brain seemed to move faster than the events unfolding around her. She felt as though she had all the time in the world. It occurred to her to relax her legs and arms, so that they wouldn't be over-extended on impact and inclined to snap. She noticed her bag sliding under the passenger seat.

And then, like the lurch of an elevator, she felt the drop begin. Air whistled in through the broken windows, and the ground rocketed towards her. The car smashed down on to the grass and bounced like a stone skipping off the surface of a lake. Harry ricocheted against the roof and doors, whacking her head against the body of the car. Finally the car crash-landed on its side, glass shattering every-where. The Mini rocked once, and then was still.

Harry's head spun. She could hear the groan of

buckling metal and the tinkle of splintered glass settling itself around her. Her head and shoulders were crushed up against the driver's window, which was now the floor of the car. She was still wearing her seatbelt. There was a warm metallic taste in her mouth. She must have bitten through her lip on impact. She tried to move her head, but it felt too heavy, as though trauma had somehow turned it to lead. She settled for a quick survey of her vital signs. Nothing seemed to be broken.

She listened for movement from outside. The Mini creaked and ticked, and she thought about all the cars she'd seen explode on TV. She should probably get out of here. But she didn't move. Maybe if she just crouched here in the dark and played dead, the guy would go away. Harry wondered if she was slightly concussed.

Suddenly, the car was flooded with light. Harry shielded her eyes, momentarily blinded. Then she twisted round in her seat and squinted through the rear window. Two globes of light blazed down on her from the road. Her whole body jolted. It was the Jeep, its headlights trained down on her like spotlights. She could make out a dark silhouette skulking down the hill, cutting in and out of the dazzling beam like someone arriving late at the cinema. Dark hat, bright white hair, face invisible.

Harry snapped off her seatbelt and clambered over the gear stick to the passenger door. Her weight tilted the car over, sending it crashing right side up. Glass sliced through her palms. She kicked open the door and tumbled out on to the grass, scrabbling to get purchase on the muck. Then she started to run.

She scudded down the hill, digging her heels in to keep from sliding down the steep incline. She could hear the sound of breathing behind her, the thud of footsteps. She tore through a clump of gorse, ignoring the prickles that pierced through her jeans.

Suddenly, the footsteps stopped. In the same instant, her pursuer toppled her with a flying tackle and slammed her to the ground. He climbed on top of her and pressed his knees into the small of her back. His weight pinned her down, crushing the breath out of her. A hand pressed against the back of her head, cramming her face into the dirt. She could taste the damp soil as it filled her nose and mouth. She tried to scream, but she couldn't breathe. Then he snatched a handful of her hair and wrenched her head backwards, and she let out a choking sob. She flailed her arms out behind her, trying to make contact, but he grabbed her left wrist and twisted it behind her back, pushing her arm upwards until she screamed again.

The man put his lips close to her ear. She could feel the warmth of his breath against her neck, and she shivered. When he spoke, she knew he was the man from the train station.

'I hear you made a deal.' His voice was harsh and rasping.

She swallowed, and tried to speak. Her lips felt parched.

'I'm just doing what you want,' she managed finally, her head arched back as he clutched her hair. 'I'm giving the money back.'

'The Prophet doesn't trust you. He doesn't trust anyone. Except me.'

'The Prophet sent you?'

'The Prophet always sends me.' He yanked her hair back even further and she cried out with the pain. 'He doesn't like it when someone tries to back out of a deal.'

She flinched, and it took effort to sound sincere. 'Why would I want to back out? Just tell me where to wire the money, and it's all his.'

He pressed his face into her hair and lowered his voice to a whisper. 'Last person who backed out of a deal ended up as just another piece of roadkill.'

Harry thought about Jonathan Spencer, flattened by an oncoming truck. She swallowed again, and felt her heartbeat throbbing up high in her throat.

'The Prophet knows I won't back out,' she said. The fingers of her right hand explored the ground beside her. There had to be a stone or a stick around, something she could use as a weapon.

'People get greedy. And when they do, it's my job to make sure they burn.'

Harry flashed on Felix, incinerated in his own home, and choked back a whimper. Her fingers touched something hard and cold. A rock.

'So what does the Prophet have in mind for me?' she said, forcing out a note of bravado. Her fingers closed over the rough granite. The rock was about the size of a grapefruit, with a jagged edge. 'Road carnage or trial by fire?'

He jerked her head back and shoved her arm higher up along her back. Harry squeezed her eyes shut and felt tears of pain springing up behind her eyelids. Her neck and throat ached and she felt as though her head might snap off.

He leaned in closer to her, his voice growing hoarser. 'With you, I get to choose.'

Then, without warning, he smashed his fist into the side of her head. Her brain swam inside her skull, and a high-pitched whine hummed in her ear. He shoved her face back down into the ground. Too late, she realized she'd released her grip on the stone.

'Stay down and start counting,' he said. 'Don't stop till you get to three hundred.'

When she didn't respond, he slapped the side of her head again, and the ringing in her ears got louder.

'Count!'

She spat out a mouthful of grit and started to count, hating the quiver she heard in her own voice. She felt him move off her back. With his weight lifted, she could breathe more easily, and she inched her nose and mouth away from the soil. She inhaled the musty smell of clay and grass, and kept on counting. She could hear his shoes rustling against the grass, the sounds growing gradually fainter.

Presently, she heard the roar of the Jeep and the chirrup of his tyres as he sped away. The valley sank back into darkness. She kept on counting. She counted all the way to four hundred before she finally gave in and sobbed into the damp earth.

CHAPTER 33

'Sorry about the damsel in distress thing,' Harry said. 'Twice in one week, too.'

She looked across at Dillon and tried to gauge his reaction, but his face was hard to read. He fired up the engine and wrenched the Lexus into a tight U-turn, his eyes fixed straight ahead. He'd hardly said a word since he'd found her in the valley.

Somehow she had managed to stumble back to her car and retrieve her bag from under the seat. She'd sunk down on to the ground, huddled against the Mini, and phoned him with trembling hands. By the time he'd found her, she'd grown cold and rigid.

She flicked another glance at him. His mouth had a zippered-up look, and his fingers were clenched on the steering wheel. Every now and then, he'd flex them open and closed, as if he was trying to make his mind up about something.

He shot her a look. 'Those cuts on your hands look nasty. So does the one over your eye. I'm taking you to A&E, you could need stitches.'

'No, I told you, I'm fine.' She made herself smile. 'Really, I am.'

'If you ask me, you look concussed.'

She shook her head, and then wished she hadn't. A sharp pain drilled through her forehead. Maybe he was right about the concussion.

'I'll be okay.' She massaged the stiffness developing at the base of her neck. 'I just need to rest.'

He frowned and turned his attention back to the road. He was dressed in jeans and an expensive leather jacket that fell loosely around his frame. The black leather looked as soft as butter, and Harry wondered what would happen if she reached out and touched it.

She cleared her throat. 'Where are we going?'

'Where would you like to go?'

Harry peered out at the black fields and hedges, and decided she'd had enough of the countryside for the time being. 'Would you mind if we went back to the city? We could go to my place, get a takeaway . . . if you like?'

Dillon met her eyes, his gaze full of questions, but he just shrugged and turned away. 'Fine.'

Harry leaned back against the headrest and closed her eyes, trying to blank him out. Right now, she could only deal with the primitive essentials, such as shelter, sleep and food. Anything more complicated than that would have to wait. Her body felt slow and sleepy as it coped with the post-adrenaline crash.

Maybe she should have prepared him better for the horrific state of her car. All she'd told him over the phone was that she'd had an accident and had gone off the road. At the time, it had seemed expedient. Anything more involved, and the wobble in her voice would have gotten the better of her.

But he'd grown silent as he'd swept his torchlight over the car, flicking back the beam in a sharp double-take as he comprehended the extent of the damage. The windscreen had shattered into a frosted web, and the other windows looked like they'd been punched out by an invisible fist. The contours of the bonnet were squished and flattened, as though the car was beginning to melt. Even Harry wondered how the hell she'd come out of it alive.

She'd stood by the Mini for several minutes, stroking its bonnet as if it was a wounded pup, not wanting to leave its side. Then, without a word, Dillon had put his hand under her elbow and guided her up the hill to his Lexus.

The Lexus was now whispering along the mountain road. Harry's head floated as the car coasted downhill, and sleep pressed down on her like a lead apron. Dillon jabbed at the brakes and Harry jerked forward, her bag almost sliding off her lap. She opened her eyes and glared at him. She was willing to bet he'd done it on purpose. What was he so pissed off about, anyway? After all, she was the one who'd been half killed.

'Aren't you even going to ask me what happened?' she said.

Dillon pounded the steering wheel with his fist, making her jump.

'I don't know, Harry – should I?' He rammed the gear stick into second and swerved round a bend. 'If I do, will you tell me the truth? Or will you just fob me off and tell me everything's fine?'

Harry's eyes widened. She opened her mouth to speak, and then closed it again with a snap.

'So you had an accident and went off the road.' He shook his head. 'That car didn't go over by itself, anyone can see that.'

'Look, if you're pissed off because of tonight –'

'Jesus, Harry, of course I'm not pissed off because of tonight.' He jammed his foot on the brakes and the car screeched to a halt. 'What do you take me for?'

Dillon raked a hand through his hair. Then he let out a long breath and turned to face her, one arm draped over the steering wheel.

'Look, we both know you're in serious trouble,' he said. He looked at her and held her gaze. For a moment she had a flash of the dark-eyed boy who'd sat in her bedroom and talked to her about life and ethics with such blazing intensity.

Then he sighed and shook his head. 'Would it kill you to let me help?'

Harry blinked and bit her lip. He was right. She'd shut him out. It was second nature to her now to rely on no one but herself. The way she saw it, that saved on disappointments. On the other hand, she'd been so busy being independent that it never occurred to her he'd feel hurt at the exclusion. She tried to look contrite, but a part of her brain hummed a cheery tune at the notion that it bothered him.

'Sorry. I'm used to handling things myself.' She shrugged. 'Looks like I'm not doing it so well this time.'

'D'you want to tell me about it?'

She nodded. 'You drive, I'll talk.' She scanned the shadows outside. 'Let's get back to civilization.'

As the Lexus glided down the mountains, Harry wondered where to begin. Then she sighed. As always, things began and ended with her father.

'I'm still piecing things together, but here's how I see it. Before he was arrested, my father stashed away a pile of money from his insider trades, and now his old buddies want to get their hands on it. The problem is, they think I have the money. Actually, for a while there, so did I, but it turns out I was wrong.'

Dillon shot her a perplexed look. Harry thought about her corrupted bank account, and made a face.

'Don't ask,' she said. 'I still feel sick about it. The upshot of it is that I made a catastrophic mistake.' She closed her eyes, dizzy at the thought of her own stupidity. 'I made a deal with my father's trading ring.'

'You what? Are you out of your mind?'

She opened her eyes and flashed him a look. 'In my defence, I was pretty desperate. I'd just found out that they'd killed someone and, for all I knew,

I was next.' She hugged her arms across her chest. 'So I made a deal. I give them the money, and they leave me alone. Otherwise, they kill me.'

Something cold slithered inside her as she thought about the guy in the mountains and what he might choose to do to her.

She shuddered. 'Naturally, that's not a deal I want to back out of if I can help it.'

Dillon was silent. Harry glanced across at him and saw his throat muscles working, as though he was having trouble swallowing.

'What are you getting into here, Harry? Who are these people?'

'There's quite a collection of them.'

She filled him in about the ring members she'd discovered so far: the Prophet, who'd fed anonymous information from JX Warner to the ring; Leon Ritch, who'd escaped prosecution by informing on his pals; Jonathan Spencer, who'd wanted out but who'd been killed to protect the Sorohan deal; Ralphy-Boy, identity unknown, but presumably the banker whom Leon had protected; Felix Roche, who'd piggy-backed on the ring's insider trades, then died because he knew who the Prophet was; and, last but not least, her own father, the only one to go to prison for the whole sorry mess.

Dillon gave a low whistle. He slowed the car to a crawl, giving her his full attention. 'How do you know all this?'

Harry explained about her meeting with Ruth

Woods. Hard to believe it was only yesterday that she'd met the journalist in the Palace Bar. She neglected to mention her hacking exploits into Felix's emails. She wasn't sure where Dillon would stand on the ethics of that one.

'So who's the ringleader in all this? Your father?'

Harry shook her head. 'The Prophet seems to be the one pulling all the strings. He's the one I made the deal with.' Then she motioned back towards the mountains. 'It was his goon that ran me off the road up there.'

'What?' Dillon swerved into the side of the road to make room for an oncoming car. 'But he could have killed you. And why do that before you've handed over the money?'

'He wasn't trying to kill me, although he very nearly did. He was trying to scare me, make sure I didn't back out of the deal.' She remembered the man's low, husky voice and her intestines shrivelled. 'He's the same guy that pushed me under the train. Maybe he was in the maze too, I don't know.'

'Jesus.'

'Leon's had someone on my tail too.' She explained about Quinney. 'I don't know if they're all working together or if they each have their own agenda, but whatever way they're organized, it's scaring the shit out of me.'

'And you've no idea who this Prophet guy is?'

Harry shook her head. Her thoughts flashed on Jude, but after all, her only grounds for suspicion were that he'd worked for JX Warner. That, and the fact that his bribery of Felix seemed a little slick for a stuffy investment banker.

'What about Ralphy-Boy?' Dillon said. 'Maybe it's him. After all, if Leon Ritch protected him, then he's got to be important.'

'I hadn't considered that.' Harry frowned. 'I'll have to see what else I can find out about him.'

His eyes drilled into hers. 'Harry, this isn't something you can handle yourself. You've got to go to the police.'

She turned away, fiddling with the strap on her bag.

Dillon threw his hands in the air, and for a second the car was driving solo. 'Come on, Harry, asking for help doesn't make you weak.'

'It's not that.'

'Don't tell me you're still worrying about your father's remission? This is your life we're talking about here.'

Harry coiled the strap around her index finger. He was probably right.

'Promise me you'll at least think about it,' he said. 'And that you'll keep me involved?'

She started to nod, and then winced. Nodding hurt, but she'd also remembered something. 'Actually, you may be more involved than you think.'

She told him about Quinney's plans to dig into his past, to try and use him to get to her. He frowned, and then turned away.

'Don't worry about me,' he said. 'I can take care of myself.'

They drove in silence for a while. Then Dillon said, 'So if you don't have the money, who does?'

Harry locked eyes with him for a moment, but she didn't answer. She reckoned they both knew the answer to that one.

By the time they got back to her apartment, it was after ten o'clock. Dillon strode past her and marched straight into the kitchen. Harry could hear him banging around in the cupboards before she'd even closed the front door.

'What have you got in this place to eat?' he called.

'Not much.'

She stood on the kitchen threshold and watched him. His back was turned to her, legs braced apart, as he examined the cupboards. He'd slung his jacket across the countertop, and in his white T-shirt he looked fit and tanned, like an ex-tennis pro.

'You must eat out a lot,' he said, closing the last of the empty cupboards.

'There's a takeaway menu here someplace.'

The galley-style kitchen was narrow, and Harry had to squeeze past him to get to the cutlery drawers. Her arm brushed against his chest and she flinched as though she'd been scorched. She turned away and busied herself with the drawer.

'I call this my Sunday-night cupboard.' She bent her head low as she rooted through the contents,

He pulled back, his gaze searching her face. His eyes were apprehensive and he hesitated. A startling thought occurred to Harry.

'Do I scare *you*?' she said.

He swallowed, and contemplated her for a moment longer. Then he nodded. 'A little.'

She grinned. She couldn't help it. The corners of his mouth twitched in response. Then he pressed one hand against the small of her back, arching her body into his groin, and bent towards her again. This time his kiss meant business. Heat flooded through her and she could feel his heartbeat hammering hard against her own body. He flicked at her lower lip with his tongue, teasing her. This time, there was definitely whimpering.

He pulled away again and Harry opened her eyes. Her face felt suffused with heat, and her eyelids were heavy.

Dillon smiled a wide, lazy smile, and led her by the hand into the bedroom. He held her gently, sensitive to the pain of her aching neck and the stinging cuts scored across her hands. For the next hour she breathed in his earthy scent and watched enthralled as he moved up and down her body, captivated by his rhythm, drawn deep into it, until finally his rhythm became her rhythm, and the words *this is Dillon, this is Dillon* ran through her head like an incantation, until the shudders that shook her body drowned them out.

Afterwards, as she watched him sleep, the fingers

of one hand laced through hers, she thought about what the Prophet had said.

Be smart. Otherwise you and everyone you care about will be in danger.

She watched Dillon's chest rise and fall, and listened to the soft sounds of his breathing. In her mind, she traced a finger over the dark brows, and touched the slight arch across the bridge of his nose, then let her finger trail along his lips, his chin, and down to his chest.

Then she turned away and stared up at the ceiling. Imogen was right. Tomorrow she'd go and visit her father.

CHAPTER 34

Harry had never been inside a prison before. It was brighter and warmer than she'd expected. She shifted on her orange plastic chair, crossing and uncrossing her legs.

She peered around at the ring of seats set back against the walls of the waiting room. The only other occupant was a woman in her sixties, dressed in a bottle-green winter coat.

A tight spasm gripped the base of Harry's neck and she massaged it with her fingers. The cuts on her hands were starting to heal, and she'd applied enough makeup to cover most of the bruises.

She peeked at her watch. There was still time to back out. She glanced over at the officer behind the glass-panelled hatch near the door. He was on the phone, his middle-aged face round and creased, and a biro stuck behind one ear. He dipped his head to look at her over the top of his glasses and gave her an encouraging smile. Harry managed a small nod in return and then looked away.

She hadn't seen her father in over six years. Somehow she'd managed to bury this fact and still get on with her life, but now it was time to dig it up and take another look.

She fiddled with the clasp on her bag. Six years was a long time. It probably wouldn't have killed her to visit him once in a while. She picked at a hangnail on her thumb. She thought about her father's track record of double-dealing and forgotten promises, searching for a reminder of just why she'd stayed away.

There were plenty of memories to choose from, even from when she was small. Like the time when she was six and her mother had been in hospital. Her father was supposed to collect her from school, but of course he'd never arrived. She'd sat on the school wall, kicking her heels, until it was almost dark. She could still recall the bewildered hurt she'd felt at being abandoned, and the way she'd shrunk from strangers as they stared and passed her by. When her father finally turned up, poker winnings in his pocket, he'd scooped her up into the air and said he'd forgotten all about her.

Harry sighed. The trouble with her father was that he never thought he'd done anything wrong. He would let people down and then be totally mystified by the effect it had on them. Her mother had withdrawn from him long ago, unable to cope. Harry understood why. It hurt to know that all along your hero was just a fraud.

'Now, ladies, they're ready for you inside.'

Harry jumped. The officer was beckoning them

over and shoving paperwork through the hatch. She took her time about getting up, letting the other woman go first.

She watched as the woman passed a gift-wrapped parcel through the hatch. Damn, maybe she should have brought her father something. Chocolates or fruit. Then she snapped her shoulders back and stepped up to the hatch. This was no time for sweets and grapes. Her father was in prison for insider trading, not in hospital with appendicitis.

The officer slid a piece of paper under the hatch.

'There's your pass docket,' he said. 'Hand it in at the main prison gate. I'll hold on to your handbag, you can collect it on your way out.' He looked at her again over the top of his glasses. 'Just follow Gracie there, she knows her way round.'

Harry thanked him and handed over her bag, pocketing the receipt. Then she followed the older woman outside.

The air felt cold and damp. The morning sky was gunmetal grey, and looked ready to unload a heavy downpour. Arbour Hill prison was located close to the city quays, but the usual traffic sounds seemed far away, as though the world had somehow been screened off.

Harry turned towards the main prison gate, and took an involuntary step backwards. The grim prison boundary wall loomed high above her, maybe fifteen or twenty feet into the air. The bleak

271

concrete seemed to stretch on and on, and she felt herself shrinking beneath it. Set into the wall was the central entrance block, a tall, Gothic-looking structure with a castellated porch. Harry watched Gracie approach the door but felt unable to move. In horror stories, this was where the vampire lived.

'Don't mind them walls,' Gracie said, without looking back. 'Give you the creeps, they would, but you get used to them.'

Harry shivered and followed her over to the steel gate, where an officer took their passes and ushered them through a heavy-duty iron door. From there, another officer led them down a narrow corridor that reminded Harry of her old primary school: green walls, hard floors and little in the way of central heating. The officer explained the basic rules of the visit as they walked. Thirty minutes per visit, one visit per week, no smoking, no touching, and no passing of contraband. He opened a door marked VISITING ROOM, and stood aside to let them in.

Harry followed Gracie into the room, unpleasantly aware of her own heartbeat. In front of her was a long wooden table, with a row of chairs set along either side. The table was unusually wide, maybe five or six feet, enough to prevent any physical contact across it.

Two prison officers sat on raised observation seats positioned at opposite ends of the room. The only person at the table was an elderly man, who looked up as Gracie sat down opposite him.

Harry hesitated, and then took a seat in the middle of the table, clasping her hands in front of her. She wished she still had her handbag so she'd have something to fiddle with. Directly opposite her was another door, and she fixed her gaze on it, waiting for her father.

Beside her, Gracie was talking in low tones to the elderly man. Harry flicked him a glance. His plump face was set back into a cushion of jowls, and he tugged at the quivering flesh beneath his chin while he listened to Gracie.

There was a soft click, and the door opposite Harry swung open. An officer stepped over the threshold and stood back against the open door, smiling at the man who passed into the room.

'See you later, Sal,' the officer said, saluting him before he left.

'*Gracias,*' the man said.

He hesitated by the door. He wore a navy-blue pullover and dark trousers, both clean and well pressed. His hair was now completely silver and his beard was thick and snowy white, giving him a nautical air. As a child, Harry had always believed her father was the real Captain Birds Eye.

Was it her imagination, or had he shrunk?

He looked at her and blinked. Harry straightened her back and crossed her ankles, tucking her feet underneath her chair. She was aware that her posture was tight, but loosening up was beyond her. There was already a fullness developing in her throat that she knew she was going to have trouble with.

He smiled at her and shook his head, holding out his arms and then letting them fall back to his sides.

'*Hija mía.*' My daughter.

For a moment, he studied the floor. Then he cleared his throat and took a seat opposite her.

'They didn't tell me it was you, Harry,' he said. 'It's so good to see you, you've no idea.'

He leaned forward and reached out across the table. Then he seemed to think better of it and pulled back, sitting with his fingers laced in front of him. Harry felt the swelling in her throat increase and tried to picture herself on the school wall, but failed.

'Look at you,' he said. 'You're so grown up. A young woman.'

His brown eyes had a cloudy look, but the eyebrows were still as black as ever. Harry dropped her gaze.

'I should've come before,' she said.

'Shush, don't talk nonsense, love. This is no place for you. You were absolutely right to stay away. I told your mother I didn't want to see any of you in here.'

'Does she come?'

His shook his head. 'We agreed it's better if she doesn't.'

Harry tried to visualise her elegant mother in a place like this, but the image wouldn't come.

Her father picked at his sleeve. 'Your mother had high expectations of life married to an investment banker. I'm afraid I didn't live up to them. It's my fault, not hers.'

'What about Amaranta? She comes in to see you, doesn't she?'

'Well, in the beginning she did, yes. She was quite a regular.' He smiled conspiratorially at her. 'You know Amaranta. Always doing her duty. But then the baby came, and naturally life got busy for her. At first she wanted to bring Ella with her, but I absolutely forbade it.' He sliced a hand through the air, palm downwards, as though he was spreading out a deck of cards. 'Under no circumstances would I allow my granddaughter to come to a place like this.'

Harry leaned back in her chair, and blinked. She'd thought she was the only one who'd chosen to stay away. 'So you don't get any visitors at all?'

He shrugged. 'Visitors can make things harder, sometimes.' He nodded in the direction of Gracie and her companion. 'Take Brendan over there. That sister of his has been in to see him every Monday for the past twenty-three years, and she sits there torturing him with details about the life and family he'll never see again. He doesn't sleep well on Monday nights.'

'What's he in here for?'

Her father avoided her gaze and didn't answer straight away. Then he shook his head.

'You're better off not knowing, love,' he said quietly.

Harry felt her eyes widen, and peeked over at

275

the elderly man. He was still plucking at the flesh on his throat with a trembling hand. He met Harry's eyes with a vacant, watery stare, and she felt her stomach dip. She looked away and studied her father's face. He seemed so much older than his sixty-four years. His skin was slack, and the lines in his forehead were deep and wavy, like the ripples left by the tide in the sand.

'Is it okay in here?' she said. 'Are you okay?'

'Don't worry about me, love. I get by.' He made a face. 'I miss the sunlight. And I can't stand someone else deciding when the lights go on and off. But I keep busy. It seems I've quite a talent for carpentry. I play a little poker, write a few letters. I write to you quite often, Harry.'

'You do? I never get any letters.'

'Oh, no, I never send them.' He smiled as if it was all just a bit of old nonsense. Then he frowned and leaned forward, stretching both arms across the table. His palms were open, offering to take her hands in his, although he must have known she couldn't reach him.

'Why did you come, Harry?' he said. 'Is something wrong? Is that why you're here?'

She sighed and felt her shoulders sag. She placed her own palms flat on the table in acknowledgement of his. There was a tug inside her chest, and she felt like a small child about to unburden herself. She took a deep breath.

'Some friends of yours have been to see me,' she began.

CHAPTER 35

Harry talked for quite a while. She watched her father curl his fingers into fists as she explained how Leon and the Prophet were closing in on her. By the time she'd described her encounter in the Dublin Mountains, his eyes were shut tight. He bent his head, and pressed his fists into his forehead. When he finally looked up, all the colour had drained from his face.

'I'm sorry.' His voice was barely a whisper. 'You were never meant to be involved. Never.' He pressed one hand against his chest and stretched the other across the table towards her. 'I'll do anything to help you, love, you know that, don't you?'

His eyes were red-rimmed, and his mouth was fixed in a determined line. Harry moved her hands closer to his. The gap between their fingers was no more than two feet, but it may as well have been a mile. She bit her lower lip and nodded. For the moment, speaking was out of the question.

'I'll talk to Leon,' her father said, straightening up. 'I'll call him and make him stay away from you.'

Harry swallowed and shook her head. 'He's not

the one we have to worry about. It's the Prophet who's calling all the shots.'

'Then tell me what you need, Harry. I'll do whatever it takes. Ask me anything.'

She looked at him and wished she had more time. There were so many things she wanted to ask him, but her thirty minutes were already running out.

'Tell me about the Sorohan deal,' she said finally.

His gaze lost focus for a moment, taking on a nostalgic look. 'It was the biggest deal we ever did. The stock was worthless after all that dot.com nonsense. And then we heard that Aventus was after it. I put in everything we had and bought up stock for the ring before anyone else could find out.'

'So you managed the funds for the whole ring?'

'For certain deals, yes. We never traded on our own information, that was a cardinal rule. It was too risky. If a leak came from Merrion & Bernstein, then someone from KWC would handle the trades, and vice versa. We'd split the profits afterwards. That way, the trades couldn't be traced back to any privileged information. It was a way of staying safe.'

'What about JX Warner? The Prophet worked there, didn't he?'

'As far as we could tell, yes. But he never did any trades. That was the way he'd operated right from the start. He'd take the money, but none of the risks.' He shook his head. 'He just got other people to do his dirty work for him.'

Harry thought about her whispering attacker the night before, and shivered. The Prophet was still getting other people to do his dirty work for him.

She pressed her arms across her chest and dragged her mind back down from the mountains. 'So for the Sorohan deal, you were in charge of the money?'

He nodded. 'Sorohan had hired JX Warner to negotiate their end of the deal. That's where the Prophet got his information. But Aventus had hired Merrion & Bernstein, so that put Leon out of the picture. KWC wasn't involved, so I was free to act.'

'What went wrong?'

He sighed. 'We broke our own cardinal rule. Leon was holding on to funds from an earlier deal and at the last minute I convinced him to buy Sorohan shares with it. It was such an opportunity, I thought it would be worth the risk, just this once. But all that activity on Sorohan shares made the Stock Exchange suspicious. Naturally, Leon's name came up in lights because of the link to Aventus and Merrion & Bernstein.' He shook his head. 'It was stupid and greedy.'

Harry looked at her hands. There was another question she had to ask, but she was having trouble getting it out.

'What about Jonathan Spencer?' she said finally, not looking at him. 'What happened to him?'

Her father's eyebrows shot up. 'You know about Jonathan?' He shook his head and sighed. 'He should never have been involved, hadn't the temperament for it. He was just a boy, same age as Amaranta. I tried to keep his name out of it at the trial. Around the time of the Sorohan deal, he told me he wanted to leave. He was terrified. I persuaded him to keep his head down and let me handle things.'

'And did you?'

He grimaced. 'I spoke to Leon, who overreacted. He was convinced Jonathan posed some kind of threat to the ring. That was nonsense, the boy wasn't going to cause any trouble. But Leon wouldn't listen. He panicked, contacted the Prophet to tell him the Sorohan deal was off.' He stared into the distance, shaking his head. 'Anyway, it all came to nothing, because the poor boy was killed in a car accident soon afterwards.'

Harry stared at her father. He seemed to have forgotten her for a moment, all his attention turned inwards. Did he really believe Jonathan's death was an accident? She closed her eyes. She hadn't the appetite to pursue the point. Instead she brought him back to the money.

'So how much did you make on the Sorohan deal?'

His eyes re-focused on her for a moment. Then he tilted his chair back on its hind legs and laced his fingers behind his head. He smiled at the ceiling and shook his head.

'About sixteen million dollars,' he said. 'All on a single deal.'

Harry did the sums. In euros, that was about twelve million.

'Where is it now?' she said. 'Did the authorities get hold of it?'

He rocked to and fro on the chair, and Harry's heart whirled around in her chest as she waited for him to answer. If he said the money was gone, she was in trouble.

He let the chair drop back with a chirp against the floor and shook his head. 'The authorities couldn't find it. I'd switched banks.' He glanced at the guards and lowered his voice. 'When Leon sold me out, he gave them details of my Credit Suisse account in the Bahamas. It was the only one he knew about. I'd opened it back in '99 when we started the ring operation, and I'd traded out of it for more than a year. It gave the authorities all the evidence they needed.'

'But there was another account?'

He nodded. 'About six months before the Sorohan deal, Credit Suisse started asking awkward questions. They didn't like the patterns they saw in my trades. Buying up shares just before a takeover can look suspicious if you do it too often. So I decided to move on to fresh territory.'

'You left the Bahamas?'

'Oh no, I was much too fond of the place.' He smiled at her. 'Sun, sand and secrecy laws, what more could a crooked banker need?'

She shook her head at him. Sometimes it was like talking to a mischievous child.

'So you just went to another bank?' she said.

'Well, I looked around. It was a question of finding

281

a bank with the right amount of discretion, if you follow me.'

Harry nodded and sighed.

'Then I met this fellow at a poker game in Nassau,' her father continued. 'Philippe Rousseau, was his name. Interesting player. Turned out he was a banker, so I told him I was on the lookout for someone to manage my investments for me.' He gave a wry smile. 'There was something about the way he played poker that made me think we'd get along. He took risks, and wasn't above a little sharp practice here and there. So we did business.'

'You opened a bank account with a stranger you met at a poker game?'

'Why not? It was a perfectly respectable bank, and highly secure. I faxed him my trading instructions using an agreed pseudonym. Any cash withdrawals or transfers out of the account had to be done in person, and arranged in advance by fax using the same codename.' He held her gaze for a moment and smiled. 'You'd have liked the name I chose.' He sighed and looked away again. 'Anyway, it suited me perfectly. And it suited him too. He copied all my trades, making a small fortune of his own. People often mimic successful trading patterns.'

Harry nodded, thinking of Felix Roche piggy-backing on the ring's trades. Then she thought of how he'd ended up, barbecued in his sleep. His copycat trades hadn't done him much good.

'Professional suicide for a banker, of course,' her father continued, unconsciously echoing her own train of thought. 'But he enjoyed the risks. I used to meet up with him every few months for a little poker and a little business. Towards the end, he was promoted to head of investments, and they put some faceless account manager in his place. Owen, or John or something. Never had any dealings with him – I'd stopped trading in the account by then.'

'But the Sorohan money is still there?'

'Oh yes.'

Harry fiddled with her watchstrap. Her half-hour was almost up. Time to get to the point. But there was still something else she wanted to know. She kept her gaze fixed on her watch, as if by not looking at him she could ward off any painful answers.

'Why did you do it?' she said.

There was a pause. 'I wish I knew what to say to you, Harry. I've had a lot of time to think in here, and I've asked myself that over and over. Why did I do it? Was it worth it? Would I do it again if I got the chance?' He sighed. 'I probably would.'

Harry's eyes whipped back up to his face. His eyebrows were raised in apology, but he held her gaze.

'It wasn't just about the money,' he said. 'That was part of it, of course, but not everything.' He frowned and seemed to grope for the right words. 'I don't know. Maybe it was all about power. With insider information, we were in control, we felt omniscient.' His eyes glowed beneath the dark brows. 'We owned the market.'

Harry stiffened. Recognition flared through her. *We owned the market.* The phrase triggered an image: herself at a keyboard, probing a network, breaking through its perimeters; slipping past the sentries, cracking the administrator account; an illicit charge stealing over her when she finally owned the network.

Her father's gaze had moved past her again, seeing something that wasn't there. He leaned forward, his hands clasped so tightly in front of him that the skin puckered.

'The danger and the risk just heightened the rush. It made me feel alive. Life's not much fun unless you go all-in once in a while.' He shook his head and slumped back in his chair, the apologetic look returning. 'Can you understand any of that, Harry?'

She couldn't answer him.

There was a slight movement to her left, and she spotted one of the guards checking his watch. Her father must have seen it too, for he leaned forward and stretched his arms towards her again.

'Look, none of this is helping you.' he said. 'Why don't you just let me handle Leon and the Prophet? I can talk to them, make them –'

She shook her head. 'Talking isn't going to make any difference. Not with the Prophet.'

'Then tell me what I can do.'

Harry took a deep breath. 'I need the money. All of it.'

He slid his hands back across the table until his elbows were tucked in against his sides. 'What?'

Harry shifted in her chair. 'I explained all this. If I don't hand over twelve million euros to the Prophet, then he's going to set his psychopath on to me. And on to others, maybe. I don't have a choice.'

Her father stared at the table, tugging at his beard. His forehead sparkled with tiny sequins of sweat.

He shook his head. 'You can't trust a fellow like that to stick to a deal. Who's to say he won't set his henchman on you even when he does get the money?'

'But at least with the money, I have some kind of bargaining power. Without it, I'm dead.' She heard her own voice rise in disbelief. How could there be any argument about this? Her life was in danger here.

Her father dragged his palms up and down over his face, as though by massaging the blood flow he could coax out an answer that would help. When he dropped his hands back to the table, he looked bleary-eyed and tired.

'They've no right to that money,' he said quietly. 'I'm the only one who's paid the price for it. Six years I've spent in this concrete box. Six years of standing in line for breakfast with paedophiles and murderers, everyone's breath so sour it turns your stomach. Six years in a place where the only way out for most people is suicide.' He breathed deeply through his nose. 'The money was the only thing that kept me going.'

Harry winced and closed her eyes, trying to drive out the images he was creating. 'I'm sorry, but I can't think of any other way out of this. Other than going to the police.'

Her father stiffened. 'There must be another way, there has to be.'

Harry looked at him, and felt something small inside her shrink even smaller.

'You're not going to help me, are you?' she said.

Even to her own ears, her voice sounded bewildered and hurt. She was back on the school wall again. A hard knot twisted up inside her chest. He was backsliding, just like he always did. What childlike part of her had ever thought it could be any different?

Suddenly, his whole demeanour changed. He met her gaze and smiled. To Harry, his smile seemed forced. Whatever the joke was, his eyes weren't in on it.

'Nonsense, of course I'm going to help you, Harry.' His gaze never wavered. 'But be reasonable, I can hardly give you the money here, can I? It's not like I have it on me.'

He turned his palms upwards and hunched his shoulders in an exaggerated Continental shrug. The gesture was more French than Spanish, and Harry had seen it before. She'd always suspected it was deliberately cultivated, rather than inherited from any Spanish lineage.

The door behind her father opened, and a prison officer stepped into the room.

'Time's up now, gentlemen,' the officer said, standing by the open door.

The elderly man to her father's left shuffled to a standing position. Gracie remained seated, intent on finishing her one-sided conversation before her brother could escape back to his cell.

Harry's father pushed his chair back, glancing at the guards. *'Hablemos esta tarde.'* Let's talk this afternoon.

'This afternoon?'

He stood up, his posture upright and relaxed. 'Meet me outside the gates at two o'clock.'

Harry frowned. 'Outside the gates? I don't understand.'

He tilted his head to one side. 'I'm getting out today. My remission came through. I thought you knew.'

Harry blinked. 'No. No, I didn't. At least, not that it was so soon.'

She thought of the phone message her mother had left. She'd probably been trying to let her know.

So after all this time, her father was coming out today. She felt flat and defeated, like a punctured tyre.

She sighed. 'So if I meet you, you'll help me.'

She didn't even bother to make it a question. What was the point, when the answer was so irrelevant?

'Of course I will, love.' He edged his way towards the door. 'Don't worry, everything will be fine.'

Harry stared after him. She didn't believe a word he said.

CHAPTER 36

Harry nudged her car back along the quays, and tried not to think about her father. She should never have gone to see him. She tightened her grip on the steering wheel and concentrated on the drive home.

The clouds were delivering on their earlier promise of rain. Her wipers whunk-whunked across the windscreen, punctuating fragments of her father's conversation as it echoed inside her head.

You were never meant to be involved.

I'll do anything to help you.

Don't worry, everything will be fine.

Harry smacked off the wipers and jammed to a halt at a red light. She propped her cheek against her fist, and watched the rain running in rivers down the windscreen until the glass looked as though it was melting.

Her father wasn't going to help her, that much was clear. He'd asked her to meet him outside the prison gates, but for what? For more evasions and apologies? Harry shook her head. She had no intention of going near those prison walls again.

The rain turned to hail and the icy pellets drilled against the car. The driver behind Harry tooted his horn and she jumped, fumbling with the gears. They felt tight and sticky. She was driving a two-year-old Nissan Micra, the temporary replacement car her insurance company had provided when they'd towed her Mini away. She'd managed to persuade them no other car had been involved in the accident and so the police had been kept out of things. The last thing she needed was another encounter with Detective Lynne. She ground the gears and sighed, thinking of her beloved Mini, whose transmission shifted as though greased in butter. She'd never drive it again.

Flipping her wipers back on, she edged forward and swung right on to O'Connell Bridge. Her intention had been to return home, but it occurred to her that the Lúbra Security office wasn't far away and that it was time she went back to work.

An image of Dillon flashed into her head: his face moving above hers, his breath on her lips. Heat stole up her thighs and something swelled inside her. He'd left her apartment before six that morning, when she was barely awake. He was flying out to Copenhagen later that day to close out a merger between Lúbra and yet another security firm. She wouldn't see him for a couple of days. Suddenly, Harry needed to hear his voice.

She groped in her bag with one hand and found her phone. She punched the speed dial and waited, but all she got was Dillon's voicemail. Probably just as well. Calling a man when you felt needy was never a good idea. Especially so early in a relationship, when personality disorders were best kept under wraps.

She sighed and flung the phone down on the passenger seat. It rang almost immediately, and she snatched it back up.

'Hello?'

'At last. We've been trying to reach you for days.'

She felt her shoulders droop. It was her sister, Amaranta.

'Sorry,' Harry said. 'I've been swamped all week.'

'We're all busy, you know.'

Harry's eyes rolled skyward at the school-mistressy tone. 'Right.'

'It's about Dad –' Amaranta began.

Harry cut her off. 'I know, he's coming out today. I've just been in to see him.'

There was a pause. Harry pictured Amaranta sitting under her stairs, straightening the notepads and pencils on the telephone desk in front of her. She'd exhibited the same neat-freak traits in their shared attic room at home. On Amaranta's side of the skipping rope, all the shoes were in rows, and the books had their edges lined up as though she'd measured them with a set square. On Harry's side of the room, things had been a lot more unpredictable.

'How does he look?' Amaranta said, finally.

Harry puffed air through her lips and wondered

how to describe the engaging, dishonest and scheming man she had just visited.

In the end, she just said, 'He looks old.'

'Did he say where he was going to stay?'

'I never thought to ask.'

There was another pause. Harry circled around College Green, driving hands-free for a moment while she changed gear. The bus driver behind her didn't appreciate the manoeuvre.

She risked a direct question. 'How come you stopped going to see him?'

'I didn't just stop, I had Ella to think about. Babies take up a lot of time, you know. Dad understood. Ella came first.'

Amaranta's tone said that was the end of the matter. Then she cleared her throat. 'Anyway, things change when you become a parent. You see things differently.'

'You mean, you see what a lousy parent our father made.'

'At least I didn't abandon him altogether.'

Great. Now she was Harry's self-appointed conscience. Did all big sisters do this?

'Like me, you mean?' Harry said.

'It was you he really wanted to see. You were always his favourite.'

There was no bitterness in Amaranta's tone. She was stating a fact, one they had both accepted many years before.

Harry felt her arms and shoulders tense as she tried to get in lane. 'Listen, I'd better go. I'm in the car, and driving conditions aren't exactly favourable.'

'Have you arranged to meet him again?'

Harry thought of the looming prison walls, and slammed the gear stick into second. 'No. No, I haven't. Look, I'll call you next week.'

She threw the phone on to the passenger seat and whirled around a corner into Kildare Street. Damn big sisters and the guilt trips they sent you on. There was no point in meeting her father. She needed his help, but he wouldn't give it. Stalemate.

A nip of misgiving bit into her gut. Maybe she should talk to him again, give him another chance. She still had some questions for him. For instance who was the Prophet? He must have had some idea, some clue to his identity. Who was Ralphy-Boy? Maybe her father knew him.

She shook her head. It didn't matter who the Prophet was. She still had to give him twelve million euros.

Cruising to a halt a few metres away from the Lúbra office, she grabbed her bag, locked the car and ran across the street, ducking her head against the stinging hailstones. She pushed through the door into the entrance hall. Annabelle, the receptionist, was on the phone, and Harry slipped past her with a quick wave, moving into the main office.

Today it was full of people. Here and there groups gathered round a desk, pointing at a screen. Her gaze swept past them to the office at the back of the room. No sign of Dillon.

Harry headed for her desk by the window, snagging a couple of How're-y'doin'-Harry's along the way, but moving too swiftly for anyone to question the cuts on her face. She sat down and powered up her laptop, listening to the ticking of hailstones against the windows as she logged in and launched her email.

'That cut wasn't there yesterday.'

She looked up to find Imogen, arms akimbo, glaring at the gash over her eye. Harry sighed.

'I know. There've been one or two developments since yesterday. But before you start in on me, I did take your advice.'

'You did?' Imogen scooted into a chair beside her. 'And?'

'It didn't go well. I'll fill you in later.'

Imogen shook her head. 'What is it about families? I always thought a smaller one like yours would be easier to get along with.' Imogen came from a family of six that squabbled and made up in ever-changing alliances. At the moment, she was on speaking terms with none of them. 'Looks like it's not that simple.'

'Believe me, it isn't.' Harry paused. It took effort to keep her voice casual. 'Is Dillon about?'

'Bachelor Boy? No, he's gone to Copenhagen.'

'Already?'

'An earlier flight came up, so he took it.' Imogen frowned. 'Something wrong?'

Harry checked her vital signs. Still needy. Damn.

She shook her head. 'I just wanted to talk to him. I'll catch him later.'

She glanced over at her screen and winced. Her head and neck movements were stiffening up; a classic case of whiplash. Maybe she should think about a chiropractor.

'Don't move.' Imogen hopped off her chair and disappeared. She returned half a minute later, holding out a glass of water and two white tablets.

'What are they?' Harry said.

'Just swallow them.'

Harry did as she was told. Imogen took the empty glass from her.

'You shouldn't be in here, you look terrible,' she said, moving back towards her own desk. 'I'll be keeping an eye on you.'

Harry waited until her friend had gone. Then, moving her neck as little as possible, she turned to check her email. Seventy-two unread messages. Things had really piled up on her since Friday. Her client caseload included three more penetration tests, two investigations into suspected computer intrusions, and an assessment of corporate security, but thankfully none of them were due straight away. She scanned her mail, checking the sender addresses in case there was anything more urgent. Then her whole body froze.

The sender's domain name seemed to pulsate from the screen. Anon.obfusc.com. A tremor shook her hand as she clutched the mouse. She gritted her teeth. Double-click.

Time to hand over the money, Harry.
Transfer it to the following account by
5 p.m. Wednesday:

SWIFT CODE: CRBSCHZ9
IBAN: CH9300762011623852957.

My sources tell me you might be stalling.
Don't. Today I'll show you what happens
to people who let me down. You have 48
hours, Harry.
The Prophet

Harry's hand flew to her mouth. Today was
Monday. What if she told him she wouldn't have
the money by 5 p.m. Wednesday? What then?
Her desk phone rang and she jumped. It was
Annabelle.
'There's a Mr Tiernan in reception to see you.'
Harry's glance shot up to the door into reception,
and then back to the Prophet's email. Her pulse
speeded up. What the hell was Jude doing here?
She tried to swallow but her mouth was dry.
'Tell him I'll be right out.'
Jude was pacing the entrance hall when she
pushed through the doors. He stopped at the sight
of her, his eyes widening as he registered her fresh
cuts and bruises.
'My God, Harry.'
She took in his appearance while he stared at hers.
The investment banker was gone. He'd swapped the

business suit for faded jeans and a T-shirt stretched tight over his torso. His fists were clenched, his biceps taut. He looked like a wrestler stoking up for a fight.

He strode towards her. Harry retreated involuntarily, then sidestepped into an empty office on her right, gesturing for him to follow. He marched in behind her and slammed the door.

'Jesus, Harry, are you okay? What the hell's going on?'

She waved a hand at her face. 'It's nothing serious.'

He took a step towards her and she tried not to flinch.

'Nothing serious?' He began counting things off on his fingers. 'I help you scam Felix Roche, he gets himself murdered, the police are interrogating me, you won't answer my calls and now I find you covered in bruises. I may not have taken things seriously before, but by God I do now, believe me.'

'Look, I appreciate the help you gave me, but there's no need for you to be involved any more.'

'Involved? The police know I called Felix the night he died. Of course I'm bloody involved.' He dragged a hand through his hair. He looked like he hadn't slept much in the last forty-eight hours. 'Anyway, Felix is on my conscience.' He paused, and held her gaze. 'So are you.'

She looked away. He touched her gently on the shoulder.

'What is it, Harry?'

She folded her arms and glared at him. 'Just how much did you tell Ashford?'

'What?'

'He was in here yesterday. You talked to him about me.'

'He asked about your accident, he sounded concerned.'

'Are you sure that's all you told him?'

Jude's eyes narrowed. 'Come on Harry, what is this? We talked about your accident, that's all. Has something changed?'

She thought of all that had changed in the last two days. What if she told him about the missing money? Her throat tightened. She couldn't risk it. He'd already talked to Ashford. Who else would he talk to? Whatever happened, the Prophet must never find out the money was gone.

She shook her head. 'Nothing's changed.'

Jude moved in close to her and grabbed her by the shoulders. She gasped as his face loomed into hers, his breath hot on her cheeks. He smelled of beer and clean male sweat.

'Is it Felix?' His fingers tightened on her shoulders. 'Maybe you talked to him that night after all. Did he tell you something? What did he say?'

'Nothing, I told you, he didn't answer.'

His eyes drilled into hers, their noses almost touching. She scoured his face for signs of the virtuous banker who never broke the rules, but found nothing. All she saw was a daredevil pilot who looked like he was capable of anything.

Suddenly, he released her arms.

'Have it your way.' He took a step back towards the door. 'But I'm not going away, Harry. None of this is.'

'Wait –'

But he opened the door and was gone.

Harry clamped her arms across her chest, rubbing her shoulders where he'd held her. She shuddered. He was right. None of this was going to go away. She thought of her deadline of forty-eight hours, and the money that wasn't there. She thought of her father waiting to meet her by the sinister prison walls.

Damn him, anyway. Why hadn't he told her where the money was? Some anonymous foreign bank, that was all she knew. Not that knowing which bank would do any good. What did she think she was going to do, hack into a secret bank account in the Bahamas? Harry closed her eyes and shook her head. Even she couldn't hope to pull off a stunt like that.

Her eyes flared open again.

Could she?

CHAPTER 37

'How's Copenhagen?'

'Cold,' Dillon said.

Harry smiled into the phone. 'That's what you get for wanting to conquer Scandinavia.' He laughed. 'Where are you?'

She shot a quick look at the long grey fortress that ran the length of Arbour Hill, its gloomy façade caged in by silver railings that glinted in the sun.

'In the car,' she said.

That much was true, at least. She had just pulled up outside the prison when Dillon had phoned. She stared across at the narrow windows set into the main entrance block. They were tall and arched, with dozens of small square panes. They could have been cathedral windows if it hadn't been for the iron bars.

She averted her gaze. Dillon would tell her to go to the police, but she couldn't do it. Whatever her father's failings, she couldn't risk sending him back behind those walls.

'I'll be finished here in a couple of days,' Dillon said. 'Maybe you could stock up that Sunday-night cupboard of yours, and we could have a night in.'

Harry rolled her eyes, mortified that he'd remembered her jumbled kitchen drawer.

'Sounds great,' she said. 'Throw in a pack of genuine Danish beer and it's a date.'

Date! Why had she said date? Deal, that's a deal, that would have worked. Harry leaned back against the headrest and closed her eyes. She wanted to ask him about the night they'd spent together, about what it had meant to him, but it was difficult to work into casual conversation. She shook her head. It occurred to her that staying celibate had its advantages.

'So how was the flight?' Harry winced. Next she'd be asking him about the weather.

'Uneventful. Except I think I was followed to the airport.'

'What?' She sat bolt upright.

'Beefy guy in a dark jacket, head like a cue ball.'

Quinney. 'Sounds like Leon's friend.'

'That's what I thought. But as far as I could tell, he didn't board the plane with me.'

'Shit. I'm sorry you got dragged into all this.'

'I told you, don't worry about me. Anyway, what's he going to do? Dig into my past and find what? There's nothing there that'll help him get to you. He'll go back to Leon empty-handed.'

'I hope so.'

'Forget about it. I have.'

Harry bit her lip, aware she was still holding out on him. Old habits didn't change overnight. She took a deep breath.

'I went to see my father this morning.'

'Wow.' There was a pause. 'Well, I'm glad. How did it go?'

'Not well. He wouldn't help. Maybe we can talk when you get back.'

'Yeah, I'd like that.' Another pause. 'Look, I'm going to shower and freshen up, but I'll call you again later. If that's okay?'

Harry found herself picturing him in the shower, and smiled. 'Yeah, that's okay. Don't forget the Danish beer.'

When Dillon rang off, she took a reading from her internal gauges. Neediness zero, lust one hundred. Better.

She checked the time: 1.45 p.m. Her father should be out soon. The sun blazed through the windscreen, heating the car upholstery to scorching point. The earlier rain clouds had purged themselves and moved on, leaving clear blue sky in their wake. Harry cranked her window open, and glanced up and down the street. Arbour Hill was a lonely stretch of road with little traffic. She had parked opposite the main prison gates, her car tucked in against the stone walls of the old Collins Military Barracks. Blind bends truncated the road in either direction, increasing the sense of isolation.

A woman in a red tracksuit rounded the bend ahead of Harry, pushing a buggy up the hill. The toddler inside was holding out a stick that plink-plinked along the prison railings.

302

Harry dragged her gaze back to the austere Victorian building that dominated the hill. The porch entrance was secured by an iron gate, like a portcullis in a castle. The prison walls seemed higher than ever, crowned here and there with tangles of thick barbed wire, vicious and thorny-looking. She thought of the collection of evil behind those walls, of the sort of half-life that was lived there, and shuddered.

Here there be dragons, she thought.

The woman with the buggy trudged past, the toddler pausing in his stick-work long enough to point at the yellow rose bushes that grew near the prison entrance. The woman pushed on, and Harry watched them disappear in her rear-view mirror.

Suddenly there was a loud clink and she whipped her gaze back to the prison. A guard stood inside the porch, unlocking the gate. He pushed it open and it swung wide, groaning like a flat violin chord. The guard stood aside, and Harry's father stepped into the sunshine.

He was wearing a navy blazer over a white crew-neck jumper and grey trousers. In one hand, he carried a blue holdall. The other he used to shield his eyes as he craned his head and looked up at the sky. Then he turned with a smile and shook the guard's hand. He could have been a naval officer about to enjoy a spot of shore leave.

He strode out along the path, the gate grinding to a close behind him. Harry watched him for a moment and wondered which persona he'd present today. White-collar criminal or successful banker? Childhood hero or failed parent? It seemed to Harry that every time she met her father, she had to reevaluate him.

She took a deep breath and got out of the car. The air was cool on her bare arms and face after the greenhouse effect of the Micra. Her father looked up at the sound of her slamming door. He gave her a hearty wave and a broad smile, all in keeping with the jolly sailor image. In spite of her misgivings, Harry found herself smiling back.

She stepped into the road, watching him as he hurried towards her. In the sunlight his face seemed bleached of colour, the black eyebrows looking artificial against his ashen skin. He moved past the yellow rose bushes, the holdall banging against the side of his leg.

Maybe everything would be okay. Maybe her father had a plan to help her. And if he didn't, she could handle it. All she needed was the name of his bank. Her social-engineering skills would take care of the rest.

Her father switched the holdall to his other hand, rattled opened the gate in the railings and stepped out into the road. Then he frowned and squinted to his left. Harry saw his eyes widen in alarm, and she followed his gaze.

The first thing she saw was the set of chrome bull-bars, wide and angry-looking. The Jeep they belonged to was thundering towards her father.

She tried to move, but her legs felt anaesthetized. She could see her father mouthing her name, but there was no sound.

Time seemed to dilate. One second felt like five. She was aware of everything all at once: the sunlight flashing off the gleaming bull-bars; her father's pale face, criss-crossed with lines; the heat radiating from the Micra behind her; the browning edges on the yellow rose petals.

Her father flung himself across the road, trying to scramble out of the Jeep's path. He slammed into her as he fell, and she crashed back against the car. Hot metal burned her flesh, and a sharp pain stabbed through her shoulder blades. Her hearing cut back in, the roar of the Jeep assaulting her eardrums. There was a loud whump, and her father sailed up into the air. Harry heard herself scream.

'Papá!'

He landed with a sickening crack on the ground a few feet away from her. The Jeep stormed off, engine screaming, tyres scuffing against the dry road. It whirled on two wheels around the bend ahead and disappeared from view.

Harry pushed herself away from the car, her arms and legs trembling. She stumbled over to her father. A heavy clot of dread sank low into her gut. He was lying motionless on his back. His eyes were closed, his skin chalky. A thread of scarlet trickled from the corner of his mouth down through the silver beard.

Today I'll show you what happens to people who let me down.

She heard the screech of a gate, the smack of running footsteps. She knelt beside her father and touched his cheek. In spite of the sun, his skin felt cold.

CHAPTER 38

Harry looked around at her family and tried to remember the last time they'd all been in the same room together. She couldn't.

Her mother sat across from her, bony hands clasped like claws across her Gucci handbag. Next to her sat Amaranta, knuckles pressed into her lips until her mouth had all but disappeared.

Her father's ventilator machine shushed and hissed into the silence, pumping air into his lungs. Harry watched the steady rise and fall of his chest, the only sign that he was still alive. The skin on his arms sagged from the bones, with bruises the colour of aubergines where they'd tried to find a vein.

Extensive internal injuries, the doctors had said. Ruptured spleen, punctured lungs, damage to the liver and kidneys. They had operated on him immediately and closed off the bleeding as much as they could. They wouldn't say whether he was going to live or die.

Harry took a deep breath. Her eyes were smarting, and the tissue in her hand had nearly disintegrated. Her feet nudged against her father's blue holdall stowed under the bed, and she shifted in her chair.

Amaranta turned red-rimmed eyes her way. 'Have you finished with the police?'

'They left about an hour ago,' Harry said. 'They're treating it as a hit and run.'

The police had questioned her for almost two hours. Lynne had watched from the sidelines again, silent but intent. She'd told them everything. Everything except the twelve million euros, that is. She looked at the narrow tubes that sprouted out of her father's flesh, trailing like worms to the bank of monitors beside the bed. Maybe she shouldn't have kept anything back. After all, what could they possibly do to him now?

She hadn't told her family anything. They assumed her cuts and bruises had happened today, and she didn't bother correcting them. There was no point. Even the police had seemed doubtful about her story, and gave her no reason to believe the cavalry was coming. They knew even less than she did.

'You should have let me talk to them,' Amaranta said.

'That wasn't my call. They didn't want to talk to you because you weren't there when it happened.'

'Well, I should have been there. He should have been coming to stay with me.' She glared at Harry. 'I offered him a room for as long as he liked. Where else was he going to stay?'

Harry shrugged. 'I told you, I don't know.'

The ventilator whooshed and sucked, and the heart monitor blipped with each passing second.

'He was coming to stay with me.' Miriam's voice was thick and low, as though someone had coated her larynx in treacle.

Harry raised her eyebrows. It was the first thing her mother had said for over an hour.

Miriam shot them a look. 'Why not? I've been on my own in that place long enough. I said he could stay for one night. Just to set him on his feet.'

Her gaze came to rest on Harry. Her eyes were watery and unfocused. Vertical lines puckered her upper lip, as though her mouth was permanently pursed on a cigarette. She sniffed and looked away again.

'I didn't know he'd made other plans,' she said.

Harry threw a can-you-believe-it look at the ceiling and got to her feet. 'I need a break. I'll be right outside.'

She stepped into the corridor and closed the door behind her. She leaned against it for a moment, breathing in the smell of sick people and canteen food.

'How is he?'

Harry spun round. It was Jude. Instinctively, she backed up against the door, as though to bar him entry.

He held up his hands. 'I'm not here for another fight. I just came to see how he is.' He paused. 'How you are.'

Harry stared at him, trying to gauge his intentions. He was back in his banker's suit, neat and pressed, although his hair stood on end where he must have ruffled his hand through it.

'How did you know he was here?' she said.

'Ashford told me. Don't ask me how he knew.' He shoved his hands deep into his pockets and glanced along the corridor. 'Hospitals and prisons. Can't stand either of them.'

'Me neither.'

He stared at his shoes. 'I should have gone to see him. In prison, I mean.'

'Why should you?' she said. 'The rest of us didn't.'

'Because I was supposed to be his friend.'

Harry took in the hunched shoulders and the hangdog look on his face. Right now it seemed absurd to think he might have meant her harm.

For a few minutes, neither of them spoke. Then, without looking up, Jude said, 'Do you think he's going to make it?'

Harry felt the question like a punch in the stomach. She shook her head and swallowed, unable to speak. Her father wouldn't die. He was supposed to go on forever. She closed her eyes. A freeze-frame of the oncoming Jeep flashed into her head: metallic black, aluminium bull-bars. Another freeze-frame, this one a close-up: the driver in a dark hat, tufts of white hair, his shoulders crouched over the wheel as he mowed her father down. She snapped her eyes open, and bit her lip. *Don't cry, don't cry, don't cry.* It was a few seconds before she could trust herself to speak.

'The doctors haven't given up on him, and neither will I,' she said eventually. 'I'd better get back.'

Jude nodded, then touched her lightly on the arm. 'I know you can look after yourself, but I'll help if you want me to.'

Before she could answer, he turned and walked away, hands back in his pockets. She watched him for a moment, chewing her lip. Then she stepped back into her father's room.

Her mother and Amaranta hadn't moved. They sat side by side, and Harry was struck by their likeness to one another, which seemed to increase with age. The same fair colouring, the same sharp bone structure, the same waspish expression. They looked up as she moved into the room. Mother and daughter presenting a united front. Reluctant to resume her seat opposite them, Harry stood at the end of the bed.

Amaranta slid the strap of her bag over her shoulder and stood up.

'Come on, Mum, I'm taking you home. You're exhausted.' She waited for her mother to move. 'You've been here for hours. We'll come back in the morning. The nurses will contact us if there's any change.'

'You go on back to your family.' Miriam tightened her grip on her handbag. 'Harry can take me home.'

311

Harry blinked, and caught a glimpse of her sister, who for the moment had forgotten to close her mouth.

Amaranta frowned. 'Now listen, Mum –'

'I want to talk to Harry.'

Harry's eyebrows shot up.

'Well, if you're sure.' Amaranta lingered for a moment, as if she expected her mother to change her mind. Then she spun on her heel and swept past Harry, drilling her with a look.

'Don't let her stay too long.'

Harry shook her head and stared after her until the door snapped shut. Then she looked back at her mother. Miriam was watching the rise and fall of her husband's chest. She fiddled with a strand of pearls at her throat. The muscle cords on her neck stood out like tree roots, and the skin that hung around them was loose and crinkled. In spite of what she'd told Amaranta, she seemed in no mood to talk, and Harry decided to wait her out.

She studied her father's face. His complexion was waxy. His bed was raised at an angle, as though at any moment he might open his eyes and want a good view of the room. Harry would have given anything to see him to open his eyes now.

'He was so glamorous when I first met him,' Miriam said suddenly. 'So dark and handsome. And so ambitious. Plans for this, ideas for that . . .' Her fingers worried at the pearls as though they were rosary beads. 'But there was nothing glamorous about being penniless. Not with two children.'

She left the pearls alone and snapped opened her handbag, digging out a gold lighter and a packet of cigarettes. Then she seemed to remember where she was, and shoved them back into the bag. Her fingers reached for the pearls again.

'Most of the time, I never knew where he was or whether he was even coming back. And when he did turn up, it could be to tell us we were homeless or to take us out to dinner. There was never any way of knowing.'

Harry wanted to ask about Ashford, but couldn't. It was one thing to know that your mother resented you, but quite another to hear her say it out loud.

'I tried to leave him once or twice,' her mother said, unconsciously broaching the subject for her. 'But it didn't work out. And Salvador always had another marvellous plan, another new deal that meant everything would be different the next time.'

She sighed and shook her head. Then she gave Harry a long look. 'You're so like him. I used to wish you weren't.'

Harry looked away. She smoothed out her powdery tissue and began folding it over on itself. It was hard to know who had disappointed Miriam most: her husband or her daughter.

'You were so close to him when you were

younger,' Miriam went on. 'Just you and him against the world. Against me.'

Harry frowned. 'It wasn't like that.'

Miriam continued as though she hadn't heard. 'He called me last week, you know. Some wild scheme. Said he was leaving for the Bahamas, starting a new life.'

Something twisted in Harry's chest. She flattened the tissue into a tight wad.

'Said he wanted to say goodbye.' Miriam frowned. 'Sal never used to say goodbye.'

Harry buried the tissue in her fist. So her father had planned to disappear again, leaving everyone else to deal with the aftermath.

'I just wondered,' Miriam said, fixing her gaze on Harry, 'was he up to something again? Was he in more trouble with the police? He used to talk to you. Did he say anything?'

Harry looked away. There was no reason not to tell her mother everything. She was entitled to know what was going on. She stared at her father's helpless body, his arms as thin as a child's. For reasons she couldn't explain, she shook her head.

'He never told me anything,' she said.

There was a gentle tap on the door, and it clicked open. Straight away she recognized the peaks of grey hair and mournful eyes: Ashford.

He stepped into the room and made straight for her mother, holding out his hands to her.

'Miriam, my dear, I'm so sorry. I came as soon as I could.'

Her mother stopped fiddling with her pearls and allowed him to grasp her hands. She looked up into his face, and the cords in her neck seemed to relax.

Ashford turned to Harry and took her hand, covering it with both of his.

'Harry, I'm so sorry.'

Miriam frowned. 'You know each other?'

'Yes, we've met.' He inclined his large head to one side and squeezed Harry's hand, his eyes full of sympathy.

Harry acknowledged him with a nod of her head, but it took effort not to pull away. His presence felt like an intrusion, an unwelcome overlap of the outside world into her private grief.

Ashford released his grip and moved around the bed until he stood by her father's shoulder. He touched the ashen forehead with the back of his fingers.

'My old friend,' he said, almost to himself. He stared down at him for a moment, as if in silent prayer. Then he turned to Harry. 'How bad is it?'

Harry shook her head. 'They won't commit themselves.'

He looked over at her mother. 'Miriam, you look worn out. How long have you been here?'

She sighed. 'Everyone keeps telling me to go home. I'm fine.'

'Well, I'm going to insist. I'll drive you there myself.'

He returned to Miriam's side, placing a hand

315

under her elbow to coax her to her feet. To Harry's surprise, she didn't resist. As he shepherded her mother gently towards the door, Harry had to swallow more than once to choke off the lump in her throat. It reminded her of the way Dillon had guided her back up the mountains, and suddenly the need to feel Dillon's arms around her was overwhelming.

Before he reached the door, Ashford turned back to Harry and handed her a business card.

'If you ever need any help, about anything at all, just call me,' he said. 'One of those numbers will always reach me.'

Harry raised her eyebrows and thanked him. Suddenly everyone wanted to help her. The door closed behind them, and for the first time she was alone in the room with her father.

She edged around the bed and sank back on to the chair she'd occupied before. Her body felt arthritic, a jarring reminder of the impact with her own car.

Her gaze came to rest on her father's face. White corrugated tubes snaked out of his mouth. Above them, his nostrils looked pinched and elongated. His hand lay on the bed and she wrapped her fingers around his.

She glanced at the card in her other hand. Blue logo, Klein, Webberly and Caulfield, Ralph Ashford, Chief Executive Officer.

Harry gaped. Ralph? Then she shook her head. It was only a name, for God's sake.

Ralphy-Boy.

Could Ashford be the fifth banker?

She remembered Ashford's visit to her office, and the silver Jag she'd seen behind her. Had he been following her after all? She thought of how Felix had laughed when they'd tried to scam him for a password using Ashford to pull rank. Had Felix known he was involved? Was he the Prophet?

Damn Ashford, and damn the Prophet, whoever he was. She had to find the money, but how? She didn't even know which bank her father had used. If only he could talk to her, help her.

She stared at the floor. The blue holdall was still at her feet and she nudged it with her shoe. Then she frowned. Her father's blue holdall. All his worldly possessions from Arbour Hill packed into a handy knapsack. The back of her neck began to tingle.

Maybe he could help her after all.

CHAPTER 39

Mathematicians love numbers. They love their symmetry and their structure, and the patterns that lie behind their subtle wizardry.

Harry knew her father was a natural mathematician. He could recite from memory the complexities of all his M&A deals and the discounting mathematics that went with them. He could also tell you the poker odds at any given moment against hitting a straight flush on the turn.

But no matter how good a head he had for numbers, even he wouldn't rely on memory to store details of an offshore bank account. Not when there was twelve million euros involved.

Harry stared at the blue holdall on the coffee table in front of her. He had to have made a record of his bank account somewhere. And everything he'd kept with him for the last six years was right here in this bag.

She pulled the holdall closer. It was the size of a large sports bag, with a double zip along the top and wide zipped pockets at either end. The bag was plump and heavy, the canvas stretched taut at the seams.

She hesitated, glancing over at the living-room window. The darkness had inked it into a black rectangle. She'd left the hospital over two hours ago, with assurances from the nurses that she'd be contacted if there was any change in her father's condition.

The living room seemed oddly quiet. Normally she found the silence soothing, but now her apartment felt empty. She was tempted to put a load of washing into the machine just to make some noise.

She turned her attention back to the bag, and tugged the top zips open. The first thing she saw were the clothes her father had been wearing when he left Arbour Hill that afternoon. Her chest contracted at the sight of them. The smart navy blazer and the white jumper had been rolled up and stuffed into the bag, presumably by one of the nurses. Gently, Harry lifted them out, smoothing their creases and folding them on the sofa beside her. Beneath those were more clothes, neatly pressed into compact stacks. One by one, she lifted everything out: shirts, ties, shoes, trousers, more jumpers.

At the bottom of the bag, she felt something hard. She lifted it out with both hands. It was a black attaché case. She set it on her lap and stroked the battered vinyl. It was scuffed and faded in places, but she would have known it anywhere.

It was the poker set she'd given her father for Christmas sixteen years before.

She squeezed the locks open and lifted the lid. Inside were eight columns of toy plastic chips: red, green, blue and white. They were slotted into grooves in the black felt lining, with spaces where some had gone missing. One of the decks of cards was gone as well, but the other lay snug in its carved-out slot.

The poker rule book was missing too, but in its place was a paperback which she immediately recognized. It was her father's own copy of *How to Play Poker and Win*. She opened it. Like hers, the inside covers were annotated with records of his poker games. She scanned the first few hands. He'd been playing Texas Hold 'Em. For each hand, he'd noted his hole cards and those of his opponents, along with the five community cards. He'd started well, with pocket aces in the first hand, but his luck hadn't held. In the second hand he'd been dealt a seven and a deuce, which was no match for his opponent's house of fives, and in the third hand his ace and two of diamonds were beaten by a weak pair of fours. Harry smiled and shook her head. By his own admission, her father was a loose player. He'd raise before he'd call, he'd bluff before he'd play straight. And above all, he'd rarely fold.

She riffled through the pages of the book, and then held it by its spine, shaking it. She didn't know what she was expecting, but nothing fell loose from its pages. She prised out a handful of chips from the case and rattled them in her hand. Then, stack by stack, she lifted them all out and piled them on to the coffee table, along with the book and the deck of cards. She pressed her fingers along the felt lining. Nothing. Sighing, she abandoned the case on to the floor and turned her attention to the holdall's side pockets.

The left pocket held a toothbrush, toothpaste, deodorant, a pair of scissors and a packet of tissues. The right pocket was more interesting. In it were her father's wallet, a set of keys, and a slim black notebook about the size of a cigarette packet. She flipped open the wallet. Inside were half a dozen credit and debit cards, all issued by Irish banks and most of them past their expiry date. There was no cash and no handy slip of paper with an offshore bank account number written on it.

Harry tossed the wallet on the table and picked up the set of keys. The key-ring was a black leather tag with the KWC logo embossed in blue and gold on both sides. There were only two keys attached to it. One was a Mercedes ignition key, belonging to the car he'd driven before he went to prison. Her mother had sold it long ago to help pay for his solicitor's fees. The other was a small silver Yale key. She looked at it and frowned. Then she strode back into the kitchen and hunted through her cutlery drawers until she found a set of keys. She selected a dull silver Yale out of the bunch and held it against her father's, lining up the valleys and notches along the blades. They were a match. It was the key to her old home in Sandymount, where her mother still lived.

Shoving the drawer back in place, she returned to the living room and flopped down on to the sofa. She picked up the black notebook and began flicking through it. It was an address book, with names and phone numbers jotted down in alphabetical order in her father's broad script. She frowned. There had to be something in here.

Starting with the letter A, she worked her way through the names. Most of them meant nothing to her, but occasionally she came across one she recognized. Amaranta was there, and under H she found her own name and mobile number. She couldn't remember giving it to her father, but Amaranta had probably passed it on.

Towards the end of the alphabet she hit a run of names that sent a buzz down her spine. Leon Ritch, Jonathan Spencer, Jude Tiernan. Harry stared at Jude's name. There was no reason why her father shouldn't have his number. They'd worked together, even been friends.

She flipped through the rest of the alphabet but there were no more entries after Jude's name. She slapped the notebook down on the table. Then she picked up the pack of cards and extracted the deck with her thumb and forefinger. They were ordinary playing cards, the design on the back a kaleidoscope of blue-and-white swirls. She fanned the cards out, examining each one front and back. They were sticky and well-thumbed, but otherwise unremarkable.

She drummed her nails on the table, chewing her bottom lip. Then she turned back to her father's clothing. She checked through the pockets of his trousers, felt inside his shoes and even pulled apart the balled-up socks. Nothing. Feeling like an intruder, she picked up his blazer and squeezed the lining. There was a faint crackle from the inside breast pocket. She thrust her hand in and pulled out a white envelope. It had her name on it. Inside, was a single sheet of white paper, headed with today's date.

It was a letter from her father. He must have written it after her visit to him earlier that day. Harry could feel her throat constrict as she began to read.

Mi queridísima Harry,

It was so good to see you today after such a long time. It made everything right again. You have no idea how proud of you I am. You have grown into such a fine, intelligent young woman. I am indebted to your mother for the strength she's shown in raising our family. I take no credit for any of it.

I know you came to me today for help, and I know I've failed you. But don't give up on me. I wouldn't hurt you for the world, and I will try not to let you down again.

But be careful of putting people up on pedestals, Harry. I love you dearly, but I am who I am. Don't judge me too harshly.
   Tu papá que te quiere

Harry brushed her thumb along his final words. *Your papa who loves you.* An image of his waxen form lying in the hospital flashed into her mind, and she swallowed hard. Then she folded the letter back into the envelope and considered his advice about pedestals. He was right. For most of her childhood, she had made him her hero, and the tumble to reality had been hard to take. She wondered was she in danger of making the same mistake with Dillon. Her teenage infatuation for him had never quite burned out, and now it was being rekindled into something else. Into love? She sighed and shoved the thought aside.

She stared at the contents of the holdall spread out in front of her.

Come on, Dad, she thought. Help me out here.

She tapped her fingernails against the address book. Names and numbers. She thought about how her father had managed his account. He'd faxed his trading instructions directly to the bank using an agreed codename. Cash withdrawals or transfers had to be done in person, with a fax notifying the bank in advance.

Was the codename masquerading as an entry in the address book, with the account number disguised as a bogus phone number? It seemed a long shot, but it was worth a try.

Using her landline, which withheld her caller id, Harry spent the next hour dialling every number in the address book. For those that were answered, she asked for the listed person by name and promptly disconnected when someone came on the line. She felt sheepish about it at first, but after the twelfth call she'd become immune. She reckoned this was how telesales people survived. After so many calls, it was easy to forget the voice on the other end was a human being.

She crossed off the numbers as she made the calls. Some were picked up by voicemail and others just rang out. She even called the numbers listed for Leon and Jonathan Spencer, both of which were diverted to answering machines. She hadn't the nerve to call Jude, and instead just checked the number against his business card. It was the same. She continued until she reached the end of the address book, but all of the numbers checked out. None of them had generated those off-tone beeps that would tell her the number didn't exist.

Harry sank back against the sofa and sighed. It wasn't conclusive. There was nothing to say the account number couldn't also be a valid phone number. But that would be a coincidence, and Harry didn't like coincidences.

She peered at the holdall in front of her and wondered if she was wasting her time. Maybe her father hadn't kept the information with him at all. It could be anywhere. Idly, she picked up the deck of cards and began dealing poker hands. The cards felt greasy from overuse, the edges ragged. She thought of her father's front-door key to the house in Sandymount, and of his plans to stay there his first night out of prison. Maybe he'd stored whatever he needed back at the house. She dealt the three flop cards and caught a ten to pair with her hole card. She shook her head. Her mother had sent her father's belongings to St Vincent de Paul the day after he was sent to prison. All traces of him had been wiped clean out of the house. She flipped over a nine on the turn and a ten on the river, giving herself three-of-a-kind, and then gathered up the cards to deal again. She decided to stick with the holdall. At this point, it was all she had.

She thought again about the trading instructions her father faxed to his bank, and wondered what the dialling code for the Bahamas was. She set down the deck of cards and went out to the hall, where she leafed through the phone book until she found it. The direct dial code for the Bahamas was 1-242.

Harry frowned. The numbers seemed familiar. She returned to the living room and flipped through the address book again, scanning the entries for the combination 1242. But after a half-hour search, she'd come up with nothing.

She picked up the cards once more and began to deal, netting pocket jacks. The flop cards didn't improve her hand, and nor did the turn, but on the river she caught another jack. Trip jacks, a winning hand.

She thought about her father's letter. Had there been anything in it, any hidden message? The notion seemed far-fetched. She scooped up the cards and dealt again, checking her hole cards. Seven of clubs, two of diamonds. Automatically, she folded and slid the other cards towards her. Even her father would have folded on a seven-two off-suit. It was the worst opening hand in Texas Hold 'Em, and the only one he'd never play.

Her hands froze in mid-shuffle. Seven-two off-suit. Her father never played it. She dropped the deck on the table and grabbed the poker book, scouring the notations on the inside cover. There it was. The second hand. 7c-2s. Seven of clubs, two of spades. Why would he play a hand like that? And why would he record it?

She examined the hand in more detail. His notations were always in the same format. His own two hole cards came first, and underneath them were his opponent's cards. In a line across from them were the five community cards. In this case, the other player had a pair of fives, noted in her father's shorthand as 5c-5d. The community cards gave his opponent a house of fives: 9d, 3c, 5s, 3h, Js.

Harry stared at the numbers. To anyone else, it was just another poker hand, but to her it was a hand she knew he'd never play. Did it have another meaning?

She found a pen and notepad and scribbled the numbers down. 7-2-5-5-9-3-5-3-J. Was it possible her father had camouflaged his bank account as a poker hand? How many digits did a Bahamian bank account number have, anyway? And what about the letter J? Did Bahamian bank accounts include letters?

She frowned, and glanced at the next poker hand in the list, where her father's ace and two of diamonds had been beaten by a pair of fours. Twos and fours. Her eyes widened and she jotted the numbers down below the first set, translating the ace as the number 1. There were three players in this hand, so there were more digits this time. 1-2 for her father's hole cards, 4-2 for the second player's, 5-1 for the third. And then the community cards: 3-8-4-6-9. She gazed at the digits in front of her. 1-2-4-2-5-1-3-8-4-6-9. The combination 1242 seemed to pulsate from the page. Was there any chance in the world she was looking at the fax number to her father's offshore bank?

There was only one way to find out. She dialled the double zero for international calls, and then followed it with the eleven digits on her pad. The line clicked as the numbers dialled out, and then shrieked in her ear. A modem.

She disconnected, her heartbeat racing. Now what? She may have dialled into a fax machine, but whose? She stared at the numbers for a moment and then dialled them again, this time replacing the final digit 9 with an 8. She was rewarded with a ringing tone, but the call wasn't picked up. She tried again, changing the last number to a 7. She checked her watch: 8.05 p.m. here, 3.05 p.m. in the Bahamas. Wherever the fax machine was, there had to be a phone extension somewhere in the same building that had a human being attached to it.

'Hello?'

Harry jumped. The voice was female and gave nothing away. This was the part Harry hadn't worked out yet. Her eyes fell on the notepad in front of her. She swallowed and adopted a businesslike tone.

'Hello, this is Central Stationery, we have a delivery here for your department but our file is incomplete. I wonder could you just confirm your full address for me?'

'Sure, no problem.' The woman's voice was slow and lilting. 'It's Investment Services, Rosenstock Bank and Trust, 322 Bay Street, Nassau.'

Harry's mouth went dry. 'That's great, thanks. And could I just double-check this fax number I have? It's 5138469. Is that the right one for the accounts department? I need to send an invoice.'

'Let me just check that.' The woman took her time. When she came back on the line, she sounded puzzled. 'No, that's a personal fax line to Owen Johnson, one of our Relationship Managers.'

Harry frowned. The name sounded familiar.

The woman went on. 'Let me just give you the right fax for accounts. It's 5138773.'

Harry thanked her and hung up. Then she stared at the name she'd written down. Owen Johnson. She shook her head. That wasn't the name of the poker-playing banker who'd managed her father's money. That was Philippe Rousseau. She frowned. Wait, hadn't he been promoted? *They put some faceless account manager in his place. Owen, or John or something.*

Owen Johnson. She drew a circle around the name, and a charge rippled down her back. She'd found a line to her father's account manager.

She tapped her pen against her teeth for a moment. Then she stepped into the small room she used as her office and powered up her laptop. Time to do a little reconnaissance on Rosenstock Bank and Trust.

CHAPTER 40

Before a burglar broke into a building, first he'd take a look at the security arrangements. How many exits were there, how many guards, where were the surveillance cameras? The same applied to a smart hacker. Before Harry broke into a system, first she'd check out the target company's security profile. What was the domain name, what were the IP addresses, what kind of Intrusion Detection System did they use?

Burglars called it casing the joint. Hackers called it footprinting an organization. Either way, such reconnaissance was essential. But it was also time-consuming, and Harry knew she'd have to take a few shortcuts.

She arched her back against her office chair, her spine snapping like dry twigs. The stiffness in her neck and shoulders was easing off, but she still felt as rickety as an old deckchair.

Leaning back over her keyboard, she typed 'rosenstockbankandtrust.com' into her browser and pulled up the bank's corporate website. She looked at the digits she'd scribbled on the pad beside her: 72559353J. Intuition told her that this was her father's account number, but she was still only guessing. She needed to know for sure.

She browsed through the web pages that gave details of the bank's organization. Rosenstock had branches all over the Caribbean: Barbados, Jamaica, Saint Lucia, the Cayman Islands, and several branches in the Bahamas. Goose-bumps sprouted along Harry's arms as she saw the branch address she'd just acquired over the phone: 322 Bay Street, Nassau, New Providence Island, Bahamas.

She continued to browse, taking notes as she went. As always, she marvelled at the amount of information corporations were prepared to divulge on their websites: organizational structure, addresses, phone numbers, fax numbers, emails, location maps, customer support numbers; all of it potential artillery for a hacker's assault.

Posted under the Careers section was an advert recruiting new helpdesk personnel for the bank, along with the email address of the Human Resources Manager. Harry read how candidates should be computer literate and friendly, with good communication skills and a willingness to help. She raised her eyebrows and thought of Sandra Nagle. Standards were obviously lower in Sheridan Bank.

She stared at the email address. It couldn't hurt to try. She composed a short email applying for the position of helpdesk operative. Next she dug up the RAT she had used to break into the KWC network. Disguising it as an innocent Word document entitled 'Resumé', she attached it to the email and hit Send. All she needed was for the HR Manager to launch the attachment. As soon as the RAT was released, it would unlock a back door in the Rosenstock network and Harry could slip inside. Unless, of course, the RAT got picked up by the bank's antivirus scanners. If the scanners were up to date enough, then that was always a possibility.

While she was at it, she figured she may as well hit the bank with a war-dialling onslaught. She noted the listed phone numbers for the Nassau branch. As with the fax and phone numbers she already had, the numbers all began with 51384, with the last two digits changing for different phone extensions. With a few deft keystrokes, Harry instructed her war-dialler to call all phone extensions from 5138400 to 5138499 until it found another modem. If the modem belonged to a computer on the Rosenstock network, then she was in.

Harry drummed her fingers on the desk. One way or another, she needed to penetrate the bank's defences and locate her father's numbered account. She didn't fool herself she'd have access to the money. Sure, she could change some numbers in a few databases, but it wouldn't move any real money around. It would be an illusion, just like the twelve million euros in her account.

Moving money online was harder than people thought.

Harry stood up and went into the kitchen to pour herself a glass of wine. As she carried it back to the office, she thought about the security of her father's account. According to him, any cash withdrawals or transfers out of the account had to be done in person, with prior notification by coded fax.

So in order to get her hands on the money, she'd need to impersonate her father and crack his codename, all in the space of two days. At this point, she didn't much like her chances.

Sighing, she sat down at her laptop and stared at the numbers on the pad. The first thing to do was to verify whether this was even her father's account. She flexed her fingers and began to type. Even if she located the bank account, she didn't expect to find her father's name attached to it. According to her information from Jude, the identities of numbered account owners were held in a file somewhere in the bank archives, and never recorded in the online systems. But as long as she could verify that this account number existed, then in her mind that would settle it.

She checked on the RAT and the war-dialling program. Neither had returned anything. She broadened the war-dialling range just in case, but she knew she couldn't afford to wait. She needed to track down the Rosenstock network and find another way inside.

Abandoning the website, she launched a query to search the public registrar databases for the domain name 'rosenstockbankandtrust.com'. Harry knew that when an organization registered its domain name on the internet, it also recorded a wealth of additional information that was invaluable to the hacker: technical employee names, phone numbers, emails, fax numbers, and most importantly, the organization's network servers and IP addresses. A computer's IP address was like its street address on the internet. It told you exactly where it was and how to find it.

Harry's search spat the data on to the screen. Her pulse raced as she copied down the numbers for the Rosenstock computers. Now that she knew where the bank's network lived, all she had to do was to sneak up to the doors and jimmy the locks.

First, though, she needed to see if anyone was at home. There was always the chance that the registered information was out of date, and that the IP addresses were no longer active. She launched a ping sweeper, a program that transmitted data packets to the target computers to check if they were alive. The Rosenstock network responded in kind. Bingo.

Next, she needed to know what software the computers were running. The thing Harry loved most about software was that it was written by human beings. And, as every hacker knew, the one thing you could rely on about human beings was that they made mistakes. Lots of them.

Hackers depended on it. No matter how smart a programmer was, he was going to leave some holes in the software. These holes, known as vulnerabilities, were widely documented in the hacker underworld. They were what the black hats used to break inside.

Harry worked the keyboard, riddling the Rosenstock computers with bogus connection attempts, trying to trick the software into identifying itself. With luck, it would be software for which there was a known vulnerability that she could use to gain access. She focused on the data scrolling up the screen in front of her, in tune with it down to her fingertips like a safecracker with her ear to the dial. In less than a minute, the software on one of the Rosenstock machines spewed back a chatty error message:

'Bad request. Server: Apache 2.0.38. Your browser sent a non-HTTP compliant message.'

She nodded, and sat back. Apache web server software was very popular, but older versions had a few well-known security holes. She tapped her nails on the desk, assessing the weapons at her disposal. Then she packaged up another command and fired it like an arrow at the Apache server. The security hole she was targeting allowed her to stuff unchecked amounts of data into Apache's storage buffers, overflowing its memory. By itself, that didn't help her much. But if the overflow data happened to contain a piece of code, then the Apache software could be tricked into executing it. And bundled into Harry's data packet was a neat chunk of code that, if launched, would give her command access to the system.

Her arrow hit the bulls-eye. In seconds, a window had popped up on to her screen, the system prompt patiently awaiting her instructions. She was in, free to roam the Rosenstock computers as if she was sitting in the Bahamas in front of them.

Harry shuddered. She felt an inexplicable urge to look over her shoulder and check that she wasn't being watched. Ignoring it, she returned to her keyboard and stole her way around the Rosenstock computer, stashing her burglar's tools as she went. Among them was a sniffer program that eaves-dropped on the network traffic flowing in and out of the machine. Within ten minutes, she'd sniffed the administrator's password off the wire and had escalated her privileges on the system. She owned the network.

Harry frowned. Instead of the usual rush of exhilaration, all she felt was a trickle of unease. As a hacker, she'd learned to trust her instincts as much as the technology, and if something didn't feel right there was usually a reason why. For now, she shook the feeling off and moved on. She was running out of time.

Using her privileged status, she tunnelled through to the rest of the Rosenstock network, drilling through any files that she passed along the way. Her eyes were trained to pick up on interesting data and there was plenty of it. Archives, log files, databases, spreadsheets, emails, confidential documents. She ploughed through it all, frowning as the responses to her commands became increasingly sluggish. Normally she could flit from file to file like a butterfly playing hopscotch, but this was more like wading through molasses. Some of her commands were rejected completely, or limited in a way she hadn't encountered before. Some of her hacking tools began to malfunction, slowing her down even more. Something wriggled at the base of her brain, but she couldn't catch hold of it.

Just as she was thinking about cutting out, she unearthed the database she'd been looking for. It was a treasure trove of banking information: account numbers, transaction histories, balance records, overdraft limits. She studied the account numbers. They were of varying lengths, but mostly they were eight digits long. None of them used any letters in their format. She launched a search for account number 72559353, both with and without the letter J, but came up with nothing.

She fiddled with the stem of her wineglass and stared at the reams of data on the screen. A strange sensation of unreality floated over her, making her feel almost light-headed. It reminded her of when she'd first seen the twelve million euros in her bank account. Optical illusions. Was she back to that? She shook her head. She felt disoriented, as though someone was playing an elaborate game of hide and seek with her, luring her like a fly following a trail of honey.

Harry's eyes flared. Shit, that was it. How had she missed it? She jerked her hand away from her glass, sending it crashing to the floor. Whipping the network cable out of her laptop, she jumped away from the desk as though the dripping wine had scalded her.

Tricked by a honeypot. What the hell was wrong with her? Any rookie hacker could have spotted it. Had her brain been so dislodged by the punches she'd taken lately that she couldn't see what was going on?

Her pulse felt as though it had flipped from sixty to one eighty in a single heartbeat. Taking deep breaths to slow it down, she dropped back on to her chair and shook her head, half-embarrassed now at her melodramatic reaction. After all, it was a honeypot, not a nuclear bomb.

A honeypot was a decoy computer, and she'd walked right into it. It was designed to lure hackers away from the real system into a fake environment where their every keystroke was recorded. People used them to protect their systems. They also used them to study how hackers operated, and to capture any new tools or zero-day exploits the hacker brought along. If a honeypot was designed well enough, a black hat would be fooled into thinking he'd accessed a server full of juicy passwords and data files, and never know he was being tracked.

Harry sighed. Rosenstock must have set up a 'Bait and Switch' honeypot. The real system was the bait, and as soon as she had intruded on it she'd been switched to a fake server. Her buffer overflow exploit must have sounded the alarm. From that point onwards, she'd been wandering through a phantom network, under surveillance the whole time.

Shit. Harry's toes and fingers curled. She'd left her tool bag of hacker tricks behind, a windfall for her pursuers.

They'd obviously set their own packet sniffer on to her and monitored her every move. She guessed that the sniffer had been badly configured and had added too much overhead to the system response times. No wonder things had seemed slow. And now she understood why some of her tools suddenly stopped working. A honeypot had to mimic a real system as far as possible, but it couldn't give a hacker complete freedom. Otherwise the hacker might springboard from it across to other networks.

Damn, maybe she shouldn't have disconnected so quickly. Maybe she could have exploited the honeypot to somehow bounce back to the real network. She shook her head. Too late now. There was no way back. She hadn't had time to wedge open any back doors. In any case, they had her IP address now and would block any further connection attempts from her. They'd collected enough forensic evidence to be used in a prosecution against her, if that was what they wanted to do.

Harry sighed, and began to power down her laptop. It probably didn't matter anyway. She suspected that the honeypot had been well-sealed with no way out. Honeypots weren't all that common in commercial networks, and she took it as a sign that Rosenstock was serious about its security.

She also took it as a given that her RAT would net her nothing. By now, the anti-virus scanners would have captured it and flung it into quarantine. Likewise, her war-dialling was a waste of time. An organization as security-conscious as Rosenstock wasn't going to leave unprotected modems lying around on its network.

Harry could feel her pulse ramping up again as she acknowledged something that perhaps she'd known all along. She glanced down at the address scribbled on her pad: 322 Bay Street, Nassau, New Providence Island, Bahamas.

She knew she wasn't going to get hold of her father's money by sitting at her desk with a laptop. She'd known what she needed to do for some time. She needed to go inside the bank.

CHAPTER 41

Harry paced around her apartment until the first half of a plan had taken shape in her head. The second half she'd have to worry about later on, but right now she had a call to make.

She checked her watch again: 9.15 p.m. here made it 4.15 p.m. in the Bahamas. She picked up her phone and dialled.

'Good afternoon, Rosenstock Bank and Trust.'

Harry grabbed a pen and paper. 'Hello, could I talk to someone about opening an account please?'

'Hold on while I transfer you.'

Harry resumed her pacing as she waited to be connected. For once, she wished the apartment was bigger, just so that she could get a good stride going.

'Hello, New Accounts, Hester speaking, how may I help you?' The woman's voice was low and unhurried.

'Hi, Hester, I'd like to open an investment account, please.'

'Certainly, madam. May I ask if you're resident here in the Bahamas?'

'No, but I plan on travelling over in the next few days. I assume I need to do this in person?'

'Yes, you'll need to meet with one of our Relationship Managers here in Nassau. They'll take you through all the paperwork and legal requirements.' Her easy Caribbean lilt made the notion of banking legalities seem almost restful.

'That's fine,' Harry said. 'Could I set something up for tomorrow afternoon?'

'I'm sure that won't be a problem. I'll just run through a few details with you first, if I may?'

'Please do.' Harry could feel the woman's good manners rubbing off on her, and wondered was she always this polite. In Harry's experience, people who dealt with the public usually behaved as though their bunions were acting up. Maybe it helped to know your customers were mostly millionaires.

'May I ask if you have a personal reference from anyone connected with the bank?'

Harry's pacing faltered for a second. 'Is that necessary?'

'It's not mandatory, no, but it can speed things up.'

Harry started to say no, but then remembered her father's first account manager, Philippe Rousseau. She wasn't ready to play that card just yet, but she would if she had to.

'Well, I do have a referee, as a matter of fact,' she said, crossing her fingers. 'Do you need that information now?'

'No, that's not necessary. You can discuss that with your Relationship Manager when you come in. Now, the bank has a minimum deposit policy on investment accounts, depending on what country you're resident in. For Canada, Europe, Asia-Pacific and Australasia, the minimum deposit is $30,000.'

Harry swallowed. Her savings were going to take a hit.

'If you live in the US it's $100,000,' Hester continued. 'And for all other countries it's $150,000.'

'Why such a difference?'

'Well, we need to verify your background, and some countries are just trickier to deal with than others.' Her soft tone became apologetic. 'I'm afraid we don't accept investments from customers in Colombia or Nigeria.'

'That won't be a problem.'

'You'll also need to bring some personal iden-tification with you, and this is very important.'

'Right, let me just make a note of this.' Harry flipped open a fresh page on her notepad. 'Okay, go ahead.'

'You'll need your original, valid passport. A copy isn't sufficient, I'm afraid, and nor is a driver's licence. And you'll need two recent utility bills to validate your legal address.'

Harry raised her eyebrows. How odd to be opening up a secret bank account with something as mundane as a utility bill. She might have been joining a video library. She made a note to herself to pack every scrap of personal documentation she could lay her hands on: driver's licence, payslips, bank statements, credit cards, tax statements from the Revenue Commissioner. If she needed to prove her identity, she wanted to be sure there were no doubts.

'You'll also need any documents necessary to establish your economic background,' Hester said.

Harry blinked. 'You mean, I need to prove where my money comes from?'

'Exactly. I'm afraid we need that to comply with anti-money-laundering laws. So, depending on the source of your funds, you'll need to provide us with, say, a copy of your employment contract and salary, or a bill of sale, or probate certification of an inheritance and so on. Naturally, all information is protected by bank secrecy laws and will remain strictly confidential.'

'Naturally.'

'If that's all in order, madam, would you like me to go ahead and set up an appointment for you?'

'Yes, please, that'd be great.'

Hester booked her in for 3.15 p.m. the following day to meet with Glen Hamilton, one of the bank's senior account managers. Harry thanked Hester for her help and hung up, belatedly realizing that the woman hadn't taken her name. But then, that was probably all part of the secrecy deal.

Harry hunted down her passport in her kitchen drawer. It was dog-eared and nearly out of date.

Then she powered up her laptop and booked a flight with Canada Airlines, departing early the next morning and arriving in Nassau at 1 p.m. local time. She knew she was cutting it fine for her appointment with the bank, but she was running out of time. The egg-timer had turned on her forty-eight hours.

Next, she logged into her online bank and transferred all her savings into her current account. She'd withdraw it at the airport. In dollars, it amounted to over eighty thousand. It might not be enough for what she had in mind, but it was all she had. She tried not to think about the plans she'd had to buy her own apartment. Along with her beloved Mini, that part of her life seemed to be a write-off for the time being.

When she got to the airport, she'd buy a guidebook to the Bahamas, with detailed maps of Nassau. Her map-reading skills had been found wanting these last few days, and she intended to do her homework this time. The last thing she needed was another navigational blackout.

It occurred to her she should leave word with someone about where she was going and why. The notion that she might not make it back alive made her thought processes jam up, like a radio getting static interference. She shook her head to clear the white-noise effect, and wondered who she should call. She had no intention of explaining things to her family. The less they knew the better. And both Dillon and Imogen would just try to talk her out of it. She needed someone who wasn't emotionally involved.

She tapped her fingers against the desk for a moment, and then snatched up her phone and dialled.

'Woods.' The journalist was as abrupt as ever.

'Ruth, it's Harry Martinez. Are you still interested in a story about my father?'

There was a pause. Harry could hear the harsh sounds of traffic at the other end of the line.

'Do you have anything for me?' Ruth said.

'I'm getting close. Just a few more days. But in the meantime, there's been a lot going on. Do you want to hear it?'

'Wait.' Paper crackled in the background. 'Okay, go ahead.'

Harry told her everything that had happened in the last few days. Ruth remained silent throughout, and it wasn't until Harry told her what had happened to her father that the reporter finally cut in.

'Jesus. Will he be okay?'

'I don't know.'

'Shit.'

There was a pause as Ruth pulled hard on a cigarette. Then she said, 'What are you going to do now?'

'The Prophet wants the money, so I'm going to the Bahamas to get it.'

'And you're just going to hand it over to him?'

'I'm not sure I have any choice. But if I can find out who he is, maybe I could expose him.'

'Or get yourself killed.'

There it was again, that buzzing white noise. Harry squeezed her eyes shut and tightened her grip on the phone.

'You could help,' Harry said eventually.

'Oh?'

'Find out about Ralph Ashford, the CEO of KWC. Where was he when the ring was in operation? Maybe he worked for JX Warner.'

'Good point. What about that other banker you mentioned – Jude Tiernan? He was in JX Warner, wasn't he?'

'Yeah, but that mightn't mean anything. He's been helping me, but that could be a front too. At this point, I don't trust anyone.'

'Let me put some pressure on Leon. He knows me. Doesn't like me, but that's because he's afraid of me. Sounds like he's in over his head here, so he might let something slide.'

'It's worth a try.'

'Right. I'll see what I can do.' Ruth hesitated. 'By the way, which hospital is Sal in?'

Harry raised her eyebrows. 'St Vincent's. Why?'

'Oh, no reason.'

Harry almost smiled. 'Visiting hours are from three to eight, if that's any help.'

'Oh. Right.'

Ruth hung up without saying goodbye. Harry dropped the phone on to the desk and hunched into a ball, bringing her feet up on to the chair. She nibbled at her lower lip.

It was always a mistake to articulate your plans. An idea that seemed ingenious when you first thought it up always sounded dumb when you said it out loud.

Harry's spine began to tingle, and it took effort not to back up against a wall. What the hell was she doing, heading off to an island thousands of miles away where she didn't even know her way around? At this stage, her plans were sketchy at best, and one vital ingredient was missing. She still didn't know the codename to her father's account.

CHAPTER 42

When Harry arrived on the island of New Providence, the first thing that struck her were the colours.

She rolled down the window of the taxi. To her right was a line of houses painted tangerine, saffron and cornflower blue. Purple bougainvillea tumbled like froth over the walls. To her left was the ocean, a strip of jade green with a lacy white hem. She felt like Dorothy, transported from the monochrome of Kansas into the brilliant Technicolor of Oz.

'First time in Nassau?'

The taxi driver tilted his head to look at her in the rearview mirror. He was young, maybe nineteen or twenty, with crisp tight curls that looked as though they might be waterproof. He'd told her his name was Ethan.

Harry managed a smile. 'Yes, first time.'

She'd been on the plane for over twelve hours, and her head was buzzing with tiredness. Even her blinking felt heavy and slow.

Ethan nodded. 'Only two reasons people come to the Bahamas –' his accent made it sound like

350

'da Bahamas' – 'business or romance.' He squinted at her in the mirror. His eyes were a surprisingly light shade of amber. 'Don't look to me like you're here for no romance.'

Harry shook her head. 'Strictly business.'

The heat from the vinyl upholstery was beginning to bake her thighs. The taxi wasn't air conditioned, unless you counted the open windows.

'Bahamas is not the place to do business, let me tell you,' Ethan said. He honked his horn at the stationary traffic in front of him. 'Everything here is slow, slow, slow.'

Harry gazed out at the hot pink blossoms and graceful palms. 'I thought that was the point.'

He shook his head and pounded the steering wheel. 'New York, now that's a place to do business. A person could do things in a hurry up there.'

Harry peered at the traffic ahead. A pair of horse-drawn surreys had turned on to the main thoroughfare in front of them. They were painted a festive yellow and red, like circus caravans. The horses clip-clopped at a steady pace, unconcerned at the congestion surrounding them.

Ethan snorted. 'See those horses? What a long, drawn-out way to get around. Gonna-Be-Glue, dat's what I call 'em.'

He pumped the accelerator and shot off like a fighter jet through a gap in the traffic. Almost immediately, he slowed down again and stopped in front of a police officer directing the gridlock. She wore a starched white tunic and white gloves, and choreographed the vehicles with ballerina-like grace. The brass buttons and soldierly stripes down the side of her skirt reminded Harry of the Bahamas' British heritage.

'You ask me, we should have left this place to the pirates,' Ethan said.

'What pirates?'

He raised his eyebrows at her in the rear-view mirror. 'You never hear of Blackbeard? Real name was Edward Teach. He practically owned New Providence a few hundred years ago. Place was overrun with pirates.' He rapped his fingers on the steering wheel. 'Sayin' goes that when a pirate slept, he didn't dream he'd died and gone to heaven, he dreamed he'd come back to Nassau.' He gunned the engine as the officer beckoned him forward. 'Nassau nothin' but a nightmare in slow motion, if you ask me.'

Harry frowned. His words had sparked off a current in her brain but almost immediately it fizzled out again. She shook her head and glanced back out at the long curved stretch of beach. The sand was like sifted flour. The aquamarine waves, larger than she'd expected, were butting unwary swimmers inland as though a giant hand had sloshed the ocean like bathwater.

A few minutes later, they turned sharp left and Ethan stopped the car. He twisted in his seat and made a sweeping gesture with one arm. 'All along here, this is Cable Beach. An' right here is your hotel.'

Harry looked out at the candy-pink façade. The Nassau Sands Hotel was built along stately lines, with a wide veranda and an entry porch fronted by Corinthian-style columns. She'd chosen it because it was a medium-budget hotel, but now that she was here it looked more like a grand Colonial home.

She thanked Ethan, tipped him generously and got out of the car. The heat swaddled her like an electric blanket. She climbed the veranda and stepped inside the hotel, and immediately felt a draught buffeting her face.

The foyer was a large, open-sided pavilion, where the missing wall exposed a blue-green view of the sea. Giant fans wheeled overhead, keeping the air on the move. The polished marble looked icy cold, and it was all she could do not to fling her sweltering body down on top of it.

Checking in took a while, but the unhurried service was a welcome change after the taxi driver's break-neck pace. Eventually, the receptionist gave her a wide smile and handed her a key.

'Welcome to da Bahamas, Ms Martinez. I hope you enjoy your stay.'

'Thanks.'

By now Harry was growing accustomed to the Bahamian accent. It was different from the stereotyped Jamaican singsong that she'd been expecting. It was smoother, more fluid; a mellow mix of British and African tones.

She found her room and noticed that the lavishness of the open foyer didn't extend behind the scenes. The décor was seventies-style floral brown, and the air carried a faint smell of drains. Harry shrugged. Five-star lobby, two-star room. It didn't matter. If everything went according to plan, she'd be out of here by tomorrow.

She flung her suitcase on the bed and peeled off her sticky clothes. She stepped into the shower to cool off under a drizzle of tepid water. Then, wrapped in a towel, she perched on the bed and took out her guidebook to the Bahamas. According to the map, Bay Street was the main thoroughfare through downtown Nassau, running east to Paradise Island Bridge and west to Cable Beach. It should be a short trip from here in a taxi.

Harry's mind flicked ahead to what she was about to do, and her mouth went dry. She still needed her father's codename. She could try to manage without it, but her chances of success that way were slim.

She tossed the guidebook on the bed and dug out the slip of paper where she'd noted down the details of her father's account. 7-2-5-5-9-3-5-3-J. What did the letter J stand for? Was it just there to complete the poker hand, or did it have a special significance? She flicked at it with her middle finger. J for what? J for Jack. Jack what? She thought of what her father had said the day she visited him in prison. *You'd have liked the name I chose.* She shook her head and sighed.

She hauled her father's blue holdall on to the bed, glad now that she'd brought it with her. She rummaged through its contents until she found her father's poker book. She poured over his flyleaf notations again until she found the reference to the card. Js. Jack of Spades. The river card. Was that her father's codename? Jack Spades? Or Jack River? She frowned. Neither felt right. Somehow she felt sure it should resonate with her more.

She closed her eyes and thought about her father. She'd gone back to the hospital late last night. According to the nurses his condition hadn't changed, but to Harry he'd seemed more shrivelled. She pictured her family there now; her mother aloof, Amaranta fussing, and an empty chair where she should have been. Harry snapped her eyes open and drove the image away. She had to leave, she'd had no choice.

She checked her watch. Time to get ready. She dropped the towel and slipped on the dress she'd bought in Dublin Airport. She'd found a small designer boutique, the sort she'd normally avoid, and bought an ivory silk embroidered dress with matching bag and shoes. Together they'd cost more than a week in the Seychelles, but the outfit looked expensive and that was the point. She'd deal with her credit-card bill later.

The silk drifted like cool water across her skin. The bodice was snug, with thin spaghetti straps that exposed enough flesh to make her worry about sunscreen. She applied more makeup than she'd normally wear, aiming for a dramatic look around the eyes to camouflage her cuts and bruises. Scraping her hair up on to the crown of her head, she twisted it into a knot so tight it made her eyes water. Then she stepped into her shoes and checked herself in the mirror. The silk's soft lustre seemed to make her skin gleam. The high topknot tugged at her hairline, lifting her eyebrows and giving her a naturally uppity expression. For the first time, she could see a strong resemblance to her mother.

She slipped on a pair of sunglasses, grabbed her bag and headed back to the foyer. Outside the hotel, she hailed a taxi and in less than five minutes had arrived in Bay Street at the doors of Rosenstock Bank.

Harry gazed up at the blue colonnaded building that housed the bank's headquarters. A sensation of weakness filled her groin. She took a few deep breaths and checked her watch again. There was almost an hour to spare before her appointment. She decided to act like a tourist for a while to try and calm her nerves. And besides, she still had one more thing to do.

She headed east down Bay Street, jostling with the throngs of holidaymakers and office workers. The street was crammed with shops. Designer boutiques selling Fendi and Gucci stood side by side with souvenir stalls selling T-shirts and pirate hats.

The sun was like a blowtorch against Harry's skin, and she decided to cross over to the shady side of the street. Taxis honked all around her and scooters zipped up and down. She ducked into the cool shade of the covered walkways, scanning the storefronts up ahead until she found what she was looking for: a mobile phone shop. Five minutes later, she'd bought a prepaid cellphone with a local Bahamian number. She tucked it safely into her bag.

Cross-checking her progress against her map, Harry strolled across Rawson Square and out to the harbour. Docked at the pier were two booming cruise ships. Seagulls squealed in circles above them, heckling the disembarking passengers. At the water's edge, vendors in small boats sold pink and green conch shells that reminded Harry of watermelons.

The wooden dock creaked beneath her feet and the air smelled of seaweed and salt. She passed by another line of market stalls, their souvenirs of Nassau on display: ceramic ornaments and straw hats, postcards and One-Eyed Jack pirate flags.

Harry froze. Something snapped into place inside her head. She stood still, afraid to move in case she dislodged it again. Water lapped at the edge of the pier, and somewhere an outboard engine throbbed. Slowly, she turned and stared at the market stalls. T-shirts, key-rings, maps and books. One-Eyed Jack flags hoisted on sticks. Harry watched the flag nearest her snapping in the breeze. A white skull and crossbones set against black, one eye socket obscured by an eye-patch.

Deuces, aces, one-eyed faces.

The childish chant popped into her head, a poker expression meaning aces, twos and one-eyed cards were wild. One-Eyed Jacks. She pictured the Jack of Spades, drawn in profile in every deck, only one eye showing. The white skull leered over at her. In her mind, she flashed on another skull and crossbones: the logo of DefCon, the hacker's convention she'd attended with her father.

You'd have liked the name I chose.

Jack of Spades. One-Eyed Jacks. Skull and crossbones.

Pirates and hackers.

She closed her eyes and another word popped into her head, the word that tied them all together. The hacker pseudonym she'd used when she was a kid. Pirata. The Spanish word for pirate.

This time it resonated, right down to her fingertips.

CHAPTER 43

'Hi, my name is Harry Martinez. I've a three-fifteen appointment with Glen Hamilton.'

Harry shifted from foot to foot while the receptionist consulted her computer screen. It felt odd to be giving out her real name when she was about to set up a scam.

Then she remembered the appointment hadn't been made for her by name and felt as though she'd committed a social gaffe. She took a quick look round the hushed lobby to see if anyone had heard. People in suits were slipping in and out of cubicles, while tellers conducted business in low discreet voices. Customers formed silent queues at the counters, like churchgoers lining up for confession. Names seemed sacrilegious in a place like this.

The receptionist turned from her screen and beamed at Harry. Then she leaned over her desk and pointed at the line of tellers on her left. The badge on her lapel said her name was Juliana.

'Go on down to the end here and take a left, and you'll see three elevators in front of you.

Take the middle one. That'll bring you up to the third floor and someone will meet you there.'

Harry thanked her and made her way to the lifts, all three of which stood open at ground level. She stepped into the one in the middle and turned to press the button for the third floor. There wasn't one. She stood with her finger pointing in mid-air, wondering what to do next. The only buttons on the metal panel were for controlling the doors and sounding the alarm. Before she could figure it out, the doors glided shut and she was moving. It must have been some kind of security lift, controlled at reception and designed to prevent snoopers like her from roaming the bank at will. The soles of Harry's feet began to tingle at the notion that she was airborne at someone else's whim.

The lift came to a halt and the doors opened. A young woman in a navy suit was waiting for her.

'This way, please.' She gestured for Harry to follow.

She escorted Harry down a corridor of beige unmarked doors. There were no signs to indicate which floor she was on or what went on inside each room. The woman opened a door on the right, identical to all the others. How could she tell them apart?

'Take a seat.' The woman stood aside to let her in. 'Glen will be with you in a moment.'

Harry thanked her and stepped inside. The door closed behind her.

In the middle of the room were four Queen

Anne chairs, grouped around a mahogany coffee table. The chairs had white padded seats and curled feet, and looked as though they'd be bad for her back. Harry knew she was meant to sit there and wait. Instead, she strayed to the window on the other side of the room. Not because she wanted to admire the view, but because next to it was a modern workstation with paperwork and a humming laptop.

For appearances' sake, she took a moment to gaze out the window. Red and blue rooftops stretched from here to the harbour, and half a mile offshore she could see Paradise Island, connected to Nassau by a bridge. Straddling the island's skyline was an astonishing structure of pink and blue, a hybrid of Disney and the Taj Mahal. Harry knew from her guidebook that it was the Atlantis Resort, some thirty-four acres of extravagant hotels, casinos and swimming lagoons.

She flicked a sideways glance at the laptop. The screensaver was on. She nudged the desk with her hip and the screen blinked back to life, only to warn her that the computer was locked. Pity.

She scanned the paperwork that littered the desk, searching for something she could use. Companies spent millions safeguarding confidential information, but in reality it was the everyday stuff that gave hackers the start they needed.

Harry spotted the perfect example taped to the wall: the bank's internal telephone list. With a quick look over her shoulder, she took out her phone and aimed its camera lens at the wall. It took her several shots, but soon she had photos spanning the entire telephone list. She could piece them together later if she needed to.

She turned her attention back to the laptop. It was a standard Dell model. The network cable was bright yellow, and she traced its route through the hole in the desk down to the network socket in the floor. Halfway down, the cable had been tagged with a strip of blue plastic marked 'port 6-47'. Harry stared at it and chewed her lip.

The door handle clicked behind her. She did a quick two-step back to the window, and turned to see a man and woman entering the room. The woman held her hand out.

'Good afternoon, I'm Glen Hamilton.' She gestured to her colleague. 'This is my deputy, Raymond Pickford.'

Harry introduced herself and shook hands. Stupid to have expected Glen to be a man. She of all people should have known better than to make gender assumptions based on a name.

Glen shepherded her away from the workstation and over to the Queen Anne chairs. 'We'll be more comfortable over here.'

Harry doubted it, but did as she was told. She took a seat opposite Glen, and watched her unzip a leather folder and settle a pad on her knees.

She looked to be in her late forties, with skin the colour of tobacco, and a tight haircut that showed off the graceful curve of her skull. Her business suit was unrelieved black, and in Harry's view could have done with a touch of colour here or there. There was an air of authority about her that reminded Harry of her last headmistress, a woman capable of spotting a lie at ten paces.

She forced herself to maintain eye contact. After all, she'd done nothing illegal. Not yet, anyway.

Glen clicked her pen into action. 'Before we begin, let me just explain that anything we discuss here will remain strictly confidential.' Her delivery was slow and precise. 'Even if you decide not to open an account with us, this visit and any information disclosed in it will be bound by banking secrecy laws.'

'That's reassuring.'

'May I ask why you chose Rosenstock Bank?'

'Well, my father banked here for years. A close family friend recommended it to him, ended up as his account manager for a while, in fact. Maybe you know him. Philippe Rousseau?' Harry searched the other woman's face, but her expression gave nothing away. 'Does he still work here?'

Glen lifted her chin and looked as though she mightn't answer, when Raymond cut in.

'Mr Rousseau is Vice President of International Client Relations,' he said, smiling at Harry. He was younger than Glen, in his early thirties perhaps, and his mild Bahamian accent was at odds with his pale Caucasian skin. 'He was promoted out of account management some years ago.'

Harry looked to Glen for confirmation. The

other woman dropped her gaze and picked at a piece of lint on her suit. Then she looked up and smiled.

'Yes, Philippe used to work for me, as a matter of fact. Up until about eight years ago.'

'Oh.' Harry frowned. 'So you took over my father's account, then?'

If that was the case, then where did Owen Johnson fit in? But Glen drew herself up.

'I had more than enough of my own clients to look after, without taking on any of Philippe's,' she said. 'No, I reassigned his workload across the rest of my team. All so that Philippe could spend his time entertaining prestigious clients.' Her smile grew brighter. 'Operating the male network, I suppose you'd call it.'

Harry raised an eyebrow and nodded. 'That's right, my father mentioned he'd met him playing poker. Can't remember where.'

'Paradise Island, probably,' Raymond said. 'Best casino in the Bahamas.' He flicked a glance at Glen and then looked away, running a hand over his head from crown to forehead. His hair was combed forward into a peak at the front, and set with so much gel it looked like an oil slick.

'Raymond, perhaps you could go and get us some coffee?' Glen's nostrils were flaring slightly.

'Of course.' He set his pen and notepad on the table and sidled out of the room, his head tilted to one side as if to avoid low-hanging branches.

Glen turned back to Harry.

'Now, perhaps we could discuss the source of your funds. For legal reasons, we can't open an account if we don't know precisely where the money comes from.'

'That makes sense.' Harry crossed her legs and the silk of her dress floated across her shins. She tried her best to look wealthy. 'Most of my money I accumulated during the dot.com boom. The software company I worked for went public in early 2000, and I had share options. Now it's mostly tied up in property and blue chip stocks. I'll just be depositing a small amount today, but eventually I plan to liquidate all my assets and move everything offshore.' She gave Glen a rueful smile and shrugged. 'I have a cheating husband I'm about to hit with divorce papers, but not before I've moved everything out of his reach.'

Glen's face was impassive. If Harry was hoping for an answering look of sisterhood, she was disappointed.

Glen made a note on her pad. 'When you've liquidated your assets and wish to deposit the funds, you'll need to produce proof of sale for us.'

'Right.' Harry swallowed and cleared her throat. The truth was, her only asset was a burnt-out Mini that in one sense was already liquidated. She had to remind herself there was no way Glen could know that.

'So you want maximum anonymity,' Glen said.

'Yes. I presume that means a numbered account?'

'There are other options, but that probably suits

365

your needs best. Your name would be replaced by a number on all documents related to your account. Apart from myself and Raymond, no one in the bank would know who you are.'

'And I can use this account to buy stocks in complete confidentiality?'

'Of course. The transactions are all conducted under the bank's name. Your name doesn't appear anywhere.'

'Sounds perfect.'

'Naturally, a numbered account comes with certain restrictions if we're to maintain that level of protection. We don't issue cheque books for numbered accounts, and teller transactions are not permitted. Withdrawals, transfers or payments must be made in person through your dedicated account manager.'

'And that would be you?'

Glen nodded. 'Or Raymond, if I'm not available. He's authorized to act in my absence.'

As if on cue, Raymond stepped back into the room carrying a tray. He lowered it on to the coffee table, teaspoons rattling. Harry noticed that his palms looked greasy, either from nerves or from smoothing them across the lard on his head. She caught his eye and gave him an encouraging smile.

Glen leaned forward. 'If you're happy to proceed, then we can get started on the paperwork.'

'Yes, let's do that.' Harry opened her bag and dug out her passport, two recent gas and electricity bills, her P60 income tax form and a bank statement showing the state of her savings account. She handed them to Glen, along with a banker's draft for $30,000. Over a third of her savings. She felt a twinge in her chest, and figured her chances of seeing the money again were slim.

Glen studied everything, and wrote her a receipt for the draft while Raymond poured coffee. Glen handed him the stack of papers without looking at him and told him to make copies. When he had gone, she extracted a form from her leather folder and passed it to Harry with a pen.

'If you wouldn't mind filling this out while we're waiting. We can take our coffee over to the desk.'

Glen moved over to the laptop and invited Harry to pull up a chair. While Glen tapped at her keyboard, Harry scanned through the form. At first glance, it looked like a routine application for opening a standard bank account. It had the usual boxes for personal information, and at the end was a section marked OFFICIAL USE ONLY, presumably for Glen to fill in. The back of the form was blank, apart from a second official box for another optional banking signatory. She began filling in the name and address details, entering her name as 'Harry (Henrietta)' for consistency with her passport.

'I told my father I'd look Philippe up while I was here,' she said, stopping herself just in time from ticking her marital status as single. That was the problem about telling lies: they criss-crossed around you like tripwires. 'Do you think I'd find him in the casino tonight?'

'I wouldn't know.' Glen drew herself up in the chair. 'By law, Bahamians are not actually allowed to gamble. But then, our Mr Rousseau is half French and half British, so the rules don't apply to him.' She punched the Enter key with unnecessary force.

Harry didn't know what prejudices Glen had had to overcome in the bank, but whatever they were, Philippe Rousseau seemed to be taking most of the heat. She continued to work through the form, ticking a box that absolved the bank from any tax declarations on her behalf. Then she came to a section headed 'Authorisation for Telephone & Fax Instructions', with a blank space underneath it entitled 'Codeword'. She swivelled the pen between her thumb and index finger.

'This codeword for phone and fax instructions,' she said. 'How does that work?'

'Well, with a numbered account we prefer you to do most of your transactions in person with myself and Raymond. That way there can be no breach of security and no uncertainty about your identification. But that's not always possible, of course. You can't always be in the Bahamas, so sometimes you need to communicate your instructions by phone or fax. We recommend you don't use your name on these communications, just to safeguard your anonymity. You authorize the bank to act on your instructions by quoting your account number and the personal codeword that's recorded on the application form.' Glen beamed at her. 'That way we know it's really you.'

Harry nodded and looked down at the empty space on the form. She felt her toes bunch up, like the curled feet on the Queen Anne chairs. Then she licked her lips and wrote down *Pirata*.

She signed her name at the bottom of the form, and then hesitated over the date. According to her father, he'd opened his own Rosenstock account about six months before the Sorohan deal. By her reckoning, that made it sometime in April 2000. She gripped the pen and scribbled down today's date: 14th April 2009. She fudged the final digit so that the head of the nine was disproportionately large. With luck, it could just as easily pass for a zero, a detail that might help later on.

She handed Glen the completed application form just as Raymond returned to the room. He stepped up to the desk and placed a sheaf of papers in front of Glen, along with an empty manila box file about the size and thickness of a bumper telephone book. Glen sorted through the documents, handing the originals back to Harry and organizing the rest into the box file. Then she signed the official section at the end of the application form. Next, she got Harry to sign a copy of her passport photo on the back and then stapled it to the front of the form. Glen signed the photograph across its face, her signature spilling over on to the page, effectively sealing it to the application.

Raymond reached over as if to do the same, but Glen waved him away.

'Just clear away the coffee,' she said.

Raymond hesitated, then did as he was told. Harry handed him her cup with a smile, then flipped her gaze back to Glen. She was securing the paperwork inside the box file by means of a spring-loaded clamp across the front. The top sheet in the stack seemed to be a list of file contents and Harry watched Glen as she ticked and initialled each entry. She must have been aware of Harry's scrutiny, for she suddenly shot her a look.

'This is your personal identification file,' she explained. 'It goes in our vaults. Only myself and Raymond know your identity, and we are the only ones authorized to access the file.'

'What happens if you both leave?'

Glen raised an eyebrow. 'In that unlikely event, your account will be passed over to a new account manager, who will be given access to the file. He or she can authenticate your fax instructions using the account number and codeword.'

Raymond chipped in. 'And your photograph has been endorsed, so when you come in to withdraw funds he can reliably identify you.'

'I see.' Harry frowned, struggling to pinpoint a weakness in the system. 'Supposing someone breaks into the vaults?'

Glen's chin lifted slightly. 'I can assure you, they've been constructed according to the highest security specifications, and are heavily protected by armed guards. I seriously doubt anyone would even try it.'

Harry nodded, and then gestured towards the laptop. 'What about your computer system? Supposing someone breaks in through there?'

Glen looked at Raymond, giving him tacit permission to respond. He leaned forward in his seat, his expression animated.

'Our IT security strategies are leading edge,' he said. 'We work with some of the best security consultants in the industry. And let me tell you, our Network Operations guys have a pretty aggressive approach to hackers. We've caught and prosecuted quite a number of them just for probing our firewalls.'

Harry thought of the honeypot and didn't doubt it.

'In any case, we don't put any of your identification data online,' Raymond continued. 'The only way of verifying your identity is through this file and, as Glen pointed out, that's extremely well guarded.'

'So what else goes in my file?'

Glen took over again. 'Documented records of any trading instructions we receive from you. Faxes, phone calls, that sort of thing.'

Harry nodded and sat back in her chair. She was running out of questions.

Glen hit a few more keys on her laptop and then closed the box file, turning it over so she could write on its spine. She copied an eight-digit number from the screen on to the file, and also on to a small white card which she handed to Harry.

'This is your account number. You'll receive formal documentation in due course, but in the meantime keep this safe. We usually advise customers to memorize it, along with the code-word, of course. Or if you can't memorize it, then camouflage it somewhere among another set of numbers, just for added security.'

Harry thought about her father's efforts to disguise his account number and code, and could understand now why he'd gone to such lengths.

'Your details will be secured in the vaults immediately.' Glen passed the box file over to Raymond and then stood up and held out her hand. 'It's been a pleasure to meet you, Ms Martinez. If you have any problems, don't hesitate to call. My direct fax and phone lines are on the card.'

Harry shook her hand, and allowed herself to be ushered out of the room. She was escorted back down the faceless corridor and into the button-free elevator. She felt her head swim as she glided down to what she hoped was the ground floor. She thought about the bank and its obsession with security. Secret elevators and unmarked doors; steel vaults and armed guards; signatures and counter-signatures; numbers and code words. Where were the chinks, where were the vulnerabilities? She shook her head. The system was tight, locked down. Besides, she was a hacker not a burglar, whatever the similarities were between them.

She was still holding the card Glen had given her, and she tucked it into her bag beside her mobile phone. Then she remembered the telephone list on the wall. The hairs at the back of her neck unfurled as she stared at her phone. The elevator came to a stop and the doors parted in front of her, but she didn't move.

She'd snapped the telephone list on a whim, but now it could turn out to be her only weapon. The system and the technology might be impenetrable, but she wasn't just a hacker. She was a social engineer. And social engineers didn't target the technology. They targeted the people that used it.

Security's weakest link: human beings.

CHAPTER 44

A social engineer needs to be good at three things: bluffing, persuading and telling downright lies. With her father as a role model, it wasn't surprising that Harry had a knack for all three.

She stared at the phone in her hotel room. As a teenager she used to set herself challenges, trying to talk strangers at the end of a phone into giving her personal information. It could have been anything from an ATM password to a grandmother's maiden name, it didn't matter. She never used the information. The point was just to acquire it, and in so doing to hone her skills in the art of sounding plausible.

But what was her target information this time? She sat cross-legged on the bed and tapped her pen against her teeth. Then she jotted down everything she'd learned about Rosenstock's security arrangements, adding to the notes she'd made from her website reconnaissance. Powering up her laptop, she downloaded the photos of the bank's internal phone list from her mobile and pieced them together. The information was legible, just about.

374

As an afterthought, she scribbled *yellow cable* in the margin on her pad, and then checked over the sum of what she'd written. It still didn't amount to much.

She unwound her legs and wandered out on to the balcony. Whatever the shortcomings of the room, the view of Cable Beach didn't disappoint. The sand looked sugar-soft, and she was close enough to hear the surf as it crashed against the shore and hissed back out to sea.

Her mind returned to her meeting with Glen Hamilton. She had to admit the bank's security was tight and, as far as she could see, the only way to penetrate it was from the inside. But where would she find an insider who was willing to take the risk? She thought about Raymond Pickford, then shook her head. He was malleable but weak, and likely to back out of things at the last minute. She needed someone in authority, someone who wouldn't be challenged.

Someone like Philippe Rousseau.

He seemed to have come a long way since his days as her father's account manager. Harry didn't know what a Vice President of International Client Relations did all day, but it sounded impressive. So impressive that the last thing he'd want was someone making accusations about his past. She remembered what her father had said about Rousseau mimicking his deals. How would it look if a Vice President of the bank had piggy-backed on insider trades?

She gripped the railings and closed her eyes. Social engineering might be a form of dishonesty, but she could rationalize its place in her world. Blackmail, on the other hand, was on a different scale of malevolence and it didn't sit well with her.

She turned away from the balcony and stepped back inside the room, returning to her notes on the bed. She needed evidence of Rousseau's copycat trades. Once she had that, she could persuade him to do anything. She stared at the phone again. So there it was, her social-engineering challenge: to somehow acquire a record of Philippe Rousseau's trades.

She scoured her notes again, this time with renewed focus. Then she picked up her pen and started sketching ideas. Ten minutes later, she made her first call. It was picked up straight away.

'Good afternoon, Rosenstock Bank and Trust, Customer Services, Webster speakin', how may I help?'

The ritual greeting was overly long and Webster seemed to take his time delivering it, clearly enjoying the lazy rhythm of his own voice.

'Hi, Webster, my name is Catalina Diego.' Harry had adopted an American twang to disguise her own accent, on the basis that she would attract less attention that way. She knew from experience that the blend of Irish and Midwest American would come out as mild Canadian.

'I'm from your Dell supplier here in Nassau,'

she continued. 'We're doing a survey to improve our services. Could you spare me a few minutes to answer some questions?'

'Sure, no problem.'

'Great, I appreciate that.' Harry smiled. Social engineering relied on the co-operation of other people, which was why Customer Service Reps were such good targets. After all, they were trained to be helpful.

'Okay, Webster, so roughly how many employees are there in your area?'

He took a moment to reply. He was probably taking a headcount around the room. 'Seems to be about twenty-five, twenty-six at the moment.'

'And what are your hours of business?'

'Seven a.m. to nine p.m. And that's seven days a week.'

'Have you ever had to call out one of our service engineers?'

'No, can't say I have personally.'

Harry continued to lead him through a series of inconsequential questions until it felt safe to broach the ones that mattered.

'Have you ever had any problems running your helpdesk software on our machines?' she said.

'No, everyt'ing works just fine. Sometimes it's a bit slow, but that's about all.'

'Really? Could be a memory issue. What helpdesk software have you got installed at the moment?'

'It's something called Customer Focus. We've had it a while.'

'I know that one.' She'd never heard of it. 'It's from Banking Solutions, right?'

'No, it's from some company called Clear Systems. Their blue and red logo's all over it.'

'Oh, that outfit.' Again, no clue. 'I've heard their reporting tools aren't that great. We can recommend a higher performance package if you need it.'

'Reports seem okay to me. I only run a few DTRs at the end of the day, and I've never had any problems.'

'DTRs?'

'Daily Transaction Reports.'

'Oh, right. What about reports on archived data? Because I know they can put a heavy load on the system. If it's slow, maybe we should consider upgrading your machines.'

'You'd need to talk to the supervisor about that. She handles all the ARs.'

Harry frowned and then her brow cleared. ARs: Archive Reports. 'Great idea, I'll do that. Could I get her name and number?'

'Sure, it's Matilda Tomlins, extension 311. But NOC handles all the hardware upgrades.' Before Harry could ask, he added, 'That's the Network Operations Centre downstairs. They handle all the technical stuff. Although sometimes you'd think they ran the entire bank, the way they carry on. You know what techies are like.'

'Believe me, I do. Okay Webster, I've just a couple more questions and then I'll let you get back to your job.'

'Take your time, I ain't goin' nowhere. Hey, what part of Canada you from, anyway?'

Harry smiled into the phone. 'Oh, all over. Toronto mostly. Now, how about your keyboard and monitor, have you ever had trouble with those?'

She finished up with a few more routine queries, and then she thanked him for his help and hung up. She scribbled down what she'd learned. As far as Webster was concerned, nothing he'd passed on was privileged information. But to Harry it was valuable insider lingo that would lend her credibility for the next stage.

She turned her attention to the Rosenstock internal phone list. Beside each name was a job title followed by a direct dial phone line. Harry skimmed down the list, noting that it seemed to cover senior management only. She jotted down the names of people working in NOC. There were three in total: Jack Belmont, Head of Network Operations; Victor Williams, NOC Security; Elliot Mitchell, NOC Support. Harry picked up the phone and dialled each one in turn. The first two calls were picked up, and she immediately disconnected. On the third call, she got through to voicemail:

'Hi, this is Elliot Mitchell. I'm out of the office from Monday 13th April till Wednesday 15th April. Please leave a message and I'll get back to you on my return. For any emergency support issues please call Jack Belmont on 5138591.'

Harry drew a big asterisk beside Elliot Mitchell's

name. Then she put in a call to Matilda Tomlins, the Customer Services supervisor. This time she used the prepaid cellphone she'd purchased on Bay Street.

'Hello, Matilda speakin'.'

'Hi, Matilda, this is Catalina downstairs in NOC Support. I'm working on that AR issue from last week.'

There was a pause. 'What AR issue?'

'Didn't Elliot Mitchell fill you in before he left?'

'No, I haven't heard anyt'ing from you people in NOC, but then that doesn't surprise me. What's this all about?'

Harry sighed, as though she didn't have time to waste on this. 'Well, it seems there's a bug in your Customer Focus reports. We're working with Clear Systems on it now, but basically the ARs have been cross-referencing into the online database instead of the archives, and now a lot of the online database pointers are corrupt.'

There was another pause, presumably while Matilda tried to follow the mumbo-jumbo.

'So what exactly does that mean?' Matilda said eventually.

'It means that some of your customer data is now being pulled from the archives instead of the online database. And that's putting a serious load on your network. Too many of your guys accessing the wrong data, and you could be out of business up there for a few hours. You can't run any DTRs today, that's for sure.'

'What are you talkin' about? I've a whole batch of DTRs due in an hour, not to mention a mountain of other things I got to get through. I can't afford to be offline.'

'Well, I'm not saying it'll definitely happen,' Harry said. 'But we had a few people down over the weekend. I was really just calling to let you know it might happen again.'

'This is crazy. Why the hell didn't I hear about this from Elliot?'

'I don't know. He's not back until Wednesday.' Harry paused. 'Look, here's what I'll do. I'll give you my cell number, and if you have any problems you can reach me directly on that. I'll do my best to get you operational.'

'Right, well. Okay, I'd certainly appreciate that. If I had to wade through all the usual NOC channels I'd be here all week.'

Harry gave her the number of her prepaid phone. 'And I'd better take your network port number while I'm here. Just so I know which one to reconnect. Do you know what it is?'

'My port number? How am I supposed to know that?'

'It's probably taped to the network cable. That's the yellow one coming out of your computer. There's usually a blue label on it somewhere.'

'I know which one my network cable is, thank you, I'm not a complete fool. Hold on a minute.'

There was another pause, and Harry pictured the woman bending down to check under the desk.

'Yes, here it is.' Matilda's voice sounded strangled, as though she was upside down. 'Port 7-45.'

'That's great. Okay, just give me a call if you need me.'

Harry disconnected and hopped off the bed. Her limbs felt jittery and she began pacing the room, timing her next move. If it came too soon after her conversation with Matilda, the supervisor might get suspicious. On the other hand, she didn't have that much time left.

She checked her watch. 4.30 p.m. here, 9.30 p.m. in Dublin. Harry took a deep breath. She had less than twenty-four hours left.

She consulted the internal phone list again for Elliot Mitchell's number. By altering the final digit, she began dialling nearby extensions, hoping to reach someone on the NOC support team. Her first two calls rang out, but the third was answered in tetchy tones by a guy identifying himself as Eric.

'Hi, Eric,' she said. 'This is Catalina from DataLink Communications. I'm upstairs working on a cabling problem for Matilda in Customer Services, and I wonder if you could help us out.'

'First I heard of any cabling problem. Network cabling's supposed to come through me.'

Harry mouthed a bad word, but kept her voice calm. 'Well, maybe it is, but all I know is Elliot Mitchell authorized an emergency call-out with us to fix this problem while he was away, and I'm on the clock here.'

'I'll need to check through the paperwork on this one. What did you say your name was?'

'Catalina. Look, I've got to leave for another call-out in ten minutes. You can waste time checking through paperwork if you like. I'll just explain to Elliot that I couldn't do my job because his support team wouldn't co-operate.'

'Who said I wouldn't co-operate? All I'm sayin' is it should've come through me.'

'Well, it's coming through you now. I need you to disable Matilda's port for a minute while I run a check on this cable. Can you just do that? It's port 7-45.'

Eric paused, and Harry could have sworn she heard him grinding his teeth.

'You'll have to wait a couple of minutes,' he said eventually. 'I can't just drop everyt'ing, you know.'

'A couple of minutes is fine. I'll call you back when I need it enabled again.'

When Harry put the phone down, she noticed she was breathing hard. The NOC link in the scam chain had always struck her as risky, and she worried she'd been too pushy. What if Eric decided to call Matilda or consult the head of NOC? It wouldn't be long before they realized that neither Catalina nor DataLink Communications existed.

Looking back on her exchange with Eric, she didn't see how she could have played it differently. The point about social engineering was to convince people they could trust you, and the method of persuasion depended on the personality of the mark. Some responded well to old-fashioned friendliness, while others were motivated by keeping in with the boss. Eric's surly disposition had called for extreme measures.

She wandered out to the balcony again, gazing out at the beach to try and calm her nerves. A banana boat was bumping its way across the water parallel to the shore. According to her guidebook, Cable Beach had been named after the transatlantic telephone cables that were laid beneath the sand in 1907, linking an isolated Bahamas with the rest of the world. Harry shivered. Odd how knowing that could make her feel more isolated than ever.

She thought about Dillon. He was probably still in Copenhagen. She hadn't seen him for two days now, and was beginning to think their night together had never happened. She stepped back inside and used the hotel phone to call his mobile. As expected, she got through to his voicemail. She left a message letting him know where she was and when she'd be coming home. She had barely hung up when her Bahamian cellphone rang. It was Matilda Tomlins and she sounded out of breath.

'Catalina? Thank the Lord, I was expectin' voicemail.'

'Hey, Matilda, everything okay?'

'I'm sweatin' here. I've gone offline, just like you said, right in the middle of a DTR. My whole machine has seized up like it has rigor mortis. You need to fix this, I can't do a thing with it.'

'Damn, I thought that might happen. Okay, well I should be free in about an hour, I'll get straight on to it then.'

'An hour? That's no good, I need to be up and runnin' here in twenty minutes max.'

'Twenty minutes? God, I don't know, Matilda. I've a lot on here. Look, I'll do my best, okay? I'll call you back.'

Harry hung up and executed a little jig. Reverse social engineering was one of her favourite techniques, where the mark was set up to ask the attacker for help. She couldn't help feeling a twinge of sympathy for Matilda, but there was nothing she could do about it. She had to play the scam out.

Harry waited ten minutes and then called Eric, asking him to re-enable Matilda's port. Five more minutes passed, and she called Matilda back.

'Hi, Matilda. You should be back in action now.'

'Hold on, let me try logging in.' There was a pause. 'Oh, thank God, it's workin'. Hey, I really appreciate you helpin' me out with this.'

'No problem. The bad news is, you could go down again at any time.'

'What?'

'That DTR problem hasn't gone away, and I'm afraid I've already left the office so I can't help you out next time.'

'You're not tellin' me I got to go through Eric?'

'I'm afraid so.' Harry paused. 'Well, there is one thing I can try. I have an idea what's causing the bug, and if I can just analyse some of the archive data I might be able to clean it up for you. But I'll need you to pull up a couple of archive reports for me.'

'Right now?'

'It could save us both a lot of headaches.'

Matilda sighed. 'Oh, all right. What do you want me to do?'

Harry pirouetted in front of the mirror and then resumed her business-like tone. 'First we need a list of trades from one of the corrupt archive accounts, and then we'll try cross-referencing against some of the transactions.'

'So what account number should I try?'

'Hold on, I've got a memo here somewhere listing all the corrupt accounts.' Harry consulted her notes for her father's bank account number. 'Okay, try this: 72559353.'

'Okay, got that. So how far back do we need to go?'

'Well, we've managed to trace the problem back to April 2000, so let's run the report from, say, April to October of that year. Can you do that?'

'Just a second.'

Harry could hear the click of keys as Matilda entered the report query. It took effort not to ask her to type faster.

'Okay, I've run that one,' Matilda said. 'It finished pretty quick, only eight different stock transactions on that account. Now what?'

'Right, save that. Now we'll try some cross-referencing to narrow down the pointer corruption.'

Harry had reverted back to mumbo-jumbo, but was betting at this point that Matilda didn't care. The supervisor just wanted her system back. 'Can you drill down into each of those eight stocks? We need a list of all other accounts that traded in those stocks over the same period. Is that possible?'

'It's possible, but it'll take forever. That's eight separate reports you're talkin' about.'

'Well, okay, let's narrow it down. Pick the four biggest trades and let's concentrate on those.'

Matilda sighed. 'I hope this is worth all the trouble.'

Harry paced the room like a clockwork soldier while Matilda ran the reports. Ten minutes later, Matilda announced they were done.

'That's great,' Harry said. 'Now, can you mail them to me? I'm almost home now. With luck I'll straighten this out in a few minutes, and then I can talk Eric through the database cleanup. Let me give you my Yahoo email account.' She gave her the email address set up in Catalina's name. 'And in the meantime, I'll call Eric and ask him to give you the VIP treatment. Just in case.'

'That'll be the day.'

Harry hung up, and then hooked her laptop into the hotel phone jack. Five minutes later, she'd downloaded Matilda's reports and was scouring the data.

The report on her father's account listed every stock he had bought or sold between April and October 2000, along with the date and the amount of money involved. Harry's eyes widened at the size of some of the trades. The other reports homed in on four specific stocks: EdenTech, CalTel, Boston Labs and, surprise, surprise, Sorohan Software. The reports listed every investment account that had traded in these stocks for the same period, along with the dates and amounts of the transactions. There must have been over two hundred accounts listed in total.

Harry waded through the data, using spreadsheet tools to sort and filter the information. After a while, some distinct patterns emerged.

First there was the pattern of her father's trades: buying low and selling high, investing for the short term. Harry guessed the stocks were bought on the strength of insider information, and sold as soon as public awareness inflated the price. Next, there was the pattern followed by the bulk of the accounts: buying stock at increasing prices, just as her father happened to be getting rid of his. Presumably these were legitimate investors acting on public M&A information.

Threaded amongst them all was a more subtle pattern, one she might have missed if she hadn't been looking out for it. The pattern was followed by only one investment account, and its premise was simple: to buy and sell stocks in close tandem with her father, the quantities on a smaller scale but the timing identical to within minutes. The duplication of trades occurred for all four stocks, on both the buy and sell legs of the transactions.

It was the pattern of a piggy-back trader, and Harry was willing to bet it belonged to Philippe Rousseau.

CHAPTER 45

Harry stared up at the floodlit luxury complex in front of her. It was a flamingo-pink palace, with archways and bridges and fairytale towers that stood over twenty storeys high. The Atlantis Resort of Paradise Island.

She clutched her handbag closer to her body. The envelopes crackled inside it, and the pulse in her neck began to throb. Water hissed all around her. Man-made waterfalls and fountains with winged horses lined the approach to the hotel. She made her way past them towards the main entrance, pinpricks of spray flicking against her skin. In spite of all the water everywhere, her mouth felt dry.

She stepped inside the hotel and for a moment stood still, struck by the grandeur that tried to recreate the legend of Atlantis. Instead of the usual lobby, Harry found herself in a huge domed rotunda. Massive pillars carved with seahorses soared sixty or seventy feet into the air. Above her, the arched ceiling was made entirely of golden shells.

The signposts told her she was in the Great Hall of Waters. She circled around it, scanning the perimeters, and tried to get her bearings. She passed a café enclosed by wall-to-wall marine aquariums. Harry could make out the blue-black shape of a giant manta ray paragliding through the waters. According to her guidebook, this was part of The Dig, an underground labyrinth of corridors with viewing tanks of the marine life outside. Harry shuddered. Ordinary mazes were bad enough, but the notion of one lined with shark-infested waters made her whole body hum.

She continued her circuit of the dome until she found what she was looking for. The entrance to the Atlantis Casino.

She stepped into the crowded room and immediately felt at home. The clicking of gaming chips filled the air, like millions of busy grasshoppers. Slot machines and gaming tables stretched ahead of her as far as she could see: blackjack, poker, roulette, craps. Dealers in bow ties manned the tables, and she could hear the occasional ding-ding of their silver bells as players tipped them out of their winnings.

Harry almost smiled. Thanks to her father, this was a familiar world. The scale of things may have been different from the casinos in Soho, but the protocol and the punters were just the same.

She fingered her bag and felt the thickness of the envelopes inside. Then she weaved her way over to the blackjack tables in the middle of the room. She ignored the lower limit games. They didn't suit her purpose, and besides, they were too crowded. Instead, she selected a table posting a minimum bet of $200. There was only one other player, an elderly man with an unlit cigarette hanging out of his mouth. She climbed up on to a stool, dug out $2,000 from the thickest envelope in her bag and placed the notes on the table, waiting for the dealer to exchange them for chips. Her father had taught her early on never to hold her cash out directly to the dealer. For security reasons, he couldn't accept anything from a punter's hands. As the dealer scooped up her buy-in stake, she noticed his light amber eyes and recognized them from the rear-view mirror. It was her taxi-driver, Ethan.

She smiled at him. 'So you have two jobs, then?'

He gave her a quizzical look, and then his brow cleared. 'Ah, da strictly-business lady.' He smiled back. 'Matter of fact, I have three. I do tours round The Dig in the morning as well.' He pushed a stack of chips in front of her and shoved the notes down a slot in the table. 'You been down there yet?'

'No, I'm not keen on sharks.'

He raised an eyebrow. 'You in the wrong place here, then.'

Harry smiled, and separated a purple chip from the rest of the stack. She placed it on the betting spot in front of her: $500. Ethan dealt the cards, sliding them out of the wooden shoe on the table. Harry caught a six and a four, while the old man next to her took a pair of eights.

'So why all the jobs?' she said, aware that the

sight of a familiar face had put her in a chatty mood.

Ethan flipped over one of his own cards, leaving the other face down. He'd drawn a nine. 'I told you, this slowcoach place is for the birds. I'm out of here just as soon as I put together enough walking-around money.'

He looked at her and waited for her to play her hand. Harry tapped the baize with her forefinger, and he flipped another card for her. A ten, making twenty in total. She sliced her hand over the cards to show she was done.

'Where are you headed, New York?' she said.

'Maybe. Or Las Vegas.' Ethan gathered up the old man's cards and chips after he'd gone bust. 'Plenty of casinos there.'

Ethan turned over his hole card. Now he had a five to go with his nine. Then he dealt himself an eight and went bust. He paid out Harry's winnings, another purple chip, and cleared away the cards.

Harry moved all her chips on to the betting spot for the next hand: a total of $2,500.

'Maybe you can help me out, Ethan.' She clasped her hands in front of her. 'I'm looking for a man called Philippe Rousseau. I heard he plays in here a lot.'

Ethan glanced over at her and then down at her stake. 'I know him. He plays poker in one of the private rooms.' He flicked the cards across the baize. 'But you don't want to tangle with those boys, they're high rollers.'

393

He dealt Harry a Queen and the Ace of spades. Blackjack.

Harry smiled. 'Maybe I'm a high roller too.'

Ethan's showing card was no match for a Blackjack. He counted out $3,750 in chips and pushed them over to her in two stacks. His expression was solemn.

'Is Rousseau here tonight?' Harry said.

'Mr Rousseau is always here.'

'So can you take me to him?'

Instead of answering, he dealt two more cards to the man with the cigarette. The second card bust the hand, and the old man climbed down from his stool, tossing Ethan a green chip as he left the table. Ethan smacked his silver bell twice with the palm of his hand, but he kept his eyes on Harry.

'People play with Mr Rousseau by special invite only,' he said, when the man had left. 'He don't let just anybody in.'

'He will if you tell him my name is Sal Martinez.'

He studied her for a moment, rattling a stack of chips through his fingers. Then he signalled to someone over her head. Harry twisted around, wondering had he summoned a bouncer to haul her outside. Instead, a young black woman wearing the dealer's waistcoated uniform came over and took his place behind the table.

'Follow me,' Ethan said.

She shovelled her chips into her bag and followed him through the crowds. He led her to an alcove with a door marked PRIVATE, and opened it with a key tied to a chain around his waist. On the other side of the door was a polished chrome lift. He used the same key in a slot on the wall to open the doors. Harry followed him inside. He punched a button marked P3. She'd expected to feel the lift floating upwards but instead it seemed to plummet through the ground. When the doors opened, she stepped out into a small vestibule decked out in gold carpets and mirrors.

'Wait here,' Ethan said, without looking at her.

He disappeared through an unmarked door. Harry did as she was told and waited, feeling like a child caught misbehaving in class. She had to remind herself that she didn't need Ethan's approval. The fact that she'd even care about it told her how isolated she was feeling. She perched on a gold-cushioned chair by the door and crossed her legs. Then she checked through the contents of her handbag, although she knew everything was there. She'd gone through it a dozen times before she left the hotel. The door opened with a click and she jumped to her feet, straightening her shoulders. Ethan gestured her inside.

'You're in,' he said, his amber eyes finally meeting hers. 'Just watch out for the sharks.'

CHAPTER 46

Harry had assumed that Ethan's warning about sharks referred to the card players. Now she wasn't so sure.

The room was the size of a concert hall, with chandeliers casting a champagne glow over thirty or forty poker tables. Spanning two entire walls in a gigantic L was a vast floor-to-ceiling aquarium.

The tanks reflected an eerie blue light into the room. A lone shark, maybe seven foot long, tacked its way through the water towards her, as though it had all the time in the world to size her up. When it reached the end of the tank, the shark butted the glass wall with its pointed snout. It seemed to stare at her with its small, dead-looking eyes.

'He's not really looking at you, you know. Sharks can't see very much.'

Harry whipped her gaze around. A tall man in his fifties was standing beside her. He was wearing a tuxedo that set off his grey hair and the sheen on his dark skin.

He held out his hand. 'Philippe Rousseau.' His nails were white and glossy, as though they had been buffed. 'You must be Sal's daughter. The resemblance is remarkable.'

Harry shook his hand. 'Yes, I know. My name's Harry. Sorry, I said my name was Sal –'

'– just to get in, yes I know. I'm intrigued.' His voice was a rich baritone, and his Caribbean inflexions had a cultivated overtone. 'Tell me, how is your father?'

His stare seemed to drill through her and she worked hard not to avert her gaze. He had to have been aware that her father had been sent to prison, but his eyes seemed to be daring her to mention it. She decided to play along, just for the time being.

'Not too good. He's in hospital. An accident.'

Rousseau's eyebrows shot up. 'I'm sorry to hear it. Roads can be so dangerous.'

She frowned, and wondered how much he already knew.

'So what can I do for you, Harry?' he went on.

She hesitated, feeling oddly vulnerable at his use of her name. Playing the role of Catalina Diego seemed so much easier than playing herself. She glanced over at the poker tables and tuned into the clack-clack of chips and the civilized murmur of conversation. She was acutely aware of the envelopes in her bag and of where her next move could take her. She took a deep breath and turned to him with a smile.

'I'd like to play.'

'Ah, the Martinez gambling instinct. I'm afraid the buy-in stake is $50,000.'

'That's not a problem.'

He considered her for a moment, and then nodded. 'Let's see if you're as good as your father.'

He led the way through the poker tables, catching handshakes from many of the players along the way. He was on first-name terms with them all, and Harry noted how well he played the role of host.

Unlike the smart casual dress code of the main casino, the rule here seemed to be formal evening wear. Tuxedos, slicked hair and wraparound sunglasses. Harry was glad of her cream silk dress.

Rousseau headed for the table with the best view of the aquarium. A few feet away from it, he turned and spoke to her in a low voice.

'You'll understand if I don't introduce you. These are high-net-worth business acquaintances, and in the Bahamas such people require anonymity. No one exchanges life stories at these tables.'

He held her gaze, and Harry nodded to show that she understood. She was not to mention her father or where he'd ended up. For the time being, she'd co-operate.

Rousseau reached the table in two strides and pulled out a chair for her opposite the dealer and facing the aquarium wall. Harry sat down. A shoal of electric-blue fish darted in unison through the water in front of her, like a platoon on parade drill: right turn, about face, forward march. The shark was nowhere to be seen.

Harry extracted the rest of her cash from the envelope and placed it on the baize. The young man on her left flashed her a smile, while his eyes did that male up-and-down thing along the length of her body.

'My favourite kind of poker player,' he said. 'A beautiful woman.'

He was in his early twenties, and his accent was pure South London. With his shaggy hairstyle and blond stubble, he could have been a member of a boy band. Harry smiled back, and then scanned the table. There were two other players, both of them women and both of them ignoring Harry.

The dealer pushed two stacks of chips towards her, one grey and one purple, in exchange for her cash. Unlike the round chips from the public tables, these were oversized oval plaques reserved for high-stakes games. Harry cupped the grey stack in one hand and let the chips clack through her fingers. They were heavier than the normal chips, and more satisfying to handle. The word 'Atlantis' was engraved on their mother-of-pearl finish in ornate blue script, along with their face value of $1,000. The purple ones were each worth $5,000.

The dealer shot his wrists out of his cuffs and fanned out a deck of cards on the baize. Then he flipped it over, mixed it flat on the table, shuffled, cut and began to deal. The game was no-limit Texas Hold 'Em.

Rousseau was seated to the dealer's left, next to

the older of the two women. She was in her fifties, her overly large mouth crammed with too many teeth. She whispered something in his ear. He responded to her in fluent French that sounded mildly flirtatious. Harry looked away. Her father had used his Spanish charm to much the same effect.

She eased back the corners of her two hole cards. Six and nine, unsuited. The woman beside her placed an opening bet of $10,000. Harry flicked her a glance. She was rail-thin, with dark circles under her eyes that suggested she hadn't slept for a year. Harry chewed her bottom lip. She'd intended to sit out the first few hands until she had a read on the other players, especially Philippe Rousseau. If he was to be her insider in Rosenstock Bank, then she needed to take her time and weigh him up for the role. And he needed a reason to take her seriously.

Six and nine, unsuited. It was the kind of opening hand she liked: not so big that it could get her into trouble, yet still with plenty of possibilities. She stopped chewing her lip and called the bet.

Boyband snatched up his chips and called. Players in a hurry usually liked their hand, so Harry put him on a top pair, maybe kings or queens. Rousseau murmured something in velvety-sounding French to the woman on his left, and took his time counting out his chips. He had quite a pile. Harry spotted a few crimson plaques each worth $100,000. He must have seen off a few unlucky players before she'd arrived. Interesting that he didn't let his corporate networking get in the way of his need to win.

Rousseau tossed his chips on the table, calling the bet, and the lady with the teeth folded. The dealer spread the three flop cards out on the table: King of clubs, seven of diamonds and eight of hearts. Harry felt the hairs on her arms perk up. Now she had six, seven, eight and nine. All she needed was a five or a ten to fill a straight.

Rousseau smiled across at Harry. 'Something for everyone there, I think.'

She held his gaze. It was up to him to open the betting. Still smiling, he moved $15,000 into the table. Harry was willing to bet he held another king, maybe with a kicker to pair the seven or eight on the board. But two pair still wouldn't beat a straight, and she had two more chances to fill it. The thin woman called, her eyes wide and staring as she parted with her chips. All she had left in front of her were a few thousand dollars. Harry wondered what kind of hole cards could have hooked her in so badly.

An indigo blue shadow loomed through the waters behind the dealer. The shark was back, prowling close to the wall of the tank. It tilted sideways, revealing the ghostly underside of its belly and the inverted U of its discontented-looking mouth. Harry averted her gaze, and made herself count up to five. Then she called.

Boyband wasn't in such a rush this time. Maybe his top pair wasn't looking so good any more. He wiped his hand across his mouth before pushing his chips into the pot. By now there was over $100,000 on the table.

The dealer flicked over the turn card. The ten of spades. Harry felt her toes curl. She'd filled her straight. She worked hard to keep her expression neutral, at the same time trying not to freeze. There was no better giveaway of a winning hand than a player who stopped breathing. She felt Rousseau's eyes on her.

'Well, well,' he said. 'Has anyone made the straight, I wonder?'

He leaned on his elbows with his hands clasped in front of him, his white nails almost fluorescent against his dark skin. He watched her for a long moment, and she'd have given anything for a pair of those wraparound sunglasses.

'Your father would try and bluff a straight,' he said. 'Like father, like daughter, perhaps?'

Harry shrugged. 'Maybe, maybe not.'

With a steady hand and no change of expression, Rousseau stacked up twenty purple chips into two piles and eased them out in front of him. $20,000.

The thin woman pressed her fingers to her mouth as if to stop her lips from trembling. She shook her head and folded.

Harry still put Rousseau on a king in the hole, with a kicker to make another pair. She gathered up her chips, and then brushed the baize with her knuckles just for good luck, a superstition she'd inherited from her father. Rousseau frowned, as though he recognized the gesture and didn't like what usually followed.

Harry shovelled all her remaining chips out in front of her. 'All-in.'

There was silence while the dealer counted her chips.

'Twenty five thousand,' he said.

Someone gasped at the table behind and Harry realized they'd acquired an audience. Boyband flicked his hole cards away in disgust and leaned back in his chair. Now it was just down to Rousseau.

When a player went all-in and raised with all he had at the table, the calling players had to reveal their hole cards. The rest of the community cards were dealt with the hands exposed and no more betting was allowed. It was the only time when bluffing and betting strategies counted for nothing; it all came down to the cards.

'All-in on your first hand,' Rousseau said, one eyebrow raised. He was no longer smiling. 'That takes guts.'

The shark was still cruising up and down, as though watching the action. Its torpedo-shaped body sliced through the water, and its curved dorsal fin reminded Harry of the Grim Reaper's scythe.

'You're either smart or reckless,' Rousseau went on. 'Your father was usually reckless.'

'He paid a price for his recklessness. Maybe for other people's recklessness, too.'

His eyes bored into hers. 'He played a loose game, took too many risks.'

'Whereas you prefer to play follow-the-leader and let other people take the risks?'

Rousseau's eyes narrowed. Harry kept her breathing level and her hands still. Be aware of the tells in yourself as well as in others, her father used to say. She took care not to nibble her lower lip, and instead leaned forward on her folded arms, waiting for Rousseau to make his move.

'Call,' he said eventually.

The pot was now over $150,000. The dealer waited for them to turn over their hole cards. Harry revealed her six and nine, and saw Rousseau's mouth tense.

'So,' he said, after a moment. 'Not a bluffer, after all.'

He flexed his fingers and flipped over his own cards. Pocket kings.

There was a murmur from the table behind as everyone worked it out. The king on the board gave Rousseau three of a kind. Harry's straight was still the stronger hand, but the river card was still to come. A fourth king could beat her. So could a full house, which he'd fill if the seven, eight or ten caught a pair.

She gave up the pretence and held her breath, waiting for the river card. The dealer flipped it over. It was her old pal, the Jack of spades. She'd won the hand.

She let out her breath and felt her limbs relax, aware of everyone else shifting in their chairs. Rousseau's chin jerked upwards and his fingers curled into fists.

'When you first came in I thought how like your father you were,' he said eventually. 'But I see I was mistaken.' His eyes seemed to pin her to the chair. 'You didn't come here just to play poker, did you?'

CHAPTER 47

'**S**o Sal is out of prison.'
Harry heard the plink-plink of ice cubes dropping into a glass. Rousseau's back was turned to her as he helped himself from a small bar at one end of the room.

They were in a private suite off the vestibule by the lifts. The room was elliptical in shape, its high domed ceiling a smaller replica of the one in the Great Hall of Waters. A regal-looking oak desk stood at one end, and behind it were two eight-foot poles bearing the British and American flags. The layout reminded Harry of the Oval Office.

She made her way over to the bar and hoisted herself up on to a stool. 'He got out yesterday.'

Rousseau held out a glass of whiskey to her but she shook her head. He took a sip from it and turned to face her, one elbow leaning against the bar. 'I thought he had another two years to go.'

'Remission for good behaviour.'

'You mentioned an accident.'

'That's right. Someone ran over him with a Jeep.'
Harry's body felt rigid, and she was surprised at

406

how normal her voice sounded. 'I don't suppose you'd know anything about that?'

He raised an eyebrow and looked bored by the question. Then he waved his drink in the air, setting the ice cubes tinkling. 'Why don't you just tell me what you came here for?'

Harry shrugged. 'It's quite simple. My father has a numbered account in your bank with about sixteen million dollars in it. I want the money.'

Rousseau stared at her for a moment, and then tilted back his head and laughed. 'That's what you came here for? To ask me for your father's money? Why don't you ask him?'

'Like I said, he was in an accident. He's incapacitated.'

'How inconvenient. But what's that got to do with me?'

'My father told me a lot about you.' She opened her bag and extracted the second envelope, placing it on the marble-topped bar between them. 'He told me all about your investments.'

Rousseau's eyes flicked down to the envelope. 'My investments are my own business.'

'Not if they show you were in collusion with a client convicted of insider trading. Now, how would that look to the executives back at Rosenstock Bank?'

His fingers tightened around his glass, the white nails blanching even whiter. 'If you're suggesting I was part of Sal's insider trading ring, then you're sadly mistaken. Besides, I'm sure you're aware of my country's banking secrecy laws, Ms Martinez. My trades are highly confidential.'

'Oh, I know all about banking secrecy, believe me. I also know that the law requires it to be lifted for serious criminal matters. Such as insider trading.' She took in the plush presidential suite. 'Looks like you'd have a lot to lose.'

Rousseau set his glass down on the marble with a crack. Then he smiled at her, just a beat too late. His front teeth were slightly crooked, and not as white as his nails. 'What exactly do you want?'

Harry picked up the envelope and extracted half a dozen sheets of folded paper. She smoothed out the creases and browsed through the pages as though she'd never seen them before.

'Remember EdenTech?' she said, after a moment. 'It was a software company listed on the NASDAQ back in 1999. Some Swiss operation bought them out in May the following year. See this?'

She turned the page so that he could see it, and pointed. It took concentration to keep her hands steady. The page was headed 'Rosenstock Bank Archives, Network Operations Centre'. It was one of Matilda's reports. She'd persuaded the receptionist at the Nassau Sands Hotel to give her access to a printer before she left.

'These are my father's archived trades,' she said. 'This entry here shows he bought 150,000 EdenTech shares for $367,000 at 2 p.m. on 28th April 2000. That was two weeks before the information about the Swiss takeover was made public.'

She pointed to an entry further down the list. 'And look at this, three weeks later he sold them again for $849,000. Nice profit.'

'So?'

'Here's another one. Boston Labs. They went bust in May 2000, couldn't even pay their staff. Then they got taken over by some big American outfit. But look, a week before anyone knows about the takeover, here's my father buying up a bunch of Boston Labs shares. And surprise, surprise, here he is selling them again two weeks later for a huge profit.'

'What's your point, Ms Martinez?' Rousseau snatched up a crystal decanter from the bar and refilled his glass. 'Sal's insider trading is hardly a secret.'

'Granted. Although the authorities never knew about this particular trading account. But you're right, none of this is news.' Harry leafed through the report. 'What is news, however, is that my father had a shadow.'

Rousseau's hand froze as he raised the glass to his lips. Harry went on.

'Someone was playing follow-the-leader with him. Whatever he bought, they bought. Whenever he sold, they sold. Happened every time. Here, let me show you.'

She slid the report towards him. She'd high-lighted some of the entries with a yellow marker.

'Less than half an hour after my father bought into EdenTech, this guy here snatched up 75,000 shares. My father sold his at 3.20 p.m. on 15th May, shortly after the takeover was announced. Five minutes later, our copycat trader sold his.' She turned a page. 'Same for Boston Labs. Mr Copycat bought 60,000 shares just six minutes after my father bought his. He offloaded them within three minutes of my father's sale.'

She checked Rousseau's face. His eyes were blank. He said nothing.

'There's plenty more,' she continued. 'CalTel, Sorohan . . . The list goes on. Once or twice might be a coincidence, but six months' worth of identical trades?' She shook her head. 'No doubt about it, someone was piggy-backing on my father's inside information. There's enough there for the authorities to blow away any bank secrecy and prepare a case for prosecution.' She tapped her finger on the second column of the tabulated report data. 'That's Mr Copycat's account number. Recognize it?'

Rousseau stared at the page, a small muscle ticking along his lower jaw. 'How did you get access to this information?'

'You'd be surprised at the sort of information I can get access to. And at the damage it can cause.'

'If you expose this copycat, whoever he is, you'll expose more of Sal's insider trades. He could be prosecuted again, sent back to prison. You'd do that to your own father?'

Harry shrugged. 'What can I say? We've never been close.'

Rousseau stared at her for a moment. 'Let me see if I understand this correctly. You're accusing me of trading on Sal's inside information, and in exchange for your silence, I'm supposed to empty his bank account and hand you his money.' He laughed and shook his head. 'I'd better tell you right now that what you're suggesting is frankly impossible. I couldn't do it even if I wanted to. That money can only be withdrawn by Sal presenting himself in person to his account manager. The bank's security is a lot tighter than you seem to realize.'

'Oh, I know all that. And don't worry, I don't want you to give me his money.'

'You don't?'

She smiled back at him, and shook her head. 'That would be too much to ask. As you pointed out, you'd never get it past the bank's security procedures.'

'Good. Well, I'm glad we understand one another.'

'What I want is a lot simpler. I just want you to switch some files.'

He narrowed his eyes. 'What files?'

Harry folded up the archive reports and began slotting them back into the envelope. 'This afternoon I opened up an account with Rosenstock Bank. I had to fill out an application form. The usual stuff, mostly. Name, address, signature, that kind of thing. Then they sealed my photograph to the form, and took copies of some other personal

411

documents. Utility bills, income tax forms and so on.' She pressed the sticky flap of the envelope back into place. 'Then they put the whole package in a special box file that had my new account number on it.'

Rousseau nodded, his eyes still wary. 'Your personal identification file. That's standard procedure.'

'Right, that's what they called it. My personal identification file. For an anonymous numbered account, it's the only way they can tell who the account owner really is, isn't it?'

Rousseau nodded again, more slowly this time.

Harry continued. 'So somewhere there's a box file with my father's account number on it. And inside that file are his personal application details. His name, his photograph, his signature, his utility bills.'

Rousseau sipped his whiskey, his eyes never leaving her face. He said nothing.

'You see where I'm going with this, don't you?' She smiled. 'I want you to switch the paperwork.'

He sucked down a deep draught of whiskey and shook his head. 'That's impossible.'

'No, not impossible. All you have to do is remove the identification paperwork out of my father's file, and replace it with the paperwork from mine. That way, when I go in tomorrow to withdraw the money from his account, the documentation will say quite clearly that the account belongs to me.'

Rousseau was still shaking his head. 'Sal's account

manager will know him. He won't be relying on the file for identification.'

'As it happens, they've never met. By the time you moved on and handed over the account, my father had stopped trading in it. And then, of course, he got arrested. He hasn't been to the Bahamas in a long time. No one has had a reason to open that file for over eight years.'

'But your photograph –'

'My passport photo's old enough not to raise any suspicions. It could easily belong to an application taken out nine years ago.'

Rousseau smirked. 'I'm sure it could. But it's signed by your banker. The rest of the documents in the file, all the transaction details, the memos, they're all signed by me. It won't match up.'

Harry smiled back at him. 'As I recall, there's space for a second signatory on the application form. My banker's deputy was about to sign it but got shooed out of the way. So there's nothing to stop you adding your name to it now and signing the photograph as well, is there?'

Rousseau took a slug of whiskey, wiping his mouth with the back of his hand. Harry forced herself to keep smiling.

'And we needn't worry about my banker's name looking out of place beside yours,' she said. 'As it happens, it's your old boss, Glen Hamilton. What could be more natural than the two of you endorsing an application form together for a new client?'

He frowned and snatched at the decanter.

'That's all very well, but what about the trading instructions in the file? They came from Sal, not you. They're signed with his personal codeword, the one he recorded on his own application form. It still won't match.'

'As luck would have it, we both picked the same codeword.' She watched his face. 'Pirata.'

She saw the flicker of recognition in his eyes, and knew that she'd got it right. She felt a buzz along her spine.

'It's still impossible,' Rousseau said. 'Those personal identification files are secured in a vault. The account managers can access them, but that's about all. I told you, I don't handle your father's account any more.'

'You're Vice President of International Client Relations. I'm sure you can get access if you try hard enough.'

'Those files are under maximum security. What am I supposed to do, sneak past half a dozen armed guards and blow up the vault?' He tugged at his bow tie. 'The only way to get hold of personal identification files is through official channels, which means signing them in and out. Do you think I'd put it on record that I had an opportunity to tamper with them?'

'Who's going to raise the alarm about any tampering? The switch will never be noticed. There's no activity on my father's account. And the file I opened today will probably lie dormant forever, because I won't be using it.'

'What about when Sal tries to get hold of his money? What then?'

'Don't worry, it won't come to that. As soon as I have the money, I'll negotiate a deal with him. He can't pursue it through the bank without putting me in the firing line, which he won't do. And besides, this isn't an account he wants to make too much noise about.' She swivelled on her seat, leaning back with her elbows against the bar. 'Relax. The switch will never come to light. Rosenstock may be hot on security, but its focus is keeping the customer's identity a secret, not worrying about it being switched.'

Rousseau gave a fake laugh and shook his head. 'You have it all worked out, don't you? But you have no idea what you're asking, none at all.'

He pushed himself away from the bar and moved into the centre of the room, spreading his arms out wide and turning in full circles like a weather vane. He came to a stop and faced her.

'Look at all this.' He held his palms upwards and gazed around him, his outstretched arms taking in the ornate domed ceiling, the presidential desk and the dreary, but probably priceless, oil paintings on the walls. 'Do you know what I've had to go through to get here? You know where I started?' He stabbed the air with his finger, pointing at her. 'I started as a gofer in this bank when I was seventeen. I fetched people's dry-cleaning, I booked their business lunches in fancy restaurants, I fetched their breakfast doughnuts. But you know what else I did?'

He started walking towards her, slapping the back of one hand into his other palm for emphasis. 'I learned to network. I learned how to make myself useful to people. To the right people. I made it my business to know the best restaurants, the best entertainment venues. I booked off-beat places no one else had heard of that made an impression on the clients. I kept notes on all the corporate players, on their wives' birthdays, their kids' names. I made myself indispensable. And I rose from running errands to almost running this damn bank.'

By now he had reached Harry. He leaned in towards her, his hands resting on the arms of her stool. She could smell the acrid fumes of whiskey on his breath.

'Now tell me,' he said. 'Why would I jeopardize all that with a suicidal move inside my own bank?'

Harry hoped he couldn't smell her fear, or the sweat that was rolling down her back. She gripped the envelope between her middle and index finger and flicked it back and forth like a windscreen wiper in front of his face. 'Think of the consequences if this got out. If it was me, I'd go for the low-risk option and just make the switch.'

Rousseau straightened up, his nostrils flaring, and Harry took the opportunity to clamber down from the stool. She tossed the envelope on to the bar and made her way over to the door.

'I've written the account numbers on the first sheet,' she said. 'I need the switch done by the time the bank opens in the morning.'

She reached the door, and with her hand on the knob, turned back to look at him. He had retrieved his whiskey from the bar, and was tossing it back in a single gulp.

'And just so you know,' she said. 'Several copies of those reports are in circulation. I can contain the information for the time being, but if anything happens to me, it's all wide open.'

Rousseau gave her a long look as he refilled his glass. She wished the threat was real, instead of something she'd only just thought of.

He leaned back against the bar and contemplated her for a moment. 'I think you're bluffing.'

'You forget, I'm not my father. I don't bluff.'

But Rousseau just saluted her with his glass and smiled.

CHAPTER 48

'About time,' Leon said. He watched Quinney grope for the folded cinema seat next to him.

'What the hell are we meeting here for?' Quinney bent down to see what he was doing. His bald head shone in the flickering light of the screen. 'This place is a fuckin' kip.'

Leon scanned the empty cinema and shrugged. The place was damp and dingy, and smelled of yesterday's rain. It hadn't had a makeover in nearly fifty years, and any day now it'd be turned into a bingo hall. Quinney was right, it was a kip. But it was also safe. Leon slunk down further in his back-row seat, pulling his anorak around him like a cocoon. He'd spent a lot of time in here over the last two days. Ever since he'd heard what had happened to Sal.

'Here's my report,' Quinney said, holding out a white envelope. Then he hesitated, and seemed to take in the empty chip bags on the floor and Leon's crumpled clothes. He pulled back his hand. 'First, the money.'

Leon snorted and reached for his pocket, pulling out an envelope of his own. 'Here.'

He watched as Quinney counted the money. The guy looked like a troll, with his bald head and thick lips. He was good at his job, but his attitude was hard to take. This was the second time Leon had hired him. The first had been five years earlier, when Maura had asked for the divorce. She'd sworn there hadn't been anyone else, but Leon hadn't believed her. Quinney had proved him right with a batch of glossy photos showing her wrapped around a tall blond man. The same man who'd ruffled his son's hair in the train station last week.

Quinney finished counting and stuffed the notes into his pocket. Then he tossed the white envelope into Leon's lap. 'Like I said on the phone, there's no sign of any money. You should've let me follow her on to the plane.'

Leon grunted. The private eye's rates were exorbitant enough without adding on bloody travel expenses. He ground his teeth. Fuck it, that money seemed further away than ever.

Quinney stood up, his seat banging against the backrest. 'These guys are out to get her, that's for sure. They've been tailing her the whole time. The names are all in the report.' He nodded towards the envelope. 'You might find some of the photographs interesting.'

He edged along the row of seats towards the exit. Leon watched him leave, his armpits growing

419

clammy under his anorak. Quinney had told him what he'd seen at Arbour Hill, about the Jeep that had slammed into Sal Martinez right outside the prison gates. A swirl of nausea started up in Leon's belly at the thought of seeing photographs.

Suddenly, the cinema lights flickered back on and Leon squinted. He'd hardly watched the film, except to know it was some feel-good comedy about a family with too many kids. He closed his eyes for a moment and despite his efforts not to, he thought about his son. Leon had returned to Blackrock Station the last couple of mornings, hoping to catch another glimpse of Richard. He'd smartened himself up, even had his suit dry-cleaned. But there'd been no sign of him.

Happy families, my arse, he thought.

He opened his eyes and fingered the envelope. Then he ripped it open and extracted a dozen or so typewritten pages and a bundle of photographs. Quinney had been following Harry Martinez for the best part of a week, and had run checks on the people who'd figured in her life. Leon thumbed through the report. It contained bios of all the main players. He tried to read it, but his gaze kept straying back to the photographs. Finally, he flung the report aside and studied the first shot. He noticed that his hands were trembling.

The photograph had been taken at night, and showed the Martinez girl getting into a sporty blue Mini. The street was lined with Victorian red-bricks and tall trees. Leon peered closer. Across the road from the girl he could make out the dark boxy shape of a Jeep. He swallowed, and checked the back of the photo. Quinney had noted her name, the date and location in blue pen. Raglan Road, Sunday, 12th April, 8.30 p.m. Three days ago.

The next photo showed a tall, dark-haired man guiding the Martinez girl up the steps of one of the old red-bricks. She had a bruise on the side of her face, and her cheeks were streaked with mud. This time, there was no sign of the Jeep.

Leon flipped to the next shot, ready to flinch, but it was a harmless snap of someone he recognized: that prig Jude Tiernan, striding out of the KWC building. Leon had butted heads with Tiernan years before, when they'd both worked for JX Warner. His lip curled at the memory. If it hadn't been for Tiernan's sanctimonious attitude, Leon might never have been fired.

He snapped the photo to the back of the pile and browsed through a few more. He felt his limbs relax. These were just shots of the girl's family: her sister coming out of Vincent's Hospital. He paused at one of a woman in her late fifties. So this was Sal's wife. With those cheekbones, she could have been Polish or Russian. Trust Sal to pick someone exotic. He frowned at the man who stood next to her in the photograph, his arm linking hers. Leon would've known that huge dome-head anywhere. What the hell was Ralphy-Boy doing cosying up to Sal's wife?

He moved on to a photograph that made his insides grow cold. It was a long-distance shot of high grey walls, of Victorian windows with iron bars. It could have been an orphanage, or an institution for the insane. But Leon knew better. He shuddered. He'd spent a year in that God-awful place. He'd shared a cell with a man called Noel, who was doing life for setting fire to his house. His wife and three children had been in it at the time. Leon's breathing grew shallow, and his fingers left sweat-prints on the glossy photo. For twelve months his world had been a bunk-bed and a toilet, with guards hammering on the door at five in the morning to make sure he hadn't died in his sleep.

He shoved the photo out of sight and breathed deeply a couple of times, as if that could expel the memory. He stared at the next shot, and it took him a moment to understand what it was. A figure lay on the ground, partially obscured by a small red car so that only the legs were visible: grey trousers, dark shoes. The girl was kneeling on the ground, her back to the camera. Leon blinked. So this was the shot he'd been dreading; no blood or gore, not even a face. His gaze lingered on what little he could see of Sal's body, and slowly he shook his head. So the poor bastard had finally got out of that brutal place, only to be mowed down. What a shitty deal.

Leon slotted the photo to the back of the bunch, thinking it was the last. But there was one more.

422

It was a close-up of a man at the wheel of a Jeep. Tufts of white-blond hair poked out like bleached straw from beneath his woollen hat. His knuckles were taut on the steering wheel, his gaze pinned on something straight ahead, oblivious to the camera. His wide, staring eyes made Leon's skin crawl. They were an eerie colourless shade, as though his pupils had disappeared, leaving only the light of insanity behind. Leon tried to wet his lips but his tongue was dry. He'd always known the Prophet used someone else to do his dirty work, but this was the first time he'd ever seen the man's face.

Leon dragged a hand across his mouth. Fuck it, maybe he was in over his head this time. Maybe he should get the hell out. Then he thought of Jonathan Spencer, and a fireball of acid burned into his gut. Jonathan had wanted out, but the Prophet hadn't let him go. Leon clutched at his abdomen. Why the fuck had the Prophet sent him that email about the girl? Why had he got him involved?

But Leon already knew the answer. The Prophet was using him, just like before. He was setting him up to take the fall. That was how the Prophet operated: from a distance, always in control but letting others take the risks. Even at the height of the trading ring's success, the Prophet had never executed a single trade. Leon, Sal and Jonathan were the ones who put their careers on the line. The Prophet took a major chunk of the proceeds but left no trace on the paper trail that led to the ring's prosecution. Even Jonathan's death had looked enough like an accident to make sure the Prophet was safe.

Leon's gaze slid back to the photograph, to those pale, psychopathic eyes. He ran a finger inside his collar as he thought about the trail leading back to him. If anything happened to Sal or the girl, he could be in deep shit. Christ, it was his PI who'd trashed her apartment, his PI who'd been tailing her. His PI had even been at Arbour Hill when Sal was struck down. Leon's heart pounded against his chest. He had the girl's bank statement, for God's sake. His address was probably somewhere on the bank's computer records. A small whimper rose in his throat. Fuck it, how had he got himself into such a stinking mess?

He snatched at the report. There had to be something here, something he could use. What had Quinney said? *The names are all in the report.* He snapped through the pages, skipping the detail. Quinney had already filled him in on the girl's movements over the phone. He skimmed through the bios, reading too fast to take it all in. Even so, he could tell Quinney had been thorough. Names, ages, families, employment histories, financial records; it was all there. The words were a blur. The name JX Warner leapt out at him, and he stared at the page. They'd always believed the Prophet was an investment banker there. A memory stirred at one of the faces. He frowned.

How long ago? Ten years? Twelve? He picked up the photos and studied them again. He hadn't known old dome-head had worked for JX Warner. But then, so had a lot of people.

He stared at the shots and then picked out two, checking the names on the back. Then he peered at the faces again. Was that the connection? He grabbed the report and flashed straight to the bios. This time he read them slowly. He knew what he was looking for, and there it was, underlined in bold. Even Quinney had seen its significance. It couldn't be a coincidence.

Leon stuffed everything back into the envelope. His fingers trembled as he fumbled with the flap. Then he barged past the empty seats and out through the drab foyer into the street. The white afternoon light jabbed at his eyes. He raced along the pavement, his breathing ragged and his heart pumping. Maybe the girl's money was out of his reach, but what if he knew who the Prophet was? That had to be worth something.

He wiped away the sweat from his forehead and shoved the envelope inside his anorak. The pain in his gut had melted away, anaesthetized by adrenaline. His knowledge was dangerous, he knew that better than anyone. But it also gave him power.

The traffic growled around him, trucks and motor-bikes alternately revving and idling in the congested streets. It was a ten-minute walk to the South Circular Road, but he picked up his pace and made

425

it in five. He turned left into St Mary's Road, the grumbling engines receding behind him. He groped for his keys. He'd shower and change while he worked out his next move.

Across the road, a dark-haired woman was leaning against the railings of his bedsit, smoking a cigarette. She caught sight of him and pushed herself upright. Leon narrowed his eyes. She looked familiar. An engine rumbled behind him as he tried to figure it out. The Big Bird frame, the helmet hairdo. Then his brow cleared. It was that nosy reporter from the court case. What the hell was she doing here?

He stepped off the kerb to cross the street, planning to push straight past her. Interfering bitch. He hadn't forgotten the sneering way she'd written about him in her articles. Sal always made time for her, he could never understand why.

The reporter shot an arm in the air and called something out to him. To hell with her, he'd other things on his mind. Suddenly, she clapped a hand to her mouth, and dropped her cigarette. She seemed to be staring over his shoulder. He checked behind him and froze.

A motorbike was charging down the middle of the road, the rider crouched forward like a jockey. The roar of the engine filled Leon's ears. He tried to move, but his feet were bags of sand. The bike stampeded towards him, gleaming black, unstoppable. Leon's feet jerked to life and he leapt sideways, but it was too late. The bike reared up like a stallion and crashed into his chest. He sailed backwards and upwards into the air, the breath expelled with a whoosh from his lungs. Houses shot past him, walls tilted. There was no pain yet.

The motorbike's rear wheel slammed into his shoulder as it coasted by. The rider bent his head down low over the side, as if searching Leon's face for signs of pain. The visor on his helmet was up, and Leon could see the pale translucent eyes, with their pinpoint pupils.

The sky slid sideways. Leon flashed on his son's smiling face. Then the ground rushed up behind him and smashed into his skull.

CHAPTER 49

'**I**s that the fax you'd like me to send for you, madam?'

Harry dragged her gaze away from the sheet of paper in her hand and stared at the hotel receptionist.

'Maybe I'll just check it over one last time,' she said.

'That's fine. Just let me know when you're ready.'

The receptionist drifted away to answer the phone. Her white cotton shirt looked crisp and cool, and Harry wondered how she managed it. Her own shirt was sticking to her like wallpaper paste.

She looked down at the fax she'd written in her hotel room. Her heartbeat drummed in her ears, and the words blurred a little. What if Rousseau hadn't made the switch? Perhaps he'd decided to call her bluff. She blinked to clear her vision, and read the fax again. It was addressed to Owen Johnson, her father's account manager.

Dear Mr Johnson,

With reference to account number 72559353, authentication code Pirata, I hereby give notice that I wish to close this account and transfer all funds to the following bank account:

SWIFT Code: CRBSCHZ9
IBAN: CH9300762011623852957

As per security procedures, I will arrange to conduct this transfer in person with you later today.

The first account number was her father's, and the second belonged to the Prophet. There was no need for a signature.

Harry checked her watch: 10.04 a.m. Even if Rousseau planned to co-operate, had she given him enough time? The last thing she needed was someone opening her father's file before her identification papers were in place. She shifted from foot to foot. The Prophet's deadline ran out at noon, Bahamas time. She had to make her move.

She handed over the fax, along with Johnson's fax number, which she'd decoded from her father's poker notes. The receptionist sauntered over to the machine behind the desk and fed the page into it. The machine beeped, and Harry watched as the woman loaded it with paper from the tall stacks on the floor. She was air-hostess elegant but slow as a mudslide, and Harry clenched her teeth to keep from screaming. Finally, her fax juddered through the machine and out the other side.

Harry raced back to her room. She reached for her phone on the bedside table and saw she'd missed three calls from Ruth Woods. She dialled the reporter's number. Voicemail. Harry left a message saying she'd call her when she got back to Dublin in the morning. Then she perched on the edge of the bed and called Rosenstock Bank. Quoting her father's account number in a businesslike tone, she fixed an appointment with Owen Johnson for 11.15 a.m.

She disconnected the call. In less than an hour, she'd be walking into Johnson's office to transfer sixteen million dollars out of his bank. The question was, would he be expecting her or her father?

She shook her head, and packed up some paperwork to take to the bank. Then she left her hotel on foot. She made her way to Bay Street, following the shade where she could. The muggy air brushed against her skin like warm cotton. By the time she reached Rosenstock Bank, her scalp was damp with sweat.

The girl on reception smiled. 'Back so soon?'

Damn, she hadn't planned on being recognized.

Juliana picked up the phone. 'Let me call through to Glen Hamilton for you.'

'No, no, don't disturb her.' Shit, the last thing she needed was Glen Hamilton breathing down her neck. 'Actually, I'm here to see Owen Johnson.'

Juliana raised her eyebrows. 'Oh, right. No problem.' She clicked a few keys on her computer.

'He's on the same floor as Glen. You remember the elevators? Take the middle one.'

Harry thanked her and followed instructions. The same Big Brother elevator carried her up to the second floor, where the same young woman escorted her along the corridor. Harry darted looks at the beige doors as she passed, half-expecting Glen to appear. Her phone vibrated at the bottom of her bag, and she slipped it out. Ruth Woods again. Harry switched off her phone. She'd contact her later.

Her escort opened a door at the end of the hall and Harry ducked inside. This time, her banker was waiting for her.

He sat behind a desk littered with papers. He was in his late fifties, with liver-brown skin and a stony expression on his face. For a moment, there was silence. Harry heard the click of the door closing behind her. Then he stood up.

'I'm Owen Johnson,' he said.

He was built like an overweight rottweiler. His barrel-shaped body was a solid mass of thick muscle and fat, and his jaw looked powerful enough to bite off her arm. Harry crossed the room and shook his hand, aware that hers was damp.

'I'm Harry Martinez,' she said.

His round, bulbous eyes bored into hers. 'I don't think we've met.'

It wasn't a question. Harry was willing to bet that Owen Johnson remembered every face he saw.

She smiled and shook her head, trying to look like a multi-millionaire instead of a hacker who told lies.

Johnson resumed his seat, and gestured for her to take the straight-backed chair opposite. She sat down. The furniture was more functional than in Glen Hamilton's office. The desk was plain and solid, the chairs sturdy. No precious antiques or silver coffee service to get in the way of business. Harry wondered if the bankers got to choose their own décor.

Johnson cleared his throat and frowned at the papers in front of him. Harry stiffened. A manila box file lay open on his desk. The spring-loaded clamp had been released and the paperwork had sprung upwards, almost filling the box. The pages were creased and well-thumbed. It had to be her father's file.

Harry cut across the silence. 'I hope you got my fax. As it says, I'd like to transfer my funds to another account as soon as possible.'

She handed him a copy of the fax. He glanced at it, but gave no indication that he'd seen it before. She dug her passport out of her bag and handed that over too. Johnson flipped it open at the photograph page and studied it with a frown. Then he extracted a document from the box file and held it up for comparison. Harry stopped breathing. She tried to read his face, but his expression didn't change. His gaze met hers. Her throat wanted to swallow but she willed the sensation away.

Without a word, Johnson snapped the passport

shut and pushed it back across the desk. He dropped the other document into the file, and Harry caught a glimpse of the photograph stapled to the top page. Signatures obliterated half the face, but there was no mistaking the mass of dark curls surrounding it. Her lungs started pumping again. It was her own application form. Rousseau had made the switch.

'May I ask if you've been satisfied with the service Rosenstock has provided?' Johnson said.

'Oh, absolutely.' Her heart was pounding. 'I'm afraid I just have other plans for the money right now.'

Johnson shifted his bulk and tilted back in his chair, making steeples out of his fingers. 'It's odd. I only saw this file once before, when I first took it over. That was eight years ago. I remember the name Martinez.' He fixed her with an unblinking stare. 'But somehow I always felt sure our Pirata client was a man.'

Harry tried to smile, but her face felt tight. 'It's probably the name. Harry, I mean. It always leaves people wrong footed.'

He tapped his fingertips together, still watching her. 'I'm sure that's it.'

Then he handed her a form from the pile of paperwork on his desk, along with her original fax. 'Perhaps you could fill this out so I can authorize the transfer.'

Harry scanned the form. It was brief and to the point, requiring details of the source and destination accounts, the amount of funds to transfer and, of course, her authentication code and signature. There was a section for Johnson to countersign at the end. She began to fill it in, copying down the account numbers from her fax.

'You used to deal with Philippe Rousseau, I believe,' Johnson said. He made it sound like an accusation.

'Yes, that's right.' Harry didn't look up, but she could feel his eyes drilling into the top of her head.

'You spoke with him last night, or so I'm told.'

Her fingers froze. 'Yes, I bumped into him at the Atlantis Casino.'

'I know. He told me.'

Harry shot him a glance. 'Oh?'

'When I went to check your file out of the vaults this morning, I found that he'd already signed it out. Naturally, as the authorized account manager I demanded to know why.'

'Naturally.' Harry kept her tone light. 'And what did he say?'

'He told me you'd met, played some poker. He said he was curious to see how your investments were doing, so he checked out the file. Strictly against security policy, of course.' Johnson smiled for the first time, a grimace that bared a mouthful of tightly packed teeth. 'But then, Mr Rousseau tends to do what he likes around here.'

Harry ducked her head and went back to the form. 'Well, I appreciate his interest.' The pen felt slippery in her fingers. 'He's known my family a long time.'

She reached the box labelled 'Transfer Amount', and hesitated.

'It's a while since I checked the balance on my account,' she said. 'Could you tell me the exact amount so I can fill this out?'

Johnson grunted, and turned to his laptop. He punched a few keys. For the first time it occurred to Harry that the account might be empty. What if someone else had got there first?

Johnson grabbed a pen and copied down some numbers from the screen. Then he shoved his pad towards her.

The numbers danced in front of her. Her head felt light, and her hearing tuned out for a moment. Almost twenty million dollars. The account had racked up interest in the last nine years.

So it was here. She was close to it. This was what they were all after: the ring, her father, the Prophet. She thought about the people who had died: Jonathan Spencer, Felix Roche. Images flashed by: a roaring Jeep, spinning mountains, a screeching train. Her head swam. But now the killing would stop. Now she'd hand everything over to the Prophet, and no one else would die.

Harry's spine felt icy. Unless he took the money and then killed her anyway. How could she trust a man who'd tried to kill her father?

She tightened her grip on the pen. She checked the time. Three minutes to twelve.

The money was the only leverage she had.

She looked at Johnson, her chin raised. 'I've changed my mind.'

'Excuse me?'

'I don't want to transfer the money.'

Johnson blinked. 'So you want to leave it in the account?'

'No. I want to withdraw it in cash. Large bills.'

Johnson leaned forward in his chair. 'Cash? But you can't walk around with that much money in cash, it's highly insecure. If you really need to move the money, I strongly advise an electronic transfer.'

Harry shook her head. 'I want cash.'

The Prophet had already accessed her bank account once. The last thing she wanted now was to place her trust in technology. She needed to feel the money in her hands.

Johnson sighed. 'But it's physically impossible to carry that amount of dollars. The largest denomination is only a hundred-dollar bill. You'd need five suitcases for the stuff.'

Harry paused. 'What's the highest denomination for euros?'

Johnson shifted in his chair. 'Five hundred.'

'So. Only one suitcase then.'

'But euros are harder to get around here.'

'Are you telling me the bank can't raise the currency?'

Johnson puffed out his chest. 'Of course Rosenstock can honour the funds, but you must

436

realize this amount of cash will take time to put together.'

'How much time?'

'Well, maybe in a day or two, we could –'

Harry cut in. 'That's too late. I need it today. I've a plane to catch.'

She saw Johnson's jaw set, and changed tack.

'Tell you what,' she said. 'You raise the cash today and I'll leave $100,000 on deposit so the account stays open. You'll still have my business. I'll write to your boss giving you credit for retaining me as a client. Otherwise, you take the blame for losing the account. Let's see, your boss is Philippe Rousseau, am I right?'

Johnson's eyes bulged, and she could see him weighing it up: the disgrace of losing a fat-cat account, or pandering to a client he didn't trust. Finally, he flung his pen on the desk.

'Very well, but it will take a few hours.'

'How many hours?'

He shrugged. 'Four, maybe five.'

'Make it three.' Harry stood up. 'Is there some-place I can wait and make some calls?'

Johnson got up from behind the desk and opened a door on his left. Harry stepped past him into a small anteroom furnished with regency chairs and a desk. When Johnson had gone, she picked up the phone and called Ruth Woods. No answer. She left a message.

'Ruth, it's Harry. It's time for your story, but we've got to move fast. I have something the

437

Prophet wants and I'm going to use it to flush him out. I need you to use your police contacts. We've got to set this bastard up. Call me back.'

Harry paced the room, hatching out a plan and trying not to think about her father. She had to involve the police now, she had no choice. One thing she knew for certain: she couldn't let go of the money.

She was still pacing the floor when Johnson finally returned. In the end, it had only taken him two hours. He led her back into his office and closed the door. Then he gestured towards his desk, which had been cleared of clutter. The only thing on its surface was a large black suitcase with wheels.

'Open it,' he said.

Harry hesitated, then she eased up the lid. The case was filled with large purple banknotes. They were bound into bundles the size of bricks, and packed together with their edges lined up. The notes looked flat and clean, as though they'd been ironed. Harry picked up a bundle, and saw more layers underneath. Like a box of chocolates, she thought. She riffled through the stack in her hand, and then ran her thumb across the top. The notes had a cottony feel, with tactile patterns along the edges. Slowly, she put the notes back in the case.

'Would you like to count it?' Johnson asked.

Harry shook her head. She lowered the lid and snapped it shut.

Johnson handed her a piece of paper. 'You'll need to sign this withdrawal form and receipt.'

Harry's hand trembled as she scrawled her signature. Johnson countersigned the forms and handed her copies, along with a plain white envelope.

'That's an authorization note from the bank. It'll get you through airport security and customs without any questions.'

Harry nodded her thanks and stuffed the envelope into her bag. Then, tensing her muscles, she grasped the case and lugged it off the desk. It yanked at her arm, and she felt a thud as the blocks of notes shifted inside. She pulled out the retractable handle and wheeled the case over to the door.

Johnson escorted her along the corridor and back down to the ground floor. Neither of them spoke. She left him in the elevator while she stepped out into the lobby, towing the suitcase behind her. Then she pushed open the doors and walked out into the sunlight with fifteen million euros.

CHAPTER 50

The plane began its descent into Dublin Airport.

Harry gripped the armrests of her seat. She hadn't slept in almost twenty-four hours. She dragged her eyelids open, keeping watch on the other passengers. She had to admit, none of them looked ready to kill her.

So far, so good. No one had stopped her at the airport, no one had asked her to open her bags. She peered out the window at the mist shifting across the aircraft's wing. According to the pilot, thick fog awaited them back in Dublin. She flexed her fingers around the armrest. What else awaited her back there?

The plane landed on time. Harry disembarked with the other passengers and made her way to the baggage carousel. Her luggage was the last to emerge, and she exhaled deeply at the sight of it. No amount of pleading with the ground staff at Nassau had convinced them to let her bags on as hand luggage, and the thought of them stowed away out of her sight had added to her anxiety.

She hauled up the black suitcase, setting it down

on its wheels, and flung her father's holdall over her shoulder. She darted a look around. No one assaulted her, and no one tried to grab her bags.

She made a detour into the Ladies' toilet, where she ran the cold tap and splashed her face until her skin felt numb. She raised her gaze to the mirror. Tiredness had cut deep purple gashes beneath her eyes. By comparison, the rest of her skin was grey. She looked like an undernourished teenager, and certainly no match for someone like the Prophet.

She closed her eyes and felt herself sway. Why hadn't she just handed over the money like she'd planned? What the hell had she been thinking? Then she shook her head. She was just tired, that was all. She'd made the right choice. The money was the only reason she was still alive.

Harry glanced around the bathroom, making sure she was alone. She clicked open the suitcase and lifted the lid a fraction. The money was still there. She snapped the case closed. Then she switched her phone on and dialled Ruth's number. She'd tried the journalist's number several times before leaving the Bahamas, but couldn't get through. No answer now either. Dammit, where was she? Harry's throat tightened. She couldn't do this alone.

Tremors vibrated along her arms and legs. Harry lowered herself on to the floor beside her bags and rested her head against her knees. She took a few deep breaths. What if someone was waiting for her out in the Arrivals hall? She shuddered and checked her watch: 12.30 p.m. Then she leaned back against her bags and closed her eyes. Maybe she'd stay here, just for a while. They couldn't get to her in here.

She stayed there for over two hours, listening to the beep of baggage carousels as other flights arrived. Trolleys clashed outside and women streamed in and out of the toilets. Harry's thighs grew numb against the hard metal. She wondered how long she could stay in here before someone threw her out.

A mob of about twenty teenagers barged into the Ladies', chattering in Gatling-gun Spanish. They looked to be about seventeen or eighteen years old. They jostled for space in front of the mirror, touching up their makeup and firing bursts of gossip across the room. The girl nearest Harry took off her watch and fiddled with the winder. '*¿Es una hora más o una hora menos?*' Are we an hour ahead or an hour behind?

No one heard her above the clamour.

'*Es una hora menos,*' Harry offered. '*Es 14.35.*'

'*Gracias.*' The girl smiled. Her eyes were the colour of cinnamon and her hair was thick and dark.

Harry blinked. Then she looked at the rest of the group, at their olive skin tones, their striking dark brows and hair. She heaved herself up off the floor and stood behind them, studying her own reflection. Thick black curls, dark eyes. Her skin was

442

paler than theirs, but for the most part she blended in. It wasn't much of a camouflage, but it might be all she had.

The girls flooded out of the Ladies'. Harry snatched up her bags and followed close behind. Outside, a swarm of Spanish students had invaded the baggage area. They moved in packs, and Harry eased into their midst. The noise was deafening. The surging throng swept her forward. She approached the Arrivals hall and ducked her head low, pretending to fiddle with her bags. Her stomach clenched. If anyone had been out there waiting, surely they'd be gone by now?

The students crushed around her, spilling into the Arrivals hall. Harry blundered forwards. The airport was jammed with people. She muscled through the crowds, eyes down, still under cover of her escorts. No one paid her any attention. Finally, she reached the main exit and peeled away from her convoy. She stopped at a car park pay station by the doors and fed money into the machine, her hands shaking. She threw a glance over her shoulder and froze.

Boxed in by the crowds a few hundred yards in front of her was a tall man in a black leather jacket. His back was towards her, a mobile phone pressed against his ear. She couldn't see his face, but the flaxen hair poking out from under his hat was unmistakable.

Heat flashed along her body. She'd seen that hair twice before: once on the Dublin mountains and once outside Arbour Hill prison. Both times, she'd almost been killed.

The blond man craned his neck over the crowds. She glimpsed his face. It was taut and pale, his expression hunted. Harry's breathing stopped. He was nodding, listening to someone on the phone. Harry edged towards the exit, tugging her case behind her. The man flinched at something that was said, and then nodded. He turned and barged back through the throng, away from her towards the Arrivals gate.

Every nerve ending screamed out for Harry to run, but she resisted. Small movements would keep her invisible. She edged nearer the doors, staring at the man's retreating back. His progress was slow, impeded by the crowds. The phone was still glued to his ear.

The automatic doors parted. She stepped towards them, glancing back over her shoulder. Another figure caught her eye, on the other side of the concourse. He was turning this way and that, scouring his surroundings. Jammed to his ear was a mobile phone. Harry flinched. She recognized his frame. Broad shoulders, rugby workhorse build. It was Jude Tiernan.

Jude stopped spinning. He glared at the man with the blond hair, his mouth tight. Then his gaze slid over to where Harry stood. Her skin turned cold. His eyes locked on hers. Then he snapped his gaze back to the blond-haired man and spoke into his phone. The other man whirled round and stared straight at Harry. His pale eyes devoured her. Harry turned and bolted through the doors.

She raced across the road to the multi-storey car park, the wheels of the case clattering behind her. She zigzagged between the parked cars, the bags dragging at her arms. If she could just get to her car. She raked her gaze across the rows of vehicles ahead, but there was no sign of the red Micra.

Her heart thudded in her ears. She wheeled to her right and scrambled up the ramp to the next level. Her footsteps slapped against the concrete, scattering echoes off the low roof. She shot a glance behind her. The blond man was sprinting towards the ramp, his arms and legs pumping.

Where the hell was her car? She spun around, the weight of the case wrenching her shoulder. Maybe she should ditch it. But what about the money? She'd need it if she ever got out of here.

Footsteps pounded behind her. Harry lurched towards the next ramp. She clambered up, the bags throwing her off-balance. A Mercedes careered down the ramp towards her. It screeched to a halt, bouncing on its suspension inches away from her. She skittered around it and tore up to the next level.

She visualized herself parking the car two days before: corkscrewing up the levels, squinting in the daylight, searching for a space. Daylight. That was it. She'd parked on the roof.

The footsteps were louder, faster. Harry tensed

her muscles and lumbered up the last few ramps. Her legs were heavy, and the bags racked her arms. Finally, daylight stabbed her eyes. The roof was deserted, apart from the rows of abandoned cars. Fog and cloud mingled together, settling over everything like grey gauze. The Nissan Micra was a splash of red right at the very back.

Harry hunkered down and scurried in between the cars, scuffing the bags along the ground behind her. Cramp seized her fingers and wrists. Footsteps whacked hard against the ground, and then stopped. Harry stiffened. She crouched even lower, listening. Then she bent her head to the ground and peered beneath the cars. Someone in trainers was creeping along a path parallel to hers. He was only two rows away from her.

Harry hunched down as low as she could and tacked her way to the last row of cars. Every few yards, she checked on the trainers. They were still tracking her. She scooted over to the Micra, finally letting go of the bags. Spasms convulsed up her arms. She found her car keys. Her fingers were stiff and shaking. She jammed the key in the door and turned the lock. Then she eased upright, keeping her head low. Her knees crackled like firewood. She squeezed the door handle, listening for footsteps. Nothing.

Slowly, she coaxed open the door. She winced, waiting for it to creak. Her reflection winced back at her from the car window. Wild hair and white face against a dark background. Then the background shifted. Harry's eyes widened. Another reflection slid out from behind hers. Ashen face, black hat, tufts of albino hair.

He grabbed her before she had time to turn around. He jerked her backwards by the hair and then slammed her head into the car door. Harry's brain reeled. She couldn't open her eyes. He wedged her up against the car with his body. He was hard and sinewy, his body odour dense. She kicked backwards, but made no contact. He grabbed her head again, this time with both hands, and smacked it off the roof of the car. Pain pulsed through her skull. Her legs buckled. She slumped against the Micra, her head spinning.

He hauled her up and yanked her arms behind her back. Cold steel slipped over her wrists. She heard tightening ratchets, then a snap. The steel cut into her skin. He covered her head with something coarse that blocked out the light. Sacking, rough and scratchy. She heard the car door open. Then he shoved her hard, and she pitched forwards across the back seat. She tried to sit up but felt seasick-dizzy and lurched down on to the floor. Her shoulders jammed between the seats, the pain in her arms excruciating.

Something heavy thudded on to the seat beside her. Her bags.

The car doors slammed shut. Then the engine sputtered to life and the Micra jolted forward, sending spasms up along her arms. Her head swam, and she felt herself drift. Images of Jude Tiernan sailed in front of her like a slide show: Jude at the KWC meeting, where he'd no business to be; Jude in White's Bar, pretending to help her get to Felix; Jude at the airport, mouthing deadly instructions into a mobile phone.

Her brain began to float. She should never have trusted him.

CHAPTER 51

Harry woke up choking. Her throat was raw, and her nostrils felt like they were on fire. She couldn't see. Something wet and heavy clung to her face. She inhaled through her nose. Fumes punched through her sinuses and made her head swim. The smell was asphyxiating, and reminded her of firelighters. Then she understood. Jesus. The sacking around her head was drenched in petrol.

She tried to inhale again, but the caustic vapours made her gag. Pain wrenched her neck and shoulders. She was lying on her side, her arms still cuffed behind her back. From the hard ground beneath her, she could tell she was no longer in the car. She twisted her head, trying to get purchase on the sacking. A small piece of it lifted away from her lower lip, admitting a tiny crack of air. She sucked it in, trying not to hyperventilate.

A scraping noise came from somewhere in front of her. Then silence.

'Who's there?' Harry said.

She hated the way her voice cracked. There was no answer. She was afraid to move in case the

449

sacking slipped back over her mouth. There it was again, a rasping sound, followed by a gentle hiss. Her body went rigid. Dear God. He was lighting matches.

Harry licked her lips, the acrid petrol burning her tongue. 'What's happening?'

'We're waiting.' His voice was ragged and harsh. He was close to her.

She cleared her throat, and tried to sound non-threatening. It wasn't hard. 'Can you at least take off the hood?'

'Not until he gets here.'

'How long will that be?'

'Not long. He followed us from the airport.'

There was another scrape. What was he doing with the lit matches? Was he blowing them out? Flicking them towards her? She imagined the sacking catching fire, her head trapped in a hood of flames, her hands bound behind her back. A scream welled up inside her and she clamped her mouth shut. No time for hysteria. She had to get away before Jude got here, before there were two of them to deal with.

She gulped in a mouthful of air.

'Maybe you could just loosen the handcuffs?' She arched her back, brushing her fingertips on the ground behind her. Nothing but dry clay.

'Not till he says,' he said.

She eased her right leg out in front of her, as though stretching her calf muscles. 'Do you always do as he says?'

She groped with her foot but felt nothing. He struck another match and her leg went still. He didn't answer her question.

'Let me guess,' she said. 'I bet you do all the dirty work while he gets all the money. Is that how it works?'

Still no answer. She risked moving her leg again and explored the ground behind her. Her foot came up against something solid. She pushed against it. There was some give in it but not much. A wooden fence, maybe.

'So what do you get out if it?' She heard a lid being unscrewed, and her leg stiffened.

'I get looked after,' he said.

'Why don't you just take the money and go? It's right there. I can't stop you, I don't even know who you are.'

There was a faint rustle, and she sensed him moving closer. Something sloshed inside a container. Without warning, a torrent of cold liquid slammed down on to her chest. She gasped, and rolled over on to her face. The reek of petrol was overwhelming. He kept on pouring, drenching her. Her shirt clung to her skin, soaked.

The deluge stopped, and she heard the lid being screwed back on to the container. He lit another match. Then he laughed, a soft snuffling sound that came through his nose.

Harry shivered. Damn her father to hell. Why hadn't he helped her? Hadn't he loved her enough to do that? She should have gone to the police, let him rot in prison for as long as he deserved, instead of trying to protect him. The scream she'd suppressed earlier surged back up inside her and threatened to erupt.

Something hissed close to her ear and then died out. She inhaled her own fumes, the petrol vapours surrounding her like an aura. Just how close did a flame need to get to her before she'd self-combust? She thought of Felix Roche, torched inside his apartment, and almost retched again.

'So you're going to set me on fire?' she said. 'Like Felix Roche?'

'I never know their names.' He sounded mildly puzzled. 'I don't know yours.'

She choked on her own suffocating smell. Would he still kill her if he knew her name?

'It's Harry,' she said. 'My name is Harry.'

Then she winced at the pleading in her voice, and clenched her fists behind her back.

'Here's a few more names for you,' she said. 'Jonathan Spencer. That was nearly nine years ago. Near the IFSC. Remember him? And my father. Sal Martinez. You tried to kill him last week on Arbour Hill.'

'The IFSC. I remember that one. There was a lot of blood.' He paused. 'But you're wrong about the one on Arbour Hill. I wasn't trying to kill him.' He lit another match. 'I was trying to kill you.'

Harry gasped. She had been the target?

The man continued. 'He saw what I was trying to do and he shoved you out of the way.' He lit another match. 'Pity he's not here to protect you now, isn't it?'

Harry pictured the deserted road outside the prison. She saw the Jeep bearing down, her father hurling himself out of its path. She remembered the stricken look on his face. For the first time she considered the possibility that he'd flung himself into the Jeep's path, not out of it; that he'd pushed her to safety, not crash-landed against her. For the first time she considered the possibility that he had saved her life.

A huge ache burned through her chest, and suddenly she was a child again, needing to be rocked in her father's arms.

A car engine revved nearby, and then cut out. A door slammed. Footsteps marched towards her, snapping on concrete, then brushing against something softer. There was a moment of silence. Then someone tugged at the sacking on her head and yanked it off.

Harry blinked at the light, her eyes smarting from the petrol fumes. She lay on a narrow clay path, her cheek pressed into the dirt. She squinted up at the blond man standing beside her. He held a large flagon of petrol, still two-thirds full. At his feet was a glass bowl filled with folded matchbooks. And on the ground next to her face, inches from her nose, was a scattering of spent matches.

An icy chill drenched through her. She sucked fresh air into her lungs, its spicy scent oddly familiar. She craned her neck to look behind her.

The wooden fence turned out to be a tall hedge, curving along a twisted path. Something stirred in her brain. Then she snapped her gaze upwards. Towering above her on all sides were more hedges, vast and dense, higher than prison walls. In front of her and behind, they circled and looped, enclosing her in a dark green tunnel. Harry shuddered. She knew where she was.

She was inside a giant maze.

CHAPTER 52

'I always knew you'd lead me to the money, Harry.'

She whipped her gaze around. Dillon was standing in front of her. He had a gun in his hand.

She stared at him, her mind blank. 'Dillon?'

'I wish you'd confided in me more.' His voice was gentle. 'I waited, but you never opened up to me.'

She tried to sit up. Pain ripped into her shoulders, and she sank back against the ground. Her brain felt woolly.

'We could have been a team,' he went on. 'Found the money together.'

She squinted up at him. Mist drifted around him like cigarette smoke. He was dressed all in black, the way he'd been when they first met. His lips twitched into his secret smile.

'I don't understand,' Harry said.

'I think you do.' He held the gun loosely, pointing it at her midriff. She stared at it, transfixed. She'd never seen a real gun before.

Dear God. Dillon. Her schoolgirl crush. Her boss. Her lover. She shuddered. Then she noticed the bags at his feet: her father's fat holdall and the black case from Rosenstock Bank. The suitcase lid was open, exposing a layer of purple banknotes.

Dillon followed her gaze and backed up a step, kneeling beside the suitcase. He plunged his hands into its depths, extracting three thick bundles of notes. He brushed them under his nose, inhaling. Then he stood up and tossed them back into the case, kicking the lid shut.

'You should have just transferred the money like I asked,' he said. 'Look at all the trouble you've caused.'

He lashed out at her father's holdall with his foot, connecting with a savage blow. Harry flinched, scuffing backwards in the dirt. He kicked it again, his face contorted. The canvas ripped open along the seam, and some of the contents slid out: her cream silk dress, her father's poker set.

The blond man gathered up the silk dress and held it to his face. Then he brought his foot back the way Dillon had, and kicked her in the stomach. She screamed and doubled over, her abdomen cramped in pain. Jesus! They really meant to do it. They were going to kill her. She hunched her shoulders, waiting for the next blow. Dillon smashed his foot into her father's poker case, and it skittered across the ground. Harry stared at the dent he'd made in the casing, and clenched her fists. Fuck them. She wasn't going to lie here just waiting to die.

She swallowed hard. 'I thought the Prophet

was a banker in JX Warner. Where the hell do you fit in?'

The blond man took aim with his leg again but Dillon waved him back with his gun.

'I fit in right at the top,' he said. 'I was head of IT Security in JX Warner for two years. I had access to more confidential information than any investment banker.'

He smiled and wiped his forehead with his sleeve. Behind him through the mist, Harry could see the red triangular flag that marked the entrance to the maze. It was only about ten yards away. It may as well have been ten miles.

'It was Leon Ritch who gave me the idea, although he never knew it,' Dillon went on. 'He got fired from JX Warner after a few shady deals. I helped put together the evidence against him, all those incriminating emails and documents that he left behind. I kept tabs on him after he left. A banker with flexible ethics was just what I needed.'

'What about my father?' Harry eyed up the hedges. They must have been twelve feet tall, and denser than reinforced concrete. 'When did you recruit him?'

'Actually, it was Leon's idea to scale things up. More sources, more money. Ashford came first, then Spencer and your father.'

'And Jude Tiernan?'

Dillon raised his eyebrows. 'The man of ethics? No chance. He'd have turned us all in.'

Harry frowned, picturing Jude at the airport,

scouring the crowds. Shit. He'd been trying to help her, not kill her.

Dillon moved in front of her, blocking her view of the exit. Even if she could run, her only choice was to go further back into the maze.

He knelt down beside her, his gaze raking her face. His hand moved out as though to touch her cheek, then he seemed to change his mind. 'Imagine how I felt when one of Leon's sources turned out to be little Pirata's father.'

Harry worked it out. 'So you didn't head-hunt me to work for Lúbra. You were using me to get to the money.'

'That's how it started out, yes.' He dropped his gaze. 'I thought if I scared you enough, you'd persuade your father to hand over the money. But you were so stubborn about going to see him. I suppose I should have expected that.'

'You scared me all right. I could have been killed on those bloody train tracks.' She shot a glance over her shoulder. Behind her the narrow path forked into three. There was another exit somewhere. But which way?

'Cameron exceeded his instructions at the train station.' Dillon gestured with his gun. 'You've met my brother Cameron, haven't you?'

Harry jerked her head around and gaped at the blond man, at his pale skin and stooped shoulders. His eyes were fixed on Dillon, like a mistreated mongrel awaiting instructions. She took in Dillon's dark looks, his casual elegance.

Then her right brain shifted, settling the pieces. Dillon had said he was adopted. This was the deadbeat younger brother who'd ended up in jail.

Harry shivered, and not just from the chill of her wet clothes. 'What about his instructions on Arbour Hill? He was trying to kill me then, wasn't he?'

Dillon pushed himself up and turned away from her. 'Scaring you wasn't working. Sal wouldn't give up the money.' He shook his head. 'What kind of father wouldn't help his own daughter?'

Harry wanted to defend her father, but what was the point? She rested her cheek against the dirt. Her neck ached from looking up at him. Her brain scrambled for something that would help her out of the maze. Phrases tumbled around in her head: simply connected and left-hand rule; man-eating Minotaur, half-man, half-bull. Fuck King Minos and his bloody labyrinth.

'I had to send Sal a warning, force his hand . . .' Dillon hung his head, his back still turned to her. 'I had to show him I could destroy something he loved.'

Her heart thudded. 'Only it went wrong, didn't it? He ended up in hospital instead of me.'

He paused, and then turned to face her. When he spoke, his voice was gentle. 'I was glad about that.'

He swallowed and looked down at the gun in his hand. Then he levelled the barrel at her face. Harry lifted her head. Not yet! Her heart raced. Ask him something else. Anything!

'What about Leon?' Her mouth was dry. 'Does he get a share of the money now?'

'Leon won't be getting a share of anything. He made a mistake when he set that bald goon of his on to me. He got too close.' He nodded towards his brother. 'Cameron took care of him.'

'You killed him?'

'He was just a scumbag, meant to take the fall if things went wrong. I made sure his messy footprints were all over everything.'

Harry thought of Leon's home address stored on her bank records; of the account statement sent to his flat; of the PI he'd hired to track her down. Dillon was right, his trail was everywhere.

'So it was you who hacked into my bank account,' she said.

He smiled. 'I had some fun with that. Especially when you promised to give me the money and then I made it disappear.'

Harry's mind clicked, like a seat belt fastening. The Sheridan Bank pen test. It had all been a set-up. Dillon knew she banked there; he paid her salary, for God's sake. And he knew about the RAT she always left as a calling card, the deliberate plant of a secret back door to test the bank's clean-up tools. But Dillon had kept the RAT out of Imogen's report. He hadn't wanted it cleaned up.

He took a step towards her, aiming the gun between her eyes. His hand shook a little. Close to, his face looked grey, with lines she hadn't noticed before. She thought of the evangelical boy of twenty-one who'd talked to her about the search for truth.

'What happened, Dillon?' she whispered. 'Wasn't all your dot.com money enough for you?'

His jaw hardened. 'Dot fucking com. Everyone in the country an overnight millionaire except me. I never got a shot at it.' His eyes lost their focus. 'When I was younger, I was always the best. Top of the pile. I had more talent than any of them. The big career, hotshot computer whiz with the best salary. How could I end up the big loser? You understand that, don't you, Harry?'

She bit her lip. 'So the dot.com was just a cover story.'

He nodded. 'Along with Lúbra Securities. Oh, it started off as a legitimate business, all right. But who the hell could turn a profit once the dot.com fucked us up? I nearly went under last year.' His nostrils flared. 'So I started thinking about the Sorohan deal, and about all that money Sal cheated me out of. That money was mine and I wanted it back.'

He caught her eye and gave her his half-smile, his gaze softening, just for a moment. Then he reached down and placed his fingers under her chin, tilting her face upwards. She shuddered at his touch, remembering the night he'd tasted her body with his mouth. Nausea quivered in her stomach.

'It's not too late for us, Harry,' he whispered. His eyes were full of heat, scouring her face, searching for something. 'Is it?'

Harry swallowed. Smile. Pretend. How hard could it be? She opened her mouth to answer, breaking eye contact just for an instant. It was a mistake. Dillon thrust her chin away, wrenching her head sideways.

'Never lie to me, Harry.' Then he stepped over to Cameron and trained the gun back on her face, steadying it with both hands. 'Get her up.'

'You said I could have some time with her,' Cameron said.

'You'll have time. Take off her cuffs.'

Cameron hauled Harry up by her arms into a standing position. Blood roared in her ears and she felt herself sway. Something throbbed in the distance. Cameron snapped off the handcuffs and her arms drifted apart, stiff and numb.

'Thanks,' she said, rubbing her wrists and hating the submission in her voice.

'I didn't do it for you.' Dillon's eyes were cold, the smile gone. 'Handcuffs are hard to explain at the scene of an accident.'

'And a petrol-soaked body isn't?' She glanced at the path behind her. She could round one of the bends in three or four strides. How long would it take him to squeeze the trigger?

Dillon shrugged. 'It doesn't really matter. No one's going to look for you out here, anyway.'

The distant throbbing grew louder, coming from above. Harry peered upwards. The sky was smothered in mist.

'Accidents are Cameron's speciality,' Dillon said,

raising his voice above the noise. 'Ever since he pushed our mother down the stairs. I found him on the top step, wasted on drugs. I had to help him stage that one, he couldn't think straight. He's been paying back the favour ever since. Haven't you, Cameron?'

Cameron hugged the flagon of petrol to his chest and stared at the ground. Suddenly the wind picked up. The massive hedges shook. Dust whipped into Harry's eyes and a furious beating noise pounded her ears.

A sky-blue helicopter broke through the haze. A powerful gust of air snatched at Harry's clothes, driving her backwards. The hedges churned and looked ready to topple over. Dillon gaped, crouching against the whirlwind, one arm shielding his face. Then he braced himself and trained the gun back on her face. The helicopter pitched towards them. A rope hung out one side, and Jude's broad frame filled the cockpit.

Harry's heart floated in her chest. Jude ripped off his headphones and yelled at her, but the whomp-whomp of the blades drowned him out. He jabbed his finger at the rope and dipped the chopper in towards her. Even from here, she could see eyes were wide and staring, his face a ghastly white.

Harry shot a look at Dillon. He'd fixed the gun in line with her eyes. She could see his throat working, his fingers flexing. The chopper hovered directly above her, the dangling rope only a few yards away. He'd kill her before she could take her first step.

Suddenly, Dillon swung his arms around and opened fire on the chopper. Bullets pierced its armour in a burst of metallic clangs. The chopper lurched sideways, dipping towards the ground. Dillon pumped more shots into its underbelly. The aircraft wavered, black smoke trickling from its tail. Then it banked left and veered across the maze, skimming the hedges. The rope and smoke trailed behind like unravelling threads.

Dillon aimed at it again. This time, Harry didn't wait. In two strides she'd reached the fork in the path, and whirled around the left-hand bend. She stumbled against the hedges, careening round blind corners. There was a crack of bullets, and she heard the chopper's engine stall. Then it looped above her, listing sideways, tilting down into the maze. The blades whacked against the hedge tops, pulverizing them like a giant blender. They dug in too deep and shattered, catapulting chunks of metal into the air. With a grinding shriek, the aircraft keeled over and crashed down behind the hedges.

For several seconds, there was silence. No engine, no whirling blades. Harry blundered along the path, her head screaming. What the hell had she done? Then she heard a blast and the unmistakable whoosh of flames. Dear God. If Jude was dead, it was all her fault.

She slammed into a wall of hedge. A junction.

Shit, which way? Her chest burned, and she felt as if she was running a fever. Left-hand rule. Place your left hand on the wall and follow it round. But surely she'd just go in circles? Scuffing footsteps sounded behind her. She shot her left palm out to the hedge and raced down the left-hand fork. The path was narrower, and the foliage crowded in. Her breath tore at her throat. Keep moving!

She lurched around in circles, following the path, spiralling in and out of dead-ends. She plunged into one tunnel after another, spinning left until her head reeled.

Then the swirling stopped. The path became wider and straighter. The foliage thinned out. The air was fresher, like a forest, and the sky seemed lighter. Ahead of her was an opening, marked by a blue flag. It looked wider than the other passageways. She scrambled towards it, whirling through. Then she caught her breath and lurched to a halt.

She was inside a circular clearing the size of a bowling green. Jude lay face down on the grass a few yards away from her. Her gut contracted. His helicopter blazed near the centre of the circle. A trail of blood stained the grass where he'd managed to drag himself clear. Beside the chopper loomed a statue, nine or ten feet tall. It was a statue of a gigantic black gladiator. He held a spear, his posture proud and erect, his shoulders broad and strong. But his head was an ugly mutation on his thick black neck. It was the head of a crazed bull.

Harry closed her eyes. Dillon's Minotaur. She'd blundered into the centre of his bloody maze.

'It's over, Harry, give it up.'

Dillon stepped into the clearing through an opening on her right. He still had the gun. Something rustled behind her. She spun round. Cameron appeared at the entrance, holding the petrol in one hand, and wheeling her black case with the other. Harry backed away, edging past Jude's body. Cameron followed, his pale eyes fixed on her face. Dillon sidestepped in parallel, keeping tabs on them both.

The heat from the flames scorched through Harry's shirt. The helicopter was only a few feet away. She radiated petrol fumes, the smell stronger than ever. If she got any closer she'd light up like a match. She stumbled backwards against the Minotaur's pedestal, the massive stone slab cool against her back. Cameron closed in on her. She could feel his hot breath on her face. He shoved the case aside and began to unscrew the flagon of petrol.

'Cameron!' Dillon took a step forward. 'Not around the fucking money. Throw me the case!'

But Cameron seemed transfixed. His lips parted, and his breathing grew shallow. Harry's eyes widened as he slipped a hand into his pocket and brought out a cigarette lighter.

'Cameron!' Dillon adjusted his sights on the gun. 'Listen to me!'

Cameron flicked the lighter with his thumb.

A three-inch flame shot into the air. He held it out towards Harry's face. She jerked away, edging round the side of the pedestal. She saw Jude stirring, raising himself up on to his knees. His shirt was blood-soaked, and his left arm hung awkwardly at his side. Dillon swung the gun round on him.

'Stay on the ground!'

Jude's head snapped up, and he froze. His skin looked raw and blistered. Cameron flicked a glance over his shoulder at him. In the same instant, Harry lunged for the case, hauling it up to her chest. Her heart thudded against its solid weight.

Cameron didn't seem to notice. He stepped closer, holding the container above Harry's head. Then he sprinkled the petrol over her hair as though he was christening her. The cold liquid trickled down her face and neck, and dripped all over the black case. The lighter flame quivered, like a snake sensing the presence of meat.

A single gunshot exploded into the air. Harry jumped and held her breath, waiting for the pain. She heard Jude yell. Cameron raised his eyebrows.

'You know, my mother's death really was an accident.' Dillon's voice sounded choked. 'He didn't kill her.'

Cameron frowned, and swayed a little. Harry's ears still rang from the gunshot.

'I made him believe he did it.' Dillon went on. 'He was so doped up he couldn't remember.'

Cameron's eyes flicked over Harry's head and he stared into the distance. A tiny muscle twitched in his left eyelid.

'After that, I could make him do anything,' Dillon said.

Cameron's shoulders slumped. Then he collapsed against Harry like an avalanche, his weight pinning her to the pedestal. She screamed, and tumbled to the ground, dropping the case. He fell with her, crushing the air out of her lungs. She dragged herself out from under him, trembling. Cameron lay face down on the grass. A large red stain spread across his back. Harry clapped both hands across her mouth, stifling a scream.

'Throw me the money, Harry, and it'll all be over,' Dillon shouted.

Harry jerked her head up. The pedestal blocked her view of him. She looked at the case beside her, and at the flagon of petrol still clutched in Cameron's hand, propped upright against the statue. It was nearly half full.

'Harry?'

She could hear his feet brush against the grass as he circled behind the statue. Her pulse raced. She grabbed the petrol. Then she snapped open the black case and up-ended the plastic container inside it. Its glug-glug action was painfully slow. Come on, come on. The flagon emptied, and she slammed the case shut. When she looked up, all she saw was the barrel of Dillon's gun.

'Throw me the bag.'

Sweat trickled down his face. His eyes slid down to Cameron's body and quickly flicked away. Close behind him, the chopper crackled, sparks hissing into the sky like fireworks.

Harry hauled herself to her feet and lugged the case up in both hands. It was even heavier now, and her arms trembled. She checked behind her. Jude was watching, wide-eyed. She turned back to Dillon. His face was white.

'You're not used to this, are you?' She was panting. 'Other people usually do your dirty work for you.'

'GIVE ME THE FUCKING BAG!'

Harry heaved the case over her shoulder, its soggy contents shifting like bricks inside. She twisted her body like a javelin thrower and hurled the case into the air. It sailed past Dillon and crashed through the side of the blazing chopper.

Dillon stared after it, and for a split second, nothing happened. Then he let out a roar and lunged after the case, barging through the flames. In the same instant, Harry spun round and yelled at Jude.

'Go!'

Jude scrambled to his feet, clutching at his useless left arm. Together they raced towards the exit in the clearing. A gusty updraught of air roared behind them, like a great wind gathering pace. Harry got to the exit first and dived headlong through, rolling for cover behind the hedge. Jude slammed to the ground beside her, yelling with pain. The roar thundered to a crescendo and then exploded, blasting through the hedges. A searing ball of heat lit up the maze, and Harry shielded her eyes against it. Branches crackled all around them. Harry clutched at her petrol-soaked clothes. Then she clambered to her feet, tugging at Jude's sleeve. She placed her right hand against the hedge wall, and staggered down the path. Left hand in, right hand out. Her legs trembled. A flickering orange light turned everything pale yellow. She followed the corkscrew track, Jude close behind, her hand never leaving the hedge wall. She finally let it drop when she saw her father's holdall and the red triangular flag of the exit beyond.

CHAPTER 53

'How much money was in the suitcase?'
Harry looked away from Detective
Lynne's steady gaze and didn't answer.
They were sitting on the lawn behind Dillon's
house. She stared at the angry red flames that
devoured the centre of the maze. Firemen were
blasting jets of water over the hedges, trying to
contain the inferno.

She allowed the silence to stretch. So did he. It
was a technique he'd been using for the last half-
hour, hoping she'd fill the silences with babble
and information. She didn't.

Lynne was the first to speak.

'We'll find it, you know.' He inclined his head
towards the flames. 'Forensics can recover almost
anything.'

Harry looked at him, taking in the lean frame,
the narrow tie. Everything about him was small
and neat, but just a little bit shabby.

'Why do you care?' she said eventually.

'The Sorohan case was never closed. We never
recovered the money.' He studied her as though
she was a chess board, and he'd just worked out

his next ten moves. 'I intend to pursue it till we do.'

Harry nodded and closed her eyes, lifting her face to the flames. She felt numb, and the heat warmed her cheeks. For a second she flashed on Dillon, diving into the blazing helicopter, screaming with rage and pain. Her fingers clutched at the grass. She swallowed, and concentrated on her tingling face and the charred smoky scent in the air.

When she opened her eyes, Lynne had disappeared. Harry frowned. Bloody man came and went like a cat. Jude caught her eye from across the lawn and came to sit beside her on the grass. She threw him a quick glance. His arm had been immobilized in a sling, and his cheeks were still wet from where they'd tried to cool the burns. His shirt was stiff with dried blood from a deep gash in his shoulder.

'You okay?' he said.

She nodded, biting her lip. For a moment, neither of them spoke. The ground by the maze looked swampy, the hedges bedraggled. The flames had finally died, and all that was left was a dark, sodden mess.

'I saw you at the airport,' Harry said eventually. 'I ran away.'

'I know.'

'How did you know I'd be there?'

'That reporter friend of yours called me this morning.'

She raised her eyebrows. 'Ruth Woods?'

He nodded. 'She'd tried your phone all day yesterday, but got no reply. In the end, she called me.'

Yesterday. Harry locked in on her movements for the previous day, adjusting for the time zones. She nodded, remembering the phone calls she'd missed as she was preparing to meet Owen Johnson.

'She'd gone to see Leon Ritch,' Jude was saying. 'He was dead before she could talk to him, but she found some kind of dossier he'd put together. He'd discovered Dillon worked in JX Warner about the same time as the Prophet.'

'That doesn't mean anything. So did you.'

'There was another connection. Leon knew about Dillon's brother. He had photos, names – he'd made the connection between them. And he had proof that he was behind your father's accident.' His eyes met hers. 'I'm sorry.'

Harry nodded and looked away, plucking at stalks of grass.

'Anyway, the reporter put the pieces together.' Then Jude's mouth tensed. 'The police would have too, if they'd found the dossier.'

'What do you mean?'

'Your bloody reporter friend kept it from them. She wanted to blow open the story before anyone could put a gag on it. If it wasn't for her, Dillon might have been picked up yesterday.' He gestured at the maze. 'And none of this would have happened.'

Harry followed his gaze. Half a dozen officers

in protective clothing swarmed into the maze, directed by a detective navigating from the viewing platform. One of the officers carried a set of large zip-up bags over one arm, like the suit covers used in the drycleaners. Jude must have seen them too.

'Body bags,' he said.

Harry swallowed and closed her eyes.

'So you came to warn me,' she said, after a moment.

He nodded. 'Someone had to. Your reporter pal had gone to ground, working on her story. I kept calling her, leaving messages, even from the airport. No response.'

She gave him a direct look and thought about the thick, impenetrable fog and his fear of flying through it. 'Thanks.'

He nodded, and they were silent for a while. Then he said, 'He never could bear failure, you know, even in college. Dillon, I mean. Always had to come first in everything.'

Harry studied her hands, unable to respond.

Jude cleared his throat. 'So you finally got hold of the Sorohan money.'

Harry shot a glance at the officers near the maze, and shook her head. 'I didn't tell the police that. I said there wasn't any money.'

'But –'

She shook her head again, fixing her eyes on his. 'What's the point in telling them now? What purpose does it serve? It would only hurt my father if we drag the money into it.'

Jude frowned. Then his brow cleared as he seemed to get it. He stared at the smouldering hedges.

'How much was there?' he said in a quiet voice.

Harry paused. 'Fifteen million euros.'

He gave a low whistle and leaned back against his elbows on the grass. Harry felt her limbs relax. She thought of the bleakness of Arbour Hill, of the inmates with their condemned souls. She thought of her father's jaunty step as he'd walked away from it all. Maybe it was stupid to lie to the police, but she knew she could never put him back there. She'd take her chances on what they might find incinerated in the maze; as far as she was concerned, her father had nothing more to hide.

But she needn't have worried about protecting her father. A few weeks later, the doctors called to say that he might die.

CHAPTER 54

The machines were the only thing keeping him alive.

'How long can they keep him like this?' Miriam said.

Harry couldn't answer. They sat together by her father's bed while Amaranta took a break outside. They spoke in whispers but, inside, Harry was screaming.

For weeks, the doctors had tried to wean him off the ventilator. Every day, he'd endured a thirty-minute trial of unassisted breathing, but each time he'd shown signs of respiratory arrest and had to be reconnected.

The nurse in charge had advised them not to be present at the weaning trials. Harry guessed she'd picked up on the family tensions and felt they'd only agitate her patient. Harry wasn't sorry. How could she bear to watch her father fight for breath, his diaphragm too weak for the burden of breathing? How could she watch him suffocate?

She stared at his frail form. His arms lay straight down by his sides, the bedclothes perfectly smooth. He looked shrunken and doll-like, but what struck Harry most was the mechanical motion of his chest.

She swallowed against the ache in her throat. So that was the difference between living and dying: the rise and fall of a spontaneous breath. Her eyes began to sting and she looked away.

'Make your mind a blank,' Miriam said in her low voice. 'It's the only way to get through it.'

Harry looked at her. Her mother's complexion was a ghostly grey. She was staring at her husband, her chin raised and her shoulders straight. Was that how her mother had coped all her life, by blanking things out?

Harry reached over and squeezed her arm. There was no response. She dropped her hand and stood up, moving towards the door to swap places with Amaranta. She left without touching her father. That would have felt too much like saying goodbye.

The weaning trials continued for several weeks.

Visitors came and went, an endless procession of friends and neighbours offering their support. Harry knew hardly any of them, but they all called her mother by her first name. Thrust into social obligation, Miriam seemed to revive, accepting people's sympathy with grace and poise. Harry was the only one close enough to notice the tremor in her hands.

Jude came to the hospital every day. His arm was still in a sling, but his facial burns were healing.

He didn't intrude but stayed out in the corridor, as if to say he was there should she need him. Harry wasn't sure what she needed any more. The only thing she was sure of was that she no longer believed in heroes.

Imogen came to see her, looking pale and shocked, no doubt still trying to absorb the truth about Dillon. She had lost a hero too, in a way. She'd brought along the newspaper that ran Ruth Woods' story, and in it Dillon's finances were stripped bare. He'd been in trouble for some time. His ambitious strategy of buying other security businesses and merging them with Lúbra had backfired. He'd paid too much for the companies he'd bought and when his own money ran out, he'd funded his acquisitions with debt he couldn't repay. By now many of the companies were worthless, and his creditors had been threatening him with bankruptcy proceedings. It seemed Dillon was better at insider trading than running a legitimate business.

When Ashford arrived, Harry felt herself freeze. She watched him clasp her mother's hands. She hadn't told the police about the connection she'd made between Ashford and Leon. After all, all she had was a name. She watched her mother battling tears, and wondered what to feel. What would it do to her mother if Ashford was sent to prison? She looked at Miriam, who'd regained her composure, and guessed that, whatever happened, her mother would probably cope.

Ashford moved towards Harry, his hand outstretched. She bit her lip. He stood in front of her, his head to one side, hair like tufts of candyfloss. She had no proof that Ashford had meant her any harm. Maybe he was a member of the ring, and maybe he wasn't. All she knew was, he was a friend of her father's. Harry studied his large sad eyes and slowly held out her hand.

After six weeks of weaning trials, there was still no improvement. At the last attempt, her father had gone into cardiac arrest and was now visibly weaker.

Harry touched her father's fingers. They were warm, but unresponsive. She stared at the sheet of paper in her mother's hand, headed in bold with the letters 'DNR'. The nurse had left it for her to sign a few minutes before, once the doctor had explained what it meant.

He'd talked of cardiac arrest and respiratory failure, and of how her father's heart and lungs had given up. He'd said that for some patients, mechanical ventilation only prolonged the dying process. They listened in silence. Even Amaranta had nothing to say.

Finally the doctor had said quietly, 'There may come a time when you feel he should no longer be resuscitated.'

DNR. Do Not Resuscitate.

Harry's mind stalled.

If his heart stopped beating they wouldn't try to bring him back.

No heroic measures.

Harry squeezed her father's fingers and stared around the hospital room, with its tubes and beeping monitors. She thought of all the things her father had taught her, all the places he'd taken her. This sterile room had nothing to do with who he was.

She glanced at her mother, who still clutched the form in her hand. Would she sign it, and consent to his death? Harry squeezed her eyes shut. How could she watch them put her father in the ground? 'Mum?'

Harry opened her eyes. Amaranta had put a hand on her mother's arm and was gesturing towards the form. Miriam turned to look at Harry, a question in her eyes. Harry swallowed and shook her head.

Slowly, her mother folded the form and put it away, unsigned, into her bag. Then she clutched her daughters' arms, first Harry's, then Amaranta's. Harry looked at her in surprise, and then grasped her hand, her throat tight. They gripped on to one another as together they watched the machine breathe for her father. And then Harry realized something she should have figured out long ago. Her father was neither fraud nor hero. In the end, he was only human.

Harry moved in with her mother for a while, in the house that had once been her home, not quite sure who was comforting whom. Her father breathed on; in, out, up down. When it looked as though it would never change, Harry left for the Bahamas.

CHAPTER 55

Harry stepped off the plane at Nassau Airport into a thick blanket of heat. She hailed a taxi outside the Arrivals hall, half-hoping the driver would be Ethan. It wasn't, of course.

She leaned back against the seat, the dawdling drive and the sleepy reggae on the radio acting like an anaesthetic. She gazed out at the fiery red and tangerine landscape. Two months ago she'd come here to defraud a bank. Today she'd come here for something entirely different.

The taxi crawled through the bustle of Bay Street and headed across Paradise Island Bridge. Sleek white yachts had gathered in the dock, a rabble of seagulls tagging along for the ride. Harry rolled down the window. The conch vendors beneath the bridge hollered out prices for the day's catch, the market stalls laden with glistening fish, golden bananas and pineapples. She inhaled the salty air, surprised at how much it felt like coming home.

The taxi dropped her off at the Atlantis Resort Hotel, where she checked into a room that made the Nassau Sands look like a youth hostel. After she'd freshened up, she made her way back down to the great domed lobby. Tightening her grip on the case in her hand, she circled the hall and stepped through the entrance to the casino.

She hesitated on the threshold just for a moment. The room was crowded, although it was still only mid-afternoon. She could hear the rattle of the chip-sorting machines and the swirling of steel roulette balls. Waitresses strolled around offering free drinks, but Harry knew the serious gamblers would all be drinking coffee. She sighed, and trudged past the gaming tables, heading for the back of the room.

Ahead of her was the cage, where a middle-aged woman sat behind bars and exchanged dollars for chips. Harry queued up behind a man wearing a Stetson, and hauled her case up on to the ledge. Then she turned to watch the gaming tables.

Directly in front of her was a high-stakes poker game, and she could tell the action was down to two players: a tight-lipped man in a business suit, and a wiry young Italian with shades. The board showed a pair of aces and the three of clubs. By the twitchy set of the Italian's shoulders, he probably wasn't holding a third ace.

Harry dragged her gaze away and turned back to her case. She brushed her fingers along a scuff-mark on the black vinyl. Dillon had added a few more dents when he'd kicked it across the ground, but otherwise her father's poker-chip case was still intact.

She pressed her thumbs to the rusty locks, snapping them open. Then she lifted the lid to peek inside. Wedged into the grooves in the felt lining were eight tight columns of chips. Two thirds of them were crimson, and the rest were evenly split between gold and sapphire blue. Harry eased out two of the crimson chips and turned them around in her fingers, admiring the soft mother-of-pearl sheen and the clacking sound they made together. They were bigger and more oval than the toy plastic chips that had originally come with the case. Harry smoothed her thumb along one ceramic surface. The casino's name was engraved across it, along with its face value. It was worth $100,000.

When she'd left Rosenstock Bank with the case of money, she'd gone back to her hotel for a while. She'd needed time to think. Then she'd headed for the Atlantis Casino. Rousseau had been furious when she'd told him what she wanted. But as long as she had evidence of his insider trades, they'd both known he had no choice. He'd vouched for her character with the casino manager, who'd happily converted most of her money into high-stakes plaques. It came to a lot of chips, even for the Atlantis, so Rousseau had enlisted the help of two other casinos to make up the shortfall. No one wanted to turn away a high roller.

There was a gasp behind her, and Harry whipped her gaze around. The dealer at the poker table had flicked over the turn card: another three.

The board was now showing two pair, aces and threes. The Italian had his head in his hands, but the man in the suit was as still as a lizard in the sun. Harry put him on a full house, with trip aces.

The man with the Stetson moved up to take his turn at the cage. Harry shuffled behind him, still fingering the plaques in her hand. She'd known as soon as she'd seen the money that she couldn't just give it all away. Images of her father had flashed in front of her: his arms reaching out to her across the prison table; his body deathly still, kept alive by tubes. She'd wanted to give him something to wake up to.

So she'd converted seven and a half million euros into chips and stacked them into her father's poker set. The rest of the money she'd kept in cash. She'd half-filled the black case from Rosenstock Bank with blocks of printer paper from her hotel, and packed the remaining banknotes into five layers across the top. One and a half million euros per layer. She'd figured there'd come a point in her setup of the Prophet when he'd want to open the case, and the banknotes might just buy her some time. Too bad she never got to set him up, but the cash had probably saved her life in the maze.

Harry stared at the chips in her hand, and felt her shoulders slump. She didn't want the money. She'd been keeping it for her father, but what use was it to him now? And it would never fill the space he'd leave behind.

The man with the Stetson moved away and Harry edged up to the woman behind the cage. She thought about Jude's lecture on market ethics; about how insider trading shattered the confidence in the fairness of the markets. She'd come back to Nassau to cash in her chips and return the money to the Fraud Bureau. It was the correct thing to do. It was what Jude would have done. And no one could hurt her father now.

The woman behind the cage tapped her pen on the desk and Harry chewed her lip. What did she care about the fairness of the market? It wasn't as if the investors would ever be recompensed, even if she gave the money back. Who knew where the money would end up?

She sighed and gave her attention to the woman behind the cage. She'd stopped tapping her pen and was staring over Harry's shoulder.

'All-in.'

Harry spun round. The Italian was pushing his entire stack of chips into the centre of the table. Among them was a tall pile of crimson plaques. Harry held her breath. The players flipped over their cards, and the spectators groaned. The Italian shoved back his chair, whipped off his shades, and paced up and down behind his chair. The man in the suit took a sip of bottled water.

Harry craned her neck to see the cards. She'd been wrong about the full house. The man in the suit had a pair of aces, putting him on four of a kind. A near-unbeatable hand. The Italian had the

485

two and four of clubs. Harry did the combinations in her head, and her eyes widened. With the ace and three of clubs already on the table, he was one card away from a straight flush; the only hand that could win him the game.

The back of Harry's neck tingled. She took a step towards the table. The Italian stopped pacing and gripped the back of his chair, his knuckles white. The dealer flipped over the river card. For a moment there was silence. Harry stretched up on her toes but she couldn't see the card. Then the crowd roared. The Italian pumped his fist high in the air and whooped like a cowboy. He turned to hug the spectators and shake his opponent's hand. Through the gap in the crowd, Harry saw the five of clubs on the table and smiled.

She put her fingers up to the back of her tingling neck. *Life's not much fun unless you go all-in once in a while.* Her father's words resonated inside her head and made her heart swell. Slowly, she turned back to the cage, slotting her plaques back into the case and gently shutting the lid.

'Sorry,' she told the woman behind the bars, 'I've changed my mind.'

She stepped over to the table and took the empty seat where the man in the suit had been. She smiled at the Italian and brushed the baize with her knuckles for good luck. Then she opened her father's poker case and lifted it on to the table.

Sept 30